PENGU

CONJU
STORIES OF THE COLOR LINE

CHARLES WADDELL CHESNUTT (1858–1932) was born in Cleveland, Ohio, where his family had moved from Fayetteville, North Carolina, to seek better economic opportunities. Shortly after the Civil War they returned to Fayetteville, where Chesnutt spent most of his childhood and young adulthood. He taught in local public schools, eventually returning to Cleveland and being admitted to the bar. He established a legal stenography business yet found himself strongly attracted to writing fiction. He published two collections of short stories, *The Conjure Woman* and *The Wife of His Youth and Other Stories of the Color Line* (1899) and three widely-reviewed novels, *The House Behind the Cedars* (1900), *The Marrow of Tradition* (1901), and *The Colonel's Dream* (1905), while devoting essays and speeches to agitation for civil rights for African Americans, especially in the South. Unable to support his family as a full-time writer, he resumed his business career but maintained until his death a respected role in African-American letters.

WILLIAM L. ANDREWS is E. Maynard Adams Professor of English and Chair of the Department of English at the University of North Carolina at Chapel Hill. He is the author of *The Literary Career of Charles W. Chesnutt* (1980) and *To Tell a Free Story: The First Century of Afro-American Autobiography, 1760-1865* (1986). He is co-editor of *The Norton Anthology of African American Literature* (1997) and *The Oxford Companion to African American Literature* (1997), and the general editor of *The Literature of the American South: A Norton Anthology* and *North American Slave Narratives, A Database and Electronic Text Library* (http://metalab.unc.edu/docsouth/neh/neh.html).

CONJURE TALES AND
STORIES OF THE COLOR LINE

―――――

CHARLES W. CHESNUTT

EDITED AND WITH AN
INTRODUCTION BY
WILLIAM L. ANDREWS

PENGUIN BOOKS

PENGUIN BOOKS
Published by the Penguin Group
Penguin Group (USA) Inc., 375 Hudson Street, New York, New York 10014, U.S.A.
Penguin Books Ltd, 80 Strand, London WC2R 0RL, England
Penguin Books Australia Ltd, 250 Camberwell Road, Camberwell, Victoria 3124, Australia
Penguin Books Canada Ltd, 10 Alcorn Avenue, Toronto, Ontario, Canada M4V 3B2
Penguin Books India (P) Ltd, 11 Community Centre, Panchsheel Park, New Delhi – 110 017, India
Penguin Books (N.Z.) Ltd, Cnr Rosedale and Airborne Roads, Albany, Auckland, New Zealand
Penguin Books (South Africa) (Pty) Ltd, 24 Sturdee Avenue,
Rosebank, Johannesburg 2196, South Africa

Penguin Books Ltd, Registered Offices: 80 Strand, London WC2R 0RL, England

First published in the United States of America as
The Collected Stories of Charles W. Chesnutt by Mentor,
an imprint of New American Library,
a division of Penguin Books USA Inc. 1992
Published in Penguin Books 2000

3 5 7 9 10 8 6 4 2

Copyright © William L. Andrews, 1992
All rights reserved

ISBN 0 14 11.8502 3

Printed in the United States of America
Set in Stempel Garamond
Designed by Sabrina Bowers

CONTENTS

Introduction by William L. Andrews *vii*
Suggestions for Further Reading *xix*
A Note on the Text *xxi*

The Goophered Grapevine 1
Po' Sandy 14
Mars Jeems's Nightmare 25
The Conjurer's Revenge 40
Sis' Becky's Pickaninny 51
The Gray Wolf's Ha'nt 63
Hot-Foot Hannibal 76
Dave's Neckliss 90
The Wife of His Youth 103
Her Virginia Mammy 115
The Sheriff's Children 133
A Matter of Principle 150
Cicely's Dream 170
The Passing of Grandison 188
Uncle Wellington's Wives 206
The Bouquet 239
The Web of Circumstance 250
Baxter's Procrustes 267

INTRODUCTION

CHARLES W. CHESNUTT was the first African-American writer of fiction to enlist the white-controlled publishing industry in the service of his social message. From 1899 to 1905, during which time he published two collections of short stories and three novels, Chesnutt reached a significant portion of the national American reading audience with his analyses and indictments of racism. His writing, which appeared at a time when the sociopolitical fortunes of black America had reached their post-Civil War nadir, brought him widespread respect among people of color, who viewed him as their foremost literary advocate. Chesnutt championed the interests of the northern black middle class, composed largely of mixed-race persons like himself. His studies of southern social conditions defended working-class blacks against the propaganda that enabled white supremacy to gain the upper hand throughout the New South by the turn of the century.

Two decades after his literary heyday, Chesnutt's popularity remained strong enough to earn him the Spingarn Medal from the National Association for the Advancement of Colored People in recognition of his "pioneer work as a literary artist depicting the life and struggles of Americans of Negro descent." Yet this appreciation in 1928 could not keep Chesnutt's books in print; forty years would elapse before his short stories and novels came back into the public eye again. Since the late 1960s, however, Chesnutt has been increasingly recognized as a literary innovator whose mastery of his craft, particularly in the short story, placed his distinctive personal signature on the pages of American literary history.

Born in Cleveland, Ohio, in 1858, the son of free black emigrés from the South, Charles Waddell Chesnutt grew up in Fayetteville,

North Carolina, during the turbulent Reconstruction era. A sensitive and bookish boy, he did not take long to discover the distinctly mixed blessing that his heritage and situation in Fayetteville posed for him. His parents belonged to what was known as the "bright mulatto" class of African Americans who enjoyed certain social and economic advantages in the color-conscious South because of their lightness of complexion. Chesnutt's white grandfather, Waddell Cade, a prosperous tobacco merchant, helped to support but never acknowledged the five children born of his unsanctioned liaison with Ann Chesnutt, a free woman of color, during the slavery era. As a result, even though his own parents had been legally married, Charles had to contend early on with the equation southern whites made between mixed blood and morally tainted blood. Resentment of this prejudice smoldered in Chesnutt throughout his life and made him permanently suspicious of any claim to privilege based on race, color, or blood.

Charles Chesnutt grew up in relative financial security and attended school regularly at an institution founded by the Freedmen's Bureau. He loved reading, particularly the classics of English and continental fiction, and showed intellectual aptitude in a variety of areas. By his late teens he had distinguished himself sufficiently to be appointed assistant principal of the normal school established for blacks in Fayetteville by the North Carolina state legislature. But the young schoolmaster chafed under the restrictions of his life in the South. He had married in 1878, and the responsibilities of a family added fuel to his ambition. Before his twenty-first birthday he had confided to his journal a plan to move to the North in order to "get employment in some literary avocation, or something leading in that direction."

"I want fame; I want money; I want to raise my children in a different rank of life from what I spring from," Chesnutt acknowledged to himself in the spring of 1881. "In my present vocation I would never accumulate a competency, with all the economy and prudence and parsimony in the world. . . . But literature pays the successful." Confident that he could succeed as a writer, Chesnutt moved to New York City in 1883 and to Cleveland in 1884, where he settled his family and launched a business career as a legal stenographer. He devoted his spare time to his much-cherished private determination to "strike for an entering wedge in the literary world."

In the mid-1880s Chesnutt broke into print inauspiciously by supplying comic sketches and mildly sentimental squibs for a national newspaper syndicate and various home journals, Sunday supplements, and humor magazines. Knowing that he needed more original material to catch the eye of the editors of the better literary magazines, Chesnutt soon decided to concentrate on what he knew best, the folklore and history of his boyhood environs in downeastern North Carolina. The popularity of Joel Chandler Harris's *Uncle Remus: His Songs and His Sayings* (1881) had proven that the folkways of southern black people could attract a sizeable literary audience. Thomas Nelson Page and other white romancers of southern life had also made a name for themselves writing stories in Negro dialect that celebrated life on the antebellum plantation. Drawing on a hoodoo tale told him by his father-in-law's gardener in Fayetteville, Chesnutt created "The Goophered Grapevine" in 1887, a story that featured southern local color of both the present and the past, and centered on an ex-slave's recollections of "conjure" practices among North Carolina blacks during the slavery era. The publication of "The Goophered Grapevine" in the prestigious *Atlantic Monthly* in the summer of 1887 marked Chesnutt's first appearance in a major American literary magazine. Within the next two years, two more conjure stories narrated by Uncle Julius McAdoo, the shrewd ex-slave raconteur of "The Goophered Grapevine," had found their way into print.

On September 26, 1889, a gratified Chesnutt wrote Albion Tourgée, whose protest fiction had inspired Chesnutt to become an author, about his recent successes and his plans for the future. The young author called attention to the recent publication of his third Uncle Julius story in the *Atlantic Monthly*, a tale entitled "Dave's Neckliss," which Chesnutt hoped "you may think the best of the series." Alluding to the fact that he had not worked the conjure element into "Dave's Neckliss," Chesnutt remarked, "I tried in this story to get out of the realm of superstition [and] into the realm of feeling and passion." The unrelieved tragedy of "Dave's Neckliss," in which Julius eulogizes an old friend whose demise he witnessed personally, revealed Chesnutt probing psychological depths in black people rarely sounded in popular southern regional writing. Sensing a turning point in his developing career as a writer, Chesnutt told Tourgée, "I think I have about used up the old Negro who serves as mouthpiece [of the conjure series], and I shall drop him in future stories, as well as much of the dialect." As if to forecast the new direction of his fiction, Chesnutt recommended that Tourgée watch for "a southern story" of his soon to appear in the *Independent*, a news and public opinion periodical. Like "Dave's Neckliss," the forthcoming story would focus on "a tragic incident," but "not of slavery exactly," instead "showing the fruits of slavery."

"It is not in dialect," Chesnutt noted pointedly, as if to call attention to the serious purpose of the story he entitled "The Sheriff's Children." In its emphasis on the consequences of miscegenation, racial hatred, mob violence, and moral compromise in the South, this story became the germ of much of Chesnutt's later protest fiction as well as his first significant study of the mulatto in American life.

In the 1890s Chesnutt tried to interest the publisher Houghton, Mifflin (the owners of the *Atlantic Monthly*) in a book of his short stories. But not until 1897, after the editor of the *Atlantic Monthly* had accepted Chesnutt's remarkable "The Wife of His Youth," did the highly respected Boston publisher encourage Chesnutt to send in the bulk of his short fiction to see if a coherent collection might be created. After reviewing the twenty-two stories that Chesnutt showed him, Walter Hines Page, editor of the *Atlantic Monthly* and a senior member of the Houghton, Mifflin firm, decided that the conjure vein might well be mined into a commercially successful book. The problem was that up to that time Chesnutt had only written three conjure stories, "The Goophered Grapevine," "Po' Sandy," and "The Conjurer's Revenge." Page urged Chesnutt to produce five or six new stories similar in style and subject to "The Goophered Grapevine" and "Po' Sandy." Even though Chesnutt had been devoting most of his efforts in the 1890s to stories about the color line in post-Civil War America, he went immediately to work on Page's assignment. Within seven weeks of Page's request, the editor had a half-dozen new conjure stories from Chesnutt. After Page selected seven of the nine stories Chesnutt had given him, and Chesnutt arranged the contents into a sequence he thought appropriate, the collection, for which Page suggested the title *The Conjure Woman*, was ready for publication in March 1899.

The Conjure Woman was favorably received as a dialect book with a difference. Although by the turn of the century the vogue of this kind of regional writing was waning, the character of wily Uncle Julius, the peculiar blend of realism and fantasy in his reminiscences of life on the plantation, and the dramatic byplay between himself and the whites who hear, judge, and record his tales, all delighted Chesnutt's reviewers. It was clear that the author had not tried to romanticize slavery or the slaveholders of the Old South. Unlike the plantation fiction of Thomas Nelson Page and his school, *The Conjure Woman* evokes a world of mean-spirited, penny-pinching masters whose preoccupation with profit limits them to a narrowly utilitarian attitude toward their slaves and life itself.

In contrast, the black protagonists of Julius's tales invoke imaginative resources that give them an empowering openness of vision and freedom of action. Through the magic of conjure, slaves in "Sis' Becky's Pickaninny" and "Mars Jeems's Nightmare" are able to resist successfully the controls wielded by their white would-be exploiters. On some occasions, as in "The Conjurer's Revenge" and "The Gray Wolf's Ha'nt," conjure is not put to such pleasing purposes; it becomes a means of wreaking vengeance in internecine struggles between slaves and free blacks. Still, whether for good or for ill, the consistent use of hoodoo practice by the black characters of *The Conjure Woman* enabled their creator to endow these men and women with a variety of desires and needs that call attention to their diverse, nonstereotypical humanity.

In his best dialect stories—"The Goophered Grapevine," "Po' Sandy," and "Dave's Neckliss," to name those most often praised by critics—Chesnutt portrayed slavery as a crucible that placed black people under almost unbearable psychological pressures and demanded of them tenacity of purpose, firmness of character, and imaginative ingenuity in order to preserve themselves, their families, and their community. Appearing during an era when most whites questioned the African American's capacity for full and equal civil rights, the stories of *The Conjure Woman* implicitly argued that, having confirmed their human dignity and heroic fortitude in the face of the worst that slavery could do, the free black man and woman were amply qualified for the rights and responsibilities of American citizenship.

While Uncle Julius's reminiscences revised popular images of masters and slaves on the Old South plantation, his interactions with his white employers, for whose entertainment and edification his tales are ostensibly intended, offered a quiet critique of the complacent rationalism of the Progressive era. John, the transplanted Ohio businessman who provides the framing for Julius's tales, usually treats him with condescension and his tales with skepticism. Yet John cannot deny that once in a while the old man has used a tale to conjure *him*, in effect, so as to gain some economic advantage at his white employer's expense.

More important to Chesnutt's purpose is Julius's persistent exploitation of a fundamental difference between John's perspective and that of his wife Annie, who responds to the ex-slave's memories in a much more heartfelt way than her husband allows himself. After learning the pathetic fate of Tenie, the slave wife in "Po' Sandy," Annie is profoundly moved to indignation and sympathy, as reflected in her statement, "What a system it was. . . . under which such things were possible!" John is appalled to think that his wife could "seriously consider the possibility of a man's being turned into a tree." But her reply—"Oh no, not that. . . . Poor Tenie!"—shows that she can look through the fantastic elements of Julius's tale to discover the tragic reality they highlight.

Annie understands that the issue in Tenie's husband's transformation into a tree is not whether such a thing is literally possible. The question instead is, what could have made a husband and wife so desperate that they might resort to such an extreme means of keeping their family together? The answer, of course, reminds Annie and the reader of "Po' Sandy" of the rootlessness and emotional instability of life under slavery. If Annie identifies with Tenie, whose husband was turned into wood, it may be partly because of her irritation with her own wooden-headed husband, whose literalistic view of the world insulates him from the disturbing realities that Julius encodes in seeming fantasy.

The Conjure Woman had been out scarcely three months when Chesnutt asked Walter Hines Page about the possibility of Houghton, Mifflin's doing a second short story collection headed by "The Wife of His Youth," a story that illuminates the manners and mores of the mixed-blood subculture in the urban North. First published in the *Atlantic Monthly* in the summer of 1898, "The Wife of His Youth" had garnered an unusual amount of favorable attention that led in turn to heightened curiosity in the literary world about the identity of Charles W. Chesnutt. Nowhere in *The Conjure Woman* or in its advertising for the book had Houghton, Mifflin announced Chesnutt's affiliation with black America, out of deference, Chesnutt would later explain, to his belief that his book should be read and reviewed on its own without regard to the racial antecedents of its author. But as positive reviews of the *The Conjure Woman* mounted, black readers and pundits demanded that Chesnutt be recognized as an African-American author whose achievements spoke well of the artistic capabilities of people of color. With a substantial audience, black as well as white, intrigued by Chesnutt and responsive to his brand of realism, Houghton, Mifflin decided in the fall of 1899 to publish a second short story collection, *The Wife of His Youth and Other Stories of the Color Line*, in time for the Christmas trade.

The majority of the stories in *The Wife of His Youth* explore the moral conflicts and psychological strains experienced by those who lived closest to the color line in Chesnutt's day, namely, mixed-race persons like himself. No black American writer before Chesnutt showed either the interest or the skill necessary to attempt a fiction of manners concerned with light-skinned, middle class African Americans. As a result, white American literature knew next to nothing about those blacks whose intellectual gifts and educational training qualified them for membership in the leadership class that W.E.B. Du Bois would later term black America's "Talented Tenth."

The image of mixed-race people in most popular American fiction of the late nineteenth century was that of the stereotypical "tragic mulatto" and mulatta, toward whom white fictionists displayed a marked ambivalence. To many whites, the tragedy of the mulatto was his selfish (and inevitably futile) obsession with "passing for white," which all but a few white writers considered to be destructive of the social fabric, as well as the racial purity, of

"Anglo-Saxon civilization." On the other hand, much white fiction of the same era portrayed the mulatta as tragic because of her self-sacrificial propensity for renouncing opportunities to pass for white, for which her creators rewarded her by letting her die a sentimental death or lose herself in some righteous cause. In *The Wife of His Youth*, Chesnutt introduced white America to mixed-race men and women whose moral standards and social goals could not be reduced to those of the standardized tragic mulatto and mulatta. Confronting head-on the ethical, social, and economic problems that mixed-race men and women actually faced, *The Wife of His Youth* portrayed the mulatto and mulatta as not only sympathetic but in important ways symbolic of America's struggle to find a solution to the problems of those who lived on the margins of its caste and class system.

The title story of *The Wife of His Youth* as well as "A Matter of Principle" and to a lesser extent "Her Virginia Mammy" analyze with both pathos and irony the aspirations and prejudices of light-skinned, middle class African Americans in "Groveland," Ohio. Many of Chesnutt's fictional models in these stories were people he knew from his own membership in the Cleveland Social Circle, an exclusive society of upwardly mobile persons of color who were reputed to discriminate against anyone with complexions darker than their own. "The Wife of His Youth" tells how a leader of the "Blue Vein Society" triumphs over his class and color prejudices by acknowledging after decades of separation his dark-skinned plantation wife. In a less pathetic and more satirical case, Chesnutt deflates the racial pretensions of Cicero Clayton, the protagonist of "A Matter of Principle," by showing how this mulatto's "principle" of dissociation from dark-skinned Negroes spoils his daughter's chance to marry a congressman. In "Her Virginia Mammy," Chesnutt broke with American social mores and literary tradition in his unhysterical depiction of the betrothal of a Boston Brahmin to a Groveland woman unaware of her black ancestry.

Chesnutt's color-line stories suggest that the largely mixed-race African American "Talented Tenth" deserved recognition, not repression, for their dedication to traditional American social and economic values. To an America that mouthed the shibboleth of the melting pot, Chesnutt presented mixed-race people's plea for admission into the mainstream as a test of the nation's conscience and its much-vaunted belief in fair play. To those who saw in his message merely a brief for racial intermarriage, the ultimate bugbear of white supremacists, Chesnutt wrote "Uncle Wellington's Wives," in which he argued that meaningful and lasting assimilation into the American mainstream depended on blacks' espousal of education and the middle class work ethic, not on intermarriage. By balancing a critique of Uncle Wellington's naïve desire for a white wife with an implicit acceptance of intermarriage between the lovers depicted in "Her Virginia Mammy," Chesnutt took the question of miscegenation out of the realm of abstract moral prohibition and made it a matter of personal ethical decision, to be judged on an individual basis in light of the social, economic, and psychological factors that most affect the persons concerned.

When Chesnutt turned to the southern scene in *The Wife of His Youth*, he focused on racial problems that resisted his faith in the ameliorative powers of the Protestant work ethic and old-fashioned rugged individualism. In "The Web of Circumstance," a former slave tries to pull himself up by his bootstraps, but a combination of adverse circumstances, racism, and betrayal leave him broken and degraded at the end of the story. In this story, and in "The Sheriff's Children," Chesnutt's pessimistic reaction to the rise of white supremacist attitudes and the eclipse of black opportunity in the "New South" of the 1890s became manifest. When the North Carolina expatriate surveyed the cancerous racism that threatened the entire social organism of the South, he could not adopt the pose of the urbane ironist that had let him write with comic imperturbability about the color consciousness of mixed-race people in the North. The problems of the South demanded a stronger rhetorical reaction. Thus, Chesnutt would sentimentalize, sensationalize, and even sermonize to force his readers to consider contemporary racial realities in the clarifying light of purely ethical considerations, unrefracted by custom, prejudice, or past traditions.

The Wife of His Youth did not sit particularly well with its reviewers or the public. Some critics, like the noted white novelist William Dean Howells, called Chesnutt a literary realist of the first order. But others were troubled by his concentration on such cheerless topics as segregation, mob violence, and, most obviously, miscegenation, which some reviewers, especially in the South, felt Chesnutt was subtly advocating. Although his publisher was disappointed by the immediate sales of his second book, Chesnutt refused to look back. In the fall of 1899, with *The Wife of His Youth* on the verge of publication, he closed his prosperous court-reporting business in Cleveland to pursue his lifelong dream—a career as a full-time author. In the next six years he published three novels of purpose, *The House Behind the Cedars* (1900), *The Marrow of Tradition* (1901), and *The Colonel's Dream* (1905), which surveyed racial problems in the postwar South and tested out a number of possible social, economic, and political solutions.

Although *The House Behind the Cedars* was generally well received and *The Marrow of Tradition* was widely reviewed as disturbing but important, by the time Chesnutt began writing *The Colonel's Dream* he knew that his experimental literary career was at an end and that he would have to return to his court-reporting business to earn a living for himself and his family. The publication of "Baxter's Procrustes," Chesnutt's last significant work of short fiction, in the *Atlantic Monthly* in 1904 may be read as the author's parting shot at the critics and reviewers who subjected him, like the protagonist of his story, to the procrustean bed of their commercial preoccupations, genteel standards, and small-minded prejudices.

In 1931, in "Post-Bellum—Pre-Harlem," an essay in literary autobiography, Chesnutt accepted the fact that writing fashions had passed him by, but he took pride in pointing out how far African-American literature and the attitude of the white literary world toward it had come since the days when he first broke into print. Although he was too modest to do so, Chesnutt might have claimed an important role in preparing the public mind in America for the advent of the New Negro author of the 1920s, for in a basic sense, the new movement followed his precedent in unmasking the false poses and images of their era in order to refocus attention on the real racial issues facing their America.

Today, historians of black American writing point out that Charles Chesnutt deserves credit for almost singlehandedly inaugurating a truly African-American literary tradition in the short story. He was the first writer to make the broad range of African-American experience his artistic province and to consider practically every issue and problem endemic to the American color line worthy of literary attention. Because he developed literary modes appropriate to his materials, Chesnutt also left to his successors a rich formal legacy that underlies major trends in twentieth-century black fiction, from the ironies of James Weldon Johnson's classic African-American fiction of manners to the magical realism of Charles Johnson's contemporary neo-slave narratives. It was Chesnutt, in other words, who first inspired black American writers—and instructed white American readers—with a body of literary work that demonstrated unquestionably the African-American fiction writer's arrival as both an artistic innovator and a social commentator on racial realities in the United States.

—WILLIAM L. ANDREWS

SUGGESTIONS FOR FURTHER READING

Andrews, William L. *The Literary Career of Charles W. Chesnutt.* Baton Rouge: Louisiana State University Press, 1980.

Bone, Robert. *Down Home: A History of Afro-American Short Fiction from Its Beginnings to the End of the Harlem Renaissance.* New York: Capricorn, 1975.

Burnette, Ricardo V., "Charles W. Chesnutt's *The Conjure Woman* Revisited," *CLA Journal* 30: 438–453 (June 1987).

Duncan, Charles. *The Absent Man: The Narrative Craft of Charles W. Chesnutt.* Athens: Ohio University Press, 1998.

Elder, Arlene A. *The "Hindered Hand": Cultural Implications of Early African-American Fiction.* Westport, CT: Greenwood Press, 1978.

Howells, William Dean. "Mr. Chesnutt's Stories." *Atlantic Monthly* 85 (1900): 699–701.

Keller, Frances Richardson. *An American Crusade: The Life of Charles Waddell Chesnutt.* Provo, Utah: Brigham Young University Press, 1978.

McElrath, Joseph R., Jr. "A Collaborative Authorship: The Charles W. Chesnutt-Walter Hines Page Relationship." In *The Professions of Authorship: Essays in Honor of Matthew J. Bruccoli*, Richard Layman and Joel Myerson, eds. Columbia: University of South Carolina Press, 1996, pp. 150–68.

———, ed. *Critical Essays on Charles W. Chesnutt.* New York: G.K. Hall, 1999.

McElrath, Joseph R., Jr., and Robert C. Leitz, III, eds. *To Be an Author: Letters of Charles W. Chesnutt, 1889–1905.* Princeton: Princeton University Press, 1997.

Render, Sylvia Lyons, ed. *The Short Fiction of Charles W. Chesnutt.* Washington, D.C.: Howard University Press, 1974.

Stepto, Robert B. " 'The Simple But Intensely Human Inner Life of Slavery': Storytelling and the Revision of History in Charles W. Chesnutt's

'Uncle Julius Stories.' " In *History and Tradition in Afro-American Culture*, Gunter H. Lenz, ed. Frankfort: Campus Verlag, 1984, pp. 29–54.

Sundquist, Eric J. *To Wake the Nations: Race in the Making of American Literature*. Cambridge, MA: Harvard University Press, 1993.

Werner, Craig. "The Framing of Charles Chesnutt: Practical Deconstruction in the Afro-American Tradition." In *Southern Literature and Literary Theory*, Jefferson Humphries, ed. Athens: University of Georgia Press, 1990, pp. 339–365.

Wideman, John Edgar. "Charles Chesnutt and the WPA Narratives: The Oral and Literate Roots of Afro-American Literature." In *The Slave's Narrative*, Charles T. Davis and Henry Louis Gates, Jr., eds. New York: Oxford University Press, 1985, pp. 59–78.

A NOTE ON THE TEXT

Conjure Tales and Stories of the Color Line reprints all the stories that appeared in Chesnutt's two books of short stories, *The Conjure Woman* (1899) and *The Wife of His Youth and Other Stories of the Color Line* (1899), in the order in which they originally appeared in these books. In addition, this volume contains the two best known and most often discussed Chesnutt stories that were published only in magazines: "Dave's Neckliss" (*Atlantic Monthly*, October 1889) and "Baxter's Procrustes" (*Atlantic Monthly*, June 1904). Over the course of his literary career, Chesnutt published sixty-one short stories, sketches, and humorous anecdotes. Of this number, approximately half were written during his literary apprenticeship for Sunday newspaper supplements, humor magazines, household journals, and the like. Of the remaining, more substantial body of Chesnutt's short fiction, the eighteen stories in *Conjure Tales and Stories of the Color Line* represent the diversity and artistry of his most enduring work in the short story.

CONJURE TALES AND
STORIES OF THE COLOR LINE

The Goophered Grapevine

SOME YEARS AGO my wife was in poor health, and our family doctor, in whose skill and honesty I had implicit confidence, advised a change of climate. I shared, from an unprofessional standpoint, his opinion that the raw winds, the chill rains, and the violent changes of temperature that characterized the winters in the region of the Great Lakes tended to aggravate my wife's difficulty, and would undoubtedly shorten her life if she remained exposed to them. The doctor's advice was that we seek, not a temporary place of sojourn, but a permanent residence, in a warmer and more equable climate. I was engaged at the time in grape-culture in northern Ohio, and, as I liked the business and had given it much study, I decided to look for some other locality suitable for carrying it on. I thought of sunny France, of sleepy Spain, of Southern California, but there were objections to them all. It occurred to me that I might find what I wanted in some one of our own Southern States. It was a sufficient time after the war for conditions in the South to have become somewhat settled; and I was enough of a pioneer to start a new industry, if I could not find a place where grape-culture had been tried. I wrote to a cousin who had gone into the turpentine business in central North Carolina. He assured me, in response to my inquiries, that no better place could be found in the South than the State and neighborhood where he lived; the climate was perfect for health, and, in conjunction with the soil, ideal for grape-culture; labor was cheap, and land could be bought for a mere song. He gave us a cordial invitation to come and visit him while we looked into the matter. We accepted the invitation, and after several days of leisurely travel, the last hundred miles of which were up a river on a sidewheel steamer, we reached our destination, a quaint old town, which I shall call Patesville, because, for one reason, that is not its name. There was a red brick markethouse in the public square, with a tall tower, which held a four-faced clock that struck the hours, and from which there pealed out a curfew at nine o'clock. There were two or three hotels, a court-house, a jail, stores, offices, and all the appurtenances of a county seat and a commercial emporium; for while Patesville numbered only four or five thousand inhabitants, of all shades of complexion, it was one of the principal towns in North Carolina, and had a considerable trade in cotton and naval stores. This business activity was not immediately apparent to my unaccustomed eyes. Indeed, when I first saw the town, there brooded over it a calm that seemed almost sabbatic in its restfulness, though I learned later on that underneath its somnolent exterior the deeper currents of life—love and hatred, joy and despair, ambition and avarice, faith and friendship—flowed not less steadily than in livelier latitudes.

We found the weather delightful at that season, the end of summer, and were hospitably entertained. Our host was a man of means and evidently regarded our visit as a pleasure, and we were therefore correspondingly at our ease, and in a position to act with the coolness of judgment desirable in making so radical a change in our lives. My cousin placed a horse and buggy at our disposal, and himself acted as our guide until I became somewhat familiar with the country.

I found that grape-culture, while it had never been carried on to any great extent, was not entirely unknown in the neighborhood. Several planters thereabouts had attempted it on a commercial scale, in former years, with greater or less success; but like most Southern industries, it had felt the blight of war and had fallen into desuetude.

I went several times to look at a place that I thought might suit me. It was a plantation of considerable extent, that had formerly belonged to a wealthy man by the name of McAdoo. The estate had been for years involved in litigation between disputing heirs, during which period shiftless cultivation had well-nigh exhausted the soil. There had been a vineyard of some extent on the place, but it had not been attended to since the war, and had lapsed into utter neglect. The vines—here partly supported by decayed and broken-down trellises, there twining themselves among the branches of the slender saplings which had sprung up among them—grew in wild and unpruned luxuriance, and the few scattered grapes they bore were the undisputed prey of the first comer. The site was admirably adapted to grape-raising; the soil, with a little attention, could not have been better; and with the native grape, the luscious scupper-nong, as my main reliance in the beginning, I felt sure that I could introduce and cultivate successfully a number of other varieties.

One day I went over with my wife to show her the place. We drove out of the town over a long wooden bridge that spanned a spreading mill-pond, passed the long white-washed fence sur-rounding the county fair-ground, and struck into a road so sandy that the horse's feet sank to the fetlocks. Our route lay partly up hill and partly down, for we were in the sand-hill country; we drove past cultivated farms, and then by abandoned fields grown up in scrub-oak and short-leaved pine, and once or twice through the solemn aisles of the virgin forest, where the tall pines, well-nigh meeting over the narrow road, shut out the sun, and wrapped us in cloistral solitude. Once, at a cross-roads, I was in doubt as to the turn to take, and we sat there waiting ten minutes—we had already caught some of the native infection of restfulness—for some human being to come along, who could direct us on our way. At length a little negro girl appeared, walking straight as an arrow, with a piggin full of water on her head. After a little patient investigation, neces-sary to overcome the child's shyness, we learned what we wished to know, and at the end of about five miles from the town reached our destination.

We drove between a pair of decayed gateposts—the gate itself had long since disappeared—and up a straight sandy lane, between two lines of rotting rail fence, partly concealed by jimson-weeds and briers, to the open space where a dwelling-house had once stood, evidently a spacious mansion, if we might judge from the ru-ined chimneys that were still standing, and the brick pillars on which the sills rested. The house itself, we had been informed, had fallen a victim to the fortunes of war.

We alighted from the buggy, walked about the yard for a while, and then wandered off into the adjoining vineyard. Upon Annie's complaining of weariness I led the way back to the yard, where a pine log, lying under a spreading elm, afforded a shady though somewhat hard seat. One end of the log was already occupied by a venerable-looking colored man. He held on his knees a hat full of grapes, over which he was smacking his lips with great gusto, and a pile of grapeskins near him indicated that the performance was no new thing. We approached him at an angle from the rear, and were close to him before he perceived us. He respectfully rose as we drew near, and was moving away, when I begged him to keep his seat.

"Don't let us disturb you," I said. "There is plenty of room for us all."

He resumed his seat with somewhat of embarrassment. While he had been standing, I had observed that he was a tall man, and, though slightly bowed by the weight of years, apparently quite vigorous. He was not entirely black, and this fact, together with the quality of his hair, which was about six inches long and very bushy, except on the top of his head, where he was quite bald, suggested a slight strain of other than negro blood. There was a shrewdness in his eyes, too, which was not altogether African, and which, as we afterwards learned from experience, was indicative of a corresponding shrewdness in his character. He went on eating the grapes, but did not seem to enjoy himself quite so well as he had apparently done before he became aware of our presence.

"Do you live around here?" I asked, anxious to put him at ease.

"Yas, suh. I lives des ober yander, behine de nex' san'-hill, on de Lumberton plank-road."

"Do you know anything about the time when this vineyard was cultivated?"

"Lawd bless you, suh, I knows all about it. Dey ain' na'er a man in dis settlement w'at won' tell you ole Julius McAdoo 'uz bawn en raise' on dis yer same plantation. Is you de Norv'n gemman w'at's gwine ter buy de ole vimya'd?"

"I am looking at it," I replied; "but I don't know that I shall care to buy unless I can be reasonably sure of making something out of it."

"Well, suh, you is a stranger ter me, en I is a stranger ter you, en we is bofe strangers ter one anudder, but 'f I 'uz in yo' place, I would n' buy dis vimya'd."

"Why not?" I asked.

"Well, I dunno whe'r you b'lieves in cunj'in' er not,—some er de w'ite folks don't, er says dey don't,—but de truf er de matter is dat dis yer ole vimya'd is goophered."

"Is what?" I asked, not grasping the meaning of this unfamiliar word.

"Is goophered,—cunju'd, bewitch'."

He imparted this information with such solemn earnestness, and with such an air of confidential mystery, that I felt somewhat interested, while Annie was evidently much impressed, and drew closer to me.

"How do you know it is bewitched?" I asked.

"I would n' spec' fer you ter b'lieve me 'less you know all 'bout de fac's. But ef you en young miss dere doan' min' lis'nin' ter a ole nigger run on a minute er two w'ile you er restin', I kin 'splain to you how it all happen'."

We assured him that we would be glad to hear how it all happened, and he began to tell us. At first the current of his memory—or imagination—seemed somewhat sluggish; but as his embarrassment wore off, his language flowed more freely, and the story acquired perspective and coherence. As he became more and more absorbed in the narrative, his eyes assumed a dreamy expression, and he seemed to lose sight of his auditors, and to be living over again in monologue his life on the old plantation.

"Ole Mars Dugal' McAdoo," he began, "bought dis place long many years befo' de wah, en I 'member well w'en he sot out all dis yer part er de plantation in scuppernon's. De vimes growed monst'us fas', en Mars Dugal' made a thousan' gallon er scuppernon' wine eve'y year.

"Now, ef dey's an'thing a nigger lub, nex' ter 'possum, en chick'n, en watermillyums, it's scuppernon's. Dey ain' nuffin dat kin stan' up side'n de scuppernon' fer sweetness; sugar ain't a suckumstance ter scuppernon'. W'en de season is nigh 'bout ober, en de grapes begin ter swivel up des a little wid de wrinkles er ole age,— w'en de skin git sof' en brown,—den de scuppernon' make you smack yo' lip en roll yo' eye en wush fer mo'; so I reckon it ain' very 'stonishin' dat niggers lub scuppernon'.

"Dey wuz a sight er niggers in de naberhood er de vimya'd.

Dere wuz ole Mars Henry Brayboy's niggers, en ole Mars Jeems McLean's niggers, en Mars Dugal's own niggers; den dey wuz a settlement er free niggers en po' buckrahs down by de Wim'l'ton Road, en Mars Dugal' had de only vimya'd in de naberhood. I reckon it ain' so much so nowadays, but befo' de wah, in slab'ry times, a nigger did n' mine goin' fi' er ten mile in a night, w'en dey wuz sump'n good ter eat at de yuther een'.

"So after a w'ile Mars Dugal' begin ter miss his scuppernon's. Co'se he 'cuse' de niggers er it, but dey all 'nied it ter de las', Mars Dugal' sot spring guns en steel traps, en he en de oberseah sot up nights once't er twice't, tel one night Mars Dugal'—he 'uz a monst'us keerless man—got his leg shot full er cow-peas. But somehow er nudder dey could n' nebber ketch none er de niggers. I dunner how it happen, but it happen des like I tell you, en de grapes kep' on agoin' des de same.

"But bimeby old Mars Dugal' fix' up a plan ter stop it. Dey wuz a cunjuh 'oman livin' down 'mongs' de free niggers on de Wim'l'ton Road, en all de darkies fum Rockfish ter Beaver Crick wuz feared er her. She could wuk de mos' powerfulles' kin' er goopher,—could make people hab fits, er rheumatiz, er make 'em des dwinel away en die; en dey say she went out ridin' de niggers at night, fer she wuz a witch 'sides bein' a cunjuh 'oman. Mars Dugal' hearn 'bout Aun' Peggy's doin's, en begun ter 'flect whe'r er no he could n' git her ter he'p him keep de niggers off'n de grapevimes. One day in de spring er de year, ole miss pack' up a basket er chick'n en poun'-cake, en a bottle er scuppernon' wine, en Mars Dugal' tuk it in his buggy en driv ober ter Aun' Peggy's cabin. He tuk de basket in, en had a long talk wid Aun' Peggy.

"De nex' day Aun' Peggy come up ter de vimya'd. De niggers seed her slippin' 'round', en dey soon foun' out what she 'uz doin' dere. Mars Dugal' had hi'ed her ter goopher de grapevimes. She sa'ntered 'roun' 'mongs' de vimes, en tuk a leaf fum dis one, en a grape-hull fum dat one, en a grape-seed fum anudder one; en den a little twig fum here, en a little pinch er dirt fum dere,—en put it all in a big black bottle, wid a snake's toof en a speckle' hen's gall en some ha'rs fum a black cat's tail, en den fill' de bottle wid scuppernon' wine. W'en she got de goopher all ready en fix', she tuk 'n went out in de woods en buried it under de root uv a red oak tree, en den come back en tole one er de niggers she done goopher de grapevimes, en a'er a nigger w'at eat dem grapes 'ud be sho ter die inside'n twel' mont's.

"Atter dat de niggers let de scuppernon's 'lone, en Mars Dugal' did n' hab no 'casion ter fine no mo' fault; en de season wuz mos' gone, w'en a strange gemman stop at de plantation one night ter see Mars Dugal' on some business; en his coachman, seein' de scuppernon's growin' so nice en sweet, slip 'roun' behine de smoke-house, en et all de scuppernon's he could hole. Nobody did n' notice it at de time, but dat night, on de way home, de gemman's hoss runned away en kill' de coachman. W'en we hearn de noos, Aun' Lucy, de cook, she up'n say she seed de strange nigger eat'n' er de scuppernon's behine de smoke-house; en den we knowed de goopher had b'en er wukkin'. Den one er de nigger chilluns runned away fum de quarters one day, en got in de scuppernon's, en died de nex' week. W'ite folks say he die' er de fevuh, but de niggers knowed it wuz de goopher. So you k'n be sho de darkies did n' hab much ter do wid dem scuppernon' vimes.

"We'en de scuppernon' season 'uz ober fer dat year, Mars Dugal' foun' he had made fifteen hund'ed gallon er wine; en one er de niggers hearn him laffin' wid de oberseah fit ter kill, en sayin' dem fifteen hund'ed gallon er wine wuz monst'us good intrus' on de ten dollars he laid out on de vimya'd. So I 'low ez he paid Aun' Peggy ten dollars fer to goopher de grapevimes.

"De goopher did n' wuk no mo' tel de nex' summer, w'en 'long to'ds de middle er de season one er de fiel' han's died; en ez dat lef' Mars Dugal' sho't er han's, he went off ter town fer ter buy anudder. He fotch de noo nigger home wid 'im. He wuz er ole nigger, er de color er a gingy-cake, en ball ez a hoss-apple on de top er his head. He wuz a peart ole nigger, do', en could do a big day's wuk.

"Now it happen dat one er de niggers on de nex' plantation, one er ole Mars Henry Brayboy's niggers, had runned away de day befo', en tuk ter de swamp, en ole Mars Dugal' en some er de yuther nabor w'ite folks had gone out wid dere guns en dere dogs fer ter he'p 'em hunt fer de nigger; en de han's on our own plantation wuz all so flusterated dat we fuhgot ter tell de noo han' 'bout de goopher on de scuppernon' vimes. Co'se he smell de grapes en see de vimes, an atter dahk de fus' thing he done wuz ter slip off ter de grapevimes 'dout sayin' nuffin ter nobody. Nex' mawnin' he tole some er de niggers 'bout de fine bait er scuppernon' he et de night befo'.

"W'en dey tole 'im 'bout de goopher on de grapevimes, he 'uz dat tarrified dat he turn pale, en look des like he gwine ter die right in his tracks. De obserseah come up en axed w'at 'uz de matter; en w'en dey tole 'im Henry be'n eatin' er de scuppernon's, en got de goopher on 'im, he gin Henry a big drink er w'iskey, en 'low dat de nex' rainy day he take 'im ober ter Aun' Peggy's, en see ef she would n' take de goopher off'n him, seein' ez he did n' know nuffin erbout it tel he done et de grapes.

"Sho nuff, it rain de nex' day, en de obserseah went ober ter Aun' Peggy's wid Henry. En Aun' Peggy say dat bein' ez Henry did n' know 'bout de goopher, en et de grapes in ign'ance er de conse-q'ences, she reckon she mought be able fer ter take de goopher off'n him. So she fotch out er bottle wid some cunjuh medicine in it, en po'd some out in a go'd fer Henry ter drink. He manage ter git it down; he say it tas'e like whiskey wid sump'n bitter in it. She 'lowed dat 'ud keep de goopher off'n him tel de spring; but w'en de sap begin ter rise in de grapevimes he ha' ter come en see her ag'in, en she tell him w'at e's ter do.

"Nex' spring, w'en de sap commence' ter rise in de scuppernon' vime, Henry tuk a ham one night. Whar'd he git de ham? *I* doan know; dey wa'n't no hams on de plantation 'cep'n' w'at 'uz in de smoke-house, but *I* never see Henry 'bout de smoke-house. But ez I wuz a-sayin', he tuk de ham ober ter Aun' Peggy's; en Aun' Peggy tole 'im dat w'en Mars Dugal' begin ter prune de grapevimes, he mus' go en take 'n scrape off de sap whar it ooze out'n de cut een's er de vimes, en 'n'int his ball head wid it; en ef he do dat once't a year de goopher would n' wuk agin 'im long ez he done it. En bein' ez he fotch her de ham, she fix' it so he kin eat all de scuppernon' he want.

"So Henry 'n'int his head wid de sap out'n de big grapevime des ha'f way 'twix' de quarters en de big house, en de goopher nebber wuk agin him dat summer. But de beatenes' thing you eber see hap-pen ter Henry. Up ter dat time he wuz ez ball ez a sweeten' 'tater, but des ez soon ez de young leaves begun ter come out on de grape-vimes, de ha'r begun ter grow out on Henry's head, en by de middle er de summer he had de bigges' head er ha'r on de plantation. Befo' dat, Henry had tol'able good ha'r 'roun' de aidges, but soon ez de young grapes begun ter come, Henry's ha'r begun to quirl all up in little balls, des like dis yer reg'lar grapy ha'r, en by de time de grapes got ripe his head look des like a bunch er grapes. Combin' it did n' do no good; he wuk at it ha'f de night wid er Jim Crow,[*] en think he git it straighten' out, but in de mawnin' de grapes 'ud be dere des de same. So he gin it up, en tried ter keep de grapes down by havin' his ha'r cut sho't.

"But dat wa'n't de quares' thing 'bout de goopher. When Henry come ter de plantation, he wuz gittin' a little ole an stiff in de j'ints. But dat summer he got des ez spry en libely ez any young nigger on de plantation; fac', he got so biggity dat Mars Jackson, de oberseah, ha' ter th'eaten ter whip 'im, ef he did n' stop cuttin' up his didos en behave hisse'f. But de mos' cur'ouses' thing happen' in de fall, when de sap begin ter go down in de grapevimes. Fus', when de grapes 'uz gethered, de knots begun ter straighten out'n Henry's ha'r; en w'en de leaves begin ter fall, Henry's ha'r 'mence' ter drap out; en when de vimes 'uz bar', Henry's head wuz baller 'n it wuz in de spring, en he begin ter git ole en stiff in de j'ints ag'in, en paid no mo' 'tention ter de gals dyoin' er de whole winter. En nex' spring, w'en he rub de sap on ag'in, he got young ag'in, en so soopl en libely dat none er de young niggers on de plantation could n' jump, ner dance, ner hoe ez much cotton ez Henry. But in de fall er de year his grapes 'mence' ter straighten out, en his j'ints ter git stiff, en his ha'r drap off, en de rheumatiz begin ter wrastle wid 'im.

"Now, ef you'd 'a' knowed ole Mars Dugal' McAdoo, you'd 'a' knowed dat it ha' ter be a mighty rainy day when he could n' fine sump'n fer his niggers ter do, en it ha' ter be a mighty little hole he could n' crawl thoo, en ha' ter be a monst'us cloudy night when a dollar git by him in de dahkness; en w'en he see how Henry git young in de spring en ole in de fall, he 'lowed ter hisse'f ez how he could make mo' money out'n Henry dan by wukkin' him in de cotton-fiel'. 'Long de nex' spring, atter de sap 'mence' ter rise, en Henry 'n'int 'is head en sta'ted fer ter git young en soopl, Mars

---

[*] A small card, resembling a currycomb in construction, and used by negroes in the rural districts instead of a comb.

Dugal' up 'n tuk Henry ter town, en sole 'im fer fifteen hunder' dollars. Co'se de man w'at bought Henry did n' know nuffin 'bout de goopher, en Mars Dugal' did n' see no 'casion fer ter tell 'im. Long to'ds de fall, w'en de sap went down, Henry begin ter git ole ag'in same ez yuzhal, en his noo marster begin ter git skeered les'n he gwine ter lose his fifteen-hunder'-dollar nigger. He sent fer a mighty fine doctor, but de med'cine did n' 'pear ter do no good; de goopher had a good holt. Henry tole de doctor 'bout de goopher, but de doctor des laff at 'im.

"One day in de winter Mars Dugal' went ter town, en wuz santerin' 'long de Main Street, when who should he meet but Henry's noo marster. Dey said 'Hoddy,' en Mars Dugal' ax 'im ter hab a see-gyar; en atter dey run on awhile 'bout de craps en de weather, Mars Dugal' ax 'im, sorter keerless, like ez ef he des thought of it,—

" 'How you like de nigger I sole you las' spring?'

"Henry's marster shuck his head en knock de ashes off'n his see-gyar.

" 'Spec' I made a bad bahgin when I bought dat nigger. Henry done good wuk all de summer, but sence de fall set in he 'pears ter be sorter pinin' away. Dey ain' nuffin per-tickler de matter wid 'im—leastways de doctor say so—'cep'n' a tech er de rheumatiz; but his ha'r is all fell out, en ef he don't pick up his strenk mighty soon, I spec' I'm gwine ter lose 'im.'

"Dey smoked on awhile, en bimeby ole mars say, 'Well, a bahgin's a bahgin, but you en me is good fren's, en I doan wan' ter see you lose all de money you paid fer dat nigger; en ef w'at you say is so, en I ain't 'sputin' it, he ain't wuf much now. I 'spec's you wukked him too ha'd dis summer, er e'se de swamps down here don't agree wid de san'-hill nigger. So you des lemme know, en ef he gits any wusser I'll be willin' ter gib yer five hund'ed dollars fer 'im, en take my chances on his livin'.'

"Sho 'nuff, when Henry begun ter draw up wid de rheumatiz en it look like he gwine ter die fer sho, his noo marster sen' fer Mars Dugal', en Mars Dugal' gin him what he promus, en brung Henry home ag'in. He tuk good keer uv 'im dyoin' er de winter,—give 'im w'iskey ter rub his rheumatiz, en terbacker ter smoke, en all he want ter eat,—'caze a nigger w'at he could make a thousan' dollars a year off'n did n' grow on eve'y huckleberry bush.

"Nex' spring, w'en de sap ris en Henry's ha'r commence' ter sprout, Mars Dugal' sole 'im ag'in, down in Robeson County dis time; en he kep' dat sellin' business up fer five year er mo'. Henry nebber say nuffin 'bout de goopher ter his noo marsters, 'caze he know he gwine ter be tuk good keer uv de nex' winter, w'en Mars Dugal' buy him back. En Mars Dugal' made 'nuff money off'n Henry ter buy anudder plantation ober on Beaver Crick.

"But 'long 'bout de een' er dat five year dey come a stranger ter stop at de plantation. De fus' day he 'uz dere he went out wid Mars Dugal' en spent all de mawnin' lookin' ober de vimya'd, en atter dinner dey spent all de evenin' playin' kya'ds. De niggers soon 'skiver' dat he wuz a Yankee, en dat he come down ter Norf C'lina fer ter l'arn de w'ite folks how to raise grapes en make wine. He promus Mars Dugal' he c'd make de grapevimes b'ar twice't ez many grapes, en dat de noo winepress he wuz a-sellin' would make mo' d'n twice't ez many gallons er wine. En ole Mars Dugal' des drunk it all in, des 'peared ter be bewitch' wid dat Yankee. W'en de darkies see dat Yankee runnin' 'roun' de vimya'd en diggin' under de grapevimes, dey shuk dere heads, en 'lowed dat dey feared Mars Dugal' losin' his min'. Mars Dugal' had all de dirt dug away fum under de roots er all de scuppernon' vimes, an' let 'em stan' dat away fer a week er mo'. Den dat Yankee made de niggers fix up a mixtry er lime en ashes en manyo, en po' it 'roun' de roots er de grapevimes. Den he 'vise Mars Dugal' fer ter trim de vimes close't, en Mars Dugal' tuck 'n done eve'ything de Yankee tole him ter do. Dyoin' all er dis time, mind yer, dis yer Yankee wuz libbin' off'n de fat er de lan', at de big house, en playin' kya'ds wid Mars Dugal' eve'y night; en dey say Mars Dugal' los' mo'n a thousan' dollars dyoin' er de week dat Yankee wuz a-ruinin' de grapevimes.

"W'en de sap ris nex' spring, ole Henry 'n'inted his head ez yuzhal, en his ha'r, 'mence' ter grow des de same ez it done eve'y year. De scuppernon' vimes growed monst's fas', en de leaves wuz greener en thicker dan dey eber be'n dyoin' my remem'ance; en Henry's ha'r growed out thicker dan eber, en he 'peared ter git younger 'n younger, en soopler 'n soopler; en seein' ez he wuz sho't er han's dat spring, havin' tuk in consid'able noo groun', Mars Dugal' 'cluded he would n' sell Henry 'tel he git de crap in en de cotton chop'. So he kep' Henry on de plantation.

"But 'long 'bout time fer de grapes ter come on de scuppernon' vimes, dey 'peared ter come a change ober 'em; de leaves withered en swivel' up, en de young grapes turn' yaller, en bimeby eve'ybody on de plantation could see dat de whole vimya'd wuz dyin'. Mars Dugal' tuk 'n water de vimes en done all he could, but 't wa'n' no use; dat Yankee had done bus' de watermillyum. One time de vimes picked up a bit, en Mars Dugal' 'lowed dey wuz gwine ter come out ag'in; but dat Yankee done dug too close under de roots, en prune de branches too close ter de vime, en all dat lime en ashes done burn' de life out'n de vimes, en dey des kep' a-with'in en a-swivelin'.

"All dis time de goopher wuz a-wukkin'. When de vimes sta'ted ter wither, Henry 'mence' ter complain er his rheumatiz; en when de leaves begin ter dry up, his ha'r 'mence' ter drap out. When de vimes fresh' up a bit, Henry 'd git peart ag'in, en when de vimes wither' ag'in, Henry 'd git ole ag'in, en des kep' gittin' mo' en mo' fitten fer nuffin; he des pined away, en pined away, en fine'ly tuk ter his cabin; en when de big vime whar he got de sap ter 'n'int his head withered en turned yaller en died, Henry died too,—des went out sorter like a cannel. Dey did n't 'pear ter be nuffin de matter wid'im, 'cep'n' de rheumatiz, but his strenk des dwinel' away 'tel he did n' hab ernuff lef' ter draw his bref. De goopher had got de under holt, en th'owed Henry dat time fer good en all.

"Mars Dugal' tuk on might'ly 'bout losin' his vimes en his nigger in de same year; en he swo' dat ef he could git holt er dat Yankee he'd wear 'im ter a frazzle, en den chaw up de frazzle; en he'd done it, too, for Mars Dugal' 'uz a monst'us brash man w'en he once git started. He sot de vimya'd out ober ag'in, but it wuz th'ee er fo' year befo' de vimes got ter b'arin' any scuppernon's.

"W'en de wah broke out, Mars Dugal' raise' a comp'ny, en went off ter fight de Yankees. He say he wuz mighty glad dat wah come, en he des want ter kill a Yankee fer eve'y dollar he los' 'long er dat grape-raisin' Yankee. En I 'spec' he would 'a' done it, too, ef de Yankees had n' s'picioned sump'n, en killed him fus'. Atter de s'render ole miss move' ter town, de niggers all scattered 'way fum de plantation, en de vimya'd ain' be'n cultervated sence."

"Is that story true?" asked Annie doubtfully, but seriously, as the old man concluded his narrative.

"It's des ez true ez I'm a-settin' here, miss. Dey's a easy way ter prove it: I kin lead de way right ter Henry's grave ober yander in de plantation buryin-groun'. En I tell yer w'at, marster, I would n' 'vise you to buy dis yer ole vimya'd, 'caze de goopher's on it yit, en dey ain' no tellin' w'en it's gwine ter crap out."

"But I thought you said all the old vines died."

"Dey did 'pear ter die, but a few un 'em come out ag'in, en is mixed in 'mongs' de yuthers. I ain' skeered ter eat de grapes, 'caze I knows de old vimes fum de noo ones; but wid strangers dey ain' no tellin' w'at mought happen. I would n' 'vise yer ter buy dis vimya'd."

I bought the vineyard, nevertheless, and it has been for a long time in a thriving condition, and is often referred to by the local press as a striking illustration of the opportunities open to Northern capital in the development of Southern industries. The luscious scuppernong holds first rank among our grapes, though we culti- vate a great many other varieties, and our income from grapes packed and shipped to the Northern markets is quite considerable. I have not noticed any developments of the goopher in the vine- yard, although I have a mild suspicion that our colored assistants do not suffer from want of grapes during the season.

I found, when I bought the vineyard, that Uncle Julius had occu- pied a cabin on the place for many years, and derived a respectable revenue from the product of the neglected grapevines. This, doubt- less, accounted for his advice to me not to buy the vineyard, though whether it inspired the goopher story I am unable to state. I believe, however, that the wages I paid him for his services as coach-man, for I gave him employment in that capacity, were more than an equivalent for anything he lost by the sale of the vineyard.

Po' Sandy

ON THE NORTHEAST CORNER of my vineyard in central North Carolina, and fronting on the Lumberton plank-road, there stood a small frame house, of the simplest construction. It was built of pine lumber, and contained but one room, to which one window gave light and one door admission. Its weather-beaten sides revealed a virgin innocence of paint. Against one end of the house, and occupying half its width, there stood a huge brick chimney: the crumbling mortar had left large cracks between the bricks; the bricks themselves had begun to scale off in large flakes, leaving the chimney sprinkled with unsightly blotches. These evidences of decay were but partially concealed by a creeping vine, which extended its slender branches hither and thither in an ambitious but futile attempt to cover the whole chimney. The wooden shutter, which had once protected the unglazed window, had fallen from its hinges, and lay rotting in the rank grass and jimson-weeds beneath. This building, I learned when I bought the place, had been used as a school-house for several years prior to the breaking out of the war, since which time it had remained unoccupied, save when some stray cow or vagrant hog had sought shelter within its walls from the chill rains and nipping winds of winter.

One day my wife requested me to build her a new kitchen. The house erected by us, when we first came to live upon the vineyard, contained a very conveniently arranged kitchen; but for some occult reason my wife wanted a kitchen in the back yard, apart from the dwelling-house, after the usual Southern fashion. Of course I had to build it.

To save expense, I decided to tear down the old school-house, and use the lumber, which was in a good state of preservation, in the construction of the new kitchen. Before demolishing the old house, however, I made an estimate of the amount of material contained in it, and found that I would have to buy several hundred feet of lumber additional, in order to build the new kitchen according to my wife's plan.

One morning old Julius McAdoo, our colored coachman, harnessed the gray mare to the rockaway, and drove my wife and me over to the sawmill from which I meant to order the new lumber. We drove down the long lane which led from our house to the plank-road; following the plank-road for about a mile, we turned into a road running through the forest and across the swamp to the sawmill beyond. Our carriage jolted over the half-rotted corduroy road which traversed the swamp, and then climbed the long hill leading to the sawmill. When we reached the mill, the foreman had gone over to a neighboring farmhouse, probably to smoke or gossip, and we were compelled to await his return before we could transact our business. We remained seated in the carriage, a few rods from the mill, and watched the leisurely movements of the mill-hands. We had not waited long before a huge pine log was placed in position, the machinery of the mill was set in motion, and the circular saw began to eat its way through the log, with a loud whir which resounded throughout the vicinity of the mill. The sound rose and fell in a sort of rhythmic cadence, which, heard from where we sat, was not unpleasing, and not loud enough to prevent conversation. When the saw started on its second journey through the log, Julius observed, in a lugubrious tone, and with a perceptible shudder:—

"Ugh! but dat des do cuddle my blood!"

"What's the matter, Uncle Julius?" inquired my wife, who is of a very sympathetic turn of mind. "Does the noise affect your nerves?"

"No, Mis' Annie," replied the old man, with emotion, "I ain' narvous; but dat saw, a-cuttin' en grindin' thoo dat stick er timber, en moanin', en groanin', en sweekin', kyars my 'memb'ance back ter ole times, en 'min's me er po' Sandy." The pathetic intonation with which he lengthened out the "po' Sandy" touched a responsive chord in our own hearts.

"And who was poor Sandy?" asked my wife, who takes a deep interest in the stories of plantation life which she hears from the lips of the older colored people. Some of these stories are quaintly humorous; others wildly extravagant, revealing the Oriental cast of the negro's imagination; while others, poured freely into the sympathetic ear of a Northern-bred woman, disclose many a tragic incident of the darker side of slavery.

"Sandy," said Julius, in reply to my wife's question, "was a nigger w'at useter b'long ter ole Mars Marrabo McSwayne. Mars Marrabo's place wuz on de yuther side'n de swamp, right nex' ter yo' place. Sandy wuz a monst'us good nigger, en could do so many things erbout a plantation, en alluz 'ten' ter his wuk so well, dat w'en Mars Marrabo's chilluns growed up en married off, dey all un 'em wanted dey daddy fer ter gin 'em Sandy fer a weddin' present. But Mars Marrabo knowed de res' would n' be satisfied ef he gin Sandy ter a'er one un 'em; so w'en dey wuz all done married, he fix it by 'lowin' one er his chilluns ter take Sandy fer a mont' er so, en den ernudder fer a mont' er so, en so on dat erway tel dey had all had 'im de same lenk er time; en den dey would all take him roun' ag'in, 'cep'n' oncet in a w'ile w'en Mars Marrabo would len' 'im ter some er his yuther kinfolks 'roun' de country, w'en dey wuz short er han's; tel bimeby it got so Sandy did n' hardly knowed whar he wuz gwine ter stay fum one week's een' ter de yuther.

"One time w'en Sandy wuz lent out ez yushal, a spekilater come erlong wid a lot er niggers, en Mars Marrabo swap' Sandy's wife off fer a noo 'oman. W'en Sandy come back, Mars Marrabo gin 'im a dollar, en 'lowed he wuz monst'us sorry fer ter break up de fambly, but de spekilater had gin 'im big boot, en times wuz hard en money skase, en so he wuz bleedst ter make de trade. Sandy tuk on some 'bout losin' his wife, but he soon seed dey want no use cryin' ober split merlasses; en bein' ez he lacked de looks er de noo 'oman, he tuk up wid her atter she'd be'n on de plantation a mont' er so.

"Sandy en his noo wife got on mighty well tergedder, en de niggers all 'mence' ter talk about how lovin' dey wuz. W'en Tenie wuz tuk sick oncet, Sandy useter set up all night wid 'er, en den go ter wuk in de mawnin' des lack he had his reg'lar sleep; en Tenie would 'a' done anythin' in de worl' for her Sandy.

"Sandy en Tenie had n' be'n libbin' tergedder fer mo' d'n two mont's befo' Mars Marrabo's old uncle, w'at libbed down in Robeson County, sent up ter fin' out ef Mars Marrabo could n' len' 'im

er hire 'im a good han' fer a mont' er so. Sandy's marster wuz one er
dese yer easy-gwine folks w'at wanter please eve'ybody, en he says
yas, he could len' 'im Sandy. En Mars Marrabo tol' Sandy fer ter git
ready ter go down ter Robeson nex' day, fer ter stay a mont' er so.

"It wuz monst'us hard on Sandy fer ter take 'im 'way fum Tenie.
It wuz so fur down ter Robeson dat he did n' hab no chance er
comin' back ter see her tel de time wuz up; he would n' 'a' mine
comin' ten er fifteen mile at night ter see Tenie, but Mars Marrabo's
uncle's plantation wuz mo' d'n forty mile off. Sandy wuz mighty
sad en cas' down atter w'at Mars Marrabo tol' 'im, en he says ter
Tenie, sezee:—

" 'I'm gittin' monst'us ti'ed er dish yer gwine roun' so much.
Here I is lent ter Mars Jeems dis mont', en I got ter do so-en-so; en
ter Mars Archie de nex' mont', en I got ter do so-en-so; den I got
ter go ter Miss Jinnie's: en hit's Sandy dis en Sandy dat, en Sandy
yer en Sandy dere, tel it 'pears ter me I ain' got no home, ner no
marster, ner no mistiss, ner no nuffin. I can't eben keep a wife: my
yuther ole 'oman wuz sol' away without my gittin' a chance fer ter
tell her good-by; en now I got ter go off en leab you, Tenie, en I
dunno whe'r I'm eber gwine ter see you ag'in er no. I wisht I wuz a
tree, er a stump, er a rock, er sump'n w'at could stay on de plantation fer a w'ile.'

"Atter Sandy got thoo talkin', Tenie did n' say naer word, but
des sot dere by de fier, studyin' en studyin'. Bimeby she up'n'
says:—

" 'Sandy, is I eber tol' you I wuz a cunjuh 'oman?'

"Co'se Sandy had n' nebber dremp' er nuffin lack dat, en he
made a great 'miration w'en he hear w'at Tenie say. Bimeby Tenie
went on:—

" 'I ain' goophered nobody, ner done no cunjuh wuk, fer fifteen
year er mo'; en w'en I got religion I made up my mine I would n'
wuk no mo' goopher. But dey is some things I doan b'lieve it's no
sin fer ter do; en ef you doan wanter be sent roun' fum pillar ter
pos', en ef you doan wanter go down ter Robeson, I kin fix things
so you won't haf ter. Ef you'll des say de word, I kin turn you ter
w'ateber you wanter be, en you kin stay right whar you wanter, ez
long ez you mineter.'

"Sandy say he doan keer; he's willin' fer ter do anythin' fer ter

stay close ter Tenie. Den Tenie ax 'im ef he doan wanter be turnt inter a rabbit.

"Sandy say, 'No, de dogs mought git atter me.'

" 'Shill I turn you ter a wolf?' sez Tenie.

" 'No, eve'ybody skeered er a wolf, en I doan want nobody ter
be skeered er me.'

" 'Shill I turn you ter a mawkin'-bird?'

" 'No, a hawk mought ketch me. I wanter be turnt inter sump'n
w'at 'll stay in one place.'

" 'I kin turn you ter a tree,' sez Tenie. 'You won't hab no mouf
ner years, but I kin turn you back oncet in a w'ile, so you kin git
sump'n ter eat, en hear w'at's gwine on.'

"Well, Sandy say dat 'll do. En so Tenie tuk 'im down by de aidge
er de swamp, not fur fum de quarters, en turnt 'im inter a big pine-
tree, en sot 'im out 'mongs' some yuther trees. En de nex' mawnin',
ez some er de fiel' han's wuz gwine long dere, dey seed a tree w'at
dey did n' 'member er habbin' seed befo'; it wuz monst'us quare, en
dey wuz bleedst ter 'low dat dey had n' 'membered right, er e'se one
er de saplin's had be'n growin' monst'us fas'.

"W'en Mars Marrabo 'skiver' dat Sandy wuz gone, he 'lowed
Sandy had runned away. He got de dogs out, but de las' place dey
could track Sandy ter wuz de foot er dat pine-tree. En dere de dogs
stood en barked, en bayed, en pawed at de tree, en tried ter climb up
on it; en w'en dey wuz tuk roun' thoo de swamp ter look fer de
scent, dey broke loose en made fer dat tree ag'in. It wuz de beatenis'
thing de w'ite folks eber hearn of, en Mars Marrabo 'lowed dat
Sandy must 'a' clim' up on de tree en jump' off on a mule er
sump'n, en rid fur ernuff fer ter spile de scent. Mars Marrabo
wanted ter 'cuse some er de yuther niggers er heppin' Sandy off, but
dey all 'nied it ter de las'; en eve'ybody knowed Tenie sot too much
sto' by Sandy fer ter he'p 'im run away whar she could n' nebber
see 'im no mo'.

"W'en Sandy had be'n gone long ernuff fer folks ter think he
done got clean away, Tenie useter go down ter de woods at night en
turn 'im back, en den dey 'd slip up ter de cabin en set by de fire en
talk. But dey ha' ter be monst'us keerful, er e'se somebody would
'a' seed 'em, en dat would 'a' spile' de whole thing; so Tenie alluz
turnt Sandy back in de mawnin' early, befo' anybody wuz a-stirrin'.

"But Sandy did n' git erlong widout his trials en tribberlations. One day a woodpecker come erlong en 'mence' ter peck at de tree; en de nex' time Sandy wuz turnt back he had a little roun' hole in his arm, des lack a sharp stick be'n stuck in it. Atter dat Tenie sot a sparrer-hawk fer ter watch de tree; en w'en de woodpecker come erlong nex' mawnin' fer ter finish his nes', he got gobble' up mos'fo' he stuck his bill in de bark.

"Nudder time, Mars Marrabo sent a nigger out in de woods fer ter chop tuppentime boxes. De man chop a box in dish yer tree, en hack' de bark up two er th'ee feet, fer ter let de tuppentime run. De nex' time Sandy wuz turnt back he had a big skyar on his lef' leg, des lack it be'n skunt; en it tuk Tenie nigh 'bout all night fer ter fix a mixtry ter kyo it up. Atter dat, Tenie sot a hawnet fer ter watch de tree; en w'en de nigger come back ag'in fer ter cut ernudder box on de yuther side'n de tree, de hawnet stung 'im so hard dat de ax slip en cut his foot nigh 'bout off.

"W'en Tenie see so many things happenin' ter de tree, she 'cluded she'd ha' ter turn Sandy ter sump'n e'se; en atter studyin' de matter ober, en talkin' wid Sandy one ebenin', she made up her mine fer ter fix up a goopher mixtry w'at would turn herse'f en Sandy ter foxes, er sump'n, so dey could run away en go some'rs whar dey could be free en lib lack w'ite folks.

"But dey ain' no tellin' w'at 's gwine ter happen in dis worl'. Tenie had got de night sot for her en Sandy ter run away, w'en dat ve'y day one er Mars Marrabo's sons rid up ter de big house in his buggy, en say his wife wuz monst'us sick, en he want his mammy ter len' 'im a 'oman fer ter nuss his wife. Tenie's mistiss say sen' Tenie; she wuz a good nuss. Young mars wuz in a tarrible hurry fer ter git back home. Tenie wuz washin' at de big house dat day, en her mistiss say she should go right 'long wid her young marster. Tenie tried ter make some 'scuse fer ter git away en hide 'tel night, w'en she would have eve'ything fix' up fer her en Sandy; she say she wanter go ter her cabin fer ter git her bonnet. Her mistiss say it doan matter 'bout de bonnet; her head-hankcher wuz good ernuff. Den Tenie say she wanter git her bes' frock; her mistiss say no, she doan need no mo' frock, en w'en dat one got dirty she could git a clean one whar she wuz gwine. So Tenie had ter git in de buggy en go 'long wid young Mars Dunkin ter his plantation, w'ich wuz mo' d'n twenty mile away; en dey wa'n't no chance er her seein' Sandy no mo' 'tel she come back home. De po' gal felt monst'us bad 'bout de way things wuz gwine on, en she knowed Sandy mus' be a wond'rin' why she did n' come en turn 'im back no mo'.

"W'iles Tenie wuz away nussin' young Mars Dunkin's wife, Mars Marrabo tuk a notion fer ter buil' 'im a noo kitchen; en bein' ez he had lots er timber on his place, he begun ter look 'roun' fer a tree ter hab de lumber sawed out'n. En I dunno how it come to be so, but he happen fer ter hit on de ve'y tree w'at Sandy wuz turnt inter. Tenie wuz gone, en dey wa'n't nobody ner nuffin fer ter watch de tree.

"De two men w'at cut de tree down say dey nebber had sech a time wid a tree befo': dey axes would glansh off, en did n' 'pear ter make no prō gress thoo de wood; en of all de creakin', en shakin', en wobblin' you eber see, dat tree done it w'en it commence' ter fall. It wuz de beatenis' thing!

"W'en dey got de tree all trim' up, dey chain it up ter a timber waggin, en start fer de sawmill. But dey had a hard time gittin' de log dere: fus' dey got stuck in de mud w'en dey wuz gwine crosst de swamp, en it wuz two er th'ee hours befo' dey could git out. W'en dey start' on ag'in, de chain kep' a-comin' loose; en dey had ter keep a-stoppin' en a-stoppin' fer ter hitch de log up ag'in. W'en dey commence' ter climb de hill ter de sawmill, de log broke loose, en roll down de hill en in 'mongs' de trees, en hit tuk nigh 'bout half a day mo' ter git it haul' up ter de sawmill.

"De nex' mawnin' atter de day de tree wuz haul' ter de sawmill, Tenie come home. W'en she got back ter her cabin, de fus' thing she done wuz ter run down ter de woods en see how Sandy wuz gittin' on. W'en she seed de stump standin' dere, wid de sap runnin' out'n it, en de limbs layin' scattered roun', she nigh 'bout went out'n her min'. She run ter her cabin, en got her goopher mixtry, en den follered de track er de timber waggin ter de sawmill. She knowed Sandy could n' lib mo' d'n a minute er so ef she turnt him back, fer he wuz all chop' up so he 'd 'a' be'n bleedst ter die. But she wanted ter turn 'im back long ernuff fer ter 'splain ter 'im dat she had n' went off a-purpose, en lef' 'im ter be chop' down en sawed up. She did n' want Sandy ter die wid no hard feelin's to'ds her.

"De han's at de sawmill had des got de big log on de kerridge, en wuz startin' up de saw, w'en dey seed a 'oman runnin' up de hill, all out er bref, cryin' en gwine on des lack she wuz plumb 'stracted. It wuz Tenie; she come right inter de mill, en th'owed herse'f on de log, right in front er de saw, a-hollerin' en cryin' ter her Sandy ter fergib her, en not ter think hard er her, fer it wa'n't no fault er hern. Den Tenie 'membered de tree did n' hab no years, en she wuz gittin' ready fer ter wuk her goopher mixtry so ez ter turn Sandy back, w'en de mill-hands kotch holt er her en tied her arms wid a rope, en fasten' her to one er de posts in de sawmill; en den dey started de saw up ag'in, en cut de log up inter bo'ds en scantlin's right befo' her eyes. But it wuz mighty hard wuk; fer of all de sweekin', en moanin', en groanin', dat log done it w'iles de saw wuz a-cuttin' thoo it. De saw wuz one er dese yer ole-timey, up-en-down saws, en hit tuk longer dem days ter saw a log 'en it do now. Dey greased de saw, but dat did n' stop de fuss; hit kep' right on, tel fin'ly dey got de log all sawed up.

"W'en de oberseah w'at run de sawmill come fum breakfas', de han's up en tell him 'bout de crazy 'oman—ez dey s'posed she wuz—w'at had come runnin' in de sawmill, a-hollerin' en gwine on, en tried ter th'ow herse'f befo' de saw. En de oberseah sent two er th'ee er de han's fer ter take Tenie back ter her marster's plantation.

"Tenie 'peared ter be out'n her min' fer a long time, en her marster ha' ter lock her up in de smoke-'ouse 'tel she got ober her spells. Mars Marrabo wuz monst'us mad, en hit would 'a' made yo' flesh crawl fer ter hear him cuss, 'caze he say de spekilater w'at he got Tenie fum had fooled 'im by wukkin' a crazy 'oman off on him. W'iles Tenie wuz lock up in de smoke-'ouse, Mars Marrabo tuk 'n' haul de lumber fum de sawmill, en put up his noo kitchen.

"W'en Tenie got quiet' down, so she could be 'lowed ter go 'roun' de plantation, she up'n' tole her marster all erbout Sandy en de pine-tree; en w'en Mars Marrabo hearn it, he 'lowed she wuz de wuss 'stracted nigger he eber hearn of. He did n' know w'at ter do wid Tenie: fus' he thought he'd put her in de po'-house; but fin'ly, seein' ez she did n' do no harm ter nobody ner nuffin, but des went 'roun' moanin', en groanin', en shakin' her head, he 'cluded ter let her stay on de plantation en nuss de little nigger chilluns w'en dey mammies wuz ter wuk in de cotton-fiel'.

"De noo kitchen Mars Marrabo buil' wuz n' much use, fer it

had n' be'n put up long befo' de niggers 'mence' ter notice quare things erbout it. Dey could hear sump'n moanin' en groanin' 'bout de kitchen in de nighttime, en w'en de win' would blow dey could hear sump'n a-hollerin' en sweekin' lack it wuz in great pain en sufferin'. En it got so atter a w'ile dat it wuz all Mars Marrabo's wife could do ter git a 'oman ter stay in de kitchen in de day-time long ernuff ter do de cookin'; en dey wa'n't naer nigger on de plantation w'at would n' rudder take forty dan ter go 'bout dat kitchen atter dark,—dat is, 'cep'n' Tenie; she did n' 'pear ter min' de ha'nts. She useter slip 'roun' at night, en set on de kitchen steps, en lean up agin de do'-jamb, en run on ter herse 'f wid some kine er foolishness w'at nobody could n' make out; fer Mars Marrabo had th'eaten' ter sen' her off'n de plantation ef she say anything ter any er de yuther niggers 'bout de pine-tree. But some-how er 'nudder de niggers foun' out all erbout it, en dey all knowed de kitchen wuz ha'nted by Sandy's sperrit. En bimeby hit got so Mars Marrabo's wife herse'f wuz skeered ter go out in de yard atter dark.

"W'en it come ter dat, Mars Marrabo tuk en to' de kitchen down, en use' de lumber fer ter buil' dat ole school-'ouse w'at you er talkin' 'bout pullin' down. De school'ouse wuz n' use' 'cep'n' in de daytime, en on dark nights folks gwine 'long de road would hear quare soun's en see quare things. Po' ole Tenie useter go down dere at night, en wander 'roun' de school'ouse; en de niggers all 'lowed she went fer ter talk wid Sandy's sperrit. En one winter mawnin', w'en one er de boys went ter school early fer ter start de fire, w'at should he fin' but po' ole Tenie, layin' on de flo', stiff, en col', en dead. Dere did n' 'pear ter be nuffin pertickler de matter wid her,— she had des grieve' herse'f ter def fer her Sandy. Mars Marrabo did n' shed no tears. He though Tenie wuz crazy, en dey wa'n't no tellin' w'at she mought do nex'; en dey ain' much room in dis worl' fer crazy w'ite folks, let 'lone a crazy nigger.

"Hit wa'n't long atter dat befo' Mars Marrabo sol' a piece er his track er lan' ter Mars Dugal' McAdoo,—*my* ole marster,—en dat's how de ole school'ouse happen to be on yo' place. W'en de wah broke out, de school stop', en de ole school'ouse be'n stannin' empty ever sence,—dat is, 'cep'n' fer de ha'nts. En folks sez dat de ole school'ouse, er any yuther house w'at got any er dat lumber in it w'at wuz sawed out'n de tree w'at Sandy wuz turnt inter, is gwine ter be ha'nted tel de las' piece er plank is rotted en crumble' inter dus'."

Annie had listened to this gruesome narrative with strained attention.

"What a system it was," she exclaimed, when Julius had finished, "under which such things were possible!"

"What things?" I asked, in amazement. "Are you seriously considering the possibility of a man's being turned into a tree?"

"Oh, no," she replied quickly, "not that;" and then she murmured absently, and with a dim look in her fine eyes, "Poor Tenie!"

We ordered the lumber, and returned home. That night, after we had gone to bed, and my wife had to all appearances been sound asleep for half an hour, she startled me out of an incipient doze by exclaiming suddenly,—

"John, I don't believe I want my new kitchen built out of the lumber in that old schoolhouse."

"You would n't for a moment allow yourself," I replied, with some asperity, "to be influenced by that absurdly impossible yarn which Julius was spinning to-day?"

"I know the story is absurd," she replied dreamily, "and I am not so silly as to believe it. But I don't think I should ever be able to take any pleasure in that kitchen if it were built out of that lumber. Besides, I think the kitchen would look better and last longer if the lumber were all new."

Of course she had her way. I bought the new lumber, though not without grumbling. A week or two later I was called away from home on business. On my return, after an absence of several days, my wife remarked to me,—

"John, there has been a split in the Sandy Run Colored Baptist Church, on the temperance question. About half the members have come out from the main body, and set up for themselves. Uncle Julius is one of the seceders, and he came to me yesterday and asked if they might not hold their meetings in the old schoolhouse for the present."

"I hope you did n't let the old rascal have it," I returned, with some warmth. I had just received a bill for the new lumber I had bought.

"Well," she replied, "I could n't refuse him the use of the house for so good a purpose."

"And I'll venture to say," I continued, "that you subscribed something toward the support of the new church?"

She did not attempt to deny it.

"What are they going to do about the ghost?" I asked, somewhat curious to know how Julius would get around this obstacle.

"Oh," replied Annie, "Uncle Julius says that ghosts never disturb religious worship, but that if Sandy's spirit *should* happen to stray into meeting by mistake, no doubt the preaching would do it good."

Mars Jeems's Nightmare

WE FOUND OLD JULIUS VERY USEFUL when we moved to our new residence. He had a thorough knowledge of the neighborhood, was familiar with the roads and the watercourses, knew the qualities of the various soils and what they would produce, and where the best hunting and fishing were to be had. He was a marvelous hand in the management of horses and dogs, with whose mental processes he manifested a greater familiarity than mere use would seem to account for, though it was doubtless due to the simplicity of a life that had kept him close to nature. Toward my tract of land and the things that were on it—the creeks, the swamps, the hills, the meadows, the stones, the trees—he maintained a peculiar personal attitude, that might be called predial rather than proprietary. He had been accustomed, until long after middle life, to look upon himself as the property of another. When this relation was no longer possible, owing to the war, and to his master's death and the dispersion of the family, he had been unable to break off entirely the mental habits of a lifetime, but had attached himself to the old plantation, of which he seemed to consider himself an appurtenance. We found him useful in many ways and entertaining in others, and my wife and I took quite a fancy to him.

Shortly after we became established in our home on the sandhills, Julius brought up to the house one day a colored boy of about seventeen, whom he introduced as his grandson, and for whom he solicited employment. I was not favorably impressed by the youth's appearance,—quite the contrary, in fact; but mainly to please the old man I hired Tom—his name was Tom—to help about the stables, weed the garden, cut wood and bring water, and in general to make himself useful about the outdoor work of the household.

My first impression of Tom proved to be correct. He turned out to be very trifling, and I was much annoyed by his laziness, his carelessness, and his apparent lack of any sense of responsibility. I kept him longer than I should, on Julius's account, hoping that he might improve; but he seemed to grow worse instead of better, and when I finally reached the limit of my patience, I discharged him.

"I am sorry, Julius," I said to the old man; "I should have liked to oblige you by keeping him; but I can't stand Tom any longer. He is absolutely untrustworthy."

"Yas, suh," replied Julius, with a deep sigh and a long shake of the head, "I knows he ain' much account, en dey ain' much 'pen'ence ter be put on 'im. But I wuz hopin' dat you mought make some 'lowance fuh a' ign'ant young nigger, suh, en gib 'im one mo' chance."

But I had hardened my heart. I had always been too easily imposed upon, and had suffered too much from this weakness. I determined to be firm as a rock in this instance.

"No, Julius," I rejoined decidedly, "it is impossible. I gave him more than a fair trial, and he simply won't do."

When my wife and I set out for our drive in the cool of the evening,—afternoon is "evening" in Southern parlance,—one of the servants put into the rockaway two large earthenware jugs. Our drive was to be down through the swamp to the mineral spring at the foot of the sand-hills beyond. The water of this spring was strongly impregnated with sulphur and iron, and, while not particularly agreeable of smell or taste, was used by us, in moderation, for sanitary reasons.

When we reached the spring, we found a man engaged in cleaning it out. In answer to an inquiry he said that if we would wait five or ten minutes, his task would be finished and the spring in such condition that we could fill our jugs. We might have driven on, and come back by way of the spring, but there was a bad stretch of road beyond, and we concluded to remain where we were until the spring should be ready. We were in a cool and shady place. It was often necessary to wait awhile in North Carolina; and our Northern energy had not been entirely proof against the influences of climate and local custom.

While we sat there, a man came suddenly around a turn of the road ahead of us. I recognized in him a neighbor with whom I had exchanged formal calls. He was driving a horse, apparently a high-spirited creature, possessing, so far as I could see at a glance, the marks of good temper and good breeding; the gentleman, I had heard it suggested, was slightly deficient in both. The horse was rearing and plunging, and the man was beating him furiously with a buggywhip. When he saw us, he flushed a fiery red, and, as he passed, held the reins with one hand, at some risk to his safety, lifted his hat, and bowed somewhat constrainedly as the horse darted by us, still panting and snorting with fear.

"He looks as though he were ashamed of himself," I observed.

"I'm sure he ought to be," exclaimed my wife indignantly. "I think there is no worse sin and no more disgraceful thing than cruelty."

"I quite agree with you," I assented.

"A man w'at 'buses his hoss is gwine ter be ha'd on de folks w'at wuks fer 'im," remarked Julius. "Ef young Mistah McLean doan min', he'll hab a bad dream one er dese days, des lack 'is grandaddy had way back yander, long yeahs befo' de wah."

"What was it about Mr. McLean's dream, Julius?" I asked. The man had not yet finished cleaning the spring, and we might as well put in time listening to Julius as in any other way. We had found some of his plantation tales quite interesting.

"Mars Jeems McLean," said Julius, "wuz de grandaddy er dis yer gent'eman w'at is des gone by us beatin' his hoss. He had a big plantation en a heap er niggers. Mars Jeems wuz a ha'd man, en monst'us stric' wid his han's. Eber sence he growed up he nebber 'peared ter hab no feelin' fer no body. W'en his daddy, ole Mars John McLean, died, de plantation en all de niggers fell ter young Mars Jeems. He had be'n bad 'nuff befo', but it wa'n't long atterwa'ds 'tel he got so dey wuz no use in libbin' at all ef you ha' ter lib roun' Mars Jeems. His niggers wuz bleedzd ter slabe fum daylight ter da'k, w'iles yuther folks's did n' hafter wuk 'cep'n' fum sun ter sun; en dey did n' git no mo' ter eat dan dey oughter, en dat de coa'ses' kin'. Dey wa'n't 'lowed ter sing, ner dance, ner play de banjo w'en Mars Jeems wuz roun' de place; fer Mars Jeems say he would n' hab no sech gwines-on,—said he bought his han's ter wuk, en not ter play, en w'en night come dey mus' sleep en res', so dey'd be ready ter git up soon in de mawnin' en go ter dey wuk fresh en strong.

"Mars Jeems did n' 'low no co'tin' er juneseyin' roun' his planta-tion,—said he wanted his niggers ter put dey min's on dey wuk, en not to be wastin' dey time wid no sech foolis'ness. En he would n' let his han's git married,—said he wuz n' raisin' niggers, but wuz raisin' cotton. En w'eneber any er de boys en gals 'ud 'mence ter git sweet on one ernudder, he'd sell one er de yuther un 'em, er sen' 'em way down in Robeson County ter his yuther plantation, whar dey could n' nebber see one ernudder.

"Ef any er de niggers eber complained, dey got fo'ty; so co'se dey did n' many un 'em complain. But dey did n' lack it, des de same, en nobody could n' blame 'em, fer dey had a ha'd time. Mars Jeems did n' make no 'lowance fer nachul bawn laz'ness, ner sickness, ner trouble in de min', ner nuffin; he wuz des gwine ter git so much wuk outer eve'y han', er know de reason w'y.

"Dey wuz one time de niggers 'lowed, fer a spell, dat Mars Jeems mought git bettah. He tuk a lackin' ter Mars Marrabo McSwayne's oldes' gal, Miss Libbie, en useter go ober dere eve'y day er eve'y ebenin', en folks said dey wuz gwine ter git married sho'. But it 'pears dat Miss Libbie heared 'bout de gwines-on on Mars Jeems's plantation, en she des 'lowed she could n' trus' herse'f wid no sech a man; dat he mought git so useter 'busin' his niggers dat he'd 'mence ter 'buse his wife atter he got useter habbin' her roun' de house. So she 'clared she wuz n' gwine ter hab nuffin mo' ter do wid young Mars Jeems.

"De niggers wuz all monst'us sorry w'en de match wuz bust' up, fer now Mars Jeems got wusser'n he wuz befo' he sta'ted sweet-hea'tin'. De time he useter spen' co'tin' Miss Libbie he put in findin' fault wid de niggers, en all his bad feelin's 'ca'se Miss Libbie th'owed 'im ober he 'peared ter try ter wuk off on de po' niggers.

"W'iles Mars Jeems wuz co'tin' Miss Libbie, two er de han's on de plantation had got ter settin' a heap er sto' by one ernudder. One un 'em wuz name' Solomon, en de yuther wuz a 'oman w'at wukked in de fiel' long er 'im—I fe'git dat 'oman's name, but it doan 'mount ter much in de tale nohow. Now, whuther 'ca'se Mars

Jeems wuz so tuk up wid his own junesey* dat he did n' paid no
'tention fer a w'ile ter w'at wuz gwine on 'twix' Solomon en his
junesey, er whuther his own co'tin' made 'im kin' er easy on de
co'tin' in de qua'ters, dey ain' no tellin'. But dey's one thing sho', dat
w'en Miss Libbie th'owed 'im ober, he foun' out 'bout Solomon en
de gal monst'us quick, en gun Solomon fo'ty, en sont de gal down
ter de Robeson County plantation, en tol' all de niggers ef he ketch
'em at any mo' sech foolishness, he wuz gwine ter skin 'em
alibe en tan dey hides befo' dey ve'y eyes. Co'se he would n' 'a' done
it, but he mought 'a' made things wusser 'n dey wuz. So you kin
'magine dey wa'n't much lub-makin' in de qua'ters fer a long time.

"Mars Jeems useter go down ter de yuther plantation sometimes
fer a week er mo', en so he had ter hab a oberseah ter look atter his
wuk w'iles he 'uz gone. Mars Jeems's oberseah wuz a po' w'ite man
name' Nick Johnson,—de niggers called 'im Mars Johnson ter his
face, but behin' his back dey useter call 'im Ole Nick, en de name
suited 'im ter a T. He wuz wusser 'n Mars Jeems ever da'ed to be.
Co'se de darkies did n' lack de way Mars Jeems used 'em, but he
wuz de marster, en had a right ter do ez he please'; but dis yer Ole
Nick wa'n't nuffin but a po' buckrah, en all de niggers 'spised 'im ez
much ez dey hated 'im, fer he did n' own nobody, en wa'n't no bettah 'n a nigger, fer in dem days any 'spectable pusson would ruther
be a nigger dan a po' w'ite man.

"Now, atter Solomon's gal had be'n sont away, he kep' feelin'
mo' en mo' bad erbout it, 'tel fin'lly he 'lowed he wuz gwine ter see
ef dey could n' be sump'n done fer ter git 'er back, en ter make
Mars Jeems treat de darkies bettah. So he tuk a peck er co'n out'n de
ba'n one night, en went ober ter see ole Aun' Peggy, de free-nigger
cunjuh 'oman down by de Wim'l'ton Road.

"Aun' Peggy listen' ter 'is tale, en ax' him some queshtuns, en
den tol' 'im she'd wuk her roots, en see w'at dey'd say 'bout it, en
ter-morrer night he sh'd come back ag'in en fetch ernudder peck er
co'n, en den she'd hab sump'n fer ter tel 'im.

"So Solomon went back de nex' night, en sho' 'nuff, Aun' Peggy
tol' 'im w'at ter do. She gun 'im some stuff w'at look' lack it be'n
made by poundin' up some roots en yarbs wid a pestle in a mo'tar.

* Sweetheart.

" 'Dis yer stuff,' sez she, 'is monst'us pow'ful kin' er goopher. You take dis home, en gin it ter de cook, ef you kin trus' her, en tell her fer ter put it in yo' marster's soup de fus' cloudy day he hab okra soup fer dinnah. Min' you follers de d'rections'.

" 'It ain' gwineter p'isen 'im, is it?' ax' Solomon, gittin' kin' er skeered; fer Solomon wuz a good man, en did n' want ter do no-body no rale ha'm.

" 'Oh, no,' sez ole Aun' Peggy, 'it's gwine ter do 'im good, but he'll hab a monst'us bad dream fus.' A mont' fum now you come down heah en lemme know how de goopher is wukkin'. Fer I ain' done much er dis kin' er cunj'in' er late yeahs, en I has ter kinder keep track un it ter see dat it doan 'complish no mo' d'n I 'lows fer it ter do. En I has ter be kinder keerful 'bout cunj'in' w'ite folks; so be sho' en lemme know, w'ateber you do, des w'at is gwine on roun' de plantation.'

"So Solomon say all right, en tuk de goopher mixtry up ter de big house en gun it ter de cook, en tol' her fer ter put it in Mars Jeems's soup de fus' cloudy day she hab okra soup fer dinnah. It happen' dat de ve'y nex' day wuz a cloudy day, en so de cook made okra soup fer Mars Jeems's dinnah, en put de powder Solomon gun her inter de soup, en made de soup rale good, so Mars Jeems eat a whole lot of it en 'peared ter enjoy it.

"De nex' mawnin' Mars Jeems tol' de oberseah he wuz gwine 'way on some bizness, en den he wuz gwine ter his yuther planta-tion, down in Robeson County, en he did n' 'spec' he'd be back fer a mont' er so.

" 'But,' sezee, 'I wants you ter run dis yer plantation fer all it's wuth. Dese yer niggers is gittin' monst'us triflin' en lazy en keer-less, en dey ain' no 'pen'ence ter be put in 'em. I wants dat stop', en w'iles I'm gone erway I wants de 'spenses cut 'way down en a heap mo' wuk done. Fac', I wants dis yer plantation ter make a reco'd dat 'll show w'at kinder oberseah you is.'

"Ole Nick did n' said nuffin but 'Yas, suh,' but de way he kinder grin' ter hisse'f en show' his big yaller teef, en snap' de rawhide he useter kyar roun' wid 'im, made col' chills run up and down de backbone er dem niggers w'at heared Mars Jeems a-talkin'. En dat night dey wuz mo'nin' en groanin' down in de qua'ters, fer de nig-gers all knowed w'at wuz comin'.

"So, sho' 'nuff, Mars Jeems went erway nex' mawnin', en de trouble begun. Mars Johnson sta'ted off de ve'y fus' day fer ter see w'at he could hab ter show Mars Jeems w'en he come back. He made de tasks bigger en de rashuns littler, en w'en de niggers had wukked all day, he'd fin' sump'n fer 'em ter do roun' de ba'n er som'ers atter da'k, fer ter keep 'em busy a' hour er so befo' dey went ter sleep.

"About th'ee er fo' days atter Mars Jeems went erway, young Mars Dunkin McSwayne rode up ter de big house one day wid a nigger settin' behin' 'im in de buggy, tied ter de seat, en ax' ef Mars Jeems wuz home. Mars Johnson wuz at de house, and he say no.

" 'Well,' sez Mars Dunkin, sezee, 'I fotch dis nigger ober ter Mistah McLean fer ter pay a bet I made wid 'im las' week w'en we wuz playin' kya'ds te'gedder. I bet 'im a nigger man, en heah 's one I reckon 'll fill de bill. He wuz tuk up de yuther day fer a stray nigger, en he could n' gib no 'count er hisse'f, en so he wuz sol' at oaction, en I bought 'im. He 's kinder brash, but I knows yo' powers, Mistah Johnson, en I reckon ef anybody kin make 'im toe de ma'k, you is de man.'

"Mars Johnson grin' one er dem grins w'at show' all his snaggle teef, en make de niggers 'low he look lack de ole debbil, en sezee ter Mars Dunkin:—

" 'I reckon you kin trus' me, Mistah Dunkin, fer ter tame any nigger wuz eber bawn. De nigger doan lib w'at I can't take down in 'bout fo' days.'

"Well, Ole Nick had 'is han's full long er dat noo nigger; en w'iles de res' er de darkies wuz sorry fer de po' man, dey 'lowed he kep' Mars Johnson so busy dat dey got along better 'n dey'd 'a' done ef de noo nigger had nebber come.

"De fus' thing dat happen', Mars Johnson sez ter dis yer noo man:—

" 'W'at 's yo' name, Sambo?'

" 'My name ain' Sambo,' 'spon' de noo nigger.

" 'Did I ax you w'at yo' name wa'n't?' sez Mars Johnson. 'You wants ter be pa'tic'lar how you talks ter me. Now, w'at is yo' name, en whar did you come fum?'

" 'I dunno my name,' sez de nigger, 'en I doan 'member whar I come fum. My head is all kin' er mix' up.'

" 'Yas,' sez Mars Johnson, 'I reckon I'll ha' ter gib you sump'n fer ter cl'ar yo' head. At de same time, it'll l'arn you some manners, en atter dis mebbe you'll say "suh" w'en you speaks ter me.'

"Well, Mars Johnson haul' off wid his rawhide en hit de noo nigger once. De noo man look' at Mars Johnson fer a minute ez ef he did n' know w'at ter make er dis yer kin' er l'arnin'. But w'en de oberseah raise' his w'ip ter hit him ag'in, de noo nigger des haul' off en made fer Mars Johnson, en ef some er de yuther niggers had n' stop' 'im, it 'peared ez ef he mought 'a' made it wa'm fer Ole Nick dere fer a w'ile. But de oberseah made de yuther niggers he'p tie de noo nigger up, en den gun 'im fo'ty, wid a dozen er so th'owed in fer good measure, fer Ole Nick wuz nebber stingy wid dem kin' er rashuns. De nigger went on at a tarrable rate, des lack a wil' man, but co'se he wuz bleedzd ter take his med'cine, fer he wuz tied up en could n' he'p hisse'f.

"Mars Johnson lock' de noo nigger up in de ba'n, en did n' gib 'im nuffin ter eat fer a day er so, 'tel he got 'im kin'er quiet' down, en den he tu'nt 'im loose en put 'im ter wuk. De nigger 'lowed he wa'n't useter wukkin', en would n' wuk, en Mars Johnson gun 'im anudder fo'ty fer laziness en impidence, en let 'im fas' a day er so mo', en den put 'im ter wuk ag'in. De nigger went ter wuk, but did n' 'pear ter know how ter han'le a hoe. It tuk des 'bout half de oberseah's time lookin' atter 'im, en dat po' nigger got mo' lashin's en cussin's en cuffin's dan any fo' yuthers on de plantation. He did n' mix wid ner talk much ter de res' er de niggers, en could n' 'pear ter git it th'oo his min' dat he wuz a slabe en had ter wuk en min' de w'ite folks, spite er de fac' dat Ole Nick gun 'im a lesson eve'y day. En fin'lly Mars Johnson 'lowed dat he could n' do nuffin wid 'im; dat ef he wuz his nigger, he'd break his sperrit er break 'is neck, one er de yuther. But co'se he wuz only sont ober on trial, en ez he did n' gib sat'sfaction, en he had n' heared fum Mars Jeems 'bout w'en he wuz comin' back; en ez he wuz feared he'd git mad some time er 'nuther en kill de nigger befo' he knowed it, he 'lowed he'd better sen' 'im back whar he come fum. So he tied 'im up en sont 'im back ter Mars Dunkin.

"Now, Mars Dunkin McSwayne wuz one er dese yer easy-gwine gent'eman w'at did n' lack ter hab no trouble wid niggers er nobody e'se, en he knowed ef Mars Ole Nick could n' git 'long wid dis nigger, nobody could. So he tuk de nigger ter town dat same day, en sol' 'im ter a trader w'at wuz gittin' up a gang er lackly niggers fer ter ship off on de steamboat ter go down de ribber ter Wim'l'ton en fum dere ter Noo Orleens.

"De nex' day atter de noo man had be'n sont away, Solomon wuz wukkin' in de cotton-fiel', en w'en he got ter de fence nex' ter de woods, at de een' er de row, who sh'd he see on de yuther side but ole Aun' Peggy. She beckon' ter 'im—de oberseah wuz down on de yuther side er de fiel',— en sez she:—

" 'W'y ain' you done come en 'po'ted ter me lack I tol' you?'

" 'W'y, law! Aun' Peggy,' sez Solomon, 'dey ain' nuffin ter 'po't. Mars Jeems went away de day atter we gun 'im de goopher mixtry, en we ain' seed hide ner hair un 'im sence, en co'se we doan know nuffin 'bout w'at 'fec' it had on 'im.'

" 'I doan keer nuffin 'bout yo' Mars Jeems now; w'at I wants ter know is w'at is be'n gwine on 'mongs' de niggers. Has you be'n gittin' 'long any better on de plantation?'

" 'No, Aun' Peggy, we be'n gittin' 'long wusser. Mars Johnson is stric'er 'n he eber wuz befo', en de po' niggers doan ha'dly git time ter draw dey bref, en dey 'lows dey mought des ez well be dead ez alibe.'

" 'Uh huh!' sez Aun' Peggy, sez she, 'I tol' you dat 'uz monst'us pow'ful goopher, en its wuk doan 'pear all at once.'

" 'Long ez we had dat noo nigger heah,' Solomon went on, 'he kep' Mars Johnson busy pa't er de time; but now he's gone erway, I s'pose de res' un us 'll ketch it wusser 'n eber.'

" 'W'at 's gone wid de noo nigger?' sez Aun' Peggy, rale quick, battin' her eyes en straight'nin' up.

" 'Ole Nick done sont 'im back ter Mars Dunkin, who had fotch 'im heah fer ter pay a gamblin' debt ter Mars Jeems,' sez Solomon, 'en I heahs Mars Dunkin has sol' 'im ter a nigger-trader up in Patesville, w'at's gwine ter ship 'im off wid a gang ter-morrer.'

"Ole Aun' Peggy 'peared ter git rale stirred up w'en Solomon tol' 'er dat, en sez she, shakin' her stick at 'im:—

" 'W'y did n' you come en tell me 'bout dis noo nigger bein' sol' erway? Did n' you promus me, ef I'd gib you dat goopher, you'd come en 'po't ter me 'bout all w'at wuz gwine on on dis plantation? Co'se I could 'a' foun' out fer myse'f, but I 'pended on yo' tellin' me, en now by not doin' it I's feared you gwine spile my cunj'in'. You come down ter my house ter-night en do w'at I tells you, er I'll put a spell on you dat'll make yo' ha'r fall out so you'll be bal', en yo' eyes drap out so you can't see, en yo teef fall out so you can't eat, en yo' years grow up so you can't heah. W'en you is foolin' wid a cunjuh 'oman lack me, you got ter min' yo' P's en Q's er dey 'll be trouble sho' 'nuff.'

"So co'se Solomon went down ter Aun' Peggy's dat night, en she gun 'im a roasted sweet'n' 'tater.

" 'You take dis yer sweet'n' 'tater,' sez she,—'I done goophered it 'speshly fer dat noo nigger, so you better not eat it yo'se'f er you'll wush you had n',—en slip off ter town, en fin' dat strange man, en gib 'im dis yer sweet'n' 'tater. He mus' eat it befo' mawnin', sho', ef he doan wanter be sol' erway ter Noo Orleens.'

" 'But s'posen de patteroles ketch me, Aun' Peggy, w'at I gwine ter do?' sez Solomon.

" 'De patteroles ain' gwine tech you, but ef you doan fin' dat nigger, *I'm* gwine git you, en you 'll fin' me wusser 'n de patteroles. Des hol' on a minute, en I'll sprinkle you wid some er dis mixtry out'n dis yer bottle, so de patteroles can't see you, en you kin rub yo' feet wid some er dis yer grease out'n dis go'd, so you kin run fas', en rub some un it on yo' eyes so you kin see in de da'k; en den you mus' fin' dat noo nigger en gib 'im dis yer 'tater, er you gwine ter hab mo' trouble on yo' han's 'n you eber had befo' in yo' life er eber will hab sence.'

"So Solomon tuk de sweet'n' 'tater en sta'ted up de road fas' ez he could go, en befo' long he retch' town. He went right 'long by de patteroles, en dey did n' 'pear ter notice 'im, en bimeby he foun' whar de strange nigger was kep', en he walked right pas' de gyard at de do' en foun' 'im. De nigger could n' see 'im, ob co'se, en he could n' 'a' seed de nigger in de da'k, ef it had n' be'n fer de stuff Aun' Peggy gun 'im ter rub on 'is eyes. De nigger wuz layin' in a co'nder, 'sleep, en Solomon des slip' up ter 'im, en hilt dat sweet'n' 'tater 'fo' de nigger's nose, en he des nach'ly retch' up wid his han', en tuck de 'tater en eat it in his sleep, widout knowin' it. W'en Solomon seed he'd done eat de 'tater, he went back en tol' Aun' Peggy, en den went home ter his cabin ter sleep, 'way 'long 'bout two o'clock in de mawnin'.

"De nex' day wuz Sunday, en so de niggers had a little time ter deyse'ves. Solomon wuz kinder 'sturb' in his min' thinkin' 'bout his junesey w'at 'uz gone away, en wond'rin' w'at Aun' Peggy had ter do wid dat noo nigger; en he had sa'ntered up in de woods so 's ter be by hisse'f a little, en at de same time ter look atter a rabbit-trap he'd sot down in de aidge er de swamp, w'en who sh'd he see stan'in' unner a tree but a w'ite man.

"Solomon did n' knowed de w'ite man at fus', 'tel de w'ite man spoke up ter 'im.

" 'Is dat you, Solomon?' sezee.

"Den Solomon reco'nized de voice.

" 'Fer de Lawd's sake, Mars Jeems! is dat you?'

" 'Yas, Solomon,' sez his marster, 'dis is me, er w'at 's lef' er me.'

"It wa'n't no wonder Solomon had n' knowed Mars Jeems at fus', fer he wuz dress' lack a po' w'ite man, en wuz barefooted, en look' monst'us pale en peaked, ez ef he'd des come th'oo a ha'd spell er sickness.

" 'You er lookin' kinder po'ly, Mars Jeems', sez Solomon. 'Is you be'n sick, suh?'

" 'No, Solomon,' sez Mars Jeems, shakin' his head, en speakin' sorter slow en sad, 'I ain' be'n sick, but I's had a monst'us bad dream,—fac', a reg'lar, nach'ul nightmare. But tell me how things has be'n gwine on up ter de plantation since I be'n gone, Solomon.'

"So Solomon up en tol' 'im 'bout de craps, en 'bout de hosses en de mules, en 'bout de cows en de hawgs. En w'en he 'mence' ter tell 'bout de noo nigger, Mars Jeems prick' up 'is yeahs en listen', en eve'y now en den he'd say, 'Uh huh! uh huh!' en nod 'is head. En bimeby, w'en he'd ax' Solomon some mo' queshtuns, he sez, sezee:—

" 'Now, Solomon, I doan want you ter say a wo'd ter nobody 'bout meetin' me heah, but I wants you ter slip up ter de house, en fetch me some clo's en some shoes,—I fergot ter tell you dat a man rob' me back yander on de road en swap' clo's wid me widout axin' me whuther er no,—but you neenter say nuffin 'bout dat, nuther. You go en fetch me some clo's heah, so nobody won't see you, en keep yo' mouf shet, en I'll gib you a dollah.'

"Solomon wuz so 'stonish' he lack ter fell ober in his tracks, w'en Mars Jeems promus' ter gib 'im a dollah. Dey su't'nly wuz a change come ober Mars Jeems, w'en he offer' one er his niggers dat much money. Solomon 'mence' ter 'spec' dat Aun' Peggy's cunj'ation had be'n wukkin' monst'us strong.

"Solomon fotch Mars Jeems some clo's en shoes, en dat same eb'nin' Mars Jeems 'peared at de house, en let on lack he des dat minute got home fum Robeson County. Mars Johnson was all ready ter talk ter 'im, but Mars Jeems sont 'im wo'd he wa'n't feelin' ve'y well dat night, en he'd see 'im ter-morrer.

"So nex' mawnin' atter breakfus' Mars Jeems sont fer de oberseah, en ax' 'im fer ter gib 'count er his styoa'dship. Ole Nick tol' Mars Jeems how much wuk be'n done, en got de books en showed 'im how much money be'n save'. Den Mars Jeems ax' 'im how de darkies be'n behabin', en Mars Johnson say dey be'n behabin' good, most un 'em, en dem w'at did n' behabe good at fus' change dey conduc' atter he got holt un 'em a time er two.

" 'All,' sezee, ' 'cep'n' de noo nigger Mistah Dunkin fotch ober heah en lef' on trial, w'iles you wuz gone.'

" 'Oh, yas,' 'lows Mars Jeems, 'tell me all 'bout dat noo nigger. I heared a little 'bout dat quare noo nigger las' night, en it wuz des too redik'lus. Tell me all 'bout dat noo nigger.'

"So seein' Mars Jeems so good-natchu'd 'bout it, Mars Johnson up en tol' 'im how he tied up de noo han' de fus' day en gun 'im fo'ty 'ca'se he would n' tell 'im 'is name.

" 'Ha, ha, ha!' sez Mars Jeems, laffin' fit ter kill, 'but dat is too funny fer any use. Tell me some mo' 'bout dat noo nigger.'

"So Mars Johnson went on en tol' 'im how he had ter starbe de noo nigger 'fo' he could make 'im take holt er a hoe.

" 'Dat wuz de beatinis' notion fer a nigger,' sez Mars Jeems, 'puttin' on airs, des lack he wuz a w'ite man! En I reckon you did n' do nuffin ter 'im?'

" 'Oh, no, suh,' sez de oberseah, grinnin' lack a chessy-cat, 'I did n' do nuffin but take de hide off'n 'im.'

"Mars Jeems lafft en lafft, 'te it 'peared lack he wuz des gwine ter bu'st. "*Tell* me some mo' 'bout dat noo nigger, oh, *tell* me some mo'. Dat noo nigger int'rusts me, he do, en dat is a fac'.'

"Mars Johnson did n' quite un'erstan' w'y Mars Jeems sh'd make sich a great 'miration 'bout de noo nigger, but co'se he want' ter please de gent'eman w'at hi'ed 'im, en so he 'splain' all 'bout how many times he had ter cowhide de noo nigger, en how he made 'im do tasks twicet ez big ez some er de yuther han's, en how he'd chain 'im up in de ba'n at night en feed 'im on co'n-bread en water.

" 'Oh! but you is a monst'us good oberseah; you is de bes' oberseah in dis county, Mistah Johnson,' sez Mars Jeems, w'en de oberseah got th'oo wid his tale; 'en dey ain' nebber be'n no nigger-breaker lack you roun' heah befo'. En you desarbes great credit fer sendin' dat nigger 'way befo' you sp'ilt 'im fer de market. Fac', you is sech a monst'us good oberseah, en you is got dis yer plantation in sech fine shape, dat I reckon I doan need you no mo'. You is got dese yer darkies so well train' dat I 'spec' I kin run 'em myse'f fum dis time on. But I does wush you had 'a' hilt on ter dat noo nigger 'tel I got home, fer I'd 'a' lack ter 'a' seed 'im, I su't'nly should.'

"De oberseah wuz so 'stonish' he did n' ha'dly know w'at ter say, but fin'lly he ax' Mars Jeems ef he would n' gib 'im a riccommen' fer ter git ernudder place.

" 'No, suh,' sez Mars Jeems, 'somehow er'nuther I doan lack yo' looks sence I come back dis time, en I'd much ruther you would n' stay roun' heah. Fac', I's feared ef I'd meet you alone in de woods some time, I mought wanter ha'm you. But layin' dat aside, I be'n lookin' ober dese yer books er yo'n w'at you kep' w'iles I wuz 'way, en fer a yeah er so back, en dere's some figgers w'at ain' des cl'ar ter me. I ain' got no time fer ter talk 'bout 'em now, but I 'spec' befo' I settles wid you fer dis las' mount', you better come up heah ter-morrer, atter I's look' de books en 'counts ober some mo', en den we'll straighten ou' business all up.'

"Mars Jeems 'lowed atterwa'ds dat he wuz des shootin' in de da'k w'en he said dat 'bout de books, but howsomeber, Mars Nick Johnson lef' dat naberhood 'twix' de nex' two suns, en nobody roun' dere nebber seed hide ner hair un 'im sence. En all de darkies t'ank de Lawd, en 'lowed it wuz a good riddance er bad rubbage.

"But all dem things I done tol' you ain' nuffin 'side'n de change w'at come ober Mars Jeems fum dat time on. Aun' Peggy's goopher had made a noo man un 'im enti'ely. De nex' day atter he come back, he tol' de han's dey neenter wuk on'y fum sun ter sun, en he cut dey tasks down so dey did n' nobody hab ter stan' ober 'em wid a rawhide er a hick'ry. En he 'lowed ef de niggers want ter hab a dance in de big ba'n any Sad'day night, dey mought hab it. En bimeby w'en Solomon seed how good Mars Jeems wuz, he ax' 'im ef he would n' please sen' down ter de yuther plantation fer his junesey. Mars Jeems say su't'nly, en gun Solomon a pass en a note ter de oberseah on de yuther plantation, en sont Solomon down ter Robeson County wid a hoss en buggy fer ter fetch his junesey back. W'en de niggers see how fine Mars Jeems gwine treat 'em, dey all tuk ter sweethea'tin' en juneseyin' en singin' en dancin', en eight er ten couples got married, en bimeby eve'ybody 'mence' ter say Mars Jeems McLean got a finer plantation, en slicker-lookin' niggers, en dat he 'uz makin' mo' cotton en co'n, dan any yuther gent'eman in de county. En Mars Jeems's own junesey, Miss Libbie, heared 'bout de noo gwines-on on Mars Jeems's plantation, en she change' her min' 'bout Mars Jeems en tuk 'im back ag'in, en 'fo' long dey had a fine weddin', en all de darkies had a feas', en dey wuz fiddlin' en dancin' en funnin' en frolic'in' fum sundown 'tel mawnin'."

"And they all lived happy ever after," I said, as the old man reached a full stop.

"Yas, suh," he said, interpreting my remarks as a question, "dey did. Solomon useter say," he added, "dat Aun' Peggy's goopher had turnt Mars Jeems ter a nigger, en dat dat noo han' wuz Mars Jeems hisse'f. But co'se Solomon did n' das' ter let on 'bout w'at he 'spicioned, en ole Aun' Peggy would 'a' 'nied it ef she had be'n ax', fer she 'd 'a' got in trouble sho', ef it 'uz knowed she'd be'n cunj'in' de w'ite folks.

"Dis yer tale goes ter show," concluded Julius sententiously, as the man came up and announced that the spring was ready for us to get water, "dat w'ite folks w'at is so ha'd en stric', en doan make no 'lowance fer po' ign'ant niggers w'at ain' had no chanst ter l'arn, is li'ble ter hab bad dreams, ter say de leas', en dat dem w'at is kin' en good ter po' people is sho' ter prosper en git 'long in de worl'."

"That is a very strange story, Uncle Julius," observed my wife, smiling, "and Solomon's explanation is quite improbable."

"Yes, Julius," said I, "that was powerful goopher. I am glad, too, that you told us the moral of the story; it might have escaped us otherwise. By the way, did you make that up all by yourself?"

The old man's face assumed an injured look, expressive more of sorrow than of anger, and shaking his head he replied:—

"No, suh, I heared dat tale befo' you er Mis' Annie dere wuz bawn, suh. My mammy tol' me dat tale w'en I wa'n't mo' d'n knee-high ter a hopper-grass."

I drove to town next morning, on some business, and did not return until noon; and after dinner I had to visit a neighbor, and did not get back until supper-time. I was smoking a cigar on the back piazza in the early evening, when I saw a familiar figure carrying a bucket of water to the barn. I called my wife.

"My dear," I said severely, "what is that rascal doing here? I thought I discharged him yesterday for good and all."

"Oh, yes," she answered, "I forgot to tell you. He was hanging round the place all the morning, and looking so down in the mouth, that I told him that if he would try to do better, we would give him one more chance. He seems so grateful, and so really in earnest in his promises of amendment, that I'm sure you'll not regret taking him back."

I was seriously enough annoyed to let my cigar go out. I did not share my wife's rose-colored hopes in regard to Tom; but as I did not wish the servants to think there was any conflict of authority in the household, I let the boy stay.

The Conjurer's Revenge

SUNDAY WAS SOMETIMES a rather dull day at our place. In the morning, when the weather was pleasant, my wife and I would drive to town, a distance of about five miles, to attend the church of our choice. The afternoons we spent at home, for the most part, occupying ourselves with the newspapers and magazines, and the contents of a fairly good library. We had a piano in the house, on which my wife played with skill and feeling. I possessed a passable baritone voice, and could accompany myself indifferently well when my wife was not by to assist me. When these resources failed us, we were apt to find it a little dull.

One Sunday afternoon in early spring,—the balmy spring of North Carolina, when the air is in that ideal balance between heat and cold where one wishes it could always remain,—my wife and I were seated on the front piazza, she wearily but conscientiously ploughing through a missionary report, while I followed the impossible career of the blonde heroine of a rudimentary novel. I had thrown the book aside in disgust, when I saw Julius coming through the yard, under the spreading elms, which were already in full leaf. He wore his Sunday clothes, and advanced with a dignity of movement quite different from his week-day slouch.

"Have a seat, Julius," I said, pointing to an empty rocking-chair.

"No, thanky, boss, I'll des set here on de top step."

"Oh, no, Uncle Julius," exclaimed Annie, "take this chair. You will find it much more comfortable."

The old man grinned in appreciation of her solicitude, and seated himself somewhat awkwardly.

"Julius," I remarked, "I am thinking of setting out scuppernong vines on that sand-hill where the three persimmontrees are; and while I'm working there, I think I'll plant watermelons between the vines, and get a little something to pay for my first year's work. The new railroad will be finished by the middle of summer, and I can ship the melons North, and get a good price for them."

"Ef you er gwine ter hab any mo' ploughin' ter do," replied Julius, "I 'spec' you'll ha' ter buy ernudder creetur, 'ca'se hit 's much ez dem hosses kin do ter 'ten' ter de wuk dey got now."

"Yes, I had thought of that. I think I'll get a mule; a mule can do more work, and does n't require as much attention as a horse."

"I would n' 'vise you ter buy no mule," remarked Julius, with a shake of his head.

"Why not?"

"Well, you may 'low hit 's all foolis'ness, but ef I wuz in yo' place, I would n' buy no mule."

"But that is n't a reason; what objection have you to a mule?"

"Fac' is," continued the old man, in a serious tone, "I doan lack ter dribe a mule. I 's alluz afeared I mought be imposin' on some human creetur; eve'y time I cuts a mule wid a hick'ry, 'pears ter me mos' lackly I 's cuttin' some er my own relations, er somebody e'se w'at can't he'p deyse'ves."

"What put such an absurd idea into your head?" I asked.

My question was followed by a short silence, during which Julius seemed engaged in a mental struggle.

"I dunno ez hit 's wuf w'ile ter tell you dis," he said, at length. "I doan ha'dly 'spec' fer you ter b'lieve it. Does you 'member dat club-footed man w'at hilt de hoss fer you de yuther day w'en you was gittin' out'n de rockaway down ter Mars Archie McMillan's sto'?"

"Yes, I believe I do remember seeing a club-footed man there."

"Did you eber see a club-footed nigger befo' er sence?"

"No, I can't remember that I ever saw a club-footed colored man," I replied, after a moment's reflection.

"You en Mis' Annie would n' wanter b'lieve me, ef I wuz ter 'low dat dat man was oncet a mule?"

"No," I replied, "I don't think it very likely that you could make us believe it."

"Why, Uncle Julius!" said Annie severely, "what ridiculous nonsense!"

This reception of the old man's statement reduced him to silence, and it required some diplomacy on my part to induce him to vouchsafe an explanation. The prospect of a long, dull afternoon was not alluring, and I was glad to have the monotony of Sabbath quiet relieved by a plantation legend.

"W'en I wuz a young man," began Julius, when I had finally prevailed upon him to tell us the story, "dat club-footed nigger—his name is Primus—use' ter b'long ter ole Mars Jim McGee ober on de Lumbe'ton plank-road. I use' ter go ober dere ter see a 'oman w'at libbed on de plantation; dat's how I come ter know all erbout it. Dis yer Primus wuz de livelies' han' on de place, alluz a-dancin', en drinkin', en runnin' roun', en singin', en pickin' de banjo; 'cep'n' once in a w'ile, w'en he'd 'low wa'n't treated right 'bout sump'n er- nudder, he'd git so sulky en stubborn dat de w'ite folks could n' ha'dly do nuffin wid 'im.

"It wuz 'gin' de rules fer any er de han's ter go 'way fum de plan- tation at night; but Primus did n' min' de rules, en went w'en he felt lack it; en de w'ite folks purten' lack dey did n' know it, fer Primus was dange'ous w'en he got in dem stubborn spells, en dey 'd ruther not fool wid 'im.

"One night in de spring er de year, Primus slip' off fum de plan- tation, en went down on de Wim'l'ton Road ter a dance gun by some er de free niggers down dere. Dey wuz a fiddle, en a banjo, en a jug gwine roun' on de outside, en Primus sung en dance' 'tel 'long 'bout two o'clock in de mawnin', w'en he start' fer home. Ez he come erlong back, he tuk a nigh-cut 'cross de cotton-fiel's en 'long by de aidge er de Min'al Spring Swamp, so ez ter git shet er de pat- teroles w'at rid up en down de big road fer ter keep de darkies fum runnin' roun' nights. Primus was sa'nt'rin' 'long, studyin' 'bout de good time he 'd had wid de gals, w'en, ez he wuz gwine by a fence co'nder, w'at sh'd he heah but sump'n grunt. He stopped a minute ter listen, en he heared sump'n grunt ag'in. Den he went ober ter de fence whar he heard de fuss, en dere, layin' in de fence co'nder, on a pile er pine straw, he seed a fine, fat shote.

"Primus look' ha'd at de shote, en den sta'ted home. But some- how er 'nudder he could n' git away fum dat shote; w'en he tuk one step for'ards wid one foot, de yuther foot 'peared ter take two steps back'ards, en so he kep' nachly gittin' closeter ter de shote. It was de beatin'es' thing! De shote des 'peared ter cha'm Primus, en fus' thing you know Primus foun' hisse'f 'way up de road wid de shote on his back.

"Ef Primus had 'a' knowed whose shote dat wuz, he 'd 'a' manage' ter git pas' it somehow er 'nudder. Ez it happen', de shote b'long ter a cunjuh man w'at libbed down in de free-nigger sett'e-ment. Co'se de cunjuh man did n' hab ter wuk his roots but a little w'ile 'fo' he foun' out who tuk his shote, en den de trouble begun. One mawnin', a day er so later, en befo' he got de shote eat up, Primus did n' go ter wuk w'en de hawn blow, en w'en de oberseah wen' ter look fer him, dey wa' no trace er Primus ter be 'skivered nowhar. W'en he did n' come back in a day or so mo', eve'ybody on de plantation 'lowed he had runned erway. His marster a'vertise' him in de papers, en offered a big reward fer 'im. De nigger-ketchers fotch out dey dogs, en track' 'im down ter de aidge er de swamp, en den de scent gun out; en dat was de las' anybody seed er Primus fer a long, long time.

"Two er th'ee weeks atter Primus disappear', his marster went ter town one Sad'day. Mars Jim was stan'in' in front er Sandy Camp-bell's bar-room, up by de ole wagon-ya'd, w'en a po' w'ite man fum down on de Wim'l'ton Road come up ter 'im en ax' 'im, kinder keerless lack, ef he did n' wanter buy a mule.

" 'I dunno,' says Mars Jim; 'it 'pen's on de mule, en on de price. Whar is de mule?'

" 'Des 'roun' heah back er ole Tom McAllister's sto',' says de po' w'ite man.

" 'I reckon I'll hab a look at de mule,' says Mars Jim, 'en ef he suit me, I dunno but w'at I mought buy 'im.'

"So de po' w'ite man tuk Mars Jim 'roun' back er de sto', en dere stood a monst'us fine mule. W'en de mule see Mars Jim, he gun a whinny, des lack he knowed him befo'. Mars Jim look' at de mule, en de mule 'peared ter be soun' en strong. Mars Jim 'lowed dey 'peared ter be sump'n fermilyus 'bout de mule's face, 'spesh'ly his eyes; but he had n' los' naer mule, en did n' hab no recommen-b'ance er habin' seed de mule befo'. He ax' de po' buckrah whar he got de mule, en de po' buckrah say his brer raise' de mule down on Rockfish Creek. Mars Jim was a little s'picious er seein' a po' w'ite man wid sech a fine creetur, but he fin'lly 'greed ter gib de man fifty dollars fer de mule,—'bout ha'f w'at a good mule was wuf dem days.

"He tied de mule behin' de buggy w'en he went home, en put 'im ter ploughin' cotton de nex' day. De mule done mighty well fer th'ee er fo' days, en den de niggers 'mence' ter notice some quare things erbout him. Dey wuz a medder on de plantation whar dey use' ter put de hosses en mules ter pastur'. Hit was fence' off fum de cornfiel' on one side, but on de yuther side'n de pastur' was a terbacker-patch w'at wa'n't fence' off, 'ca'se de beastisses doan none un 'em eat terbacker. Dey doan know w'at 's good! Terbacker is lack religion, de good Lawd made it fer people, en dey ain' no yuther creetur w'at kin 'preciate it. De darkies notice' dat de fus' thing de new mule done, w'en he was turnt inter de pastur', wuz ter make fer de terbacker-patch. Co'se dey did n' think nuffin un it, but nex' mawnin', w'en dey went ter ketch 'im, dey 'skivered dat he had eat up two whole rows er terbacker plants. Atter dat dey had ter put a halter on 'im, en tie 'im ter a stake, er e'se dey would n' 'a' been naer leaf er terbacker lef' in de patch.

"Ernudder day one er de han's, name' 'Dolphus, hitch' de mule up, en dribe up here ter dis yer vimya'd,—dat wuz w'en ole Mars Dugal' own' dis place. Mars Dugal' had kilt a yearlin', en de naber w'ite folks all sont ober fer ter git some fraish beef, en Mars Jim had sont 'Dolphus fer some too. Dey wuz a wine-press in de ya'd whar 'Dolphus lef' de mule a-stan'in', en right in front er de press dey wuz a tub er grape-juice, des pressed out, en a little ter one side a bairl erbout half full er wine w'at had be'n stan'in' two er th'ee days, en had begun ter git sorter sha'p ter de tas'e. Dey wuz a couple er bo'ds on top er dis yer bairl, wid a rock laid on 'em ter hol' 'em down. Ez I wuz a-sayin', 'Dolphus lef' de mule stan'in' in de ya'd, en went inter de smoke-house fer ter git de beef. Bimeby, w'en he come out, he seed de mule a-stagg'rin' 'bout de ya'd; en 'fo' 'Dolphus could git dere ter fin' out w'at wuz de matter, de mule fell right ober on his side, en laid dere des' lack he was dead.

"All de niggers 'bout de house run out dere fer ter see w'at wuz de matter. Some say de mule had de colic; some say one thing en some ernudder; 'tel bimeby one er de han's seed de top wuz off'n de bairl, en run en looked in.

" 'Fo' de Lawd!' he say, 'dat mule drunk! he be'n drinkin' de wine.' En sho' 'nuff, de mule had pas' right by de tub er fraish grape-juice en push' de kiver off'n de bairl, en drunk two er th'ee gallon er de wine w'at had been stan'in' long ernough fer ter begin ter git sha'p.

"De darkies all made a great 'miration 'bout de mule gittin' drunk. Dey never had n' seed nuffin lack it in dey bawn days. Dey po'd water ober de mule, en tried ter sober 'im up; but it wa'n't no use, en 'Dolphus had ter take de beef home on his back, en leabe de mule dere, 'tel he slep' off 'is spree.

"I doan 'member whe'r I tol' you er no, but w'en Primus disappear' fum de plantation, he lef' a wife behin' 'im—a monst'us good-lookin' yaller gal, name' Sally. W'en Primus had be'n gone a mont' er so, Sally 'mence' fer ter git lonesome, en tuk up wid ernudder young man name' Dan, w'at b'long' on de same plantation. One day dis yer Dan tuk de noo mule out in de cotton-fiel' fer ter plough, en w'en dey wuz gwine 'long de tu'n-row, who sh'd he meet but dis yer Sally. Dan look' 'roun' en he did n' see de oberseah nowhar, so he stop' a minute fer ter run on wid Sally.

" 'Hoddy, honey,' sezee. 'How you feelin' dis mawnin'?'

" 'Fus' rate,' 'spon' Sally.

"Dey wuz lookin' at one ernudder, en dey did n' naer one un 'em pay no 'tention ter de mule, who had turnt 'is head 'roun' en wuz lookin' at Sally ez ha'd ez he could, en stretchin' 'is neck en raisin' 'is years, en whinnyin' kinder sof' ter hisse'f.

" 'Yas, honey,' 'lows Dan, 'en you gwine ter feel fus' rate long ez you sticks ter me. Fer I's a better man dan dat low-down runaway nigger Primus dat you be'n wastin' yo' time wid.'

"Dan had let go de plough-handle, en had put his arm 'roun' Sally, en wuz des gwine ter kiss her, w'en sump'n ketch' 'im by de scruff er de neck en flung 'im 'way ober in de cotton-patch. W'en he pick' 'isse'f up, Sally had gone kitin' down de tu'n-row, en de mule wuz stan'in' dere lookin' ez ca'm en peaceful ez a Sunday mawnin'.

"Fus' Dan had 'lowed it wuz de oberseah w'at had cotch' 'im wastin' 'is time. But dey wa'n't no oberseah in sight, so he 'cluded it must 'a' be'n de mule. So he pitch' inter de mule en lammed 'im ez ha'd ez he could. De mule tuk it all, en 'peared ter be ez 'umble ez a mule could be; but w'en dey wuz makin' de turn at de een' er de row, one er de plough-lines got under de mule's hin' leg. Dan retch' down ter git de line out, sorter keerless like, w'en de mule haul' off en kick him clean ober de fence inter a brier-patch on de yuther side.

"Dan wuz mighty so' fum 'is woun's en scratches, en wuz laid up fer two er th'ee days. One night de noo mule got out'n de pastur', en went down to de quarters. Dan wuz layin' dere on his pallet, w'en he heard sump'n bangin' erway at de side er his cabin. He raise' up on one shoulder en look' roun', w'en w'at should he see but de noo mule's head stickin' in de winder, wid his lips drawed back over his toofs, grinnin' en snappin' at Dan des' lack he wanter eat 'im up. Den de mule went roun' ter de do', en kick' erway lack he wanter break de do' down, 'tel bimeby somebody come 'long en driv him back ter de pastur'. W'en Sally come in a little later fum de big house, whar she'd be'n waitin' on de w'ite folks, she foun' po' Dan nigh 'bout dead, he wuz so skeered. She 'lowed Dan had had de nightmare; but w'en dey look' at de do', dey seed de marks er de mule's huffs, so dey could n' be no mistake 'bout w'at had happen.'

"Co'se de niggers tol' dey marster 'bout de mule's gwineson. Fust he did n' pay no 'tention ter it, but atter a w'ile he tol' 'em ef dey did n' stop dey foolis'ness, he gwine tie some un 'em up. So atter dat dey did n' say nuffin mo' ter dey marster, but dey kep' on noticin' de mule's quare ways des de same.

" 'Long 'bout de middle er de summer dey wuz a big camp-meetin' broke out down on de Wim'l'ton Road, en nigh 'bout all de po' w'ite folks en free niggers in de settlement got 'ligion, en lo en behol'! 'mongs' 'em wuz de cunjuh man w'at own' de shote w'at cha'med Primus.

"Dis cunjuh man wuz a Guinea nigger, en befo' he wuz sot free had use' ter b'long ter a gent'eman down in Sampson County. De cunjuh man say his daddy wuz a king, er a guv'ner, er some sorter w'at-you-may-call-'em 'way ober yander in Affiky whar de niggers come fum, befo' he was stoled erway en sol' ter de spekilaters. De cunjuh man had he'ped his marster out'n some trouble ernudder wid his goopher, en his marster had sot him free, en bought him a trac' er land down on de Wim'l'ton Road. He purten' ter be a cow-doctor, but eve'ybody knowed w'at he r'al'y wuz.

"De cunjuh man had n' mo' d'n come th'oo good, befo' he wuz

tuk sick wid a col' w'at he kotch kneelin' on de groun' so long at de mou'ners' bench. He kep' gittin' wusser en wusser, en bimeby de rheumatiz tuk holt er 'im, en drawed him all up, 'tel one day he sont word up ter Mars Jim McGee's plantation, en ax' Pete, de nigger w'at tuk keer er de mules, fer ter come down dere dat night en fetch dat mule w'at his marster had bought fum de po' w'ite man dyoin' er de summer.

"Pete did n' know w'at de cunjuh man wuz dribin' at, but he did n' daster stay way; en so dat night, w'en he'd done eat his bacon en his hoe-cake, en drunk his 'lasses-en-water, he put a bridle on de mule, en rid 'im down ter de cunjuh man's cabin. W'en he got ter de do', he lit en hitch' de mule, en den knock' at de do'. He felt mighty jubous 'bout gwine in, but he was bleedst ter do it; he knowed he could n' he'p 'isse'f.

" 'Pull de string,' sez a weak voice, en w'en Pete lif' de latch en went in, de cunjuh man was layin' on de bed, lookin' pale en weak, lack he did n' hab much longer fer ter lib.

" 'Is you fotch' de mule?' sezee.

"Pete say yas, en de cunjuh man kep' on.

" 'Brer Pete,' sezee, 'I 's be'n a monst'us sinner man, en I 's done a power er wickedness endyoin' er my days; but de good Lawd is wash' my sins erway, en I feels now dat I 's boun' fer de kingdom. En I feels, too, dat I ain' gwine ter git up fum dis bed no mo' in dis worl', en I wants ter ondo some er de harm I done. En dat's de reason, Brer Pete, I sont fer you ter fetch dat mule down here. You 'member dat shote I was up ter yo' plantation inquirin' 'bout las' June?'

" 'Yas,' says Brer Pete, 'I 'member yo' axin' 'bout a shote you had los'.'

" 'I dunno whe'r you eber I'arnt it er no,' says de cunjuh man, 'but I done knowed yo' marster's Primus had tuk de shote, en I wuz boun' ter git eben wid 'im. So one night I cotch' 'im down by de swamp on his way ter a candy-pullin', en I th'owed a goopher mixtry on 'im, en turnt 'im ter a mule, en got a po' w'ite man ter sell de mule, en we 'vided de money. But I doan want ter die 'tel I turn Brer Primus back ag'in.'

"Den de cunjuh man ax' Pete ter take down one er two go'ds off'n a she'f in de corner, en one er two bottles wid some kin' er mixtry in 'em, en set 'em on a stool by de bed; en den he ax' 'im ter fetch de mule in.

"W'en de mule come in de do', he gin a snort, en started fer de bed, des lack he was gwine ter jump on it.

" 'Hol' on dere, Brer Primus!' de cunjuh man hollered. 'I's monst'us weak, en ef you 'mence on me, you won't nebber hab no chance fer ter git turn' back no mo'.'

"De mule seed de sense er dat, en stood still. Den de cunjuh man tuk de go'ds en bottles, en 'mence' ter wuk de roots en yarbs, en de mule 'mence' ter turn back ter a man,—fust his years, den de res' er his head, den his shoulders en arms. All de time de cunjuh man kep' on wukkin' his roots; en Pete en Primus could see he wuz gittin' weaker en weaker all de time.

" 'Brer Pete,' sezee, bimeby, 'gimme a drink er dem bitters out'n dat green bottle on de she'f yander. I 's gwine fas', en it 'll gimme strenk fer ter finish dis wuk.'

"Brer Pete look' up on de mantelpiece, en he seed a bottle in de corner. It was so da'k in de cabin he could n' tell whe'r it wuz a green bottle er no. But he hilt de bottle ter de cunjuh man's mouf, en he tuck a big mouff'l. He had n' mo' d'n swallowed it befo' he 'mence' ter holler.

" 'You gimme de wrong bottle, Brer Pete; dis yer bottle 's got pizen in it, en I 's done fer dis time, sho'. Hol' me up, fer de Lawd's sake! 'tel I git th'oo turnin' Brer Primus back.'

"So Pete hilt him up, en he kep' on wukkin' de roots, 'tel he got de goopher all tuk off'n Brer Primus 'cep'n' one foot. He had n' got dis foot mo' d'n half turnt back befo' his strenk gun out enti'ely, en he drap' de roots en fell back on de bed.

" 'I can't do no mo' fer you, Brer Primus,' sezee, 'but I hopes you will fergib me fer w'at harm I done you. I knows de good Lawd done fergib me, en I hope ter meet you bofe in glory. I sees de good angels waitin' fer me up yander, wid a long w'ite robe en a starry crown, en I'm on my way ter jine 'em.' En so de cunjuh man died, en Pete en Primus went back ter de plantation.

"De darkies all made a great 'miration w'en Primus come back. Mars Jim let on lack he did n' b'lieve de tale de two niggers tol'; he sez Primus had runned erway, en stay' 'tel he got ti'ed er de swamps, en den come back on him ter be fed. He tried ter 'count fer

de shape er Primus' foot by sayin' Primus got his foot smash', er
snake-bit, er sump'n, w'iles he wuz erway, en den stayed out in de
woods whar he could n' git it kyoed up straight, 'stidder comin'
long home whar a doctor could 'a' 'tended ter it. But de niggers all
notice' dey marster did n' tie Primus up, ner take on much 'ca'se
de mule wuz gone. So dey 'lowed dey marster must 'a' had his
s'picions 'bout dat cunjah man."

My wife had listened to Julius's recital with only a mild interest.
When the old man had finished it she remarked:—

"That story does not appeal to me, Uncle Julius, and is not up to
your usual mark. It is n't pathetic, it has no moral that I can discover, and I can't see why you should tell it. In fact, it seems to me
like nonsense."

The old man looked puzzled as well as pained. He had not
pleased the lady, and he did not seem to understand why.

"I'm sorry, ma'm," he said reproachfully, "ef you doan lack dat
tale. I can't make out w'at you means by some er dem wo'ds you
uses, but I'm tellin' nuffin but de truf. Co'se I did n' see de cunjuh
man tu'n 'im back, fer I wuz n' dere; but I be'n hearin' de tale fer
twenty-five yeahs, en I ain' got no 'casion fer ter 'spute it. Dey 's so
many things a body knows is lies, dat dey ain' no use gwine roun'
findin' fault wid tales dat mought des ez well be so ez not. F' instance, dey 's a young nigger gwine ter school in town, en he come
out heah de yuther day en 'lowed dat de sun stood still en de yeath
turnt roun' eve'y day on a kinder axletree. I tol' dat young nigger ef
he did n' take hisse'f 'way wid dem lies, I'd take a buggy-trace ter
'im; fer I sees de yeath stan'in still all de time, en I sees de sun gwine
roun' it, en ef a man can't b'lieve w'at 'e sees, I can't see no use in
libbin'—mought 's well die en be whar we can't see nuffin. En ernudder thing w'at proves de tale 'bout dis ole Primus is de way he
goes on ef anybody ax' him how he come by dat club-foot. I axed
'im one day, mighty perlite en civil, en he call' me a' ole fool, en got
so mad he ain' spoke ter me sence. Hit 's monst'us quare. But dis a
quare worl', anyway yer kin fix it," concluded the old man, with a
weary sigh.

"Ef you makes up yo' min' not ter buy dat mule, suh," he added,
as he rose to go, "I knows a man w'at 's got a good hoss he wants
ter sell,—leas'ways dat 's w'at I heared. I'm gwine ter pra'rmeetin'

ter-night, en I'm gwine right by de man's house, en ef you'd lack ter look at de hoss, I'll ax 'im ter fetch him roun'."

"Oh, yes," I said, "you can ask him to stop in, if he is passing. There will be no harm in looking at the horse, though I rather think I shall buy a mule."

Early next morning the man brought the horse up to the vineyard. At that time I was not a very good judge of horse-flesh. The horse appeared sound and gentle, and, as the owner assured me, had no bad habits. The man wanted a large price for the horse, but finally agreed to accept a much smaller sum, upon payment of which I became possessed of a very fine-looking animal. But alas for the deceitfulness of appearances! I soon ascertained that the horse was blind in one eye, and that the sight of the other was very defective; and not a month elapsed before my purchase developed most of the diseases that horse-flesh is heir to, and a more worthless, broken-winded, spavined quadruped never disgraced the noble name of horse. After worrying through two or three months of life, he expired one night in a fit of the colic. I replaced him with a mule, and Julius henceforth had to take his chances of driving some metamorphosed unfortunate.

Circumstances that afterwards came to my knowledge created in my mind a strong suspicion that Julius may have played a more than unconscious part in this transaction. Among other significant facts was his appearance, the Sunday following the purchase of the horse, in a new suit of store clothes, which I had seen displayed in the window of Mr. Solomon Cohen's store on my last visit to town, and had remarked on account of their striking originality of cut and pattern. As I had not recently paid Julius any money, and as he had no property to mortgage, I was driven to conjecture to account for his possession of the means to buy the clothes. Of course I would not charge him with duplicity unless I could prove it, at least to a moral certainty, but for a long time afterwards I took his advice only in small doses and with great discrimination.

Sis' Becky's Pickaninny

WE HAD NOT LIVED in North Carolina very long before I was able to note a marked improvement in my wife's health. The ozone-laden air of the surrounding piney woods, the mild and equable climate, the peaceful leisure of country life, had brought about in hopeful measure the cure we had anticipated. Toward the end of our second year, however, her ailment took an unexpected turn for the worse. She became the victim of a settled melancholy, attended with vague forebodings of impending misfortune.

"You must keep up her spirits," said our physician, the best in the neighboring town. "This melancholy lowers her tone too much, tends to lessen her strength, and, if it continue too long, may be fraught with grave consequences."

I tried various expedients to cheer her up. I read novels to her. I had the hands on the place come up in the evening and serenade her with plantation songs. Friends came in sometimes and talked, and frequent letters from the North kept her in touch with her former home. But nothing seemed to rouse her from the depression into which she had fallen.

One pleasant afternoon in spring, I placed an armchair in a shaded portion of the front piazza, and filling it with pillows led my wife out of the house and seated her where she would have the pleasantest view of a somewhat monotonous scenery. She was scarcely placed when old Julius came through the yard, and, taking off his tattered straw hat, inquired, somewhat anxiously:—

"How is you feelin' dis afternoon, ma'm?"

"She is not very cheerful, Julius," I said. My wife was apparently without energy enough to speak for herself.

The old man did not seem inclined to go away, so I asked him to sit down. I had noticed, as he came up, that he held some small object in his hand. When he had taken his seat on the top step, he kept fingering this object,—what it was I could not quite make out.

"What is that you have there, Julius?" I asked, with mild curiosity.

"Dis is my rabbit foot, suh."

This was at a time before this curious superstition had attained its present jocular popularity among white people, and while I had heard of it before, it had not yet outgrown the charm of novelty.

"What do you do with it?"

"I kyars it wid me fer luck, suh."

"Julius," I observed, half to him and half to my wife, "your people will never rise in the world until they throw off these childish superstitions and learn to live by the light of reason and common sense. How absurd to imagine that the fore-foot of a poor dead rabbit, with which he timorously felt his way along through a life surrounded by snares and pitfalls, beset by enemies on every hand, can promote happiness or success, or ward off failure or misfortune!"

"It is ridiculous," assented my wife, with faint interest.

"Dat's w'at I tells dese niggers roun' heah," said Julius. "De fo'-foot ain' got no power. It has ter be de hin'-foot, suh,—de lef' hin'-foot er a grabe-ya'd rabbit, killt by a cross-eyed nigger on a da'k night in de full er de moon."

"They must be very rare and valuable," I said.

"Dey is kinder ska'ce, suh, en dey ain' no 'mount er money could buy mine, suh. I mought len' it ter anybody I sot sto' by, but I would n' sell it, no indeed, suh, I would n'."

"How do you know it brings good luck?" I asked.

" 'Ca'se I ain' had no bad luck sence I had it, suh, en I 's had dis rabbit foot fer fo'ty yeahs. I had a good marster befo' de wah, en I wa'n't sol' erway, en I wuz sot free; en dat 'uz all good luck."

"But that does n't prove anything," I rejoined. "Many other people have gone through a similar experience, and probably more than one of them had no rabbit's foot."

"Law, suh! you doan hafter prove 'bout de rabbit foot! Eve'ybody knows dat; leas'ways eve'ybody roun' heah knows it. But ef it has ter be prove' ter folks w'at wa'n't bawn en raise' in dis naberhood, dey is a' easy way ter prove it. Is I eber tol' you de tale er Sis' Becky en her pickaninny?"

"No," I said, "let us hear it." I thought perhaps the story might interest my wife as much or more than the novel I had meant to read from.

"Dis yer Becky," Julius began, "useter b'long ter ole Kunnel Pen'leton, who owned a plantation down on de Wim'l'ton Road, 'bout ten miles fum heah, des befo' you gits ter Black Swamp. Dis yer Becky wuz a fiel-han', en a monst'us good 'un. She had a husban' oncet, a nigger w'at b'longed on de nex' plantation, but de man w'at owned her husban' died, en his lan' en his niggers had ter be sol' fer ter pay his debts. Kunnel Pen'leton 'lowed he 'd 'a' bought dis nigger, but he had be'n bettin' on hoss races, en did n' hab no money, en so Becky's husban' wuz sol' erway ter Fuhginny.

"Co'se Becky went on some 'bout losin' her man, but she could n' he'p herse'f; en 'sides dat, she had her pickaninny fer ter comfo't her. Dis yer little Mose wuz de cutes', blackes', shiny-eyedes' little nigger you eber laid eyes on, en he wuz ez fon' er his mammy ez his mammy wuz er him. Co'se Becky had ter wuk en did n' hab much time ter was'e wid her baby. Ole Aun' Nancy, de plantation nuss down at de qua'ters, useter take keer er little Mose in de daytime, en atter de niggers come in fum de cotton-fiel' Becky 'ud git her chile en kiss 'im en nuss 'im, en keep 'im 'tel mawnin'; en on Sundays she 'd hab 'im in her cabin wid her all day long.

"Sis' Becky had got sorter useter gittin' 'long widout her husban', w'en one day Kunnel Pen'leton went ter de races. Co'se w'en he went ter de races, he tuk his hosses, en co'se he bet on 'is own hosses, en co'se he los' his money; fer Kunnel Pen'leton did n' nebber hab no luck wid his hosses, ef he did keep hisse'f po' projeckin' wid 'em. But dis time dey wuz a hoss name' Lightnin' Bug, w'at b'longed ter ernudder man, en dis hoss won de sweep-stakes; en Kunnel Pen'leton tuk a lackin' ter dat hoss, en ax' his owner w'at he wuz willin' ter take fer 'im.

" 'I'll take a thousan' dollahs fer dat hoss,' sez dis yer man, who had a big plantation down to'ds Wim'l'ton, whar he raise' hosses fer ter race en ter sell.

"Well, Kunnel Pen'leton scratch' 'is head, en wonder whar he wuz gwine ter raise a thousan' dollahs; en he did n' see des how he could do it, fer he owed ez much ez he could borry a'ready on de skyo'ity he could gib. But he wuz des boun' ter hab dat hoss, so sezee:—

"'I'll gib you my note fer 'leven hund'ed dollahs fer dat hoss.'

"De yuther man shuck 'is head, en sezee:—

"'Yo' note, suh, is better'n gol', I doan doubt; but I is made it a rule in my bizness not ter take no notes fum nobody. Howsomeber, suh, ef you is kinder sho't er fun's, mos' lackly we kin make some kin' er bahg'in. En w'iles we is talkin', I mought is well say dat I needs ernudder good nigger down on my place. Ef you is got a good one ter spar', I mought trade wid you.'

"Now, Kunnel Pen'leton did n' r'ally hab no niggers fer ter spar', but he 'lowed ter hisse'f he wuz des bleedzd ter hab dat hoss, en so he sez, sezee:—

"'Well, I doan lack ter, but I reckon I'll haf ter. You come out ter my plantation ter-morrer en look ober my niggers, en pick out de one you wants.'

"So sho' 'nuff nex' day dis yer man come out ter Kunnel Pen'leton's place en rid roun' de plantation en glanshed at de niggers, en who sh'd he pick out fum 'em all but Sis' Becky.

"'I needs a noo nigger 'oman down ter my place,' sezee, 'fer ter cook en wash, en so on; en dat young 'oman 'll des fill de bill. You gimme her, en you kin hab Lightnin' Bug.'"

"Now, Kunnel Pen'leton did n' lack ter trade Sis' Becky, 'ca'se she wuz nigh 'bout de bes' fiel'-han' he had; en 'sides, Mars Kunnel did n' keer ter take de mammies 'way fum dey chillun w'iles de chillun wuz little. But dis man say he want Becky, er e'se Kunnel Pen'leton could n' hab de race hoss.

"'Well,' sez de kunnel, 'you kin hab de 'oman. But I doan lack ter sen' her 'way fum her baby. W'at 'll you gimme fer dat nigger baby?'

"'I doan want de baby,' sez de yuther man. 'I ain' got no use fer de baby.'

"'I tell yer w'at I'll do,' 'lows Kunnel Pen'leton, 'I'll th'ow dat pickaninny in fer good measure.'

"But de yuther man shuck his head. 'No,' sezee, 'I's much erbleedzd, but I doan raise niggers; I raises hosses, en I doan wanter

be both'rin' wid no nigger babies. Nemmine de baby. I'll keep dat
'oman so busy she'll fergit de baby; fer niggers is made ter wuk, en
dey ain' got no time fer no sich foolis'ness ez babies.'

"Kunnel Pen'leton did n' wanter hu't Becky's feelin's,—fer Kunnel Pen'leton wuz a kin'-hea'ted man, en nebber lack' ter make no
trouble fer nobody,—en so he tol' Becky he wuz gwine sen' her
down ter Robeson County fer a day er so, ter he'p out his son-in-
law in his wuk; en bein' ez dis yuther man wuz gwine dat way, he
had ax' 'im ter take her 'long in his buggy.

" 'Kin I kyar little Mose wid me, marster?' ax' Sis' Becky.

" 'N-o,' sez de kunnel, ez ef he wuz studyin' whuther ter let her
take 'im er no; 'I reckon you better let Aun' Nancy look atter yo'
baby fer de day er two you 'll be gone, en she 'll see dat he gits ernuff ter eat 'tel you gits back.'

"So Sis' Becky hug' en kiss' little Mose, en tol' 'im ter be a
good little pickaninny, en take keer er hisse'f, en not fergit his
mammy w'iles she wuz gone. En little Mose put his arms roun' his
mammy en lafft en crowed des lack it wuz monst'us fine fun fer
his mammy ter go 'way en leabe 'im.

"Well, dis yer hoss trader sta'ted out wid Becky, en bimeby, atter
dey 'd gone down de Lumbe'ton Road fer a few miles er so, dis man
tu'nt roun' in a diffe'nt d'rection, en kep' goin' dat erway, 'tel
bimeby Sis' Becky up 'n ax' 'im ef he wuz gwine ter Robeson
County by a noo road.

" 'No, nigger,' sezee, 'I ain' gwine ter Robeson County at all. I 's
gwine ter Bladen County, whar my plantation is, en whar I raises all
my hosses.'

" 'But how is I gwine ter git ter Mis' Laura's plantation down in
Robeson County?' sez Becky, wid her hea't in her mouf, fer she
'mence' ter git skeered all er a sudden.

" 'You ain' gwine ter git dere at all,' sez de man. 'You b'longs ter
me now, fer I done traded my bes' race hoss fer you, wid yo' ole
marster. Ef you is a good gal, I'll treat you right, en ef you doan behabe yo'se'f,—w'y, w'at e'se happens 'll be yo' own fault.'

"Co'se Sis' Becky cried en went on 'bout her pickaninny, but
co'se it did n' do no good, en bimeby dey got down ter dis yer
man's place, en he put Sis' Becky ter wuk, en fergot all 'bout her
habin' a pickaninny.

"Meanw'iles, w'en ebenin' come, de day Sis' Becky wuz tuk 'way, little Mose 'mence' ter git res'less, en bimeby, w'en his mammy did n' come, he sta'ted ter cry fer 'er. Aun' Nancy fed 'im en rocked 'im en rocked 'im, en fin'lly he des cried en cried 'tel he cried hisse'f ter sleep.

"De nex' day he did n' 'pear ter be as peart ez yushal, en w'en night come he fretted en went on wuss'n he did de night befo'. De nex' day his little eyes 'mence' ter lose dey shine, en he would n' eat nuffin, en he 'mence' ter look so peaked dat Aun' Nancy tuk 'n kyared 'im up ter de big house, en showed 'im ter her ole missis, en her ole missis gun her some med'cine fer 'im, en 'lowed ef he did n' git no better she sh'd fetch 'im up ter de big house ag'in, en dey 'd hab a doctor, en nuss little Mose up dere. Fer Aun' Nancy's ole missis 'lowed he wuz a lackly little nigger en wu'th raisin'.

"But Aun' Nancy had I'arn' ter lack little Mose, en she did n' wanter hab 'im tuk up ter de big house. En so w'en he did n' git no better, she gethered a mess er green peas, and tuk de peas en de baby, en went ter see ole Aun' Peggy, de cunjuh 'oman down by de Wim'l'ton Road. She gun Aun' Peggy de mess er peas, en tol' her all 'bout Sis' Becky en little Mose.

" 'Dat is a monst'us small mess er peas you is fotch' me,' sez Aun' Peggy, sez she.

" 'Yas, I knows,' 'lowed Aun' Nancy, 'but dis yere is a monst'us small pickaninny.'

" 'You'll hafter fetch me sump'n mo',' sez Aun' Peggy, 'fer you can't 'spec' me ter was'e my time diggin' roots en wukkin' cunj' ation fer nuffin.'

" 'All right,' sez Aun' Nancy, 'I'll fetch you sump'n mo' nex' time.'

" 'You bettah,' sez Aun' Peggy, 'er e'se dey 'll be trouble. W'at dis yer little pickaninny needs is ter see his mammy. You leabe 'im heah 'tel ebenin' en I 'll show 'im his mammy.'

"So w'en Aun' Nancy had gone 'way, Aun' Peggy tuk 'n wukked her roots, en tu'nt little Mose ter a hummin'-bird, en sont 'im off fer ter fin' his mammy.

So little Mose flewed, en flewed, en flewed away, 'tel bimeby he got ter de place whar Sis' Becky b'longed. He seed his mammy wukkin' roun' de ya'd, en he could tell fum lookin' at her dat she

wuz trouble' in her min' 'bout sump'n, en feelin' kin' er po'ly. Sis'
Becky heared sump'in hummin' roun' en roun' her, sweet en low.
Fus' she 'lowed it wuz a hummin'-bird; den she thought it sounded
lack her little Mose croonin' on her breas' way back yander on de
ole plantation. En she des 'magine' it wuz her little Mose, en it
made her feel bettah, en she went on 'bout her wuk pearter 'n she 'd
done sence she 'd be'n down dere. Little Mose stayed roun' 'tel late
in de ebenin', en den flewed back ez hard ez he could ter Aun'
Peggy. Ez fer Sis' Becky, she dremp all dat night dat she wuz holdin'
her pickaninny in her arms, en kissin' him, en nussin' him, des lack
she useter do back on de ole plantation whar he wuz bawn. En fer
th'ee er fo' days Sis' Becky went 'bout her wuk wid mo' sperrit dan
she'd showed sence she 'd be'n down dere ter dis man's plantation.

"De nex' day atter he come back, little Mose wuz mo' pearter en
better 'n he had be'n fer a long time. But to'ds de een' er de week he
'mence' ter git res'less ag'in, en stop' eatin', en Aun' Nancy kyared
'im down ter Aun' Peggy once mo', en she tu'nt 'im ter a mawkin'-
bird dis time, en sont 'im off ter see his mammy ag'in.

"It did n' take him long fer ter git dere, en w'en he did, he seed
his mammy standin' in de kitchen, lookin' back in de d'rection little
Mose wuz comin' fum. En dey wuz tears in her eyes, en she look'
mo' po'ly en peaked 'n she had w'en he wuz down dere befo'. So
little Mose sot on a tree in de ya'd en sung, en sung, en sung, des fittin' ter split his th'oat. Fus' Sis' Becky did n' notice 'im much, but
dis mawkin'-bird kep' stayin' roun' de house all day, en bimeby Sis'
Becky des 'magine' dat mawkin'-bird wuz her little Mose crowin'
en crowin', des lack he useter do w'en his mammy would come
home at night fum de cotton-fiel'. De mawkin'-bird stayed roun'
dere 'mos' all day, en w'en Sis' Becky went out in de ya'd one time,
dis yer mawkin'-bird lit on her shoulder en peck' at de piece er
bread she wuz eatin', en fluttered his wings so dey rub' up agin de
side er her head. En w'en he flewed away 'long late in de ebenin',
des 'fo' sundown, Sis' Becky felt mo' better 'n she had sence she had
heared dat hummin'-bird a week er so pas'. En dat night she dremp
'bout ole times ag'in, des lack she did befo'.

"But dis yer totin' little Mose down ter ole Aun' Peggy, en dis
yer gittin' things fer ter pay de cunjuh 'oman, use' up a lot er Aun'
Nancy's time, en she begun ter git kinder ti'ed. 'Sides dat, w'en Sis'

Becky had be'n on de plantation, she had useter he'p Aun' Nancy wid de young uns ebenin's en Sundays; en Aun' Nancy 'mence' ter miss 'er monst'us, 'speshly sence she got a tech er de rheumatiz herse'f, en so she 'lows ter ole Aun' Peggy one day:—

" 'Aun' Peggy, ain' dey no way you kin fetch Sis' Becky back home?'

" 'Huh!' sez Aun' Peggy, 'I dunno 'bout dat. I 'll hafter wuk my roots en fin' out whuther I kin er no. But it 'll take a monst'us heap er wuk, en I can't was'e my time fer nuffin. Ef you 'll fetch me sump'n ter pay me fer my trouble, I reckon we kin fix it.'

"So nex' day Aun' Nancy went down ter see Aun' Peggy ag'in.

" 'Aun' Peggy,' sez she, 'I is fotch' you my bes' Sunday head-hankercher. Will dat do?'

"Aun' Peggy look' at de head-hankercher, en run her han' ober it, en sez she:—

" 'Yas, dat 'll do fus'-rate. I's be'n wukkin' my roots sence you be'n gone, en I 'lows mos' lackly I kin git Sis' Becky back, but it 's gwine take fig'rin' en studyin' ez well ez cunj'in'. De fus' thing ter do 'll be ter stop fetchin' dat pickaninny down heah, en not sen' 'im ter see his mammy no mo'. Ef he gits too po'ly, you lemme know, en I'll gib you some kin' er mixtry fer ter make 'im fergit Sis' Becky fer a week er so. So 'less'n you comes fer dat, you neenter come back ter see me no mo' 'tel I sen's fer you.'

"So Aun' Peggy sont Aun' Nancy erway, en de fus' thing she done wuz ter call a hawnet fum a nes' unner her eaves.

" 'You go up ter Kunnel Pen'leton's stable, hawnet,' sez she, 'en sting de knees er de race hoss name' Lightnin' Bug. Be sho' en git de right one.'

"So de hawnet flewed up ter Kunnel Pen'leton's stable en stung Lightnin' Bug roun' de laigs, en de nex' mawnin' Lightnin' Bug's knees wuz all swoll' up, twice't ez big ez dey oughter be. W'en Kunnel Pen'leton went out ter de stable en see de hoss's laigs, hit would 'a' des made you trimble lack a leaf fer ter heah him cuss dat hoss trader. Howsomeber, he cool' off bimeby en tol' de stable boy fer ter rub Lightnin' Bug's laigs wid some linimum. De boy done ez his marster tol' 'im, en by de nex' day de swellin' had gone down consid'able. Aun' Peggy had sont a sparrer, w'at had a nes' in one er de trees close ter her cabin, fer ter watch w'at wuz gwine on 'roun' de big house, en w'en dis yer sparrer tol' 'er de hoss wuz gittin' ober de swellin', she sont de hawnet back fer ter sting 'is knees some mo', en de nex' mawnin' Lightnin' Bug's laigs wuz swoll' up wuss 'n befo'.

"Well, dis time Kunnel Pen'leton wuz mad th'oo en th'oo, en all de way 'roun', en he cusst dat hoss trader up en down, fum *A* ter *Izzard.* He cusst so ha'd dat de stable boy got mos' skeered ter def, en went off en hid hisse'f in de hay.

"Ez fer Kunnel Pen'leton, he went right up ter de house en got out his pen en ink, en tuk off his coat en roll' up his sleeves, en writ a letter ter dis yer hoss trader, en sezee:—

" 'You is sol' me a hoss w'at is got a ringbone er a spavin er sump'n, en w'at I paid you fer wuz a soun' hoss. I wants you ter sen' my nigger 'oman back en take yo' ole hoss, er e'se I 'll sue you, sho 's you bawn.'

"But dis yer man wa'n't skeered a bit, en he writ back ter Kunnel Pen'leton dat a bahg'in wuz a bahg'in; dat Lightnin' Bug wuz soun' w'en he sol' 'im, en ef Kunnel Pen'leton did n' knowed ernuff 'bout hosses ter take keer er a fine racer, dat wuz his own fune'al. En he say Kunnel Pen'leton kin sue en be cusst fer all he keer, but he ain' gwine ter gib up de nigger he bought en paid fer.

"W'en Kunnel Pen'leton got dis letter he wuz madder 'n he wuz befo', 'spheshly 'ca'se dis man 'lowed he did n' know how ter take keer er fine hosses. But he could n' do nuffin but fetch a lawsuit, en he knowed, by his own 'spe'ience, dat lawsuits wuz slow ez de seben-yeah eetch and cos' mo' d'n dey come ter, en he 'lowed he better go slow en wait awhile.

"Aun' Peggy knowed w'at wuz gwine on all dis time, en she fix' up a little bag wid some roots en one thing en ernudder in it, en gun it ter dis sparrer er her'n, en tol' 'im ter take it 'way down yander whar Sis' Becky wuz, en drap it right befo' de do' er her cabin, so she 'd be sho' en fin' it de fus' time she come out'n de do'.

"One night Sis' Becky dremp' her pickaninny wuz dead, en de nex' day she wuz mo'nin en groanin' all day. She dremp' de same dream th'ee nights runnin', en den, de nex' mawnin' atter de las' night, she foun' dis yer little bag de sparrer had drap' in front her do'; en she 'lowed she'd be'n cunju'd, en wuz gwine ter die, en ez long ez her pickaninny wuz dead dey wa'n't no use tryin' ter do

nuffin nohow. En so she tuk 'n went ter bed, en tol' her marster she
'd be'n conju'd en wuz gwine ter die.

"Her marster lafft at her, en argyed wid her, en tried ter 'suade
her out'n dis yer fool notion, ez he called it,—fer he wuz one er
dese yer w'ite folks w'at purten' dey doan b'liebe in cunj'in',—but
hit wa'n't no use. Sis' Becky kep' gittin' wusser en wusser, 'tel
fin'lly dis yer man 'lowed Sis' Becky wuz gwine ter die, sho' 'nuff.
En ez he knowed dey had n' be'n nuffin de matter wid Lightnin'
Bug w'en he traded 'im, he 'lowed mebbe he could kyo' 'im en fetch
'im roun' all right, leas'ways good 'nuff ter sell ag'in. En anyhow, a
lame hoss wuz better 'n a dead nigger. So he sot down en writ Kunnel Pen'leton a letter.

" 'My conscience,' sezee, 'has be'n troublin' me 'bout dat ringbone' hoss I sol' you. Some folks 'lows a hoss trader ain' got no
conscience, but dey doan know me, fer dat is my weak spot en de
reason I ain' made no mo' money hoss tradin'. Fac' is,' sezee, 'I is
got so I can't sleep nights fum studyin' 'bout dat spavin' hoss; en I
is made up my min' dat, w'iles a bahg'in is a bahg'in, en you seed
Lightnin' Bug befo' you traded fer 'im, principle is wuth mo' d'n
money er hosses er niggers. So ef you 'll sen' Lightnin' Bug down
heah, I'll sen' yo' nigger 'oman back, en we 'll call de trade off, en
be ez good frien's ez we eber wuz, en no ha'd feelin's.'

"So sho' 'nuff, Kunnel Pen'leton sont de hoss back. En w'en de
man w'at come ter bring Lightnin' Bug tol' Sis' Becky her pickaninny wa'n't dead, Sis' Becky wuz so glad dat she 'lowed she wuz
gwine ter try ter lib 'tel she got back whar she could see little Mose
once mo'. En w'en she retch' de ole plantation en seed her baby
kickin' en crowin' en holdin' out his little arms to'ds her, she wush'
she was n' cunju'd en did n' hafter die. En w'en Aun' Nancy tol' 'er
all 'bout Aun' Peggy, Sis' Becky went down ter see de cunjuh
'oman, en Aun' Peggy tol' her she had cunju'd her. En den Aun'
Peggy tuk de goopher off'n her, en she got well, en stayed on de
plantation, en raise' her pickaninny. En w'en little Mose growed up,
he could sing en whistle des lack a mawkin'bird, so dat de w'ite
folks useter hab 'im come up ter de big house at night, en whistle en
sing fer 'em, en dey useter gib 'im money en vittles en one thing er
ernudder, w'ich he alluz tuk home ter his mammy; fer he knowed
all 'bout w'at she had gone th'oo. He tu'nt out ter be a sma't man,

en l'arnt de blacksmif trade; en Kunnel Pen'leton let 'im hire his time. En bimeby he bought his mammy en sot her free, en den he bought hisse'f, en tuk keer er Sis' Becky ez long ez dey bofe libbed."

My wife had listened to this story with greater interest than she had manifested in any subject for several days. I had watched her furtively from time to time during the recital, and had observed the play of her countenance. It had expressed in turn sympathy, indignation, pity, and at the end lively satisfaction.

"That is a very ingenious fairy tale, Julius," I said, "and we are much obliged to you."

"Why, John!" said my wife severely, "the story bears the stamp of truth, if ever a story did."

"Yes," I replied, "especially the humming-bird episode, and the mocking-bird digression, to say nothing of the doings of the hornet and the sparrow."

"Oh, well, I don't care," she rejoined, with delightful animation; "those are mere ornamental details and not at all essential. The story is true to nature, and might have happened half a hundred times, and no doubt did happen, in those horrid days before the war."

"By the way, Julius," I remarked, "your story does n't establish what you started out to prove,—that a rabbit's foot brings good luck."

"Hit 's plain 'nuff ter me, suh," replied Julius. "I bet young missis dere kin 'splain it herse'f."

"I rather suspect," replied my wife promptly, "that Sis' Becky had no rabbit's foot."

"You is hit de bull's-eye de fus' fire, ma'm," assented Julius. "Ef Sis' Becky had had a rabbit foot, she nebber would 'a' went th'oo all dis trouble."

I went into the house for some purpose, and left Julius talking to my wife. When I came back a moment later, he was gone.

My wife's condition took a turn for the better from this very day, and she was soon on the way to ultimate recovery. Several weeks later, after she had resumed her afternoon drives, which had been interrupted by her illness, Julius brought the rockaway round to the front door one day, and I assisted my wife into the carriage.

"John," she said, before I had taken my seat, "I wish you would look in my room, and bring me my handkerchief. You will find it in the pocket of my blue dress."

I went to execute the commission. When I pulled the handkerchief out of her pocket, something else came with it and fell on the floor. I picked up the object and looked at it. It was Julius's rabbit's foot.

The Gray Wolf's Ha'nt

IT WAS A RAINY DAY at the vineyard. The morning had dawned bright and clear. But the sky had soon clouded, and by nine o'clock there was a light shower, followed by others at brief intervals. By noon the rain had settled into a dull, steady downpour. The clouds hung low, and seemed to grow denser instead of lighter as they discharged their watery burden, and there was now and then a muttering of distant thunder. Outdoor work was suspended, and I spent most of the day at the house, looking over my accounts and bringing up some arrears of correspondence.

Towards four o'clock I went out on the piazza, which was broad and dry, and less gloomy than the interior of the house, and composed myself for a quiet smoke. I had lit my cigar and opened the volume I was reading at that time, when my wife, whom I had left dozing on a lounge, came out and took a rocking-chair near me.

"I wish you would talk to me, or read to me—or something," she exclaimed petulantly. "It's awfully dull here today."

"I'll read to you with pleasure," I replied, and began at the point where I had found my bookmark:—

" 'The difficulty of dealing with transformations so many-sided as those which all existences have undergone, or are undergoing, is such as to make a complete and deductive interpretation almost hopeless. So to grasp the total process of redistribution of matter and motion as to see simultaneously its several necessary results in their actual interdependence is scarcely possible. There is, however, a mode of rendering the process as a whole tolerably comprehensible. Though the genesis of the rearrangement of every evolving aggregate is in itself one, it presents to our intelligence' "—

"John," interrupted my wife, "I wish you would stop reading that nonsense and see who that is coming up the lane."

I closed my book with a sigh. I had never been able to interest my wife in the study of philosophy, even when presented in the simplest and most lucid form.

Some one was coming up the lane; at least, a huge faded cotton umbrella was making progress toward the house, and beneath it a pair of nether extremities in trousers was discernible. Any doubt in my mind as to whose they were was soon resolved when Julius reached the steps and, putting the umbrella down, got a good dash of the rain as he stepped up on the porch.

"Why in the world, Julius," I asked, "did n't you keep the umbrella up until you got under cover?"

"It's bad luck, suh, ter raise a' umbrella in de house, en w'iles I dunno whuther it's bad luck ter kyar one inter de piazzer er no, I 'lows it's alluz bes' ter be on de safe side. I did n' s'pose you en young missis 'u'd be gwine on yo' dribe ter-day, but bein' ez it's my pa't ter take you ef you does, I 'lowed I'd repo't fer dooty, en let you say whuther er no you wants ter go."

"I'm glad you came, Julius," I responded. "We don't want to go driving, of course, in the rain, but I should like to consult you about another matter. I'm thinking of taking in a piece of new ground. What do you imagine it would cost to have that neck of woods down by the swamp cleared up?"

The old man's countenance assumed an expression of unwonted seriousness, and he shook his head doubtfully.

"I dunno 'bout dat, suh. It mought cos' mo', en it mought cos' less, ez fuh ez money is consarned. I ain' denyin' you could cl'ar up dat trac' er lan' fer a hund'ed er a couple er hund'ed dollahs,—ef you wants ter cl'ar it up. But ef dat 'uz my trac' er lan', I would n' 'sturb it, no, suh, I would n'; sho's you bawn, I would n'."

"But why not?" I asked.

"It ain' fittin' fer grapes, fer noo groun' nebber is."

"I know it, but"—

"It ain' no yeathly good fer cotton, 'ca'se it's too low."

"Perhaps so; but it will raise splendid corn."

"I dunno," rejoined Julius deprecatorily. "It's so nigh de swamp dat de 'coons'll eat up all de cawn."

"I think I'll risk it," I answered.

"Well, suh," said Julius, "I wushes you much joy er yo' job. Ef you has bad luck er sickness er trouble er any kin', doan blame *me*. You can't say ole Julius did n' wa'n you."

"Warn him of what, Uncle Julius?" asked my wife.

"Er de bad luck w'at follers folks w'at 'sturbs dat trac' er lan'. Dey is snakes en sco'pions in dem woods. En ef you manages ter 'scape de p'isen animals, you is des boun' ter hab a ha'nt ter settle wid,—ef you doan hab two."

"Whose haunt?" my wife demanded, with growing interest.

"De gray wolf's ha'nt, some folks calls it,—but I knows better."

"Tell us about it, Uncle Julius," said my wife. "A story will be a godsend to-day."

It was not difficult to induce the old man to tell a story, if he were in a reminiscent mood. Of tales of the old slavery days he seemed indeed to possess an exhaustless store,—some weirdly grotesque, some broadly humorous; some bearing the stamp of truth, faint, perhaps, but still discernible; others palpable inventions, whether his own or not we never knew, though his fancy doubtless embellished them. But even the wildest was not without an element of pathos,—the tragedy, it might be, of the story itself; the shadow, never absent, of slavery and of ignorance; the sadness, always, of life as seen by the fading light of an old man's memory.

"Way back yander befo' de wah," began Julius, "ole Mars Dugal' McAdoo useter own a nigger name' Dan. Dan wuz big en strong en hearty en peaceable en good-nachu'd most er de time, but dange'ous ter aggervate. He alluz done his task, en nebber had no trouble wid de w'ite folks, but woe be unter de nigger w'at 'lowed he c'd fool wid Dan, fer he wuz mos' sho' ter git a good lammin'. Soon ez eve'ybody foun' Dan out, dey did n' many un 'em 'temp' ter 'sturb 'im. De one dat did would 'a' wush' he had n', ef he could 'a' libbed long ernuff ter do any wushin'.

"It all happen' dis erway. Dey wuz a cunjuh man w'at libbed ober t' other side er de Lumbe'ton Road. He had be'n de only cunjuh doctor in de naberhood fer lo! dese many yeahs, 'tel ole Aun' Peggy sot up in de bizness down by de Wim'l'ton Road. Dis cunjuh man had a son w'at libbed wid 'im, en it wuz dis yer son w'at got mix' up wid Dan,—en all 'bout a 'oman.

"Dey wuz a gal on de plantation name' Mahaly. She wuz a monst'us lackly gal,—tall en soopl', wid big eyes, en a small foot, en a lively tongue, en w'en Dan tuk ter gwine wid 'er eve'ybody 'lowed dey wuz well match', en none er de yuther nigger men on de plantation das' ter go nigh her, fer dey wuz all feared er Dan.

"Now, it happen' dat dis yer cunjuh man's son wuz gwine 'long de road one day, w'en who sh'd come pas' but Mahaly. En de minute dis man sot eyes on Mahaly, he 'lowed he wuz gwine ter hab her fer hisse'f. He come up side er her en 'mence' ter talk ter her; but she did n' paid no 'tention ter 'im, fer she wuz studyin' 'bout Dan, en she did n' lack dis nigger's looks nohow. So w'en she get ter whar she wuz gwine, dis yer man wa'n't no fu'ther 'long dan he wuz w'en he sta'ted.

"Co'se, atter he had made up his min' fer ter git Mahaly, he 'mence' ter 'quire 'roun', en soon foun' out all 'bout Dan, en w'at a dange'ous nigger he wuz. But dis man 'lowed his daddy wuz a cunjuh man, en so he'd come out all right in de een'; en he kep' right on atter Mahaly. Meanw'iles Dan's marster had said dey could git married ef dey wanter, en so Dan en Mahaly had tuk up wid one ernudder, en wuz libbin' in a cabin by deyse'ves, en wuz des wrop' up in one ernudder.

"But dis yer cunjuh man's son did n' 'pear ter min' Dan's takin' up wid Mahaly, en he kep' on hangin' 'roun' des de same, 'tel fin'lly one day Mahaly sez ter Dan, sez she:—

" 'I wush you'd do sump'n ter stop dat free nigger man fum follerin' me 'roun'. I doan lack him nohow, en I ain' got no time fer ter was'e wid no man but you.'

"Co'se Dan got mad w'en he heared 'bout dis man pest'rin' Mahaly, en de nex' night, w'en he seed dis nigger comin' 'long de road, he up en ax' 'im w'at he mean by hangin' 'roun' his 'oman. De man did n' 'spon' ter suit Dan, en one wo'd led ter ernudder, 'tel bimeby dis cunjuh man's son pull' out a knife en sta'ted ter stick it in Dan; but befo' he could git it drawed good, Dan haul' off en hit 'im in de head so ha'd dat he nebber got up. Dan 'lowed he'd come to atter a w'ile en go 'long 'bout his bizness, so he went off en lef' 'im layin' dere on de groun'.

"De nex' mawnin' de man wuz foun' dead. Dey wuz a great 'miration made 'bout it, but Dan did n' say nuffin, en none er de

yuther niggers had n' seed de fight, so dey wa'n't no way ter
tell who done de killin'. En bein' ez it wuz a free nigger, en dey
wa'n't no w'ite folks 'speshly int'rusted, dey wa'n't nuffin done
'bout it, en de conjuh man come en tuk his son en kyared 'im 'way
en buried 'im.

"Now, Dan had n' meant ter kill dis nigger, en w'iles he knowed
de man had n' got no mo' d'n he desarved, Dan 'mence' ter worry
mo' er less. Fer he knowed dis man's daddy would wuk his roots en
prob'ly fin' out who had killt 'is son, en make all de trouble fer 'im
he could. En Dan kep' on studyin' 'bout dis 'tel he got so he did n'
ha'dly das' ter eat er drink fer fear dis cunjuh man had p'isen' de
vittles er de water. Fin'lly he 'lowed he'd go ter see Aun' Peggy, de
noo cunjuh 'oman w'at had moved down by de Wim'l'ton Road, en
ax her fer ter do sump'n ter pertec' 'im fum dis cunjuh man. So he
tuk a peck er 'taters en went down ter her cabin one night.

"Aun' Peggy heard his tale, en den sez she:—

" 'Dat cunjuh man is mo' d'n twice't ez ole ez I is, en he kin
make monst'us powe'ful goopher. W'at you needs is a life-cha'm,
en I'll make you one ter-morrer; it 's de on'y think w'at 'll do you
any good. You leabe me a couple er ha'rs fum yo' head, en fetch me
a pig ter-morrer night fer ter roas', en w'en you come I'll hab de
cha'm all ready for you.'

"So Dan went down ter Aun' Peggy de nex' night,—wid a young
shote,—en Aun' Peggy gun 'im de cha'm. She had tuk de ha'rs Dan
had lef' wid 'er, en a piece er red flannin, en some roots en yarbs, en
had put 'em in a little bag made out'n 'coon-skin.

" 'You take dis cha'm,' sez she, 'en put it in a bottle er a tin box,
en bury it deep unner de root er a live-oak tree, en ez long ez it
stays dere safe en soun', dey ain' no p'isen kin p'isen you, dey ain'
no rattlesnake kin bite you, dey ain' no sco'pion kin sting you. Dis
yere cunjuh man mought do one thing er 'nudder ter you, but he
can't kill you. So you neenter be at all skeered, but go 'long 'bout
yo' bizness en doan bother yo' min'.'

"So Dan went down by de ribber, en 'way up on de bank he
buried de cha'm deep unner de root er a live-oak tree, en kivered it
up en stomp' de dirt down en scattered leaves ober de spot, en den
went home wid his min' easy.

"Sho' 'nuff, dis yer cunjuh man wukked his roots, des ez Dan had 'spected he would, en soon I'arn' who killt his son. En co'se he made up his min' fer ter git eben wid Dan. So he sont a rattlesnake fer ter sting 'im, but de rattlesnake say de nigger's heel wuz so ha'd he could n' git his sting in. Den he sont his jay-bird fer ter put p'isen in Dan's vittles, but de p'isen did n' wuk. Den de cunjuh man 'low' he'd double Dan all up wid de rheumatiz, so he could n' git 'is han' ter his mouf ter eat, en would hafter sta've ter def; but Dan went ter Aun' Peggy, en she gun 'im a' 'intment ter kyo de rheumatiz. Den de cunjuh man 'lowed he 'd bu'n Dan up wid a fever, but Aun' Peggy tol' 'im how ter make some yarb tea fer dat. Nuffin dis man tried would kill Dan, so fin'lly de cunjuh man 'lowed Dan mus' hab a life-cha'm.

"Now, dis yer jay-bird de cunjuh man had wuz a monst'us sma't creeter,—fac', de niggers 'lowed he wuz de ole Debbil hisse'f, des settin' roun' waitin' ter kyar dis ole man erway w'en he'd retch' de een' er his rope. De cunjuh man sont dis jay-bird fer ter watch Dan en fin' out whar he kep' his cha'm. De jay-bird hung roun' Dan fer a week er so, en one day he seed Dan go down by de ribber en look at a live-oak tree; en den de jay-bird went back ter his marster, en tol' 'im he 'spec' de nigger kep' his life-cha'm under dat tree.

"De cunjuh man lafft en lafft, en he put on his bigges' pot, en fill' it wid his stronges' roots, en b'iled it en b'iled it, 'tel bimeby de win' blowed en blowed, 'tel it blowed down de live-oak tree. Den he stirred some more roots in de pot, en it rained en rained 'tel de water run down de ribber bank en wash' Dan's life-cha'm inter de ribber, en de bottle went bobbin' down de current des ez onconsarned ez ef it wa'n't takin' po' Dan's chances all 'long wid it. En den de cunjuh man lafft some mo', en 'lowed ter hisse'f dat he wuz gwine ter fix Dan now, sho' 'nuff; he wa'n't gwine ter kill 'im des yet, fer he could do sump'n ter 'im w'at would hu't wusser 'n killin'.

"So dis cunjuh man 'mence' by gwine up ter Dan's cabin eve'y night, en takin' Dan out in his sleep en ridin' 'im roun' de roads en fiel's ober de rough groun'. In de mawnin' Dan would be ez ti'ed ex ef he had n' be'n ter sleep. Dis kin' er thing kep' up fer a week er so, en Dan had des 'bout made up his min' fer ter go en see Aun' Peggy ag'in, w'en who sh'd he come across, gwine 'long de road one day, to'ds sundown, but dis yer cunjuh man. Dan felt kinder skeered at fus'; but den he 'membered 'bout his life-cha'm, w'ich he had n' be'n ter see fer a week er so, en 'lowed wuz safe en soun' unner der live-oak tree, en so he hilt up 'is head en walk' 'long, des lack he did n' keer nuffin 'bout dis man no mo' d'n any yuther nigger. W'en he got close ter de cunjuh man, dis cunjuh man sez, sezee:—

" 'Hoddy, Brer Dan? I hopes you er well?'

"W'en Dan seed de cunjuh man wuz in a good humor en did n' 'pear ter bear no malice, Dan 'lowed mebbe de cunjuh man had n' foun' out who killt his son, en so he 'termine' fer ter let on lack he did n' know nuffin, en so sezee:—

" 'Hoddy, Unk' Jube?'—dis ole cunjuh man's name wuz Jube. 'I's p'utty well, I thank you. How is you feelin' dis mawnin'?'

" 'I's feelin' ez well ez a' ole nigger could feel w'at had los' his only son, en his main 'pen'ence in 'is ole age.

" 'But den my son wuz a bad boy,' sezee, 'en I could n' 'spec' nuffin e'se. I tried ter l'arn him de arrer er his ways en make him go ter chu'ch en pra'r-meetin'; but it wa'n't no use. I dunno who killt 'im, en I doan wanter know, fer I'd be mos' sho' ter fin' out dat my boy had sta'ted de fuss. Ef I 'd 'a' had a son lack you, Brer Dan, I 'd 'a' be'n a proud nigger; oh, yas, I would, sho's you bawn. But you ain' lookin' ez well ez you oughter, Brer Dan. Dey's sump'n de matter wid you, en w'at 's mo', I 'spec' you dunno w'at it is.'

"Now, dis yer kin' er talk nach'ly th'owed Dan off'n his gya'd, en fus' thing he knowed he wuz talkin' ter dis old cunjuh man des lack he wuz one er his bes' frien's. He tol' 'im all 'bout not feelin' well in de mawnin', en ax' 'im ef he could tell w'at wuz de matter wid 'im.

" 'Yas,' sez de cunjuh man. 'Dey is a witch be'n ridin' you right 'long. I kin see de marks er de bridle on yo' mouf. En I 'll des bet yo' back is raw whar she 's be'n beatin' you.'

" 'Yas,' 'spon' Dan, 'so it is.' He had n' notice it befo', but now he felt des lack de hide had be'n tuk off'n 'im.

" 'En yo' thighs is des raw whar de spurrers has be'n driv' in you,' sez de cunjuh man. 'You can't see de raw spots, but you kin feel 'em.'

" 'Oh, yas,' 'lows Dan, 'dey does hu't pow'ful bad.'

" 'En w'at's mo',' sez de cunjuh man, comin' up close ter Dan en whusp'in' in his yeah, 'I knows who it is be'n ridin' you.'

" 'Who is it?' ax' Dan. 'Tell me who it is.'

" 'It's a' ole nigger 'oman down by Rockfish Crick. She had a pet rabbit, en you cotch' 'im one day, en she 's been squarin' up wid you eber sence. But you better stop her, er e'se you'll be rid ter def in a mont' er so.'

" 'No,' sez Dan, 'she can't kill me, sho'.'

" 'I dunno how dat is,' said de cunjuh man, 'but she kin make yo' life mighty mis'able. Ef I wuz in yo' place, I'd stop her right off.'

" 'But how is I gwine ter stop her?' ax' Dan. 'I dunno nuffin 'bout stoppin' witches.'

" 'Look a heah, Dan,' sez de yuther; 'you is a good young man. I lacks you monst'us well. Fac', I feels lack some er dese days I mought buy you fum yo' marster, ef I could eber make money er-nuff at my bizness dese hard times, en 'dop' you fer my son. I lacks you so well dat I 'm gwine ter he'p you get rid er dis yer witch fer good en all; fer des ez long ez she libs, you is sho' ter hab trouble, en trouble, en mo' trouble.'

" 'You is de bes' frien' I got, Unk' Jube,' sez Dan, 'en I'll 'member yo' kin'ness ter my dyin' day. Tell me how I kin git rid er dis yer ole witch w'at 's be'n ridin' me so ha'd.'

" 'In de fus' place,' sez de cunjuh man, 'dis ole witch nebber comes in her own shape, but eve'y night, at ten o'clock, she tu'ns herse'f inter a black cat, en runs down ter yo' cabin en bridles you, en mounts you, en dribes you out th'oo de chimbly, en rides you ober de roughes' places she kin fin'. All you got ter do is ter set fer her in de bushes 'side er yo' cabin, en hit her in de head wid a rock er a lighterd-knot w'en she goes pas'.'

" 'But,' sez Dan, 'how kin I see her in de da'k? En s'posen I hits at her en misses her? Er s'posen I des woun's her, en she gits er-way,—w'at she gwine do ter me den?'

" 'I is done studied 'bout all dem things,' sez de cunjuh man, 'en it 'pears ter me de bes' plan fer you ter foller is ter lemme tu'n you ter some creetur w'at kin see in de da'k, en w'at kin run des ez fas' ez a cat, en w'at kin bite, en bite fer ter kill; en den you won't hafter hab no trouble atter de job is done. I dunno whuther you'd lack dat er no, but dat is de sho'es' way.'

" 'I doan keer,' 'spon' Dan. 'I 'd des ez lief be anything fer a' hour er so, ef I kin kill dat ole witch. You kin do des w'at you er mineter.'

" 'All right, den,' sez de cunjuh man, 'you come down ter my cabin at half-past nine o'clock ter-night, en I 'll fix you up.'

"Now, dis cunjuh man, w'en he had got th'oo talkin' wid Dan, kep' on down de road 'long de side er de plantation, 'tel he met Mahaly comin' home fum wuk des atter sundown.

" 'Hoddy do, ma'm,' sezee; 'is yo' name Sis' Mahaly, w'at b'longs ter Mars Dugal' McAdoo?'

" 'Yas,' s'pon' Mahaly, 'dat's my name, en I b'longs ter Mars Dugal'.'

" 'Well,' sezee, 'yo' husban' Dan wuz down by my cabin dis ebenin', en he got bit by a spider er sump'n, en his foot is swoll' up so he can't walk. En he ax' me fer ter fin' you en fetch you down dere ter he'p 'im home.'

"Co'se Mahaly wanter see w'at had happen' ter Dan, en so she sta'ted down de road wid de cunjuh man. Ez soon ez he got her inter his cabin, he shet de do', en sprinkle' some goopher mixtry on her, en tu'nt her ter a black cat. Den he tuk 'n put her in a bairl, en put a bo'd on de bairl, en a rock on de bo'd, en lef' her dere 'tel he got good en ready fer ter use her.

" 'Long 'bout half-pas' nine o'clock Dan come down ter de cunjuh man's cabin. It wuz a wa'm night, en de do' wuz stan'in' open. De cunjuh man 'vited Dan ter come in, en pass' de time er day wid 'im. Ez soon ez Dan 'mence' talkin', he heared a cat miauin' en scratchin' en gwine on at a tarrable rate.

" 'W'at 's all dat fuss 'bout?' ax' Dan.

" 'Oh, dat ain' nuffin but my ole gray tomcat,' sez de cunjuh man. 'I has ter shet 'im up sometimes fer ter keep 'im in nights, en co'se he doan lack it.

" 'Now,' 'lows de cunjuh man, 'lemme tell you des w'at you is got ter do. W'en you ketches dis witch, you mus' take her right by de th'oat en bite her right th'oo de neck. Be sho' yo' teef goes th'oo at de fus' bite, en den you won't nebber be bothe'd no mo' by dat witch. En w'en you git done, come back heah en I'll tu'n you ter yo'se'f ag'in, so you kin go home en git yo' night's res'.'

"Den de cunjuh man gun Dan sump'n nice en sweet ter drink out'n a new go'd, en in 'bout a minute Dan foun' hisse'f tu'nt ter a gray wolf; en soon ez he felt all fo' er his noo feet on de groun', he sta'ted off fas' ez he could fer his own cabin, so he could be sho' en be dere time ernuff ter ketch de witch, en put a' een' ter her kyarin's-on.

"Ez soon ez Dan wuz gone good, de cunjuh man tuk de rock off'n de bo'd, en de bo'd off'n de bairl, en out le'p' Mahaly en sta'ted fer ter go home, des lack a cat er a 'oman er anybody e'se would w'at wuz in trouble; en it wa'n't many minutes befo' she wuz gwine up de path ter her own do'.

"Meanw'iles, w'en Dan had retch' de cabin, he had hid hisse'f in a bunch er jimson weeds in de ya'd. He had n' wait' long befo' he seed a black cat run up de path to'ds de do'. Des ez soon ez she got close ter 'im, he le'p' out en ketch' her by de th'oat, en got a grip on her, des lack de cunjuh man had tol' 'im ter do. En lo en behol'! no sooner had de blood 'mence' ter flow dan de black cat tu'nt back ter Mahaly, en Dan seed dat he had killt his own wife. En w'iles her bref wuz gwine she call' out:

"'O Dan! O my husban'! come en he'p me! come en sabe me fum dis wolf w'at 's killin' me!'

"W'en po' Dan sta'ted to'ds her, ez any man nach'ly would, it des made her holler wuss en wuss; fer she did n' knowed dis yer wolf wuz her Dan. En Dan des had ter hide in de weeds, en grit his teef en hol' hisse'f in, 'tel she passed out'n her mis'ry, callin' fer Dan ter de las', en wond'rin w'y he did n' come en he'p her. En Dan 'lowed ter hisse'f he'd ruther 'a' be'n killt a dozen times 'n ter 'a' done w'at he had ter Mahaly.

"Dan wuz mighty nigh 'stracted, but w'en Mahaly wuz dead en he got his min' straighten' out a little, it did n' take 'im mo' d'n a minute er so fer ter see th'oo all de cunjuh man's lies, en how de cunjuh man had fooled 'im en made 'im kill Mahaly, fer ter git eben wid 'im fer de killin' er his son. He kep' gittin' madder en madder, en Mahaly had n' much mo' d'n drawed her' las bref befo' he sta'ted back ter de cunjuh man's cabin ha'd ez he could run.

"W'en he got dere, de do' wuz stan'in' open; a lighterd-knot wuz flick'rin' on de h'a'th, en de ole cunjuh man wuz settin' dere noddin' in de corner. Dan le'p' in de do' en jump' fer dis man's th'oat, en got de same grip on 'im w'at de cunjuh man had tol' 'im 'bout half a' hour befo'. It wuz ha'd wuk dis time, fer de ole man's neck wuz monst'us tough en stringy, but Dan hilt on long ernuff ter be sho' his job wuz done right. En eben den he did n' hol' on long ernuff; fer w'en he tu'nt de cunjuh man loose en he fell ober on de flo', de cunjuh man rollt his eyes at Dan, en sezee:—

" 'I 's eben wid you, Brer Dan, en you er eben wid me; you killt my son en I killt yo' 'oman. En ez I doan want no mo' d'n w'at 's fair 'bout dis thing, ef you'll retch up wid yo' paw en take down dat go'd hangin' on dat peg ober de chimbly, en take a sip er dat mixtry, it 'll tu'n you back ter a nigger ag'in, en I kin die mo' sad'sfied 'n ef I lef' you lack you is.'

"Dan nebber 'lowed fer a minute dat a man would lie wid his las' bref, en co'se he seed de sense er gittin' tu'nt back befo' de cunjuh man died; so he clumb on a chair en retch' fer de go'd, en tuk a sip er de mixtry. En ez soon ez he 'd done dat de cunjuh man lafft his las' laf, en gapsed out wid 'is las' gaps:—

" 'Uh huh! I reckon I 's square wid you now fer killin' me, too; fer dat goopher on you is done fix' en sot now fer good, en all de cunj'in' in de worl' won't nebber take it off.

'Wolf you is en wolf you stays,
All de rest er yo' bawn days.'

"Co'se Brer Dan could n' do nuffin. He knowed it wa'n't no use, but he clumb up on de chimbly en got down de go'ds en bottles en yuther cunjuh fixin's, en tried 'em all on hisse'f, but dey did n' do no good. Den he run down ter ole Aun' Peggy, but she did n' know de wolf langwidge, en could n't 'a' tuk off dis yuther goopher no-how, eben ef she 'd 'a' unnerstood w'at Dan wuz sayin'. So po' Dan wuz bleedgd ter be a wolf all de rest er his bawn days.

"Dey foun' Mahaly down by her own cabin nex' mawnin', en eve'ybody made a great 'miration 'bout how she'd be'n killt. De niggers 'lowed a wolf had bit her. De w'ite folks say no, dey ain' be'n no wolves 'roun' dere fer ten yeahs er mo'; en dey did n' know w'at ter make out'n it. En w'en dey could n' fin' Dan nowhar, dey 'lowed he 'd quo'lled wid Mahaly en killt her, en run erway; en dey did n' know w'at ter make er dat, fer Dan en Mahaly wuz de mos' lovin' couple on de plantation. Dey put de dawgs on Dan's scent, en track' 'im down ter ole Unk' Jube's cabin, en foun' de ole man dead, en dey did n' know w'at ter make er dat; en den Dan's scent gun out, en dey did n' know w'at ter make er dat. Mars Dugal' tuk on a heap 'bout losin' two er his bes' han's in one day, en ole missis 'lowed it wuz a jedgment on 'im fer sump 'n he 'd done. But dat fall de craps wuz monst'us big, so Mars Dugal' say de Lawd had temper' de win' ter de sho'n ram, en make up ter 'im fer w'at he had los.'

"Dey buried Mahaly down in dat piece er low groun' you er talkin' 'bout cl'arin' up. Ez fer po' Dan, he did n' hab nowhar e'se ter go, so he des stayed 'roun' Mahaly's grabe, w'en he wa'n't out in de yuther woods gittin' sump'n ter eat. En sometimes, w'en night would come, de niggers useter heah him howlin' en howlin' down dere, des fittin' ter break his hea't. En den some mo' un 'em said dey seed Mahaly's ha'nt dere 'bun'ance er times, colloguin' wid dis gray wolf. En eben now, fifty yeahs sence, long atter ole Dan has died en dried up in de woods, his ha'nt en Mahaly's hangs 'roun' dat piece er low groun', en eve'body w'at goes 'bout dere has some bad luck er 'nuther; fer ha'nts doan lack ter be 'sturb' on dey own stompin'-groun'."

The air had darkened while the old man related this harrowing tale. The rising wind whistled around the eaves, slammed the loose window-shutters, and, still increasing, drove the rain in fiercer gusts into the piazza. As Julius finished his story and we rose to seek shelter within doors, the blast caught the angle of some chimney or gable in the rear of the house, and bore to our ears a long, wailing note, an epitome, as it were, of remorse and hopelessness.

"Dat 's des lack po' ole Dan useter howl," observed Julius, as he reached for his umbrella, "en w'at I be'n tellin' you is de reason I doan lack ter see dat neck er woods cl'ared up. Co'se it b'longs ter you, en a man kin do ez he choose' wid 'is own. But ef you gits rheumatiz er fever en agur, er ef you er snake-bit er p'isen' wid some yarb er 'nuther, er ef a tree falls on you, er a ha'nt runs you en makes you git 'stracted in yo' min', lack some folks I knows w'at went foolin' 'roun' dat piece er lan', you can't say I neber wa'ned you, suh, en tol' you w'at you mought look fer en be sho' ter fin'."

When I cleared up the land in question, which was not until the following year, I recalled the story Julius had told us, and looked in vain for a sunken grave or perhaps a few weather-bleached bones of some denizen of the forest. I cannot say, of course, that some one had not been buried there; but if so, the hand of time had long since removed any evidence of the fact. If some lone wolf, the last of his pack, had once made his den there, his bones had long since crumbled into dust and gone to fertilize the rank vegetation that formed the undergrowth of this wild spot. I did find, however, a bee-tree in the woods, with an ample cavity in its trunk, and an opening through which convenient access could be had to the stores of honey within. I have reason to believe that ever since I had bought the place, and for many years before, Julius had been getting honey from this tree. The gray wolf's haunt had doubtless proved useful in keeping off too inquisitive people, who might have interfered with his monopoly.

Hot-Foot Hannibal

"I HATE YOU AND DESPISE YOU! I wish never to see you or speak to you again!"

"Very well; I will take care that henceforth you have no opportunity to do either."

These words—the first in the passionately vibrant tones of my sister-in-law, and the latter in the deeper and more restrained accents of an angry man—startled me from my nap. I had been dozing in my hammock on the front piazza, behind the honeysuckle vine. I had been faintly aware of a buzz of conversation in the parlor, but had not at all awakened to its import until these sentences fell, or, I might rather say, were hurled upon my ear. I presume the young people had either not seen me lying there,—the Venetian blinds opening from the parlor windows upon the piazza were partly closed on account of the heat,—or else in their excitement they had forgotten my proximity.

I felt somewhat concerned. The young man, I had remarked, was proud, firm, jealous of the point of honor, and, from my observation of him, quite likely to resent to the bitter end what he deemed a slight or an injustice. The girl, I knew, was quite as high-spirited as young Murchison. I feared she was not so just, and hoped she would prove more yielding. I knew that her affections were strong and enduring, but that her temperament was capricious, and her sunniest moods easily overcast by some small cloud of jealousy or pique. I had never imagined, however, that she was capable of such intensity as was revealed by these few words of hers. As I say, I felt concerned. I had learned to like Malcolm Murchison, and had heartily consented to his marriage with my ward; for it was in that capacity that I had stood for a year or two to my wife's younger sister, Mabel. The match thus rudely broken off had promised to be another link binding me to the kindly Southern people among whom I had not long before taken up my residence.

Young Murchison came out of the door, cleared the piazza in two strides without seeming aware of my presence, and went off down the lane at a furious pace. A few moments later Mabel began playing the piano loudly, with a touch that indicated anger and pride and independence and a dash of exultation, as though she were really glad that she had driven away forever the young man whom the day before she had loved with all the ardor of a first passion.

I hoped that time might heal the breach and bring the two young people together again. I told my wife what I had overheard. In return she gave me Mabel's version of the affair.

"I do not see how it can ever be settled," my wife said. "It is something more than a mere lovers' quarrel. It began, it is true, because she found fault with him for going to church with that hateful Branson girl. But before it ended there were things said that no woman of any spirit could stand. I am afraid it is all over between them."

I was sorry to hear this. In spite of the very firm attitude taken by my wife and her sister, I still hoped that the quarrel would be made up within a day or two. Nevertheless, when a week had passed with no word from young Murchison, and with no sign of relenting on Mabel's part, I began to think myself mistaken.

One pleasant afternoon, about ten days after the rupture, old Julius drove the rockaway up to the piazza, and my wife, Mabel, and I took our seats for a drive to a neighbor's vineyard, over on the Lumberton plank-road.

"Which way shall we go," I asked,—"the short road or the long one?"

"I guess we had better take the short road," answered my wife. "We will get there sooner."

"It's a mighty fine dribe roun' by de big road, Mis' Annie," observed Julius, "en it doan take much longer to git dere."

"No," said my wife, "I think we will go by the short road. There is a bay-tree in blossom near the mineral spring, and I wish to get some of the flowers."

"I 'spec's you 'd fin' some bay-trees 'long de big road, ma'am," suggested Julius.

"But I know about the flowers on the short road, and they are the ones I want."

We drove down the lane to the highway, and soon struck into the short road leading past the mineral spring. Our route lay partly through a swamp, and on each side the dark, umbrageous foliage, unbroken by any clearing, lent to the road solemnity, and to the air a refreshing coolness. About half a mile from the house, and about half-way to the mineral spring, we stopped at the tree of which my wife had spoken, and reaching up to the low-hanging boughs, I gathered a dozen of the fragrant white flowers. When I resumed my seat in the rockaway, Julius started the mare. She went on for a few rods, until we had reached the edge of a branch crossing the road, when she stopped short.

"Why did you stop, Julius?" I asked.

"I did n', suh," he replied. " 'T wuz de mare stop'. G' 'long dere, Lucy! W'at you mean by dis foolis'ness?"

Julius jerked the reins and applied the whip lightly, but the mare did not stir.

"Perhaps you had better get down and lead her," I suggested. "If you get her started, you can cross on the log and keep your feet dry."

Julius alighted, took hold of the bridle, and vainly essayed to make the mare move. She planted her feet with even more evident obstinacy.

"I don't know what to make of this," I said. "I have never known her to balk before. Have you, Julius?"

"No, suh," replied the old man. "I neber has. It's a cu'ous thing ter me, suh."

"What's the best way to make her go?"

"I 'spec's, suh, dat ef I 'd tu'n her 'roun', she 'd go de udder way."

"But we want her to go this way."

"Well, suh, I 'low ef we des set heah fo' er fibe minutes, she 'll sta't up by herse'f."

"All right," I rejoined; "it is cooler here than any place I have struck to-day. We'll let her stand for a while, and see what she does."

We had sat in silence for a few minutes, when Julius suddenly ejaculated, "Uh huh! I knows w'y dis mare doan go. It des flash' 'cross my recommemb'ance."

"Why is it, Julius?" I inquired.

" 'Ca'se she sees Chloe."

"Where is Chloe?" I demanded.

"Chloe's done be'n dead dese fo'ty years er mo'," the old man returned. "Her ha'nt is settin' ober yander on de udder side er de branch, unner dat willer-tree, dis blessed minute."

"Why, Julius!" said my wife, "do you see the haunt?"

"No'm," he answered, shaking his head, "I doan see 'er, but de mare sees 'er."

"How do you know?" I inquired.

"Well, suh, dis yer is a gray hoss, en dis yer is a Friday; en a gray hoss kin alluz see a ha'nt w'at walks on Friday."

"Who was Chloe?" said Mabel.

"And why does Chloe's haunt walk?" asked my wife.

"It 's all in de tale, ma'm," Julius replied, with a deep sigh. "It 's all in de tale."

"Tell us the tale," I said. "Perhaps, by the time you get through, the haunt will go away and the mare will cross."

I was willing to humor the old man's fancy. He had not told us a story for some time; and the dark and solemn swamp around us; the amber-colored stream flowing silently and sluggishly at our feet, like the waters of Lethe; the heavy, aromatic scent of the bays, faintly suggestive of funeral wreaths,—all made the place an ideal one for a ghost story.

"Chloe," Julius began in a subdued tone, "use' ter b'long ter ole Mars' Dugal' McAdoo,—my old marster. She wuz a lackly gal en a smart gal, en ole mis' tuk her up ter de big house, en l'arnt her ter wait on de w'ite folks, 'tel bimeby she come ter be mis's own maid, en 'peared ter 'low she run de house herse'f, ter heah her talk erbout it. I wuz a young boy den, en use' ter wuk 'bout de stables, so I knowed eve'ythin' dat wuz gwine on 'roun' de plantation.

"Well, one time Mars' Dugal' wanted a house boy, en sont down ter de qua'ters fer ter hab Jeff en Hannibal come up ter de big house nex' mawnin'. Ole marster en ole mis' look' de two boys ober, en 'sco'sed wid deyse'ves fer a little w'ile, en den Mars' Dugal' sez, sezee:—

" 'We lacks Hannibal de bes', en we gwine ter keep him. Heah, Hannibal, you 'll wuk at de house fum now on. En ef you er a good nigger en min's yo' bizness, I'll gib you Chloe fer a wife nex' spring. You other nigger, you Jeff, you kin go back ter de qua'ters. We ain' gwine ter need you.'

"Now Chloe had be'n stan'in' dere behin' ole mis' dyoin' all er dis yer talk, en Chloe made up her min' fum de ve'y fus' minute she sot eyes on dem two dat she did n' lack dat nigger Hannibal, en wa'n't neber gwine keer fer 'im, en she wuz des ez sho' dat she lack' Jeff, en wuz gwine ter set sto' by 'im, whuther Mars' Dugal' tuk 'im in de big house er no; en so co'se Chloe wuz monst'us sorry w'en ole Mars' Dugal' tuk Hannibal en sont Jeff back. So she slip' roun' de house en waylaid Jeff on de way back ter de qua'ters, en tol' 'im not ter be down-hea'ted, fer she wuz gwine ter see ef she could n' fin' some way er 'nuther ter git rid er dat nigger Hannibal, en git Jeff up ter de house in his place.

"De noo house boy kotch' on monst'us fas', en it wa'n't no time ha'dly befo' Mars' Dugal' en ole mis' befo 'mence' ter 'low Hannibal wuz de bes' house boy dey eber had. He wuz peart en soopl', quick ez lightnin', en sha'p ez a razor. But Chloe did n' lack his ways. He wuz so sho' he wuz gwine ter git 'er in de spring, dat he did n' 'pear ter 'low he had ter do any co'tin', en w'en he 'd run 'cross Chloe 'bout de house, he 'd swell roun' 'er in a biggity way en say:—

" 'Come heah en kiss me, honey. You gwine ter be mine in de spring. You doan 'pear ter be ez fon' er me ez you oughter be.'

"Chloe did n' keer nuffin fer Hannibal, en had n' keered nuffin fer 'im, en she sot des ez much sto' by Jeff ez she did de day she fus' laid eyes on 'im. En de mo' fermilyus dis yer Hannibal got, de mo' Chloe let her min' run on Jeff, en one ebenin' she went down ter de qua'ters en watch', 'tel she got a chance fer ter talk wid 'im by hisse'f. En she tol' Jeff fer ter go down en see ole Aun' Peggy, de cunjuh 'oman down by de Wim'l'ton Road, en ax her ter gib 'im sump'n ter he'p git Hannibal out'n de big house, so de w'ite folks 'u'd sen' fer Jeff ag'in. En bein' ez Jeff did n' hab nuffin ter gib Aun' Peggy, Chloe gun 'im a silber dollah en a silk han'kercher fer ter pay her wid, fer Aun' Peggy neber lack ter wuk fer nobody fer nuffin.

"So Jeff slip' off down ter Aun' Peggy's one night, en gun 'er de present he brung, en tol' 'er all 'bout 'im en Chloe en Hannibal, en ax' 'er ter he'p 'im out. Aun' Peggy tol' 'im she 'd wuk 'er roots, en fer 'im ter come back de nex' night, en she 'd tell 'im w'at she c'd do fer 'im.

"So de nex' night Jeff went back, en Aun' Peggy gun 'im a baby doll, wid a body made out'n a piece er co'n-stalk, en wid splinters fer a'ms en laigs, en a head made out'n elderberry peth, en two little red peppers fer feet.

" 'Dis yer baby doll,' sez she, 'is Hannibal. Dis yer peth head is Hannibal's head, en dese yer pepper feet in Hannibal's feet. You take dis en hide it unner de house, on de sill unner de do', whar Hannibal 'll hafter walk ober it eve'y day. En ez long ez Hannibal comes anywhar nigh dis baby doll, he 'll be des lack it is,—light-headed en hot-footed; en ef dem two things doan git 'im inter trouble mighty soon, den I'm no cunjuh 'oman. But w'en you git Hannibal out'n de house, en git all th'oo wid dis baby doll, you mus' fetch it back ter me, fer it's monst'us powerful goopher, en is liable ter make mo' trouble ef you leabe it layin' roun'.'

"Well, Jeff tuk de baby doll, en slip' up ter de big house, en whis-tle' ter Chloe, en w'en she come out he tol' 'er w'at ole Aun' Peggy had said. En Chloe showed 'im how ter git unner de house, en w'en he had put de cunjuh doll on de sill, he went 'long back ter de qua'ters—en des waited.

"Nex' day, sho' 'nuff, de goopher 'mence' ter wuk. Hannibal sta'ted in de house soon in de mawnin' wid a armful er wood ter make a fire, en he had n' mo' d'n got 'cross de do'-sill befo' his feet begun ter bu'n so dat he drap' de armful er wood on de flo' en woke ole mis' up a' hour sooner 'n yushal, en co'se ole mis' did n' lack dat, en spoke sha'p erbout it.

"W'en dinner-time come, en Hannibal wuz help'n' de cook kyar de dinner f'm de kitchen inter de big house, en wuz gittin' close ter de do' whar he had ter go in, his feet sta'ted ter bu'n en his head be-gun ter swim, en he let de big dish er chicken en dumplin's fall right down in de dirt, in de middle er de ya'd, en de w'ite folks had ter make dey dinner dat day off'n col' ham en sweet'n' 'taters.

"De nex' mawnin' he overslep' hisse'f, en got inter mo' trouble. Atter breakfus', Mars' Dugal' sont 'im ober ter Mars' Marrabo Ut-ley's fer ter borry a monkey wrench. He oughter be'n back in ha'f a' hour, but he come pokin' home 'bout dinner-time wid a screw-driver stidder a monkey wrench. Mars' Dugal' sont ernudder nigger back wid de screw-driver, en Hannibal did n' git no dinner. 'Long in de afternoon, ole mis' sot Hannibal ter weedin' de flowers in de front gya'den, en Hannibal dug up all de bulbs ole mis' had sont er-way fer, en paid a lot er money fer, en tuk 'em down ter de hawg-pen by de ba'nya'd, en fed 'em ter de hawgs. W'en ole mis' come out in de cool er de ebenin', en seed w'at Hannibal had done, she wuz mos' crazy, en she wrote a note en sont Hannibal down ter de oberseah wid it.

"But w'at Hannibal got fum de oberseah did n' 'pear ter do no good. Eve'y now en den 'is feet 'd 'mence ter torment 'im, en 'is min' 'u'd git all mix' up, en his conduc' kep' gittin' wusser en wusser, 'tel fin'lly de w'ite folks could n' stan' it no longer, en Mars' Dugal' tuk Hannibal back down ter de qua'ters.

" 'Mr. Smif', sez Mars' Dugal' ter de oberseah, 'dis yer nigger has done got so triflin' yer lately dat we can't keep 'im at de house no mo', en I 's fotch' 'im ter you ter be straighten' up. You 's had 'ca-sion ter deal wid 'im once, so he knows w'at ter expec'. You des take 'im in han', en lemme know how he tu'ns out. En w'en de han's comes in fum de fiel' dis ebenin' you kin sen' dat yaller nig-ger Jeff up ter de house. I'll try 'im, en see ef he's any better 'n Hannibal.'

"So Jeff went up ter de big house, en pleas' Mars' Dugal' en ole mis' en de res' er de fambly so well dat dey all got ter lackin' 'im fus'rate; en dey 'd 'a' fergot all 'bout Hannibal, ef it had n' be'n fer de bad repo'ts w'at come up fum de qua'ters 'bout 'im fer a mont' er so. Fac' is, dat Chloe en Jeff wuz so int'rusted in one ernudder sence Jeff be'n up ter de house, dat dey fergot all 'bout takin' de baby doll back ter Aun' Peggy, en it kep' wukkin' fer a w'ile, en makin' Hannibal's feet bu'n mo' er less, 'tel all de folks on de plan-tation got ter callin' 'im Hot-Foot Hannibal. He kep' gittin' mo' en mo' triflin', 'tel he got de name er bein' de mos' no 'countes' nigger on de plantation, en Mars' Dugal' had ter th'eaten ter sell 'im in de spring, w'en bimeby de goopher quit wukkin', en Hannibal 'mence' ter pick up some en make folks set a little mo' sto' by 'im.

"Now, dis yer Hannibal was a monst'us sma't nigger, en w'en he got rid er dem so' feet, his min' kep' runnin' on 'is udder troubles. Heah th'ee er fo' weeks befo' he 'd had a' easy job, waitin' on de w'ite folks, libbin' off'n de fat er de lan', en promus' de fines' gal on de plantation fer a wife in de spring, en now heah he wuz back in de co'n-fiel', wid de oberseah a-cussin' en a-r'arin' ef he did n' get a ha'd tas' done; wid nuffin but co'n bread en bacon en merlasses ter eat; en all de fiel'-han's makin' rema'ks, en pokin' fun at 'im 'ca'se he'd be'n sont back fum de big house ter de fiel'. En de mo' Hanni-bal studied 'bout it de mo' madder he got, 'tel he fin'lly swo' he wuz gwine ter git eben wid Jeff en Chloe, ef it wuz de las' ac'.

"So Hannibal slipped 'way fum de qua'ters one Sunday en hid in de co'n up close ter de big house, 'tel he see Chloe gwine down de road. He waylaid her, en sezee:—

" 'Hoddy, Chloe?'

" 'I ain' got no time fer ter fool wid fiel'-han's,' sez Chloe, tossin' her head; 'w'at you want wid me, Hot-Foot?'

" 'I wants ter know how you en Jeff is gittin' 'long.'

" 'I 'lows dat's none er yo' bizness, nigger. I doan see w'at 'casion any common fiel-han' has got ter mix in wid de 'fairs er folks w'at libs in de big house. But ef it 'll do you any good ter know, I mought say dat me en Jeff is gittin' 'long mighty well, en we gwine ter git married in de spring, en you ain' gwine ter be 'vited ter de weddin' nuther.'

" 'No, no!' sezee, 'I would n' 'spec' ter be 'vited ter de wed-din',—a common, low-down fiel'-han' lack *I* is. But I 's glad ter heah you en Jeff is gittin' 'long so well. I did n' knowed but w'at he had 'mence' ter be a little ti'ed.'

" 'Ti'ed er me? Dat's rediklus!' sez Chloe. 'W'y, dat nigger lubs me so I b'liebe he 'd go th'oo fire en water fer me. Dat nigger is des wrop' up in me.'

" 'Uh huh,' sez Hannibal, 'den I reckon it mus' be some udder nigger w'at meets a 'oman down by de crick in de swamp eve'y Sunday ebenin', ter say nuffin 'bout two er th'ee times a week.'

" 'Yas, hit is ernudder nigger, en you is a liah w'en you say it wuz Jeff.'

" 'Mebbe I is a liah, en mebbe I ain' got good eyes. But 'less'n I *is* a liah, en 'less'n I *ain'* got good eyes, Jeff is gwine ter meet dat 'oman dis ebenin' 'long 'bout eight o'clock right down dere by de crick in de swamp 'bout half-way betwix' dis plantation en Mars' Marrabo Utley's.'

"Well, Chloe tol' Hannibal she did n' b'liebe a wo'd he said, en call' 'im a low-down nigger, who wuz tryin' ter slander Jeff 'ca'se he wuz mo' luckier 'n he wuz. But all de same, she could n' keep her min' fum runnin' on w'at Hannibal had said. She 'membered she'd heared one er de niggers say dey wuz a gal ober at Mars' Marrabo Utley's plantation w'at Jeff use' ter go wid some befo' he got 'quaninted wid Chloe. Den she 'mence' ter figger back, en sho' 'nuff, dey wuz two er th'ee times in de las' week w'en she 'd be'n he'pin' de ladies wid dey dressin' en udder fixin's in de ebenin', en Jeff mought 'a' gone down ter de swamp widout her knowin' 'bout it at all. En den she 'mence' ter 'member little things w'at she had n' tuk no notice of befo', en w'at 'u'd make it 'pear lack Jeff had sump'n on his min'.

"Chloe set a monst'us heap er sto' by Jeff, en would 'a' done mos' anythin' fer 'im, so long ez he stuck ter her. But Chloe wuz a mighty jealous 'oman, en w'iles she did n' b'liebe w'at Hannibal said, she seed how it *could* 'a' be'n so, en she 'termine' fer ter fin' out fer herse'f whuther it *wuz* so er no.

"Now, Chloe had n' seed Jeff all day, fer Mars' Dugal' had sont Jeff ober ter his daughter's house, young Mis' Ma'g'ret's, w'at libbed 'bout fo' miles fum Mars' Dugal's, en Jeff wuz n' 'spected home 'tel ebenin'. But des atter supper wuz ober, en w'iles de ladies wuz settin' out on de piazzer, Chloe slip' off fum de house en run down de road,—dis yer same road we come; en w'en she got mos'ter de crick—dis yer same crick right befo' us—she kin' er kep' in de bushes at de side er de road, 'tel fin'lly she seed Jeff settin' on de bank on de udder side er de crick,—right unner dat ole willer-tree droopin' ober de water yander. En eve'y now en den he 'd git up en look up de road to'ds Mars' Marrabo's on de udder side er de swamp.

"Fus' Chloe felt lack she'd go right ober de crick en gib Jeff a piece er her min'. Den she 'lowed she better be sho' befo' she done anythin'. So she helt herse'f in de bes' she could, gittin' madder en madder eve'y minute, 'tel bimeby she seed a 'oman comin' down de road on de udder side fum to'ds Mar's Marrabo Utley's plantation.

En w'en she seed Jeff jump up en run to'ds dat 'oman, en th'ow his a'ms roun' her neck, po' Chloe did n' stop ter see no mo', but des tu'nt roun' en run up ter de house, en rush' up on de piazzer, en up en tol' Mars' Dugal' en ole mis' all 'bout de baby doll, en all 'bout Jeff gittin de goopher fum Aun' Peggy, en 'bout w'at de goopher had done ter Hannibal.

"Mars' Dugal' wuz monst'us mad. He did n' let on at fus' lack he b'liebed Chloe, but w'en she tuk en showed 'im whar ter fin' de baby doll, Mars' Dugal' tu'nt w'ite ez chalk.

" 'W'at debil's wuk is dis?' sezee. 'No wonder de po' nigger's feet eetched. Sump'n got ter be done ter l'arn dat ole witch ter keep her han's off'n my niggers. En ez fer dis yer Jeff, I'm gwine ter do des w'at I promus', so de darkies on dis plantation 'll know I means w'at I sez.'

"Fer Mars' Dugal' had warned de han's befo' 'bout foolin' wid cunju'ation; fac', he had los' one er two niggers hisse'f fum dey bein' goophered, en he would 'a' had old Aun' Peggy whip' long ago, on'y Aun' Peggy wuz a free 'oman, en he wuz 'feard she'd cunjuh him. En w'iles Mars' Dugal' say he did n' b'liebe in cunj'in' en sich, he 'peared ter 'low it wuz bes' ter be on de safe side, en let Aun' Peggy alone.

"So Mars' Dugal' done des ez he say. Ef ole mis' had ple'd fer Jeff, he mought 'a' kep' 'im. But ole mis' had n' got ober losin' dem bulbs yit, en she neber said a wo'd. Mars' Dugal' tuk Jeff ter town nex' day en' sol' 'im ter a spekilater, who sta'ted down de ribber wid 'im nex' mawnin' on a steamboat, fer ter take 'im ter Alabama.

"Now, w'en Chloe tol' ole Mar's Dugal' 'bout dis yer baby doll en dis udder goopher, she had n' ha'dly 'lowed Mar's Dugal' would sell Jeff down Souf. Howsomeber, she wuz so mad wid Jeff dat she 'suaded herse'f she did n' keer; en so she hilt her head up en went roun' lookin' lack she wuz rale glad 'bout it. But one day she wuz walkin' down de road, w'en who sh'd come 'long but dis yer Hannibal.

"W'en Hannibal seed 'er, he bus' out laffin' fittin' fer ter kill; 'Yah, yah, yah! ho, ho, ho! ha, ha, ha! Oh, hol' me, honey, hol' me, er I 'll laf myse'f ter def. I ain' nebber laf' so much sence I be'n bawn.'

" 'W'at you laffin' at, Hot-Foot?'

" 'Yah, yah, yah! W'at I laffin' at? W'y, I's laffin' at myse'f, tooby sho',—laffin' ter think w'at a fine 'oman I made.'

"Chloe tu'nt pale, en her hea't come up in her mouf.

" 'W'at you mean nigger?' sez she, ketchin' holt er a bush by de road fer ter stiddy herse'f. 'W'at you mean by de kin' er 'oman you made?'

" 'W'at do I mean? I means dat I got squared up wid you fer treatin' me de way you done, en I got eben wid dat yaller nigger Jeff fer cuttin' me out. Now, he's gwine ter know w'at it is ter eat co'n bread en merlasses once mo', en wuk fum daylight ter da'k, en ter hab a oberseah dribin' 'im fum one day's een' ter de udder. I means dat I sont wo'd ter Jeff dat Sunday dat you wuz gwine ter be ober ter Mars' Marrabo's visitin' dat ebenin', en you want 'im ter meet you down by de crick on de way home en go de rest er de road wid you. En den I put on a frock en a sunbonnet, en fix' myse'f up ter look lack a 'oman; en w'en Jeff seed me comin', he run ter meet me, en you seed 'im,—fer I'd be'n watchin' in de bushes befo' en 'skivered you comin' down de road. En now I reckon you en Jeff bofe knows w'at it means ter mess wid a nigger lack me.'

"Po' Chloe had n' heared mo' d'n half er de las' part er w'at Hannibal said, but she had heared 'nuff to l'arn dat dis nigger had fooled her en Jeff, en dat po' Jeff had n' done nuffin, en dat fer lovin' her too much en goin' ter meet her she had cause' 'im ter be sol' erway whar she'd neber, neber see 'im no mo'. De sun mought shine by day, de moon by night, de flowers mought bloom, en de mawkin'-birds mought sing, but po' Jeff wuz done los' ter her fereber en fereber.

"Hannibal had n' mo' d'n finish' w'at he had ter say, w'en Chloe's knees gun 'way unner her, en she fell down in de road, en lay dere half a' hour er so befo' she come to. W'en she did, she crep' up ter de house des ez pale ez a ghos'. En fer a mont' er so she crawled roun' de house, en 'peared ter be so po'ly dat Mars' Dugal' sont fer a doctor; en de doctor kep' on axin' her questions 'tel he foun' she wuz des pinin' erway fer Jeff.

"W'en he tol' Mars' Dugal', Mar's Dugal' lafft, en said he'd fix dat. She could hab de noo house boy fer a husban'. But ole mis' say, no, Chloe ain' dat kin'er gal, en dat Mars' Dugal' sh'd buy Jeff back.

"So Mars' Dugal' writ a letter ter dis yer spekilater down ter

Wim'l'ton, en tol' ef he ain' done sol' dat nigger Souf w'at he bought fum 'im, he'd lack ter buy 'im back ag'in. Chloe 'mence' ter pick up a little w'en ole mis' tol' her 'bout dis letter. Howsomeber, bimeby Mars' Dugal' got a' answer fum de spekilater, who said he wuz monst'us sorry, but Jeff had fell ove'boa'd er jumped off'n de steamboat on de way ter Wim'l'ton, en got drownded, en co'se he could n' sell 'im back, much ez he'd lack ter 'bleedge Mars' Dugal.'

"Well, atter Chloe heared dis, she wa'n't much mo' use ter nobody. She pu'tended ter do her wuk, en ole mis' put up wid her, en had de doctor gib her medicine, en let 'er go ter de circus, en all so'ts er things fer ter take her min' off'n her troubles. But dey did n' none un 'em do no good. Chloe got ter slippin' down here in de ebenin' des lack she 'uz comin' ter meet Jeff, en she 'd set dere unner dat willer-tree on de udder side, en wait fer 'im, night atter night. Bimeby she got so bad de w'ite folks sont her ober ter young Mis' Ma'g'ret's fer ter gib her a change; but she runned erway de fus' night, en w'en dey looked fer 'er nex' mawnin', dey foun' her co'pse layin' in de branch yander, right 'cross fum whar we 're settin' now.

"Eber sence den," said Julius in conclusion, "Chloe's ha'nt comes eve'y ebenin' en sets down unner dat willer-tree en waits fer Jeff, er e'se walks up en down de road yander, lookin' en lookin', en waitin' en waitin', fer her sweethea't w'at ain' neber, neber come back ter her no mo'."

There was silence when the old man had finished, and I am sure I saw a tear in my wife's eye, and more than one in Mabel's.

"I think, Julius," said my wife, after a moment, "that you may turn the mare around and go by the long road."

The old man obeyed with alacrity, and I noticed no reluctance on the mare's part.

"You are not afraid of Chloe's haunt, are you?" I asked jocularly.

My mood was not responded to, and neither of the ladies smiled.

"Oh, no," said Annie, "but I've changed my mind. I prefer the other route."

When we had reached the main road and had proceeded along it for a short distance, we met a cart driven by a young negro, and on the cart were a trunk and a valise. We recognized the man as Malcolm Murchison's servant, and drew up a moment to speak to him.

"Who's going away, Marshall?" I inquired.

"Young Mistah Ma'colm gwine 'way on de boat ter Noo Yo'k dis ebenin', suh, en I'm takin' his things down ter de wharf, suh."

This was news to me, and I heard it with regret. My wife looked sorry, too, and I could see that Mabel was trying hard to hide her concern.

"He's comin' 'long behin', suh, en I' 'spec's you 'll meet 'im up de road a piece. He's gwine ter walk down ez fur ez Mistah Jim Williams's, en take de buggy fum dere ter town. He 'spec's ter be gone a long time, suh, en say prob'ly he ain' neber comin' back."

The man drove on. There were a few words exchanged in an undertone between my wife and Mabel, which I did not catch. Then Annie said: "Julius, you may stop the rock-away a moment. There are some trumpet-flowers by the road there that I want. Will you get them for me, John?"

I sprang into the underbrush, and soon returned with a great bunch of scarlet blossoms.

"Where is Mabel?" I asked, noting her absence.

"She has walked on ahead. We shall overtake her in a few minutes."

The carriage had gone only a short distance when my wife discovered that she had dropped her fan.

"I had it where we were stopping. Julius, will you go back and get it for me?"

Julius got down and went back for the fan. He was an unconscionably long time finding it. After we got started again we had gone only a little way, when we saw Mabel and young Murchison coming toward us. They were walking arm in arm, and their faces were aglow with the light of love.

I do not know whether or not Julius had a previous understanding with Malcolm Murchison by which he was to drive us round by the long road that day, nor do I know exactly what motive influenced the old man's exertions in the matter. He was fond of Mabel, but I was old enough, and knew Julius well enough, to be skeptical of his motives. It is certain that a most excellent understanding existed between him and Murchison after the reconciliation, and that when the young people set up housekeeping over at the old Murchison place, Julius had an opportunity to enter their service. For some reason or other, however, he preferred to remain with us. The mare, I might add, was never known to balk again.

Dave's Neckliss

"HAVE SOME DINNER, Uncle Julius?" said my wife.

It was a Sunday afternoon in early autumn. Our two women-servants had gone to a camp-meeting some miles away, and would not return until evening. My wife had served the dinner, and we were just rising from the table when Julius came up the lane, and, taking off his hat, seated himself on the piazza.

The old man glanced through the open door at the dinner-table, and his eyes rested lovingly upon a large sugar-cured ham, from which several slices had been cut, exposing a rich pink expanse that would have appealed strongly to the appetite of any hungry Christian.

"Thanky, Miss Annie," he said, after a momentary hesitation. "I dunno ez I keers ef I does tas'e a piece er dat ham, ef yer 'll cut me off a slice un it."

"No," said Annie, "I won't. Just sit down to the table and help yourself; eat all you want, and don't be bashful."

Julius drew a chair up to the table, while my wife and I went out on the piazza. Julius was in my employment; he took his meals with his own family, but when he happened to be about our house at mealtimes, my wife never let him go away hungry.

I threw myself into a hammock, from which I could see Julius through an open window. He ate with evident relish, devoting his attention chiefly to the ham, slice after slice of which disappeared in the spacious cavity of his mouth. At first the old man ate rapidly, but after the edge of his appetite had been taken off he proceeded in a more leisurely manner. When he had cut the sixth slice of ham (I kept count of them from a lazy curiosity to see how much he *could* eat) I saw him lay it on his plate; as he adjusted the knife and fork to cut it into smaller pieces, he paused, as if struck by a sudden thought, and a tear rolled down his rugged cheek and fell upon the slice of ham before him. But the emotion, whatever the thought that caused it, was transitory, and in a moment he continued his dinner. When he was through eating, he came out on the porch, and resumed his seat with the satisfied expression of countenance that usually follows a good dinner.

"Julius," I said, "you seemed to be affected by something a moment ago. Was the mustard so strong that it moved you to tears?"

"No, suh, it wa'n't de mustard; I wuz studyin' 'bout Dave."

"Who was Dave, and what about him?" I asked.

The conditions were all favorable to storytelling. There was an autumnal languor in the air, and a dreamy haze softened the dark green of the distant pines and the deep blue of the Southern sky. The generous meal he had made had put the old man in a very good humor. He was not always so, for his curiously undeveloped nature was subject to moods which were almost childish in their variableness. It was only now and then that we were able to study, through the medium of his recollection, the simple but intensely human inner life of slavery. His way of looking at the past seemed very strange to us; his view of certain sides of life was essentially different from ours. He never indulged in any regrets for the Arcadian joyousness and irresponsibility which was a somewhat popular conception of slavery; his had not been the lot of the petted houseservant, but that of the toiling fieldhand. While he mentioned with a warm appreciation the acts of kindness which those in authority had shown to him and his people, he would speak of a cruel deed, not with the indignation of one accustomed to quick feeling and spontaneous expression, but with a furtive disapproval which suggested to us a doubt in his own mind as to whether he had a right to think or to feel, and presented to us the curious psychological spectacle of a mind enslaved long after the shackles had been struck off from the limbs of its possessor. Whether the sacred name of liberty ever set his soul aglow with a generous fire; whether he had more than the most elementary ideas of love, friendship, patriotism, religion—things which are half, and the better half, of life to us; whether he even realized, except in a vague, uncertain way, his own degradation, I do not know. I fear not; and if not, then centuries of repression had borne their legitimate fruit. But in the simple human feeling, and still more in the undertone of sadness which pervaded his stories, I thought I could see a spark which, fanned by favoring breezes and fed by the memories of the past, might become in his children's children a glowing flame of sensibility, alive to every thrill of human happiness or human woe.

"Dave use' ter b'long ter my old marster," said Julius; "he wuz raise' on dis yer plantation, en I kin 'member all erbout 'im, fer I wuz old 'nuff ter chop cotton w'en it all happen'. Dave wuz a tall man, en monst'us strong: he could do mo' wuk in a day dan any yuther two niggers on de plantation. He wuz one er dese yer solemn kine er men, en nebber run on wid much foolishness, like de yuther darkies. He use' ter go out in de woods en pray; en w'en he hear de han's on de plantation cussin' en gwine on wid dere dancin' en foolishness, he use' ter tell 'em 'bout religion en jedgmen'-day, w'en dey would haf ter gin account fer eve'y idle word en all dey yuther sinful kyarin's-on.

"Dave had l'arn' how ter read de Bible. Dey wuz a free nigger boy in de settlement w'at wuz monst'us smart, en could write en ci-pher, en wuz alluz readin' books er papers. En Dave had hi'ed dis free boy fer ter l'arn 'im how ter read. Hit wuz 'g'in' de law, but co'se none er de niggers did n' say nuffin ter de w'ite folks 'bout it. Howsomedever, one day Mars Walker—he wuz de oberseah— foun' out Dave could read. Mars Walker wa'n't nuffin but a po' bockrah, en folks said he could n' read ner write hisse'f, en co'se he did n' lack ter see a nigger w'at knowed mo' d'n he did; so he went en tole Mars Dugal'. Mars Dugal' sont fer Dave, en ax' 'im 'bout it.

"Dave did n't hardly knowed w'at ter do; but he could n' tell no lie, so he 'fessed he could read de Bible a little by spellin' out de words. Mars Dugal' look' mighty solemn.

" 'Dis yer is a se'ious matter,' sezee; 'it 's 'g'in' de law ter l'arn niggers how ter read, er 'low 'em ter hab books. But w'at yer l'arn out'n dat Bible, Dave?'

"Dave wa'n't no fool, ef he wuz a nigger, en sezee:

" 'Marster, I l'arns dat it's a sin fer ter steal, er ter lie, er fer ter want w'at doan b'long ter yer; en I l'arns fer ter love de Lawd en ter 'bey my marster.'

"Mars Dugal' sorter smile' en laf' ter hisse'f, like he 'uz might'ly tickle' 'bout sump'n, en sezee:

" 'Doan 'pear ter me lack readin' de Bible done yer much harm, Dave. Dat's w'at I wants all my niggers fer ter know. Yer keep right on readin', en tell de yuther han's w'at yer be'n tellin' me. How would yer lack fer ter preach ter de niggers on Sunday?'

"Dave say he'd be glad fer ter do w'at he could. So Mars Dugal' tole de oberseah fer ter let Dave preach ter de niggers, en tell 'em w'at wuz in de Bible, en it would he'p ter keep 'em fum stealin' er runnin' erway.

"So Dave 'mence' ter preach, en done de han's on de plantation a heap er good, en most un 'em lef' off dey wicked ways, en 'mence' ter love ter hear 'bout God, en religion, en de Bible; en dey done dey wuk better, en did n' gib de oberseah but mighty little trouble fer ter manage 'em.

"Dave wuz one er dese yer men w'at did n' keer much fer de gals—leastways he did n' 'tel Dilsey come ter de plantation. Dilsey wuz a monst'us peart, good-lookin', gingybread-colored gal—one er dese yer high-steppin' gals w'at hol's dey heads up, en won' stan' no foolishness fum no man. She had b'long' ter a gemman over on Rockfish, w'at died, en whose 'state ha' ter be sol' fer ter pay his debts. En Mars Dugal' had be'n ter de oction, en w'en he seed dis gal a-cryin' en gwine on 'bout bein' sol' erway fum her ole mammy, Aun' Mahaly, Mars Dugal' bid 'em bofe in, en fotch 'em ober ter our plantation.

"De young nigger men on de plantation wuz des wil' atter Dilsey, but it did n' do no good, en none un 'em could n' git Dilsey fer dey junesey,* 'tel Dave 'mence' fer ter go roun' Aun' Mahaly's cabin. Dey wuz a fine-lookin' couple, Dave en Dilsey wuz, bofe tall, en well-shape', en soopl'. En dey sot a heap by one ernudder. Mars Dugal' seed 'em tergedder one Sunday, en de nex' time he seed Dave atter dat, sezee:

" 'Dave, w'en yer en Dilsey gits ready fer ter git married, I ain' got no rejections. Dey 's a poun' er so er chawin'ter-backer up at de house, en I reckon yo' mist'iss kin fine a frock en a ribbin er two fer

---

* Sweetheart.

Dilsey. Youer bofe good niggers, en yer neenter be feared er bein'
sol' 'way fum one ernudder long ez I owns dis plantation; en I
'spec's ter own it fer a long time yit.'

"But dere wuz one man on de plantation w'at did n' lack ter see
Dave en Dilsey tergedder ez much ez ole marster did. W'en Mars
Dugal' went ter de sale whar he got Dilsey en Mahaly, he bought ernudder han', by de name er Wiley. Wiley wuz one er dese yer
shiny-eyed, double-headed little niggers, sha'p ez a steel trap, en sly
ez de fox w'at keep out'n it. Dis yer Wiley had be'n pesterin' Dilsey
'fo' she come ter our plantation, en had nigh 'bout worried de life
out'n her. She did n' keer nuffin fer 'im, but he pestered her so she
ha' ter th'eaten ter tell her marster fer ter make Wiley let her 'lone.
W'en he come ober to our place it wuz des ez bad, 'tel bimeby Wiley seed dat Dilsey had got ter thinkin' a heap 'bout Dave, en den he
sorter hilt off aw'ile, en purten' lack he gin Dilsey up. But he wuz
one er dese yer 'ceitful niggers, en w'ile he wuz laffin' en jokin' wid
de yuther han's 'bout Dave en Dilsey, he wuz settin' a trap fer ter
ketch Dave en git Dilsey back fer hisse'f.

"Dave en Dilsey made up dere min's fer ter git married long
'bout Christmas time, w'en dey 'd hab mo' time fer a weddin'. But
'long 'bout two weeks befo' dat time ole mars 'mence' ter lose a
heap er bacon. Eve'y night er so somebody 'ud steal a side er bacon,
er a ham, er a shoulder, er sump'n, fum one er de smoke'ouses. De
smoke'ouses wuz lock', but somebody had a key, en manage' ter git
in some way er 'nudder. Dey 's mo' ways 'n one ter skin a cat, en
dey 's mo' d'n one way ter git in a smoke'ouse—leastways dat 's
w'at I hearn say. Folks w'at had bacon fer ter sell did n' hab no
trouble 'bout gittin' rid un it. Hit wuz 'g'in de law fer ter buy
things fum slabes; but Lawd! dat law did n' 'mount ter a hill er peas.
Eve'y week er so one er dese yer big covered waggins would come
'long de road, peddlin' terbacker en w'iskey. Dey wuz a sight er
room in one er dem big waggins, en it wuz monst'us easy fer ter
swop off bacon fer sump'n ter chaw er ter wa'm yer up in de win-
tertime. I s'pose de peddlers did n' knowed dey wuz breakin' de
law, caze de niggers alluz went at night, en stayed on de dark side er
de waggin; en it wuz mighty hard fer ter tell *w'at* kine er folks
dey wuz.

"Atter two er th'ee hund'ed er meat had be'n stole', Mars Walker call all de niggers up one ebenin', en tol' 'em dat de fus' nigger he cot stealin' bacon on dat plantation would git sump'n fer ter 'member it by long ez he lib'. En he say he'd gin fi' dollars ter de nigger w'at 'skiver' de rogue. Mars Walker say he s'picion' one er two er de niggers, but he could n' tell fer sho, en co'se dey all 'nied it w'en he 'cuse em un it.

"Dey wa'n't no bacon stole' fer a week er so, 'tel one dark night w'en somebody tuk a ham fum one er de smoke'ouses. Mars Walker des cusst awful w'en he foun' out de ham wuz gone, en say he gwine ter sarch all de niggers' cabins; w'en dis yer Wiley I wuz tellin' yer 'bout up'n say he s'picion' who tuk de ham, fer he seed Dave comin' 'cross de plantation fum to'ds de smoke'ouse de night befo'. W'en Mars Walker hearn dis fum Wiley, he went en sarch' Dave's cabin, en foun' de ham hid under de flo'.

"Eve'ybody wuz 'stonish'; but dere wuz de ham. Co'se Dave 'nied it ter de las', but dere wuz de ham. Mars Walker say it wuz des ez he 'spected: he did n' b'lieve in dese yer readin' en prayin' niggers; it wuz all 'pocrisy, en sarve' Mars Dugal' right fer 'lowin' Dave ter be readin' books w'en it wuz 'g'in' de law.

"W'en Mars Dugal' hearn 'bout de ham, he say he wuz might'ly 'ceived en dissapp'inted in Dave. He say he would n' nebber hab no mo' conference in no nigger, en Mars Walker could do des ez he wuz a mineter wid Dave er any er de res' er de niggers. So Mars Walker tuk'n tied Dave up en gin 'im forty; en den he got some er dis yer wire clof w'at dey uses fer ter make sifters out'n, en tuk'n wrap' it roun' de ham en fasten it tergedder at de little een'. Den he tuk Dave down ter de blacksmif shop, en had Unker Silas, de plantation blacksmif, fasten a chain ter de ham, en den fasten de yuther een' er de chain roun' Dave's neck. En den he says ter Dave, sezee:

" 'Now, suh, yer 'll wear dat neckliss fer de nex' six mont's; en I 'spec's yer ner none er de yuther niggers on dis plantation won' steal no mo' bacon dyoin' er dat time.'

"Well, it des 'peared ez if fum dat time Dave did n' hab nuffin but trouble. De niggers all turnt ag'in' 'im, caze he be'n de 'casion er Mars Dugal' turnin' 'em all ober ter Mars Walker. Mars Dugal' wa'n't a bad marster hisse'f, but Mars Walker wuz hard ez a rock. Dave kep' on sayin' he did n' take de ham, but none un 'em did n' b'lieve 'im.

"Dilsey wa'n't on de plantation w'en Dave wuz 'cused er stealin' de bacon. Ole mist'iss had sont her ter town fer a week er so fer ter wait on one er her darters w'at had a young baby, en she did n' fine out nuffin 'bout Dave's trouble 'tel she got back ter de plantation. Dave had patien'ly endyoed de finger er scawn, en all de hard words w'at de niggers pile' on 'im, caze he wuz sho' Dilsey would stan' by 'im, en would n' b'lieve he wuz a rogue, ner none er de yuther tales de darkies wuz tellin' 'bout 'im.

"W'en Dilsey come back fum town, en got down fum behine de buggy whar she b'en ridin' wid ole mars, de fus' nigger 'ooman she met says ter her—

" 'Is yer seed Dave, Dilsey?'

" 'No, I ain' seed Dave,' says Dilsey.

" 'Yes des oughter look at dat nigger; reckon yer would n' want 'im fer yo' junesey no mo'. Mars Walker cotch 'im stealin' bacon, en gone en fasten' a ham roun' his neck, so he can't git it off'n hisse'f. He sut'nly do look quare.' En den de 'ooman bus' out laffin' fit ter kill herse'f. W'en she got thoo laffin' she up'n tole Dilsey all 'bout de ham, en all de yuther lies w'at de niggers be'n tellin' on Dave.

"W'en Dilsey started down ter de quarters, who should she meet but Dave, comin' in fum de cotton-fiel'. She turnt her head ter one side, en purten' lack she did n' seed Dave.

" 'Dilsey!' sezee.

"Dilsey walk' right on, en did n' notice 'im.

" '*Oh*, Dilsey!'

"Dilsey did n' paid no 'tention ter 'im, en den Dave knowed some er de niggers be'n tellin' her 'bout de ham. He felt monst'us bad, but he 'lowed ef he could des git Dilsey fer ter listen ter 'im for a minute er so, he could make her b'lieve he did n' stole de bacon. It wuz a week er two befo' he could git a chance ter speak ter her ag'in; but fine'ly he cotch her down by de spring one day, en sezee:

" 'Dilsey, w'at fer yer won' speak ter me, en purten' lack yer doan see me? Dilsey, yer knows me too well fer ter b'lieve I'd steal, er do dis yuther wick'ness de niggers is all layin' ter me—yer *knows* I would n' do dat, Dilsey. Yer ain' gwine back on yo' Dave, is yer?'

"But w'at Dave say did n' hab no 'fec' on Dilsey. Dem lies folks b'en tellin' her had p'isen' her min' 'g'in' Dave.

" 'I doan wanter talk ter no nigger,' says she, 'w'at be'n whip' fer stealin', en w'at gwine roun' wid sich a lookin' thing ez dat hung roun' his neck. I's a 'spectable gal, *I* is. W'at yer call dat, Dave? Is dat a cha'm fer to keep off witches, er is it a noo kine er neckliss yer got?'

"Po' Dave did n' knowed w'at ter do. De las' one he had 'pended on fer ter stan' by 'im had gone back on 'im, en dey did n' 'pear ter be nuffin mo' wuf libbin' fer. He could n' hol' no mo' pra'r-meetin's, fer Mars Walker would n' 'low 'im ter preach, en de darkies would n' 'a' listen' ter 'im ef he had preach.' He did n' eben hab his Bible fer ter comfort hisse'f wid, fer Mars Walker had tuk it er-way fum 'im en burnt it up, en say ef he ketch any mo' niggers wid Bibles on de plantation he 'd do 'em wuss'n he done Dave.

"En ter make it still harder fer Dave, Dilsey tuk up wid Wiley. Dave could see him gwine up ter Aun' Mahaly's cabin, en settin' out on de bench in de moonlight wid Dilsey, en singin' sinful songs en playin' de banjer. Dave use' ter scrouch down behine de bushes, en wonder w'at de Lawd sen' 'im all dem tribberlations fer.

"But all er Dave's yuther troubles wa'n't nuffin side er dat ham. He had wrap' de chain roun' wid a rag, so it did n' hurt his neck; but w'eneber he went ter wuk, dat ham would be in his way; he had ter do his task, howsomedever, des de sam ez ef he did n' hab de ham. W'eneber he went ter lay down, dat ham would be in de way. Ef he turn ober in his sleep, dat ham would be tuggin' at his neck. It wuz de las' thing he seed at night, en de fus' thing he seed in de mawnin'. W'eneber he met a stranger, de ham would be de fus' thing de stranger would see. Most un 'em would 'mence' ter laf, en whareber Dave went he could see folks p'intin' at him, en year 'em sayin':

" 'W'at kine er collar dat nigger got roun' his neck?' er, ef dey knowed 'im, 'Is yer stole any mo' hams lately?' er 'W'at yer take fer yo' neckliss, Dave?' er some joke er 'nuther 'bout dat ham.

"Fus' Dave did n' mine it so much, caze he knowed he had n' done nuffin. But bimeby he got so he could n' stan' it no longer, en he'd hide hisse'f in de bushes w'eneber he seed anybody comin', en alluz kep' hisse'f shet up in his cabin atter he come in fum wuk.

"It wuz monst'us hard on Dave, en bimeby, w'at wid dat ham eberlastin' en etarnally draggin' roun' his neck, he 'mence' fer ter do en say quare things, en make de niggers wonder ef he wa'n't gittin'

out'n his mine. He got ter gwine roun' talkin' ter hisse'f, en singin'
cornshuckin' songs, en laffin' fit ter kill 'bout nuffin. En one day he
tole one er de niggers he had 'skivered a noo way fer ter raise
hams—gwine ter pick 'em off'n trees, en save de expense er
smoke'ouses by kyoin' 'em in de sun. En one day he up'n tole Mars
Walker he got sump'n pertickler fer ter say ter 'im; en he tuk Mars
Walker off ter one side, en tole 'im he wuz gwine ter show 'im a
place in de swamp whar dey wuz a whole trac' er lan' covered wid
ham trees.

"W'en Mars Walker hearn Dave talkin' dis kine er fool-talk, en
w'en he seed how Dave wuz 'mencin' ter git behine in his wuk, en
w'en he ax' de niggers en dey tole 'im how Dave be'n gwine on, he
'lowed he reckon' he 'd punish' Dave ernuff, en it mou't do mo'
harm dan good fer ter keep de ham on his neck any longer. So he
sont Dave down ter de blacksmif shop en had de ham tuk off. Dey
wa'n't much er de ham lef' by dat time, fer de sun had melt all de
fat, en de lean had all swivel' up, so dey wa'n't but th'ee er fo'
poun's lef'.

"W'en de ham had be'n tuk off'n Dave, folks kinder stopped
talkin' 'bout 'im so much. But de ham had be'n on his neck so long
dat Dave had sorter got use' ter it. He look des lack he 'd los'
sump'n fer a day er so atter de ham wuz tuk off, en did n' 'pear
ter know w'at ter do wid hisse'f; en fine'ly he up'n tuk'n tied a
lighterd-knot ter a string, en hid it under de flo' er his cabin, en
w'en nobody wuz n' lookin' he'd take it out en hang it roun' his
neck, en go off in de woods en holler en sing; en he allus tied it
roun' his neck w'en he went ter sleep. Fac', it 'peared lack Dave
done gone clean out'n his mine. En atter a w'ile he got one er de
quarest notions you eber hearn tell un. It wuz 'bout dat time dat I
come back ter de plantation fer ter wuk—I had be'n out ter Mars
Dugal's yuther place on Beaver Crick for a mont' er so. I had hearn
'bout Dave en de bacon, en 'bout w'at wuz gwine on on de plantation; but I did n' b'lieve w'at dey all say 'bout Dave, fer I knowed
Dave w'n't dat kine er man. One day atter I come back, me'n Dave
wuz choppin' cotton tergedder, w'en Dave lean' on his hoe, en motion' fer me ter come ober close ter 'im; en den he retch ober en
w'ispered ter me.

" 'Julius,' sezee, 'did yer knowed yer wuz wukkin' long yer wid a ham?'

"I could n' 'magine w'at he meant. 'G'way fum yer, Dave,' says I. 'Yer ain' wearin' no ham no mo'; try en fergit 'bout dat; 't ain' gwine ter do yer no good fer ter 'member it.'

" 'Look a-yer, Julius,' sezee, 'kin yer keep a secret?'

" 'Co'se I kin, Dave,' says I. 'I doan go roun' tellin' people w'at yuther folks says ter me.'

" 'Kin I trus' yer, Julius? Will yer cross yo' heart?'

"I cross' my heart. 'Wush I may die ef I tells a soul,' says I.

"Dave look' at me des lack he wuz lookin' thoo me en 'way on de yuther side er me, en sezee:

" 'Did yer knowed I wuz turnin' ter a ham, Julius?'

"I tried ter 'suade Dave dat dat wuz all foolishness, en dat he ought n't ter be talkin' dat-a-way—hit wa'n't right. En I tole 'im ef he'd des be patien', de time would sho'ly come w'en eve'ything would be straighten' out, en folks would fine out who de rale rogue wuz w'at stole de bacon. Dave 'peared ter listen ter w'at I say, en promise' ter do better, en stop gwine on dat-a-way; en it seem lack he pick' up a bit w'en he seed dey wuz one pusson did n' b'lieve dem tales 'bout 'im.

"Hit wa'n't long atter dat befo' Mars Archie McIntyre, ober on de Wimbleton road, 'mence' ter complain 'bout somebody stealin' chickens fum his hen'ouse. De chickens kep' on gwine, en at las' Mars Archie tole de han's on his plantation dat he gwine ter shoot de fus' man he ketch in his hen'ouse. In less'n a week atter he gin dis warnin', he cotch a nigger in de hen'ouse, en fill' 'im full er squir'l-shot. W'en he got a light, he 'skivered it wuz a strange nigger; en w'en he call' one er his own sarven's, de nigger tole 'im it wuz our Wiley. W'en Mars Archie foun' dat out, he sont ober ter our plantation fer ter tell Mars Dugal' he had shot one er his niggers, en dat he could sen' ober dere en git w'at wuz lef' un 'im.

"Mars Dugal' wuz mad at fus'; but w'en he got ober dere en hearn how it all happen', he did n' hab much ter say. Wiley wuz shot so bad he wuz sho' he wuz gwine ter die, so he up'n says ter ole marster:

" 'Mars Dugal',' sezee, 'I knows I's be'n a monst'us bad nigger, but befo' I go I wanter git sump'n off'n my mine. Dave did n' steal dat bacon w'at wuz tuk out'n de smoke-'ouse. *I* stole it all, en I hid de ham under Dave's cabin fer ter th'ow de blame on him—en may de good Lawd fergib me fer it.'

"Mars Dugal' had Wiley tuk back ter de plantation, en sont fer a doctor fer ter pick de shot out'n 'im. En de ve'y next' mawnin' Mars Dugal' sont fer Dave ter come up ter de big house; he felt kinder sorry fer de way Dave had be'n treated. Co'se it wa'n't no fault er Mars Dugal's, but he wuz gwine ter do w'at he could fer ter make up fer it. So he sont word down ter de quarters fer Dave en all de yuther han's ter 'semble up in de yard befo' de big house at sun up nex' mawnin'.

"Yearly in de mawnin' de niggers all swarm' up in de yard. Mars Dugal' wuz feelin' so kine dat he had brung up a bairl er cider, en tole de niggers all fer ter he'p deyselves.

"All de han's on de plantation come but Dave; en bimeby, w'en it seem lack he wa'n't comin', Mars Dugal' sont a nigger down ter de quarters ter look fer 'im. De sun wuz gittin' up, en dey wuz a heap er wuk ter be done, en Mars Dugal' sorter got ti'ed waitin'; so he up'n says:

" 'Well, boys en gals, I sont fer yer all up yer fer ter tell yer dat all dat 'bout Dave's stealin' er de bacon wuz a mistake, ez I s'pose yer all done hearn befo' now, en I 's mighty sorry it happen'. I wants ter treat all my niggers right, en I wants yer all ter know dat I sets a heap by all er my han's w'at is hones' en smart. En I want yer all ter treat Dave des lack yer did befo' dis thing happen', en mine w'at he preach ter yer; fer Dave is a good nigger, en has had a hard row ter hoe. En de fus' one I ketch sayin' anythin' 'g'in' Dave, I'll tell Mister Walker ter gin 'im forty. Now take ernudder drink er cider all roun', en den git at dat cotton, fer I wanter git dat Persimmon Hill trac' all pick' ober terday.'

"W'en de niggers wuz gwine 'way, Mars Dugal' tole me fer ter go en hunt up Dave, en bring 'im up ter de house. I went down ter Dave's cabin, but could n' fine 'im dere. Den I look' roun' de plantation, en in de aidge er de woods, en 'long de road; but I could n' fine no sign er Dave. I wuz 'bout ter gin up de sarch, w'en I happen' fer ter run 'cross a foot-track w'at look' lack Dave's. I had wukked 'long wid Dave so much dat I knowed his tracks: he had a monst'us long foot, wid a holler instep, w'ich wuz sump'n skase 'mongs' black folks. So I follered dat track 'cross de fiel' fum de quarters 'tel I get ter de smoke'ouse. De fus' thing I notice' wuz smoke comin' out'n de cracks: it wuz cu'ous, caze dey had n' be'n no hogs kill' on de plantation fer six mont' er so, en all de bacon in de smoke'ouse wuz done kyoed. I could n' 'magine fer ter sabe my life w'at Dave wuz doin' in dat smoke'ouse. I went up ter de do' en hollered:

" 'Dave!'

"Dey did n' nobody answer. I did n' wanter open de do', fer w'ite folks is monst'us pertickler 'bout dey smoke'ouses; en ef de oberseah had a-come up en cotch me in dere, he mou't not wanter b'lieve I wuz des lookin' fer Dave. So I sorter knock at de do' en call' out ag'in:

" 'O Dave, hit's me—Julius! Doan be skeered. Mars Dugal' wants yer ter come up ter de big house—he done 'skivered who stole de ham.'

"But Dave did n' answer. En w'en I look' roun' ag'in en did n' seed none er his tracks gwine way fum de smoke'ouse, I knowed he wuz in dere yit, en I wuz 'termine' fer ter fetch 'im out; so I push de do' open en look in.

"Dey wuz a pile er bark burnin' in de middle er de flo', en right ober de fier, hangin' fum one er de rafters, wuz Dave; dey wuz a rope roun' his neck, en I did n' haf ter look at his face mo' d'n once fer ter see he wuz dead.

"Den I knowed how it all happen'. Dave had kep' on gittin' wusser en wusser in his mine, 'tel he des got ter b'lievin' he wuz all done turnt ter a ham; en den he had gone en built a fier, en tied a rope roun' his neck, des lack de hams wuz tied, en had hung hisse'f up in de smoke'ouse fer ter kyo.

"Dave wuz buried down by the swamp, in de plantation buryin' groun'. Wiley did n' died fum de woun' he got in Mars McIntyre's hen'ouse; he got well atter a w'ile, but Dilsey would n' hab nuffin mo' ter do wid 'im, en 't wa'n't long 'fo' Mars Dugal' sol' 'im ter a spekilater on his way souf—he say he did n' want no sich a nigger on de plantation, ner in de county, ef he could he'p it. En w'en de een' er de year come, Mars Dugal' turnt Mars Walker off, en run de plantation hisse'f atter dat.

"Eber sence den," said Julius in conclusion, "w'eneber I eats ham, it min's me er Dave. I lacks ham, but I nebber kin eat mo' d'n two er th'ee poun's befo' I gits ter studyin' 'bout Dave, en den I has ter stop en leab de res' fer ernudder time."

There was a short silence after the old man had finished his story, and then my wife began to talk to him about the weather, on which subject he was an authority. I went into the house. When I came out, half an hour later, I saw Julius disappearing down the lane, with a basket on his arm.

At breakfast, next morning, it occurred to me that I should like a slice of ham. I said as much to my wife.

"Oh, no, John," she responded, "you shouldn't eat anything so heavy for breakfast."

I insisted.

"The fact is," she said, pensively, "I couldn't have eaten any more of that ham, so I gave it to Julius."

The Wife of His Youth

I

MR. RYDER WAS GOING to give a ball. There were several reasons why this was an opportune time for such an event.

Mr. Ryder might aptly be called the dean of the Blue Veins. The original Blue Veins were a little society of colored persons organized in a certain Northern city shortly after the war. Its purpose was to establish and maintain correct social standards among a people whose social condition presented almost unlimited room for improvement. By accident, combined perhaps with some natural affinity, the society consisted of individuals who were, generally speaking, more white than black. Some envious outsider made the suggestion that no one was eligible for membership who was not white enough to show blue veins. The suggestion was readily adopted by those who were not of the favored few, and since that time the society, though possessing a longer and more pretentious name, had been known far and wide as the "Blue Vein Society," and its members as the "Blue Veins."

The Blue Veins did not allow that any such requirement existed for admission to their circle, but, on the contrary, declared that character and culture were the only things considered; and that if most of their members were light-colored, it was because such persons, as a rule, had had better opportunities to qualify themselves for membership. Opinions differed, too, as to the usefulness of the society. There were those who had been known to assail it violently as a glaring example of the very prejudice from which the colored race had suffered most; and later, when such critics had succeeded in getting on the inside, they had been heard to maintain with zeal and earnestness that the society was a lifeboat, an anchor, a bulwark and a shield,—a pillar of cloud by day and of fire by night, to guide their people through the social wilderness. Another alleged prerequisite for Blue Vein membership was that of free birth; and while there was really no such requirement, it is doubtless true that very few of the members would have been unable to meet it if there had been. If there were one or two of the older members who had come up from the South and from slavery, their history presented enough romantic circumstances to rob their servile origin of its grosser aspects.

While there were no such tests of eligibility, it is true that the Blue Veins had their notions on these subjects, and that not all of them were equally liberal in regard to the things they collectively disclaimed. Mr. Ryder was one of the most conservative. Though he had not been among the founders of the society, but had come in some years later, his genius for social leadership was such that he had speedily become its recognized adviser and head, the custodian of its standards, and the preserver of its traditions. He shaped its social policy, was active in providing for its entertainment, and when the interest fell off, as it sometimes did, he fanned the embers until they burst again into a cheerful flame.

There were still other reasons for his popularity. While he was not as white as some of the Blue Veins, his appearance was such as to confer distinction upon them. His features were of a refined type, his hair was almost straight; he was always neatly dressed; his manners were irreproachable, and his morals above suspicion. He had come to Groveland a young man, and obtaining employment in the office of a railroad company as messenger had in time worked himself up to the position of stationery clerk, having charge of the distribution of the office supplies for the whole company. Although the lack of early training had hindered the orderly development of a naturally fine mind, it had not prevented him from doing a great deal of reading or from forming decidedly literary tastes. Poetry was his passion. He could repeat whole pages of the great English poets; and if his pronunciation was sometimes faulty, his eye, his voice, his gestures, would respond to the changing sentiment with a precision that revealed a poetic soul and disarmed criticism. He was economical, and had saved money; he owned and occupied a very comfortable house on a respectable street. His residence was hand-somely furnished, containing among other things a good library, es-pecially rich in poetry, a piano, and some choice engravings. He generally shared his house with some young couple, who looked after his wants and were company for him; for Mr. Ryder was a single man. In the early days of his connection with the Blue Veins he had been regarded as quite a catch, and young ladies and their mothers had manœuvred with much ingenuity to capture him. Not, however, until Mrs. Molly Dixon visited Groveland had any woman ever made him wish to change his condition to that of a married man.

Mrs. Dixon had come to Groveland from Washington in the spring, and before the summer was over she had won Mr. Ryder's heart. She possessed many attractive qualities. She was much younger than he; in fact, he was old enough to have been her father, though no one knew exactly how old he was. She was whiter than he, and better educated. She had moved in the best colored society of the country, at Washington, and had taught in the schools of that city. Such a superior person had been eagerly welcomed to the Blue Vein Society, and had taken a leading part in its activities. Mr. Ryder had at first been attracted by her charms of person, for she was very good looking and not over twenty-five; then by her refined man-ners and the vivacity of her wit. Her husband had been a govern-ment clerk, and at his death had left a considerable life insurance. She was visiting friends in Groveland, and, finding the town and the people to her liking, had prolonged her stay indefinitely. She had not seemed displeased at Mr. Ryder's attentions, but on the contrary had given him every proper encouragement; indeed, a younger and less cautious man would long since have spoken. But he had made up his mind, and had only to determine the time when he would ask her to be his wife. He decided to give a ball in her honor, and at some time during the evening of the ball to offer her his heart and hand. He had no special fears about the outcome, but, with a little touch of romance, he wanted the surroundings to be in harmony with his own feelings when he should have received the answer he expected.

Mr. Ryder resolved that this ball should mark an epoch in the social history of Groveland. He knew, of course,—no one could know better,—the entertainments that had taken place in past years, and what must be done to surpass them. His ball must be worthy of the lady in whose honor it was to be given, and must, by the quality of its guests, set an example for the future. He had observed of late a growing liberality, almost a laxity, in social matters, even among members of his own set, and had several times been forced to meet in a social way persons whose complexions and callings in life were hardly up to the standard which he considered proper for the society to maintain. He had a theory of his own.

"I have no race prejudice," he would say, "but we people of mixed blood are ground between the upper and the nether millstone. Our fate lies between absorption by the white race and extinction in the black. The one does n't want us yet, but may take us in time. The other would welcome us, but it would be for us a backward step. 'With malice towards none, with charity for all,' we must do the best we can for ourselves and those who are to follow us. Self-preservation is the first law of nature."

His ball would serve by its exclusiveness to counteract leveling tendencies, and his marriage with Mrs. Dixon would help to further the upward process of absorption he had been wishing and waiting for.

II

The ball was to take place on Friday night. The house had been put in order, the carpets covered with canvas, the halls and stairs decorated with palms and potted plants; and in the afternoon Mr. Ryder sat on his front porch, which the shade of a vine running up over a wire netting made a cool and pleasant lounging place. He expected to respond to the toast "The Ladies" at the supper, and from a volume of Tennyson—his favorite poet—was fortifying himself with apt quotations. The volume was open at "A Dream of Fair Women." His eyes fell on these lines, and he read them aloud to judge better of their effect:—

"*At length I saw a lady within call,*
  Stiller than chisell'd marble, standing there;
 A daughter of the gods, divinely tall,
   And most divinely fair."

He marked the verse, and turning the page read the stanza beginning,—

  "*O sweet pale Margaret,*
    O rare pale Margaret."

He weighed the passage a moment, and decided that it would not
do. Mrs. Dixon was the palest lady he expected at the ball, and she
was of a rather ruddy complexion, and of lively disposition and
buxom build. So he ran over the leaves until his eye rested on the
description of Queen Guinevere:—

  "*She seem'd a part of joyous Spring:*
  A gown of grass-green silk she wore,
  Buckled with golden clasps before;
  A light-green tuft of plumes she bore
  Closed in a golden ring.

                * * * * * *

  "*She look'd so lovely, as she sway'd*
  The rein with dainty finger-tips,
  A man had given all other bliss,
  And all his worldly worth for this,
  To waste his whole heart in one kiss
  Upon her perfect lips."

As Mr. Ryder murmured these words audibly, with an appreciative thrill, he heard the latch of his gate click, and a light footfall
sounding on the steps. He turned his head, and saw a woman standing before his door.

She was a little woman, not five feet tall, and proportioned to her
height. Although she stood erect, and looked around her with very
bright and restless eyes, she seemed quite old; for her face was
crossed and re-crossed with a hundred wrinkles, and around the
edges of her bonnet could be seen protruding here and there a tuft
of short gray wool. She wore a blue calico gown of ancient cut, a little red shawl fastened around her shoulders with an old-fashioned
brass brooch, and a large bonnet profusely ornamented with faded

red and yellow artificial flowers. And she was very black,—so black that her toothless gums, revealed when she opened her mouth to speak, were not red, but blue. She looked like a bit of the old plantation life, summoned up from the past by the wave of a magician's wand, as the poet's fancy had called into being the gracious shapes of which Mr. Ryder had just been reading.

He rose from his chair and came over to where she stood.

"Good-afternoon, madam," he said.

"Good-evenin', suh," she answered, ducking suddenly with a quaint curtsy. Her voice was shrill and piping, but softened somewhat by age. "Is dis yere whar Mistuh Ryduh lib, suh?" she asked, looking around her doubtfully, and glancing into the open windows, through which some of the preparations for the evening were visible.

"Yes," he replied, with an air of kindly patronage, unconsciously flattered by her manner, "I am Mr. Ryder. Did you want to see me?"

"Yas, suh, ef I ain't 'sturbin' of you too much."

"Not at all. Have a seat over here behind the vine, where it is cool. What can I do for you?"

" 'Scuse me, suh," she continued, when she had sat down on the edge of a chair, " 'scuse me, suh, I's lookin for my husban'. I heerd you wuz a big man an' had libbed heah a long time, an' I 'lowed you would n't min' ef I'd come roun' an' ax you ef you'd ever heerd of a merlatter man by de name er Sam Taylor 'quirin' roun' in de chu'ches ermongs' de people fer his wife 'Liza Jane?"

Mr. Ryder seemed to think for a moment.

"There used to be many such cases right after the war," he said, "but it has been so long that I have forgotten them. There are very few now. But tell me your story, and it may refresh my memory."

She sat back farther in her chair so as to be more comfortable, and folded her withered hands in her lap.

"My name's 'Liza," she began, " 'Liza Jane. W'en I wuz young I us'ter b'long ter Marse Bob Smif, down in ole Missoura. I wuz bawn down dere. W'en I wuz a gal I wuz married ter a man named Jim. But Jim died, an' after dat I married a merlatter man named Sam Taylor. Sam wuz free-bawn, but his mammy and daddy died, an' de w'ite folks 'prenticed him ter my marster fer ter work fer 'im 'tel he wuz growed up. Sam worked in de fiel', an' I wuz de cook. One day Ma'y Ann, old miss's maid, came rushin' out ter de kitchen, an' says she, ' 'Liza Jane, ole marse gwine sell yo' Sam down de ribber.'

" 'Go way f'm yere,' says I; 'my husban's free!'

" 'Don' make no diff'ence. I heerd ole marse tell ole miss he wuz gwine take yo' Sam 'way wid 'im ter-morrow, fer he needed money, an' he knowed whar he could git a t'ousan' dollars for Sam an' no questions axed.'

"W'en Sam come home f'm de fiel' dat night, I tole him 'bout ole marse gwine steal 'im, an' Sam run erway. His time wuz mos' up, an' he swo' dat w'en he wuz twenty-one he would come back an' he'p me run erway, er else save up de money ter buy my freedom. An' I know he'd 'a' done it, fer he thought a heap er me, Sam did. But w'en he come back he did n' fin' me, fer I wuz n' dere. Ole marse had heerd dat I warned Sam, so he had me whip' an' sol' down de ribber.

"Den de wah broke out, an' w'en it wuz ober de cullud folks wuz scattered. I went back ter de ole home; but Sam wuz n' dere, an' I could n' l'arn nuffin' 'bout 'im. But I knowed he 'd be'n dere to look fer me an' had n' foun' me, an' had gone erway ter hunt fer me.

"I's be'n lookin' fer 'im eber sence," she added simply, as though twenty-five years were but a couple of weeks, "an' I knows he's be'n lookin' fer me. Fer he sot a heap er sto' by me, Sam did, an' I know he's be'n huntin' fer me all dese years,—'less'n he's be'n sick er sump'n, so he could n' work, er out'n his head, so he could n' 'member his promise. I went back down de ribber, fer I 'lowed he'd gone down dere lookin' fer me. I's be'n ter Noo Orleens, an' Atlanty, an' Charleston, an' Richmon'; an' w'en I'd be'n all ober de Souf I come ter de Norf. Fer I knows I'll fin' 'im some er dese days," she added softly, "er he 'll fin' me, an' den we 'll bofe be as happy in freedom as we wuz in de ole days befo' de wah." A smile stole over her withered countenance as she paused a moment, and her bright eyes softened into a faraway look.

This was the substance of the old woman's story. She had wandered a little here and there. Mr. Ryder was looking at her curiously when she finished.

"How have you lived all these years?" he asked.

"Cookin', suh. I's a good cook. Does you know anybody w'at needs a good cook, suh? I's stoppin' wid a cullud fam'ly roun' de corner yonder 'tel I kin git a place."

"Do you really expect to find your husband? He may be dead long ago."

She shook her head emphatically. "Oh no, he ain' dead. De signs an' de tokens tells me. I dremp three nights runnin' on'y dis las' week dat I foun' him."

"He may have married another woman. Your slave marriage would not have prevented him, for you never lived with him after the war, and without that your marriage does n't count."

"Would n' make no diff'ence wid Sam. He would n' marry no yuther 'ooman 'tel he foun' out 'bout me. I knows it," she added. "Sump'n 's be'n tellin' me all dese years dat I's gwine fin' Sam 'fo' I dies."

"Perhaps he's outgrown you, and climbed up in the world where he would n't care to have you find him."

"No, indeed, suh," she replied, "Sam ain' dat kin' er man. He wuz good ter me, Sam wuz, but he wuz n' much good ter nobody e'se, fer he wuz one er de triflin'es' han's on de plantation. I 'spec's ter haf ter suppo't 'im w'en I fin' 'im, fer he nebber would work 'less'n he had ter. But den he wuz free, an' he did n' git no pay fer his work, an' I don' blame 'im much. Mebbe he's done better sence he run erway, but I ain' 'spectin' much."

"You may have passed him on the street a hundred times during the twenty-five years, and not have known him; time works great changes."

She smiled incredulously. "I'd know 'im 'mongs' a hund'ed men. Fer dey wuz n' no yuther merlatter man like my man Sam, an' I could n' be mistook. I 's toted his picture roun' wid me twenty-five years."

"May I see it?" asked Mr. Ryder. "It might help me to remember whether I have seen the original."

As she drew a small parcel from her bosom he saw that it was fastened to a string that went around her neck. Removing several wrappers, she brought to light an old-fashioned daguerreotype in a black case. He looked long and intently at the portrait. It was faded with time, but the features were still distinct, and it was easy to see what manner of man it had represented.

He closed the case, and with a slow movement handed it back to her.

"I don't know of any man in town who goes by that name," he said, "nor have I heard of any one making such inquiries. But if you will leave me your address, I will give the matter some attention, and if I find out anything I will let you know."

She gave him the number of a house in the neighborhood, and went away, after thanking him warmly.

He wrote the address on the fly-leaf of the volume of Tennyson, and, when she had gone, rose to his feet and stood looking after her curiously. As she walked down the street with mincing step, he saw several persons whom she passed turn and look back at her with a smile of kindly amusement. When she had turned the corner, he went upstairs to his bedroom, and stood for a long time before the mirror of his dressing-case, gazing thoughtfully at the reflection of his own face.

III

At eight o'clock the ballroom was a blaze of light and the guests had begun to assemble; for there was a literary programme and some routine business of the society to be gone through with before the dancing. A black servant in evening dress waited at the door and directed the guests to the dressing-rooms.

The occasion was long memorable among the colored people of the city; not alone for the dress and display, but for the high average of intelligence and culture that distinguished the gathering as a whole. There were a number of school-teachers, several young doctors, three or four lawyers, some professional singers, an editor, a lieutenant in the United States army spending his furlough in the city, and others in various polite callings; these were colored, though most of them would not have attracted even a casual glance because of any marked difference from white people. Most of the ladies were in evening costume, and dress coats and dancing pumps were the rule among the men. A band of string music, stationed in an alcove behind a row of palms, played popular airs while the guests were gathering.

The dancing began at half past nine. At eleven o'clock supper was served. Mr. Ryder had left the ballroom some little time before the intermission, but reappeared at the supper-table. The spread was worthy of the occasion, and the guests did full justice to it. When the coffee had been served, the toast-master, Mr. Solomon Sadler, rapped for order. He made a brief introductory speech, complimenting host and guests, and then presented in their order the toasts of the evening. They were responded to with a very fair display of after-dinner wit.

"The last toast," said the toast-master, when he reached the end of the list, "is one which must appeal to us all. There is no one of us of the sterner sex who is not at some time dependent upon woman,—in infancy for protection, in manhood for companionship, in old age for care and comforting. Our good host has been trying to live alone, but the fair faces I see around me to-night prove that he too is largely dependent upon the gentler sex for most that makes life worth living,—the society and love of friends,—and rumor is at fault if he does not soon yield entire subjection to one of them. Mr. Ryder will now respond to the toast,—The Ladies."

There was a pensive look in Mr. Ryder's eyes as he took the floor and adjusted his eyeglasses. He began by speaking of woman as the gift of Heaven to man, and after some general observations on the relations of the sexes he said: "But perhaps the quality which most distinguishes woman is her fidelity and devotion to those she loves. History is full of examples, but has recorded none more striking than one which only to-day came under my notice."

He then related, simply but effectively, the story told by his visitor of the afternoon. He gave it in the same soft dialect, which came readily to his lips, while the company listened attentively and sympathetically. For the story had awakened a responsive thrill in many hearts. There were some present who had seen, and others who had heard their fathers and grandfathers tell, the wrongs and sufferings of this past generation, and all of them still felt, in their darker moments, the shadow hanging over them. Mr. Ryder went on:—

"Such devotion and confidence are rare even among women.

There are many who would have searched a year, some who would have waited five years, a few who might have hoped ten years; but for twenty-five years this woman has retained her affection for and her faith in a man she has not seen or heard of in all that time.

"She came to me to-day in the hope that I might be able to help her find this long-lost husband. And when she was gone I gave my fancy rein, and imagined a case I will put to you.

"Suppose that this husband, soon after his escape, had learned that his wife had been sold away, and that such inquiries as he could make brought no information of her whereabouts. Suppose that he was young, and she much older than he; that he was light, and she was black; that their marriage was a slave marriage, and legally binding only if they chose to make it so after the war. Suppose, too, that he made his way to the North, as some of us have done, and there, where he had larger opportunities, had improved them, and had in the course of all these years grown to be as different from the ignorant boy who ran away from fear of slavery as the day is from the night. Suppose, even, that he had qualified himself, by industry, by thrift, and by study, to win the friendship and be considered worthy the society of such people as these I see around me to-night, gracing my board and filling my heart with gladness; for I am old enough to remember the day when such a gathering would not have been possible in this land. Suppose, too, that, as the years went by, this man's memory of the past grew more and more indistinct, until at last it was rarely, except in his dreams, that any image of his by-gone period rose before his mind. And then suppose that accident should bring to his knowledge the fact that the wife of his youth, the wife he had left behind him,—not one who had walked by his side and kept pace with him in his upward struggle, but one upon whom advancing years and a laborious life had set their mark,—was alive and seeking him, but that he was absolutely safe from recognition or discovery, unless he chose to reveal himself. My friends, what would the man do? I will presume that he was one who loved honor, and tried to deal justly with all men. I will even carry the case further, and suppose that perhaps he had set his heart upon another, whom he had hoped to call his own. What would he do, or rather what ought he to do, in such a crisis of a lifetime?

"It seemed to me that he might hesitate, and I imagined that I was an old friend, a near friend, and that he had come to me for advice; and I argued the case with him. I tried to discuss it impartially. After we had looked upon the matter from every point of view, I said to him, in words that we all know:—

'*This above all: to thine own self be true,*
And it must follow, as the night the day,
Thou canst not then be false to any man.'

"Then, finally, I put the question to him, 'Shall you acknowledge her?'

"And now, ladies and gentlemen, friends and companions, I ask you, what should he have done?"

There was something in Mr. Ryder's voice that stirred the hearts of those who sat around him. It suggested more than mere sympathy with an imaginary situation; it seemed rather in the nature of a personal appeal. It was observed, too, that his look rested more especially upon Mrs. Dixon, with a mingled expression of renunciation and inquiry.

She had listened, with parted lips and streaming eyes. She was the first to speak: "He should have acknowledged her."

"Yes," they all echoed, "he should have acknowledged her."

"My friends and companions," responded Mr. Ryder, "I thank you, one and all. It is the answer I expected, for I knew your hearts."

He turned and walked toward the closed door of an adjoining room, while every eye followed him in wondering curiosity. He came back in a moment, leading by the hand his visitor of the afternoon, who stood startled and trembling at the sudden plunge into this scene of brilliant gayety. She was neatly dressed in gray, and wore the white cap of an elderly woman.

"Ladies and gentlemen," he said, "this is the woman, and I am the man, whose story I have told you. Permit me to introduce to you the wife of my youth."

Her Virginia Mammy

I

THE PIANIST HAD STRUCK UP a lively two-step, and soon the floor was covered with couples, each turning on its own axis, and all revolving around a common center, in obedience perhaps to the same law of motion that governs the planetary systems. The dancing-hall was a long room, with a waxed floor that glistened with the reflection of the lights from the chandeliers. The walls were hung in paper of blue and white, above a varnished hard wood wainscoting; the monotony of surface being broken by numerous windows draped with curtains of dotted muslin, and by occasional engravings and colored pictures representing the dances of various nations, judiciously selected. The rows of chairs along the two sides of the room were left unoccupied by the time the music was well under way, for the pianist, a tall colored woman with long fingers and a muscular wrist, played with a verve and a swing that set the feet of the listeners involuntarily in motion.

The dance was sure to occupy the class for a quarter of an hour at least, and the little dancing-mistress took the opportunity to slip away to her own sitting-room, which was on the same floor of the block, for a few minutes of rest. Her day had been a hard one. There had been a matinée at two o'clock, a children's class at four, and at eight o'clock the class now on the floor had assembled.

When she reached the sitting-room she gave a start of pleasure. A young man rose at her entrance, and advanced with both hands extended—a tall, broad-shouldered, fair-haired young man, with a frank and kindly countenance, now lit up with the animation of pleasure. He seemed about twenty-six or twenty-seven years old.

His face was of the type one instinctively associates with intellect and character, and it gave the impression, besides, of that intangible something which we call race. He was neatly and carefully dressed, though his clothing was not without indications that he found it necessary or expedient to practice economy.

"Good-evening, Clara," he said, taking her hands in his; "I've been waiting for you five minutes. I supposed you would be in, but if you had been a moment later I was going to the hall to look you up. You seem tired to-night," he added, drawing her nearer to him and scanning her features at short range. "This work is too hard; you are not fitted for it. When are you going to give it up?"

"The season is almost over," she answered, "and then I shall stop for the summer."

He drew her closer still and kissed her lovingly. "Tell me, Clara," he said, looking down into her face,—he was at least a foot taller than she,—"when I am to have my answer."

"Will you take the answer you can get to-night?" she asked with a wan smile.

"I will take but one answer, Clara. But do not make me wait too long for that. Why, just think of it! I have known you for six months."

"That is an extremely long time," said Clara, as they sat down side by side.

"It has been an age," he rejoined. "For a fortnight of it, too, which seems longer than all the rest, I have been waiting for my answer. I am turning gray under the suspense. Seriously, Clara dear, what shall it be? or rather, when shall it be? for to the other question there is but one answer possible."

He looked into her eyes, which slowly filled with tears. She repulsed him gently as he bent over to kiss them away.

"You know I love you, John, and why I do not say what you wish. You must give me a little more time to make up my mind before I can consent to burden you with a nameless wife, one who does not know who her mother was"—

"She was a good woman, and beautiful, if you are at all like her."

"Or her father"—

"He was a gentleman and a scholar, if you inherited from him your mind or your manners."

"It is good of you to say that, and I try to believe it. But it is a serious matter; it is a dreadful thing to have no name."

"You are known by a worthy one, which was freely given you, and is legally yours."

"I know—and I am grateful for it. After all, though, it is not my real name; and since I have learned that it was not, it seems like a garment—something external, accessory, and not a part of myself. It does not mean what one's own name would signify."

"Take mine, Clara, and make it yours; I lay it at your feet. Some honored men have borne it."

"Ah yes, and that is what makes my position the harder. Your great-grandfather was governor of Connecticut."

"I have heard my mother say so."

"And one of your ancestors came over in the *Mayflower*."

"In some capacity—I have never been quite clear whether as ship's cook or before the mast."

"Now you are insincere, John; but you cannot deceive me. You never spoke in that way about your ancestors until you learned that I had none. I know you are proud of them, and that the memory of the governor and the judge and the Harvard professor and the *Mayflower* pilgrim makes you strive to excel, in order to prove yourself worthy of them."

"It did until I met you, Clara. Now the one inspiration of my life is the hope to make you mine."

"And your profession?"

"It will furnish me the means to take you out of this; you are not fit for toil."

"And your book—your treatise that is to make you famous?"

"I have worked twice as hard on it and accomplished twice as much since I have hoped that you might share my success."

"Oh! if I but knew the truth!" she sighed, "or could find it out! I realize that I am absurd, that I ought to be happy. I love my parents—my foster-parents—dearly. I owe them everything. Mother—poor, dear mother!—could not have loved me better or cared for me more faithfully had I been her own child. Yet—I am ashamed to say it—I always felt that I was not like them, that there was a subtle difference between us. They were contented in prosperity, resigned in misfortune; I was ever restless, and filled with vague ambitions.

They were good, but dull. They loved me, but they never said so. I feel that there is warmer, richer blood coursing in my veins than the placid stream that crept through theirs."

"There will never be any such people to me as they were," said her lover, "for they took you and brought you up for me."

"Sometimes," she went on dreamily, "I feel sure that I am of good family, and the blood of my ancestors seems to call to me in clear and certain tones. Then again when my mood changes, I am all at sea—I feel that even if I had but simply to turn my hand to learn who I am and whence I came, I should think from taking the step, for fear that what I might learn would leave me forever unhappy."

"Dearest," he said, taking her in his arms, while from the hall and down the corridor came the softened strains of music, "put aside these unwholesome fancies. Your past is shrouded in mystery. Take my name, as you have taken my love, and I'll make your future so happy that you won't have time to think of the past. What are a lot of musty, mouldy old grandfathers, compared with life and love and happiness? It's hardly good form to mention one's ancestors nowadays, and what's the use of them at all if one can't boast of them?"

"It's all very well of you to talk that way," she rejoined. "But suppose you should marry me, and when you become famous and rich, and patients flock to your office, and fashionable people to your home, and everyone wants to know who you are and whence you came, you'll be obliged to bring out the governor, and the judge, and the rest of them. If you should refrain, in order to forestall embarrassing inquiries about *my* ancestry, I should have deprived you of something you are entitled to, something which has a real social value. And when people found out all about you, as they eventually would from some source, they would want to know—we Americans are a curious people—who your wife was, and you could only say"—

"The best and sweetest woman on earth, whom I love unspeakably."

"You know that is not what I mean. You could only say—a Miss Nobody, from Nowhere."

"A Miss Hohlfelder, from Cincinnati, the only child of worthy German parents, who fled from their own country in '49 to escape political persecution—an ancestry that one surely need not be ashamed of."

"No; but the consciousness that it was not true would be always with me, poisoning my mind, and darkening my life and yours."

"Your views of life are entirely too tragic, Clara," the young man argued soothingly. "We are all worms of the dust, and if we go back far enough, each of us has had millions of ancestors; peasants and serfs, most of them; thieves, murderers, and vagabonds, many of them, no doubt; and therefore the best of us have but little to boast of. Yet we are all made after God's own image, and formed by his hand, for his ends; and therefore not to be lightly despised, even the humblest of us, least of all by ourselves. For the past we can claim no credit, for those who made it died with it. Our destiny lies in the future."

"Yes," she sighed, "I know all that. But I am not like you. A woman is not like a man; she cannot lose herself in theories and generalizations. And there are tests that even all your philosophy could not endure. Suppose you should marry me, and then some-time, by the merest accident, you should learn that my origin was the worst it could be—that I not only had no name, but was not en-titled to one."

"I cannot believe it," he said, "and from what we do know of your history it is hardly possible. If I learned it, I should forget it, unless, perchance, it should enhance your value in my eyes, by stamping you as a rare work of nature, an exception to the law of heredity, a triumph of pure beauty and goodness over the grosser limitations of matter. I cannot imagine, now that I know you, any-thing that could make me love you less. I would marry you just the same—even if you were one of your dancing-class to-night."

"I must go back to them," said Clara, as the music ceased.

"My answer," he urged, "give me my answer!"

"Not to-night, John," she pleaded. "Grant me a little longer time to make up my mind—for your sake."

"Not for my sake, Clara, no."

"Well—for mine." She let him take her in his arms and kiss her again.

"I have a patient yet to see to-night," he said as he went out. "If

I am not detained too long, I may come back this way—if I see the lights in the hall still burning. Do not wonder if I ask you again for my answer, for I shall be unhappy until I get it."

II

A stranger entering the hall with Miss Hohlfelder would have seen, at first glance, only a company of well-dressed people, with nothing to specially distinguish them from ordinary humanity in temperate climates. After the eye had rested for a moment and begun to separate the mass into its component parts, one or two dark faces would have arrested its attention; and with the suggestion thus offered, a closer inspection would have revealed that they were nearly all a little less than white. With most of them this fact would not have been noticed, while they were alone or in company with one another, though if a fair white person had gone among them it would perhaps have been more apparent. From the few who were undistinguishable from pure white, the colors ran down the scale by minute gradations to the two or three brown faces at the other extremity.

It was Miss Hohlfelder's first colored class. She had been somewhat startled when first asked to take it. No person of color had ever applied to her for lessons; and while a woman of that race had played the piano for her for several months, she had never thought of colored people as possible pupils. So when she was asked if she would take a class of twenty or thirty, she had hesitated, and begged for time to consider the application. She knew that several of the more fashionable dancing-schools tabooed all pupils, singly or in classes, who labored under social disabilities—and this included the people of at least one other race who were vastly farther along in the world than the colored people of the community where Miss Hohlfelder lived. Personally she had no such prejudice, except perhaps a little shrinking at the thought of personal contact with the dark faces of whom Americans always think when "colored people" are spoken of. Again, a class of forty pupils was not to be despised, for she taught for money, which was equally current and desirable, regardless of its color. She had consulted her foster-parents, and after them her lover. Her foster-parents, who were

German-born, and had never become thoroughly Americanized, saw no objection. As for her lover, he was indifferent.

"Do as you please," he said. "It may drive away some other pupils. If it should break up the business entirely, perhaps you might be willing to give me a chance so much the sooner."

She mentioned the matter to one or two other friends, who expressed conflicting opinions. She decided at length to take the class, and take the consequences.

"I don't think it would be either right or kind to refuse them for any such reason, and I don't believe I shall lose anything by it."

She was somewhat surprised, and pleasantly so, when her class came together for their first lesson, at not finding them darker and more uncouth. Her pupils were mostly people whom she would have passed on the street without a second glance, and among them were several whom she had known by sight for years, but had never dreamed of as being colored people. Their manners were good, they dressed quietly and as a rule with good taste, avoiding rather than choosing bright colors and striking combinations—whether from natural preference, or because of a slightly morbid shrinking from criticism, of course she could not say. Among them, the dancing-mistress soon learned, there were lawyers and doctors, teachers, telegraph operators, clerks, milliners and dressmakers, students of the local college and scientific school, and, somewhat to her awe at the first meeting, even a member of the legislature. They were mostly young, although a few light-hearted older people joined the class, as much for company as for the dancing.

"Of course, Miss Hohlfelder," explained Mr. Solomon Sadler, to whom the teacher had paid a compliment on the quality of the class, "the more advanced of us are not numerous enough to make the fine distinctions that are possible among white people; and of course as we rise in life we can't get entirely away from our brothers and our sisters and our cousins, who don't always keep abreast of us. We do, however, draw certain lines of character and manners and occupation. You see the sort of people we are. Of course we have no prejudice against color, and we regard all labor as honorable, provided a man does the best he can. But we must have standards that will give our people something to aspire to."

The class was not a difficult one, as many of the members were already fairly good dancers. Indeed the class had been formed as much for pleasure as for instruction. Music and hall rent and a knowledge of the latest dances could be obtained cheaper in this way than in any other. The pupils had made rapid progress, displaying in fact a natural aptitude for rhythmic motion, and a keen susceptibility to musical sounds. As their race had never been criticized for these characteristics, they gave them full play, and soon developed, most of them, into graceful and indefatigable dancers. They were now almost at the end of their course, and this was the evening of the last lesson but one.

Miss Hohlfelder had remarked to her lover more than once that it was a pleasure to teach them. "They enter into the spirit of it so thoroughly, and they seem to enjoy themselves so much."

"One might think," he suggested, "that the whitest of them would find their position painful and more or less pathetic; to be so white and yet to be classed as black—so near and yet so far."

"They don't accept our classification blindly. They do not acknowledge any inferiority; they think they are a great deal better than any but the best white people," replied Miss Hohlfelder. "And since they have been coming here, do you know," she went on, "I hardly think of them as any different from other people. I feel perfectly at home among them."

"It is a great thing to have faith in one's self," he replied. "It is a fine thing, too, to be able to enjoy the passing moment. One of your greatest charms in my eyes, Clara, is that in your lighter moods you have this faculty. You sing because you love to sing. You find pleasure in dancing, even by way of work. You feel the *joie de vivre*—the joy of living. You are not always so, but when you are so I think you most delightful."

Miss Hohlfelder, upon entering the hall, spoke to the pianist and then exchanged a few words with various members of the class. The pianist began to play a dreamy Strauss waltz. When the dance was well under way Miss Hohlfelder left the hall again and stepped into the ladies' dressing-room. There was a woman seated quietly on a couch in a corner, her hands folded on her lap.

"Good-evening, Miss Hohlfelder. You do not seem as bright as usual to-night."

Miss Hohlfelder felt a sudden yearning for sympathy. Perhaps it was the gentle tones of the greeting; perhaps the kindly expression of the soft though faded eyes that were scanning Miss Hohlfelder's features. The woman was of the indefinite age between forty and fifty. There were lines on her face which, if due to years, might have carried her even past the half-century mark, but if caused by trouble or ill health might leave her somewhat below it. She was quietly dressed in black, and wore her slightly wavy hair low over her ears, where it lay naturally in the ripples which some others of her sex so sedulously seek by art. A little woman, of clear olive complexion and regular features, her face was almost a perfect oval, except as time had marred its outline. She had been in the habit of coming to the class with some young women of the family she lived with, part boarder, part seamstress and friend of the family. Sometimes, while waiting for her young charges, the music would jar her nerves, and she would seek the comparative quiet of the dressing-room.

"Oh, I'm all right, Mrs. Harper," replied the dancing-mistress, with a brave attempt at cheerfulness,—"just a little tired, after a hard day's work."

She sat down on the couch by the elder woman's side. Mrs. Harper took her hand and stroked it gently, and Clara felt soothed and quieted by her touch.

"There are tears in your eyes and trouble in your face. I know it, for I have shed the one and known the other. Tell me, child, what ails you? I am older than you, and perhaps I have learned some things in the hard school of life that may be of comfort or service to you."

Such a request, coming from a comparative stranger, might very properly have been resented or lightly parried. But Clara was not what would be called self-contained. Her griefs seemed lighter when they were shared with others, even in spirit. There was in her nature a childish strain that craved sympathy and comforting. She had never known—or if so it was only in a dim and dreamlike past—the tender, brooding care that was her conception of a mother's love. Mrs. Hohlfelder had been fond of her in a placid way, and had given her every comfort and luxury her means permitted. Clara's ideal of maternal love had been of another and more romantic type; she had thought of a fond, impulsive mother, to whose bosom she could fly when in trouble or distress, and to whom she could communicate her sorrows and trials; who would dry her tears and soothe her with caresses. Now, when even her kind foster-mother was gone, she felt still more the need of sympathy and companionship with her own sex; and when this little Mrs. Harper spoke to her so gently, she felt her heart respond instinctively.

"Yes, Mrs. Harper," replied Clara with a sigh, "I am in trouble, but it is trouble that not you nor anyone else can heal."

"You do not know, child. A simple remedy can sometimes cure a very grave complaint. Tell me your trouble, if it is something you are at liberty to tell."

"I have a story," said Clara, "and it is a strange one,—a story I have told to but one other person, one very dear to me."

"He must be dear to you indeed, from the tone in which you speak of him. Your very accents breathe love."

"Yes, I love him, and if you saw him—perhaps you have seen him, for he has looked in here once or twice during the dancing-lessons—you would know why I love him. He is handsome, he is learned, he is ambitious, he is brave, he is good; he is poor, but he will not always be so; and he loves me, oh, so much!"

The other woman smiled. "It is not so strange to love, nor yet to be loved. And all lovers are handsome and brave and fond."

"That is not all of my story. He wants to marry me." Clara paused, as if to let this statement impress itself upon the other.

"True lovers always do," said the elder woman.

"But sometimes, you know, there are circumstances which prevent them."

"Ah yes," murmured the other reflectively, and looking at the girl with deeper interest, "circumstances which prevent them. I have known of such a case."

"The circumstance which prevents us from marrying is my story."

"Tell me your story, child, and perhaps, if I cannot help you otherwise, I can tell you one that will make yours seem less sad."

"You know me," said the young woman, "as Miss Hohlfelder; but that is not actually my name. In fact I do not know my real name, for I am not the daughter of Mr. and Mrs. Hohlfelder, but only an adopted child. While Mrs. Hohlfelder lived, I never knew that I was not her child. I knew I was very different from her and father,—I mean Mr. Hohlfelder. I knew they were fair and I was dark; they were stout and I was slender; they were slow and I was quick. But of course I never dreamed of the true reason of this difference. When mother—Mrs. Hohlfelder—died, I found among her things one day a little packet, carefully wrapped up, containing a child's slip and some trinkets. The paper wrapper of the packet bore an inscription that awakened my curiosity. I asked father Hohlfelder whose the things had been, and then for the first time I learned my real story.

"I was not their own daughter, he stated, but an adopted child. Twenty-three years ago, when he had lived in St. Louis, a steamboat explosion had occurred up the river, and on a piece of wreckage floating down stream, a girl baby had been found. There was nothing on the child to give a hint of its home or parentage; and no one came to claim it, though the fact that a child had been found was advertised all along the river. It was believed that the infant's parents must have perished in the wreck, and certainly no one of those who were saved could identify the child. There had been a passenger list on board the steamer, but the list, with the officer who kept it, had been lost in the accident. The child was turned over to an orphan asylum, from which within a year it was adopted by the two kindhearted and childless German people who brought it up as their own. I was that child."

The woman seated by Clara's side had listened with strained attention. "Did you learn the name of the steam-boat?" she asked quietly, but quickly, when Clara paused.

"The *Pride of St. Louis*," answered Clara. She did not look at Mrs. Harper, but was gazing dreamily toward the front, and therefore did not see the expression that sprang into the other's face,—a look in which hope struggled with fear, and yearning love with both,—nor the strong effort with which Mrs. Harper controlled herself and moved not one muscle while the other went on.

"I was never sought," Clara continued, "and the good people who brought me up gave me every care. Father and mother—I can never train my tongue to call them anything else—where very good to me. When they adopted me they were poor; he was a pharmacist with a small shop. Later on he moved to Cincinnati, where he made and sold a popular 'patent' medicine and amassed a fortune. Then I went to a fashionable school, was taught French, and deportment, and dancing. Father Hohlfelder made some bad investments, and lost most of his money. The patent medicine fell off in popularity. A year or two ago we came to this city to live. Father bought this block and opened the little drug store below. We moved into the rooms upstairs. The business was poor, and I felt that I ought to do something to earn money and help support the family. I could dance; we had this hall, and it was not rented all the time, so I opened a dancing-school."

"Tell me, child," said the other woman, with restrained eagerness, "what were the things found upon you when you were taken from the river?"

"Yes," answered the girl, "I will. But I have not told you all my story, for this is but the prelude. About a year ago a young doctor rented an office in our block. We met each other, at first only now and then, and afterwards oftener; and six months ago he told me that he loved me."

She paused, and sat with half opened lips and dreamy eyes, looking back into the past six months.

"And the things found upon you"—

"Yes, I will show them to you when you have heard all my story. He wanted to marry me, and has asked me every week since. I have told him that I love him, but I have not said I would marry him. I don't think it would be right for me to do so, unless I could clear up this mystery. I believe he is going to be great and rich and famous, and there might come a time when he would be ashamed of me. I don't say that I shall never marry him; for I have hoped—I have a presentiment that in some strange way I shall find out who I am, and who my parents were. It may be mere imagination on my part, but somehow I believe it is more than that."

"Are you sure there was no mark on the things that were found upon you?" said the elder woman.

"Ah yes," sighed Clara, "I am sure, for I have looked at them a hundred times. They tell me nothing, and yet they suggest to me many things. Come," she said, taking the other by the hand, "and I will show them to you."

She led the way along the hall to her sitting-room, and to her bedchamber beyond. It was a small room hung with paper showing a pattern of morning-glories on a light ground, with dotted muslin curtains, a white iron bedstead, a few prints on the wall, a rocking-chair—a very dainty room. She went to the maple dressing-case, and opened one of the drawers.

As they stood for a moment, the mirror reflecting and framing their image, more than one point of resemblance between them was emphasized. There was something of the same oval face, and in Clara's hair a faint suggestion of the wave in the older woman's; and though Clara was fairer of complexion, and her eyes were gray and the other's black, there was visible, under the influence of the momentary excitement, one of those indefinable likenesses which are at times encountered,—sometimes marking blood relationship, sometimes the impress of a common training; in one case perhaps a mere earmark of temperament, and in another the index of a type. Except for the difference in color, one might imagine that if the younger woman were twenty years older the resemblance would be still more apparent.

Clara reached her hand into the drawer and drew out a folded packet, which she unwrapped, Mrs. Harper following her movements meanwhile with a suppressed intensity of interest which Clara, had she not been absorbed in her own thoughts, could not have failed to observe.

When the last fold of paper was removed there lay revealed a child's muslin slip. Clara lifted it and shook it gently until it was unfolded before their eyes. The lower half was delicately worked in a lacelike pattern, revealing an immense amount of patient labor.

The elder woman seized the slip with hands which could not disguise their trembling. Scanning the garment carefully, she seemed to be noting the pattern of the needlework, and then, pointing to a certain spot, exclaimed:—

"I thought so! I was sure of it! Do you not see the letters—M.S.?"

"Oh, how wonderful!" Clara seized the slip in turn and scanned the monogram. "How strange that you should see that at once and that I should not have discovered it, who have looked at it a hundred times! And here," she added, opening a small package which had been inclosed in the other, "is my coral necklace. Perhaps your keen eyes can find something in that."

It was a simple trinket, at which the older woman gave but a glance—a glance that added to her emotion.

"Listen, child," she said, laying her trembling hand on the other's arm. "It is all very strange and wonderful, for that slip and necklace, and, now that I have seen them, your face and your voice and your ways, all tell me who you are. Your eyes are your father's eyes, your voice is your father's voice. The slip was worked by your mother's hand."

"Oh!" cried Clara, and for a moment the whole world swam before her eyes.

"I was on the *Pride of St. Louis,* and I knew your father—and your mother."

Clara, pale with excitement, burst into tears, and would have fallen had not the other woman caught her in her arms. Mrs. Harper placed her on the couch, and, seated by her side, supported her head on her shoulder. Her hands seemed to caress the young woman with every touch.

"Tell me, oh, tell me all!" Clara demanded, when the first wave of emotion had subsided. "Who were my father and my mother, and who am I?"

The elder woman restrained her emotion with an effort, and answered as composedly as she could,—

"There were several hundred passengers on the *Pride of St. Louis* when she left Cincinnati on that fateful day, on her regular trip to New Orleans. Your father and mother were on the boat—and I was on the boat. We were going down the river, to take ship at New Orleans for France, a country which your father loved."

"Who was my father?" asked Clara. The woman's words fell upon her ear like water on a thirsty soil.

"Your father was a Virginia gentleman, and belonged to one of the first families, the Staffords, of Melton County."

Clara drew herself up unconsciously, and into her face there came a frank expression of pride which became it wonderfully, set-

ting off a beauty that needed only this to make it all but perfect of
its type.

"I knew it must be so," she murmured. "I have often felt it.
Blood will always tell. And my mother?"

"Your mother—also belonged to one of the first families of Virginia, and in her veins flowed some of the best blood of the Old
Dominion."

"What was her maiden name?"

"Mary Fairfax. As I was saying, your father was a Virginia gentleman. He was as handsome a man as ever lived, and proud, oh, so
proud!—and good, and kind. He was a graduate of the University
and had studied abroad."

"My mother—was she beautiful?"

"She was much admired, and your father loved her from the moment he first saw her. Your father came back from Europe, upon his
father's sudden death, and entered upon his inheritance. But he had
been away from Virginia so long, and had read so many books, that
he had outgrown his home. He did not believe that slavery was
right, and one of the first things he did was to free his slaves. His
views were not popular, and he sold out his lands a year before the
war, with the intention of moving to Europe."

"In the mean time he had met and loved and married my
mother?"

"My mother was a Virginia belle, was she not?"

"The Fairfaxes," answered Mrs. Harper, "were the first of the
first families, the bluest of the blue-bloods. The Miss Fairfaxes were
all beautiful and all social favorites."

"What did my father do then, when he had sold out in Virginia?"

"He went with your mother and you—you were then just a year
old—to Cincinnati, to settle up some business connected with his
estate. When he had completed his business, he embarked on the
Pride of St. Louis with you and your mother and a colored nurse."

"And how did you know about them?" asked Clara.

"I was one of the party. I was"—

"You were the colored nurse?—my 'mammy,' they would have
called you in my old Virginia home?"

"Yes, child, I was—your mammy. Upon my bosom you have
rested; my breasts once gave you nourishment; my hands once

ministered to you; my arms sheltered you, and my heart loved you and mourned you like a mother loves and mourns her firstborn."

"Oh, how strange, how delightful!" exclaimed Clara. "Now I understand why you clasped me so tightly, and were so agitated when I told you my story. It is too good for me to believe. I am of good blood, of an old and aristocratic family. My presentiment has come true. I can marry my lover, and I shall owe all my happiness to you. How can I ever repay you?"

"You can kiss me, child, kiss your mammy."

Their lips met, and they were clasped in each other's arms. One put into the embrace all of her new-found joy, the other all the suppressed feeling of the last half hour, which in turn embodied the unsatisfied yearning of many years.

The music had ceased and the pupils had left the hall. Mrs. Harper's charges had supposed her gone, and had left for home without her. But the two women, sitting in Clara's chamber, hand in hand, were oblivious to external things and noticed neither the hour nor the cessation of the music.

"Why, dear mammy," said the young woman musingly, "did you not find me, and restore me to my people?"

"Alas, child! I was not white, and when I was picked up from the water, after floating miles down the river, the man who found me kept me prisoner for a time, and, there being no inquiry for me, pretended not to believe that I was free, and took me down to New Orleans and sold me as a slave. A few years later the war set me free. I went to St. Louis but could find no trace of you. I had hardly dared to hope that a child had been saved, when so many grown men and women had lost their lives. I made such inquiries as I could, but all in vain."

"Did you go to the orphan asylum?"

"The orphan asylum had been burned and with it all the records. The war had scattered the people so that I could find no one who knew about a lost child saved from a river wreck. There were many orphans in those days, and one more or less was not likely to dwell in the public mind."

"Did you tell my people in Virginia?"

"They, too, were scattered by the war. Your uncles lost their lives on the battlefield. The family mansion was burned to the ground.

Your father's remaining relatives were reduced to poverty, and moved away from Virginia."

"What of my mother's people?"

"They are all dead. God punished them. They did not love your father, and did not wish him to marry your mother. They helped to drive him to his death."

"I am alone in the world, then, without kith or kin," murmured Clara, "and yet, strange to say, I am happy. If I had known my people and lost them, I should be sad. They are gone, but they have left me their name and their blood. I would weep for my poor father and mother if I were not so glad."

Just then some one struck a chord upon the piano in the hall, and the sudden breaking of the stillness recalled Clara's attention to the lateness of the hour.

"I had forgotten about the class," she exclaimed. "I must go and attend to them."

They walked along the corridor and entered the hall. Dr. Winthrop was seated at the piano, drumming idly on the keys.

"I did not know where you had gone," he said. "I knew you would be around, of course, since the lights were not out, and so I came in here to wait for you."

"Listen, John, I have a wonderful story to tell you."

Then she told him Mrs. Harper's story. He listened attentively and sympathetically, at certain points taking his eyes from Clara's face and glancing keenly at Mrs. Harper, who was listening intently. As he looked from one to the other he noticed the resemblance between them, and something in his expression caused Mrs. Harper's eyes to fall, and then glance up appealingly.

"And now," said Clara, "I am happy. I know my name. I am a Virginia Stafford. I belong to one, yes, to two of what were the first families of Virginia. John, my family is as good as yours. If I remember my history correctly, the Cavaliers looked down upon the Roundheads."

"I admit my inferiority," he replied. "If you are happy I am glad."

"Clara Stafford," mused the girl. "It is a pretty name."

"You will never have to use it," her lover declared, "for now you will take mine."

"Then I shall have nothing left of all that I have found"—

"Except your husband," asserted Dr. Winthrop, putting his arm around her, with an air of assured possession.

Mrs. Harper was looking at them with moistened eyes in which joy and sorrow, love and gratitude, were strangely blended. Clara put out her hand to her impulsively.

"And my mammy," she cried, "my dear Virginia mammy."

The Sheriff's Children

BRANSON COUNTY, NORTH CAROLINA, is in a sequestered district of one of the staidest and most conservative States of the Union. Society in Branson County is almost primitive in its simplicity. Most of the white people own the farms they till, and even before the war there were no very wealthy families to force their neighbors, by comparison, into the category of "poor whites."

To Branson County, as to most rural communities in the South, the war is the one historical event that overshadows all others. It is the era from which all local chronicles are dated,—births, deaths, marriages, storms, freshets. No description of the life of any Southern community would be perfect that failed to emphasize the all pervading influence of the great conflict.

Yet the fierce tide of war that had rushed through the cities and along the great highways of the country had comparatively speaking but slightly disturbed the sluggish current of life in this region, remote from railroads and navigable streams. To the north in Virginia, to the west in Tennessee, and all along the seaboard the war had raged; but the thunder of its cannon had not disturbed the echoes of Branson County, where the loudest sounds heard were the crack of some hunter's rifle, the baying of some deep-mouthed hound, or the yodel of some tuneful negro on his way through the pine forest. To the east, Sherman's army had passed on its march to the sea; but no straggling band of "bummers" had penetrated the confines of Branson County. The war, it is true, had robbed the county of the flower of its young manhood; but the burden of taxation, the doubt and uncertainty of the conflict, and the sting of ultimate defeat, had been borne by the people with an apathy that robbed misfortune of half its sharpness.

The nearest approach to town life afforded by Branson County is found in the little village of Troy, the county seat, a hamlet with a population of four or five hundred.

Ten years make little difference in the appearance of these remote Southern towns. If a railroad is built through one of them, it infuses some enterprise; the social corpse is galvanized by the fresh blood of civilization that pulses along the farthest ramifications of our great system of commercial highways. At the period of which I write, no railroad had come to Troy. If a traveler, accustomed to the bustling life of cities, could have ridden through Troy on a summer day, he might easily have fancied himself in a deserted village. Around him he would have seen weather-beaten houses, innocent of paint, the shingled roofs in many instances covered with a rich growth of moss. Here and there he would have met a razor-backed hog lazily rooting his way along the principal thoroughfare; and more than once he would probably have had to disturb the slumbers of some yellow dog, dozing away the hours in ardent sunshine, and reluctantly yielding up his place in the middle of the dusty road.

On Saturdays the village presented a somewhat livelier appearance, and the shade trees around the court-house square and along Front Street served as hitching-posts for a goodly number of horses and mules and stunted oxen, belonging to the farmer-folk who had come in to trade at the two or three local stores.

A murder was a rare event in Branson County. Every well-informed citizen could tell the number of homicides committed in the county for fifty years back, and whether the slayer, in any given instance, had escaped, either by flight or acquittal, or had suffered the penalty of the law. So, when it became known in Troy early one Friday morning in summer, about ten years after the war, that old Captain Walker, who had served in Mexico under Scott, and had left an arm on the field of Gettysburg, had been foully murdered during the night, there was intense excitement in the village. Business was practically suspended, and the citizens gathered in little groups to discuss the murder, and speculate upon the identity of the murderer. It transpired from testimony at the coroner's inquest, held during the morning, that a strange mulatto had been seen going in the di-

Capt Walker Murder

rection of Captain Walker's house the night before, and had been met going away from Troy early Friday morning, by a farmer on his way to town. Other circumstances seemed to connect the stranger with the crime. The sheriff organized a posse to search for him, and early in the evening, when most of the citizens of Troy were at supper, the suspected man was brought in and lodged in the county jail.

By the following morning the news of the capture had spread to the farthest limits of the county. A much larger number of people than usual came to town that Saturday—bearded men in straw hats and blue homespun shirts, and butternut trousers of great amplitude of material and vagueness of outline; women in homespun frocks and slat-bonnets, with faces as expressionless as the dreary sandhills which gave them a meagre sustenance.

The murder was almost the sole topic of conversation. A steady stream of curious observers visited the house of mourning, and gazed upon the rugged face of the old veteran, now stiff and cold in death; and more than one eye dropped a tear at the remembrance of the cheery smile, and the joke—sometimes superannuated, generally feeble, but always good-natured—with which the captain had been wont to greet his acquaintances. There was a growing sentiment of anger among these stern men, toward the murderer who had thus cut down their friend, and a strong feeling that ordinary justice was too slight a punishment for such a crime.

Toward noon there was an informal gathering of citizens in Dan Tyson's store.

"I hear it 'lowed that Square Kyahtah's too sick ter hol' co'te this evenin'," said one, "an' that the purlim'nary hearin' 'll haf ter go over 'tel nex' week."

A look of disappointment went round the crowd.

"Hit 's the durndes', meanes' murder ever committed in this caounty," said another, with moody emphasis.

"I s'pose the nigger 'lowed the Cap'n had some green-backs," observed a third speaker.

"The Cap'n," said another, with an air of superior information, "has left two bairls of Confedrit money, which he 'spected 'ud be good some day er nuther."

This statement gave rise to a discussion of the speculative value of Confederate money; but in a little while the conversation returned to the murder.

"Hangin' air too good fer the murderer," said one; "he oughter be burnt, stidier bein' hung."

There was an impressive pause at this point, during which a jug of moonlight whiskey went the round of the crowd.

"Well," said a round-shouldered farmer, who, in spite of his peaceable expression and faded gray eye, was known to have been one of the most daring followers of a rebel guerrilla chieftain, "what air yer gwine ter do about it? Ef you fellers air gwine ter set down an' let a wuthless nigger kill the bes' white man in Branson, an' not say nuthin' ner do nuthin', *I'll* move outen the caounty."

This speech gave tone and direction to the rest of the conversation. Whether the fear of losing the round-shouldered farmer operated to bring about the result or not is immaterial to this narrative; but, at all events, the crowd decided to lynch the negro. They agreed that this was the least that could be done to avenge the death of their murdered friend, and that it was a becoming way in which to honor his memory. They had some vague notions of the majesty of the law and the rights of the citizen, but in the passion of the moment these sunk into oblivion; a white man had been killed by a negro.

"The Cap'n was an ole sodger," said one of his friends solemnly. "He 'll sleep better when he knows that a co'temartial has be'n hilt an' jestice done."

By agreement the lynchers were to meet at Tyson's store at five o'clock in the afternoon, and proceed thence to the jail, which was situated down the Lumberton Dirt Road (as the old turnpike antedating the plank-road was called), about half a mile south of the court-house. When the preliminaries of the lynching had been arranged, and a committee appointed to manage the affair, the crowd dispersed, some to go to their dinners, and some to secure recruits for the lynching party.

It was twenty minutes to five o'clock, when an excited negro, panting and perspiring, rushed up to the back door of Sheriff Campbell's dwelling, which stood at a little distance from the jail and somewhat farther than the latter building from the court-house. A turbaned colored woman came to the door in response to the negro's knock.

"Hoddy, Sis' Nance."

"Hoddy, Brer Sam."

"Is de shurff in," inquired the negro.

"Yas, Brer Sam, he's eatin' his dinner," was the answer.

"Will yer ax 'im ter step ter de do' a minute, Sis' Nance?"

The woman went into the dining-room, and a moment later the sheriff came to the door. He was a tall, muscular man, of a ruddier complexion than is usual among Southerners. A pair of keen, deep-set gray eyes looked out from under bushy eyebrows, and about his mouth was a masterful expression, which a full beard, once sandy in color, but now profusely sprinkled with gray, could not entirely conceal. The day was hot; the sheriff had discarded his coat and vest, and had his white shirt open at the throat.

"What do you want, Sam?" he inquired of the negro, who stood hat in hand, wiping the moisture from his face with a ragged shirt-sleeve.

"Shurff, dey gwine ter hang de pris'ner w'at's lock' up in de jail. Dey're comin' dis a-way now. I wuz layin' down on a sack er corn down at de sto', behine a pile er flour-bairls, w'en I hearn Doc' Cain en Kunnel Wright talkin' erbout it. I slip' outen de back do', en run here as fas' as I could. I hearn you say down ter de sto' once't dat you would n't let nobody take a pris'ner 'way fum you wid-out walkin' over yo' dead body, en I thought I'd let you know 'fo' dey come, so yer could pertec' de pris'ner."

The sheriff listened calmly, but his face grew firmer, and a determined gleam lit up his gray eyes. His frame grew more erect, and he unconsciously assumed the attitude of a soldier who momentarily expects to meet the enemy face to face.

"Much obliged, Sam," he answered. "I'll protect the prisoner. Who's coming?"

"I dunno who-all *is* comin'," replied the negro. "Dere's Mistah McSwayne, en Doc' Cain, en Maje' McDonal', en Kunnel Wright, en a heap er yuthers. I wuz so skeered I done furgot mo' d'n half un em. I spec' dey mus' be mos' here by dis time, so I'll git outen de way, fer I don' want nobody fer ter think I wuz mix' up in dis business." The negro glanced nervously down the road toward the town, and made a movement as if to go away.

"Won't you have some dinner first?" asked the sheriff.

The negro looked longingly in at the open door, and sniffed the appetizing odor of boiled pork and collards.

"I ain't got no time fer ter tarry, Shurff," he said, "but Sis' Nance mought gin me sump'n I could kyar in my han' en eat on de way."

A moment later Nancy brought him a huge sandwich of split corn-pone, with a thick slice of fat bacon inserted between the halves, and a couple of baked yams. The negro hastily replaced his ragged hat on his head, dropped the yams in the pocket of his capacious trousers, and, taking the sandwich in his hand, hurried across the road and disappeared in the woods beyond.

The sheriff reëntered the house, and put on his coat and hat. He then took down a double-barreled shotgun and loaded it with buckshot. Filling the chambers of a revolver with fresh cartridges, he slipped it into the pocket of the sack-coat which he wore.

A comely young woman in a calico dress watched these proceedings with anxious surprise.

"Where are you going, father?" she asked. She had not heard the conversation with the negro.

"I am goin' over to the jail," responded the sheriff. "There's a mob comin' this way to lynch the nigger we've got locked up. But they won't do it," he added, with emphasis.

"Oh, father! don't go!" pleaded the girl, clinging to his arm; "they'll shoot you if you don't give him up."

"You never mind me, Polly," said her father reassuringly, as he gently unclasped her hands from his arm. "I'll take care of myself and the prisoner, too. There ain't a man in Branson County that would shoot me. Besides, I have faced fire too often to be scared away from my duty. You keep close in the house," he continued, "and if any one disturbs you just use the old horse-pistol in the top bureau drawer. It's a little old-fashioned, but it did good work a few years ago."

The young girl shuddered at this sanguinary allusion, but made no further objection to her father's departure.

The sheriff of Branson was a man far above the average of the community in wealth, education, and social position. His had been one of the few families in the county that before the war had owned large estates and numerous slaves. He had graduated at the State University at Chapel Hill, and had kept up some acquaintance with current literature and advanced thought. He had traveled some in his youth, and was looked up to in the county as an authority on all subjects connected with the outer world. At first an ardent supporter of the Union, he had opposed the secession movement in his native State as long as opposition availed to stem the tide of public opinion. Yielding at last to the force of circumstances, he had entered the Confederate service rather late in the war, and served with distinction through several campaigns, rising in time to the rank of colonel. After the war he had taken the oath of allegiance, and had been chosen by the people as the most available candidate for the office of sheriff, to which he had been elected without opposition. He had filled the office for several terms, and was universally popular with his constituents.

Colonel or Sheriff Campbell, as he was indifferently called, as the military or civil title happened to be most important in the opinion of the person addressing him, had a high sense of the responsibility attaching to his office. He had sworn to do his duty faithfully, and he knew what his duty was, as sheriff, perhaps more clearly than he had apprehended it in other passages of his life. It was, therefore, with no uncertainty in regard to his course that he prepared his weapons and went over to the jail. He had no fears for Polly's safety.

The sheriff had just locked the heavy front door of the jail behind him when a half dozen horsemen, followed by a crowd of men on foot, came round a bend in the road and drew near the jail. They halted in front of the picket fence that surrounded the building, while several of the committee of arrangements rode on a few rods farther to the sheriff's house. One of them dismounted and rapped on the door with his riding-whip.

"Is the sheriff at home?" he inquired.

"No, he has just gone out," replied Polly, who had come to the door.

"We want the jail keys," he continued.

"They are not here," said Polly. "The sheriff has them himself." Then she added, with assumed indifference, "He is at the jail now."

The man turned away, and Polly went into the front room, from which she peered anxiously between the slats of the green blinds of a window that looked toward the jail. Meanwhile the messenger returned to his companions and announced his discovery. It looked as though the sheriff had learned of their design and was preparing to resist it.

One of them stepped forward and rapped on the jail door.

"Well, what is it?" said the sheriff, from within.

"We want to talk to you, Sheriff," replied the spokesman.

There was a little wicket in the door; this the sheriff opened, and answered through it.

"All right, boys, talk away. You are all strangers to me, and I don't know what business you can have." The sheriff did not think it necessary to recognize anybody in particular on such an occasion; the question of identity sometimes comes up in the investigation of these extra-judicial executions.

"We're a committe of citizens and we want to get into the jail."

"What for? It ain't much trouble to get into jail. Most people want to keep out."

The mob was in no humor to appreciate a joke, and the sheriff's witticism fell dead upon an unresponsive audience.

"We want to have a talk with the nigger that killed Cap'n Walker."

"You can talk to that nigger in the court-house, when he's brought out for trial. Court will be in session here next week. I know what you fellows want, but you can't get my prisoner to-day. Do you want to take the bread out of a poor man's mouth? I get seventy-five cents a day for keeping this prisoner, and he's the only one in jail. I can't have my family suffer just to please you fellows."

One or two young men in the crowd laughed at the idea of Sheriff Campbell's suffering for want of seventy-five cents a day; but they were frowned into silence by those who stood near them.

"Ef yer don't let us in," cried a voice, "we'll bu's' the do' open."

"Bust away," answered the sheriff, raising his voice so that all could hear. "But I give you fair warning. The first man that tries it will be filled with buckshot. I'm sheriff of this county; I know my duty, and I mean to do it."

"What's the use of kicking, Sheriff?" argued one of the leaders of the mob. "The nigger is sure to hang anyhow; he richly deserves it; and we've got to do something to teach the niggers their places, or white people won't be able to live in the county."

"There's no use talking, boys," responded the sheriff. "I'm a white man outside, but in this jail I'm sheriff; and if this nigger's to be hung in this county, I propose to do the hanging. So you fellows might as well right-about-face, and march back to Troy. You've had a pleasant trip, and the exercise will be good for you. You know *me*. I've got powder and ball, and I've faced fire before now, with nothing between me and the enemy, and I don't mean to surrender this jail while I'm able to shoot." Having thus announced his determination, the sheriff closed and fastened the wicket, and looked around for the best position from which to defend the building.

The crowd drew off a little, and the leaders conversed together in low tones.

The Branson County jail was a small, two-story brick building, strongly constructed, with no attempt at architectural ornamentation. Each story was divided into two large cells by a passage running from front to rear. A grated iron door gave entrance from the passage to each of the four cells. The jail seldom had many prisoners in it, and the lower windows had been boarded up. When the sheriff had closed the wicket, he ascended the steep wooden stairs to the upper floor. There was no window at the front of the upper passage, and the most available position from which to watch the movements of the crowd below was the front window of the cell occupied by the solitary prisoner.

The sheriff unlocked the door and entered the cell. The prisoner was crouched in a corner, his yellow face, blanched with terror, looking ghastly in the semi-darkness of the room. A cold perspiration had gathered on his forehead, and his teeth were chattering with affright.

"For God's sake, Sheriff," he murmured hoarsely, "don't let 'em lynch me; I did n't kill the old man."

The sheriff glanced at the cowering wretch with a look of mingled contempt and loathing.

"Get up," he said sharply. "You will probably be hung sooner or later, but it shall not be to-day, if I can help it. I'll unlock your fetters, and if I can't hold the jail, you'll have to make the best fight you can. If I'm shot, I'll consider my responsibility at an end."

There were iron fetters on the prisoner's ankles, and handcuffs on his wrists. These the sheriff unlocked, and they fell clanking to the floor.

"Keep back from the window," said the sheriff. "They might shoot if they saw you."

The sheriff drew toward the window a pine bench which formed a part of the scanty furniture of the cell, and laid his revolver upon it. Then he took his gun in hand, and took his stand at the side of the window where he could with least exposure of himself watch the movements of the crowd below.

The lynchers had not anticipated any determined resistance. Of course they had looked for a formal protest, and perhaps a sufficient show of opposition to excuse the sheriff in the eye of any stickler for legal formalities. They had not, however, come prepared to fight a battle, and no one of them seemed willing to lead an attack upon the jail. The leaders of the party conferred together with a good deal of animated gesticulation, which was visible to the sheriff from his outlook, though the distance was too great for him to hear what was said. At length one of them broke away from the group, and rode back to the main body of the lynchers, who were restlessly awaiting orders.

"Well, boys," said the messenger, "we'll have to let it go for the present. The sheriff says he'll shoot, and he's got the drop on us this time. There ain't any of us that want to follow Cap'n Walker jest yet. Besides, the sheriff is a good fellow, and we don't want to hurt 'im. But," he added, as if to reassure the crowd, which began to show signs of disappointment, "the nigger might as well say his prayers, for he ain't got long to live."

There was a murmur of dissent from the mob, and several voices insisted that an attack be made on the jail. But pacific counsels finally prevailed, and the mob sullenly withdrew.

The sheriff stood at the window until they had disappeared around the bend in the road. He did not relax his watchfulness when the last one was out of sight. Their withdrawal might be a mere feint, to be followed by a further attempt. So closely, indeed, was his attention drawn to the outside, that he neither saw nor heard the prisoner creep stealthily across the floor, reach out his hand and secure the revolver which lay on the bench behind the sheriff, and creep as noiselessly back to his place in the corner of the room.

A moment after the last of the lynching party had disappeared there was a shot fired from the woods across the road; a bullet whistled by the window and buried itself in the wooden casing a few inches from where the sheriff was standing. Quick as thought, with the instinct borne of a semi-guerilla army experience, he raised his gun and fired twice at the point from which a faint puff of smoke showed the hostile bullet to have been sent. He stood a moment watching, and then rested his gun against the window, and reached behind him mechanically for the other weapon. It was not on the bench. As the sheriff realized this fact, he turned his head and looked into the muzzle of the revolver.

"Stay where you are, Sheriff," said the prisoner, his eyes glistening, his face almost ruddy with excitement.

The sheriff mentally cursed his own carelessness for allowing him to be caught in such a predicament. He had not expected anything of the kind. He had relied on the negro's cowardice and subordination in the presence of an armed white man as a matter of course. The sheriff was a brave man, but realized that the prisoner had him at an immense disadvantage. The two men stood thus for a moment, fighting a harmless duel with their eyes.

"Well, what do you mean to do?" asked the sheriff with apparent calmness.

"To get away, of course," said the prisoner, in a tone which caused the sheriff to look at him more closely, and with an involuntary feeling of apprehension; if the man was not mad, he was in a state of mind akin to madness, and quite as dangerous. The sheriff felt that he must speak the prisoner fair, and watch for a chance to turn the tables on him. The keen-eyed, desperate man before him was a different being altogether from the groveling wretch who had begged so piteously for life a few minutes before.

At length the sheriff spoke:—

"Is this your gratitude to me for saving your life at the risk of my own? If I had not done so, you would now be swinging from the limb of some neighboring tree."

"True," said the prisoner, "you saved my life, but for how long? When you came in, you said Court would sit next week. When the crowd went away they said I had not long to live. It is merely a choice of two ropes."

"While there's life there's hope." replied the sheriff. He uttered this commonplace mechanically, while his brain was busy in trying to think out some way of escape. "If you are innocent you can prove it."

The mulatto kept his eye upon the sheriff. "I did n't kill the old man," he replied; "but I shall never be able to clear myself. I was at his house at nine o'clock. I stole from it the coat that was on my back when I was taken. I would be convicted, even with a fair trial, unless the real murderer were discovered beforehand."

The sheriff knew this only too well. While he was thinking what argument next to use, the prisoner continued:—

"Throw me the keys—no, unlock the door."

The sheriff stood a moment irresolute. The mulatto's eye glittered ominously. The sheriff crossed the room and unlocked the door leading into the passage.

"Now go down and unlock the outside door."

The heart of the sheriff leaped within him. Perhaps he might make a dash for liberty, and gain the outside. He descended the narrow stairs, the prisoner keeping close behind him.

The sheriff inserted the huge iron key into the lock. The rusty bolt yielded slowly. It still remained for him to pull the door open.

"Stop!" thundered the mulatto, who seemed to divine the sheriff's purpose. "Move a muscle, and I'll blow your brains out."

The sheriff obeyed; he realized that his chance had not yet come.

"Now keep on that side of the passage, and go back upstairs."

Keeping the sheriff under cover of the revolver, the mulatto followed him up the stairs. The sheriff expected the prisoner to lock him into the cell and make his own escape. He had about come to the conclusion that the best thing he could do under the circumstances was to submit quietly, and take his chances of recapturing the prisoner after the alarm had been given. The sheriff had faced death more than once upon the battlefield. A few minutes before, well armed, and with a brick wall between him and them, he had dared a hundred men to fight; but he felt instinctively that the desperate man confronting him was not to be trifled with, and he was too prudent a man to risk his life against such heavy odds. He had Polly to look after, and there was a limit beyond which devotion to duty would be quixotic and even foolish.

"I want to get away," said the prisoner, "and I don't want to be captured; for if I am I know I will be hung on the spot. I am afraid," he added somewhat reflectively, "that in order to save myself I shall have to kill you."

"Good God!" exclaimed the sheriff in involuntary terror; "you would not kill the man to whom you owe your own life."

"You speak more truly than you know," replied the mulatto. "I indeed owe my life to you."

The sheriff started. He was capable of surprise, even in that moment of extreme peril. "Who are you?" he asked in amazement.

"Tom, Cicely's son," returned the other. He had closed the door and stood talking to the sheriff through the grated opening. "Don't you remember Cicely—Cicely whom you sold, with her child, to the speculator on his way to Alabama?"

The sheriff did remember. He had been sorry for it many a time since. It had been the old story of debts, mortgages, and bad crops. He had quarreled with the mother. The price offered for her and her child had been unusually large, and he had yielded to the combination of anger and pecuniary stress.

"Good God!" he gasped, "you would not murder your own father?"

"My father?" replied the mulatto. "It were well enough for me to claim the relationship, but it comes with poor grace from you to ask anything by reason of it. What father's duty have you ever performed for me? Did you give me your name, or even your protection? Other white men gave their colored sons freedom and money, and sent them to the free States. *You* sold *me* to the rice swamps."

"I at least gave you the life you cling to," murmured the sheriff.

"Life?" said the prisoner, with a sarcastic laugh. "What kind of a life? You gave me your own blood, your own features,—no man need look at us together twice to see that,—and you gave me a black mother. Poor wretch! She died under the lash, because she had enough womanhood to call her soul her own. You gave me a white man's spirit, and you made me a slave, and crushed it out."

"But you are free now," said the sheriff. He had not doubted, could not doubt, the mulatto's word. He knew whose passions coursed beneath that swarthy skin and burned in the black eyes opposite his own. He saw in this mulatto what he himself might have become had not the safeguards of parental restraint and public opinion been thrown around him.

"Free to do what?" replied the mulatto. "Free in name, but despised and scorned and set aside by the people to whose race I belong far more than to my mother's."

"There are schools," said the sheriff. "You have been to school." He had noticed that the mulatto spoke more eloquently and used better language than most Branson County people.

"I have been to school, and dreamed when I went that it would work some marvelous change in my condition. But what did I learn? I learned to feel that no degree of learning or wisdom will change the color of my skin and that I shall always wear what in my own country is a badge of degradation. When I think about it seriously I do not care particularly for such a life. It is the animal in me, not the man, that flees the gallows. I owe you nothing," he went on, "and expect nothing of you; and it would be no more than justice if I should avenge upon you my mother's wrongs and my own. But still I hate to shoot you; I have never yet taken human life—for I did *not* kill the old captain. Will you promise to give no alarm and make no attempt to capture me until morning, if I do not shoot?"

So absorbed were the two men in their colloquy and their own tumultuous thoughts that neither of them had heard the door below move upon its hinges. Neither of them had heard a light step come stealthily up the stairs, nor seen a slender form creep along the darkening passage toward the mulatto.

The sheriff hesitated. The struggle between his love of life and his sense of duty was a terrific one. It may seem strange that a man who could sell his own child into slavery should hesitate at such a moment, when his life was trembling in the balance. But the baleful influence of human slavery poisoned the very fountains of life, and created new standards of right. The sheriff was conscientious; his conscience had merely been warped by his environment. Let no one ask what his answer would have been; he was spared the necessity of a decision.

"Stop," said the mulatto, "you need not promise. I could not trust you if you did. It is your life for mine; there is but one safe way for me; you must die."

He raised his arm to fire, when there was a flash—a report from the passage behind him. His arm fell heavily at his side, and the pistol dropped at his feet.

The sheriff recovered first from his surprise, and throwing open the door secured the fallen weapon. Then seizing the prisoner he thrust him into the cell and locked the door upon him; after which he turned to Polly, who leaned half-fainting against the wall, her hands clasped over her heart.

"Oh, father, I was just in time!" she cried hysterically, and, wildly sobbing, threw herself into her father's arms.

"I watched until they all went away," she said. "I heard the shot from the woods and I saw you shoot. Then when you did not come out I feared something had happened, that perhaps you had been wounded. I got out the other pistol and ran over here. When I found the door open, I knew something was wrong, and when I heard voices I crept upstairs, and reached the top just in time to hear him say he would kill you. Oh, it was a narrow escape!"

When she had grown somewhat calmer, the sheriff left her standing there and went back into the cell. The prisoner's arm was bleeding from a flesh wound. His bravado had given place to a stony apathy. There was no sign in his face of fear or disappointment or feeling of any kind. The sheriff sent Polly to the house for cloth, and bound up the prisoner's wound with a rude skill acquired during his army life.

"I'll have a doctor come and dress the wound in the morning," he said to the prisoner. "It will do very well until then, if you will keep quiet. If the doctor asks you how the wound was caused, you can say that you were struck by the bullet fired from the woods. It would do you no good to have it known that you were shot while attempting to escape."

The prisoner uttered no word of thanks or apology, but sat in sullen silence. When the wounded arm had been bandaged, Polly and her father returned to the house.

The sheriff was in an unusually thoughtful mood that evening. He put salt in his coffee at supper, and poured vinegar over his pancakes. To many of Polly's questions he returned random answers. When he had gone to bed he lay awake for several hours.

In the silent watches of the night, when he was alone with God, there came into his mind a flood of unaccustomed thoughts. An hour or two before, standing face to face with death, he had experienced a sensation similar to that which drowning men are said to feel—a kind of clarifying of the moral faculty, in which the veil of the flesh, with its obscuring passions and prejudices, is pushed aside for a moment, and all the acts of one's life stand out, in the clear light of truth, in their correct proportions and relations,—a state of mind in which one sees himself as God may be supposed to see him. In the reaction following his rescue, this feeling had given place for a time to far different emotions. But now, in the silence of midnight, something of this clearness of spirit returned to the sheriff. He saw that he had owed some duty to this son of his,—that neither law nor custom could destroy a responsibility inherent in the nature of mankind. He could not thus, in the eyes of God at least, shake off the consequences of his sin. Had he never sinned, this wayward spirit would never have come back from the vanished past to haunt him. As these thoughts came, his anger against the mulatto died away, and in its place there sprang up a great pity. The hand of parental authority might have restrained the passions he had seen burning in the prisoner's eyes when the desperate man spoke the words which had seemed to doom his father to death. The sheriff felt that he might have saved this fiery spirit from the slough of slavery; that he might have sent him to the free North, and given him there, or in some other land, an opportunity to turn to usefulness and honorable pursuits the talents that had run to crime, perhaps to madness; he might, still less, have given this son of his the poor simulacrum of liberty which men of his caste could possess in a slave-holding community; or least of all, but still something, he might have kept the boy on the plantation, where the burdens of slavery would have fallen lightly upon him.

The sheriff recalled his own youth. He had inherited an honored name to keep untarnished; he had had a future to make; the picture of a fair young bride had beckoned him on to happiness. The poor wretch now stretched upon a pallet of straw between the brick walls of the jail had had none of these things,—no name, no father, no mother—in the true meaning of motherhood,—and until the past few years no possible future, and then one vague and shadowy in its outline, and dependent for form and substance upon the slow solution of a problem in which there were many unknown quantities.

From what he might have done to what he might yet do was an easy transition for the awakened conscience of the sheriff. It occurred to him, purely as a hypothesis, that he might permit his prisoner to escape; but his oath of office, his duty as sheriff, stood in the way of such a course, and the sheriff dismissed the idea from his mind. He could, however, investigate the circumstances of the murder, and move Heaven and earth to discover the real criminal, for he no longer doubted the prisoner's innocence; he could employ counsel for the accused, and perhaps influence public opinion in his favor. An acquittal once secured, some plan could be devised by which the sheriff might in some degree atone for his crime against this son of his—against society—against God.

When the sheriff had reached this conclusion he fell into an unquiet slumber, from which he awoke late the next morning.

He went over to the jail before breakfast and found the prisoner lying on his pallet, his face turned to the wall; he did not move when the sheriff rattled the door.

"Good-morning," said the latter, in a tone intended to waken the prisoner.

There was no response. The sheriff looked more keenly at the recumbent figure; there was an unnatural rigidity about its attitude.

He hastily unlocked the door and, entering the cell, bent over the prostrate form. There was no sound of breathing; he turned the body over—it was cold and stiff. The prisoner had torn the bandage from his wound and bled to death during the night. He had evidently been dead several hours.

A Matter of Principle

I

"WHAT OUR COUNTRY NEEDS in its treatment of the race problem," observed Mr. Cicero Clayton at one of the monthly meetings of the Blue Vein Society, of which he was a prominent member, "is a clearer conception of the brotherhood of man."

The same sentiment in much the same words had often fallen from Mr. Clayton's lips,—so often, in fact, that the younger members of the society sometimes spoke of him—among themselves of course—as "Brotherhood Clayton." The sobriquet derived its point from the application he made of the principle involved in this oft-repeated proposition.

The fundamental article of Mr. Clayton's social creed was that he himself was not a negro.

"I know," he would say, "that the white people lump us all together as negroes, and condemn us all to the same social ostracism. But I don't accept this classification, for my part, and I imagine that, as the chief party in interest, I have a right to my opinion. People who belong by half or more of their blood to the most virile and progressive race of modern times have as much right to call themselves white as others have to call them negroes."

Mr. Clayton spoke warmly, for he was well informed, and had thought much upon the subject; too much, indeed, for he had not been able to escape entirely the tendency of too much concentration upon one subject to make even the clearest minds morbid.

"Of course we can't enforce our claims, or protect ourselves from being robbed of our birthright; but we can at least have principles, and try to live up to them the best we can. If we are not

150

accepted as white, we can at any rate make it clear that we object to being called black. Our protest cannot fail in time to impress itself upon the better class of white people; for the Anglo-Saxon race loves justice, and will eventually do it, where it does not conflict with their own interests."

Whether or not the fact that Mr. Clayton meant no sarcasm, and was conscious of no inconsistency in this eulogy, tended to establish the racial identity he claimed may safely be left to the discerning reader.

In living up to his creed Mr. Clayton declined to associate to any considerable extent with black people. This was sometimes a little inconvenient, and occasionally involved a sacrifice of some pleasure for himself and his family, because they would not attend entertainments where many black people were likely to be present. But they had a social refuge in a little society of people like themselves; they attended, too, a church, of which nearly all the members were white, and they were connected with a number of the religious and benevolent associations open to all good citizens, where they came into contact with the better class of white people, and were treated, in their capacity of members, with a courtesy and consideration scarcely different from that accorded to other citizens.

Mr. Clayton's racial theory was not only logical enough, but was in his own case backed up by substantial arguments. He had begun life with a small patrimony, and had invested his money in a restaurant, which by careful and judicious attention had grown from a cheap eating-house into the most popular and successful confectionery and catering establishment in Groveland. His business occupied a double store on Oakwood Avenue. He owned houses and lots, and stocks and bonds, had good credit at the banks, and lived in a style befitting his income and business standing. In person he was of olive complexion, with slightly curly hair. His features approached the Cuban or Latin-American type rather than the familiar broad characteristic of the mulatto, this suggestion of something foreign being heightened by a Vandyke beard and a carefully waxed and pointed mustache. When he walked to church on Sunday mornings with his daughter Alice, they were a couple of such striking appearance as surely to attract attention.

Miss Alice Clayton was queen of her social set. She was young, she was handsome. She was nearly white; she frankly confessed her sorrow that she was not entirely so. She was accomplished and amiable, dressed in good taste, and had for her father by all odds the richest colored man—the term is used with apologies to Mr. Clayton, explaining that it does not necessarily mean a negro—in Groveland. So pronounced was her superiority that really she had but one social rival worthy of the name,—Miss Lura Watkins, whose father kept a prosperous livery stable and lived in almost as good style as the Claytons. Miss Watkins, while good-looking enough, was not so young nor quite so white as Miss Clayton. She was popular, however, among their mutual acquaintances, and there was a good-natured race between the two as to which should make the first and best marriage.

Marriages among Miss Clayton's set were serious affairs. Of course marriage is always a serious matter, whether it be a success or a failure, and there are those who believe that any marriage is better than no marriage. But among Miss Clayton's friends and associates matrimony took on an added seriousness because of the very narrow limits within which it could take place. Miss Clayton and her friends, by reason of their assumed superiority to black people, or perhaps as much by reason of a somewhat morbid shrinking from the curiosity manifested toward married people of strongly contrasting colors, would not marry black men, and except in rare instances white men would not marry them. They were therefore restricted for a choice to the young men of their own complexion. But these, unfortunately for the girls, had a wider choice. In any State where the laws permit freedom of the marriage contract, a man, by virtue of his sex, can find a wife of whatever complexion he prefers; of course he must not always ask too much in other respects, for most women like to better their social position when they marry. To the number thus lost by "going on the other side," as the phrase went, add the worthless contingent whom no self-respecting woman would marry, and the choice was still further restricted; so that it had become fashionable, when the supply of eligible men ran short, for those of Miss Clayton's set who could afford it to go traveling; ostensibly for pleasure, but with the serious hope that they might meet their fate away from home.

Miss Clayton had perhaps a larger option than any of her associ-

social promotion via marriage

ates. Among such men as there were she could have taken her choice. Her beauty, her position, her accomplishments, her father's wealth, all made her eminently desirable. But, on the other hand, the same things rendered her more difficult to reach, and harder to please. To get access to her heart, too, it was necessary to run the gauntlet of her parents, which, until she had reached the age of twenty-three, no one had succeeded in doing safely. Many had called, but none had been chosen.

There was, however, one spot left unguarded, and through it Cupid, a veteran sharpshooter, sent a dart. Mr. Clayton had taken into his service and into his household a poor relation, a sort of cousin several times removed. This boy—his name was Jack—had gone into Mr. Clayton's service at a very youthful age,—twelve or thirteen. He had helped about the housework, washed the dishes, swept the floors, taken care of the lawn and the stable for three or four years, while he attended school. His cousin had then taken him into the store, where he had swept the floor, washed the windows, and done a class of work that kept fully impressed upon him the fact that he was a poor dependent. Nevertheless he was a cheerful lad, who took what he could get and was properly grateful, but always meant to get more. By sheer force of industry and affability and shrewdness, he forced his employer to promote him in time to a position of recognized authority in the establishment. Any one outside of the family would have perceived in him a very suitable husband for Miss Clayton; he was of about the same age, or a year or two older, was as fair of complexion as she, when she was not powdered, and was passably good-looking, with a bearing of which the natural manliness had been no more warped than his training and racial status had rendered inevitable; for he had early learned the law of growth, that to bend is better than to break. He was sometimes sent to accompany Miss Clayton to places in the evening, when she had no other escort, and it is quite likely that she discovered his good points before her parents did. That they should in time perceive them was inevitable. But even then, so accustomed were they to looking down upon the object of their former bounty, that they only spoke of the matter jocularly.

"Well, Alice," her father would say in his bluff way, "you'll not be absolutely obliged to die an old maid. If we can't find anything better for you, there's always Jack. As long as he does n't take to some other girl, you can fall back on him as a last chance. He'd be glad to take you to get into the business."

Miss Alice had considered the joke a very poor one when first made, but by occasional repetition she became somewhat familiar with it. In time it got around to Jack himself, to whom it seemed no joke at all. He had long considered it a consummation devoutly to be wished, and when he became aware that the possibility of such a match had occurred to the other parties in interest, he made up his mind that the idea should in due course of time become an accomplished fact. He had even suggested as much to Alice, in a casual way, to feel his ground; and while she had treated the matter lightly, he was not without hope that she had been impressed by the suggestion. Before he had had time, however, to follow up this lead, Miss Clayton, in the spring of 187-, went away on a visit to Washington.

The occasion of her visit was a presidential inauguration. The new President owed his nomination mainly to the votes of the Southern delegates in the convention, and was believed to be correspondingly well disposed to the race from which the Southern delegates were for the most part recruited. Friends of rival and unsuccessful candidates for the nomination had more than hinted that the Southern delegates were very substantially rewarded for their support at the time when it was given; whether this was true or not the parties concerned know best. At any rate the colored politicians did not see it in that light, for they were gathered from near and far to press their claims for recognition and patronage. On the evening following the White House inaugural ball, the colored people of Washington gave an "inaugural" ball at a large public hall. It was under the management of their leading citizens, among them several high officials holding over from the last administration, and a number of professional and business men. This ball was the most noteworthy social event that colored circles up to that time had ever known. There were many visitors from various parts of the country. Miss Clayton attended the ball, the honors of which she carried away easily. She danced with several partners, and was introduced to innumerable people whom she had never seen before, and whom she hardly expected ever to meet again. She went away from the ball, at four o'clock in the morning, in a glow of triumph, and with a confused impression of senators and representatives and lawyers and doctors of all shades, who had sought an introduction, led her through the dance, and overwhelmed her with compliments. She returned home the next day but one, after the most delightful week of her life.

II

One afternoon, about three weeks after her return from Washington, Alice received a letter through the mail. The envelope bore the words "House of Representatives" printed in one corner, and in the opposite corner, in a bold running hand, a Congressman's frank, "Hamilton M. Brown, M. C." The letter read as follows:—

> House of Representatives,
> Washington, D. C., March 30, 187-.

Miss Alice Clayton, Groveland.

Dear Friend (if I may be permitted to call you so after so brief an acquaintance),—I remember with sincerest pleasure our recent meeting at the inaugural ball, and the sensation created by your beauty, your amiable manners, and your graceful dancing. Time has so strengthened the impression I then received, that I should have felt inconsolable had I thought it impossible ever to again behold the charms which had brightened the occasion of our meeting and eclipsed by their brilliancy the leading belles of the capital. I had hoped, however, to have the pleasure of meeting you again, and circumstances have fortunately placed it in my power to do so at an early date. You have doubtless learned that the contest over the election in the Sixth Congressional District of South Carolina has been decided in my favor, and that I now have the honor of representing my native State at the national capital. I have just been appointed a member of a special committee to visit and inspect the Sault River and the Straits of Mackinac, with reference to the needs of lake navigation. I have made arrangements to start a week ahead of the other members of the committee, whom I am to meet in Detroit on the 20th. I shall leave here on the 2d, and will arrive in Groveland on the 3d, by the 7.30 evening express. I shall remain in Groveland several days, in the course of which I shall be pleased to call, and renew the acquaintance so auspiciously begun in Washington, which it is my fondest hope may ripen into a warmer friendship.

If you do not regard my visit as presumptuous, and do not write me in the mean while forbidding it, I shall do myself the pleasure of waiting on you the morning after my arrival in Groveland.

With renewed expressions of my sincere admiration and profound esteem, I remain,

SINCERELY YOURS,
HAMILTON M. BROWN, M.C.

To Alice, and especially to her mother, this bold and flowery letter had very nearly the force of a formal declaration. They read it over again and again, and spent most of the afternoon discussing it. There were few young men in Groveland eligible as husbands for so superior a person as Alice Clayton, and an addition to the number would be very acceptable. But the mere fact of his being a Congressman was not sufficient to qualify him; there were other considerations.

"I've never heard of this Honorable Hamilton M. Brown," said Mr. Clayton. The letter had been laid before him at the supper-table. "It's strange, Alice, that you have n't said anything about him before. You must have met lots of swell folks not to recollect a Congressman."

"But he was n't a Congressman then," answered Alice; "he was only a claimant. I remember Senator Bruce, and Mr. Douglass; but there were so many doctors and lawyers and politicians that I could n't keep track of them all. Still I have a faint impression of a Mr. Brown who danced with me."

She went into the parlor and brought out the dancing programme she had used at the Washington ball. She had decorated it with a bow of blue ribbon and preserved it as a souvenir of her visit.

"Yes," she said, after examining it, "I must have danced with him. Here are the initials—'H. M. B.' "

"What color is he?" asked Mr. Clayton, as he plied his knife and fork.

"I have a notion that he was rather dark—darker than any one I had ever danced with before."

"Why did you dance with him?" asked her father. "You were n't obliged to go back on your principles because you were away from home."

"Well, father, 'when you're in Rome'—you know the rest. Mrs. Clearweather introduced me to several dark men, to him among others. They were her friends, and common decency required me to be courteous."

"If this man is black, we don't want to encourage him. If he's the right sort, we'll invite him to the house."

"And make him feel at home," added Mrs. Clayton, on hospitable thoughts intent.

"We must ask Sadler about him to-morrow," said Mr. Clayton, when he had drunk his coffee and lighted his cigar. "If he's the right man he shall have cause to remember his visit to Groveland. We'll show him that Washington is not the only town on earth."

The uncertainty of the family with regard to Mr. Brown was soon removed. Mr. Solomon Sadler, who was supposed to know everything worth knowing concerning the colored race, and everybody of importance connected with it, dropped in after supper to make an evening call. Sadler was familiar with the history of every man of negro ancestry who had distinguished himself in any walk of life. He could give the pedigree of Alexander Pushkin, the titles of scores of Dumas's novels (even Sadler had not time to learn them all), and could recite the whole of Wendell Phillips's lecture on Toussaint l'Ouverture. He claimed a personal acquaintance with Mr. Frederick Douglass, and had been often in Washington, where he was well known and well received in good colored society.

"Let me see," he said reflectively, when asked for information about the Honorable Hamilton M. Brown. "Yes, I think I know him. He studied at Oberlin just after the war. He was about leaving there when I entered. There were two H. M. Browns there—a Hamilton M. Brown and a Henry M. Brown. One was stout and dark and the other was slim and quite light; you could scarcely tell him from a dark white man. They used to call them 'light Brown' and 'dark Brown.' I did n't know either of them except by sight, for they were there only a few weeks after I went in. As I remember them, Hamilton was the fair one—a very good-looking, gentlemanly fellow, and, as a I heard, a good student and a fine speaker."

"Do you remember what kind of hair he had?" asked Mr. Clayton.

"Very good indeed; straight, as I remember it. He looked something like a Spaniard or a Portuguese."

"Now that you describe him," said Alice, "I remember quite well dancing with such a gentleman; and I'm wrong about my 'H. M. B.' The dark man must have been some one else; there are two others on my card that I can't remember distinctly, and he was probably one of those."

"I guess he's all right, Alice," said her father when Sadler had gone away. "He evidently means business, and we must treat him white. Of course he must stay with us; there are no hotels in Groveland while he is here. Let's see—he'll be here in three days. That is n't very long, but I guess we can get ready. I'll write a letter this afternoon—or you write it, and invite him to the house, and say I'll meet him at the depot. And you may have *carte blanche* for making the preparations."

"We must have some people to meet him."

"Certainly; a reception is the proper thing. Sit down immediately and write the letter and I'll mail it first thing in the morning, so he'll get it before he has time to make other arrangements. And you and your mother put your heads together and make out a list of guests, and I'll have the invitations printed to-morrow. We will show the darkeys of Groveland how to entertain a Congressman."

It will be noted that in moments of abstraction or recitement Mr. Clayton sometimes relapsed into forms of speech not entirely consistent with his principles. But some allowance must be made for his atmosphere; he could no more escape from it than the leopard can change his spots, or the—. In deference to Mr. Clayton's feelings the quotation will be left incomplete.

Alice wrote the letter on the spot and it was duly mailed, and sped on its winged way to Washington.

The preparations for the reception were made as thoroughly and elaborately as possible on so short a notice. The invitations were issued; the house was cleaned from attic to cellar; an orchestra was engaged for the evening; elaborate floral decorations were planned and the flowers ordered. Even the refreshments, which ordinarily, in the household of a caterer, would be mere matter of familiar detail, became a subject of serious consultation and study.

The approaching event was a matter of very much interest to the fortunate ones who were honored with invitations, and this for several reasons. They were anxious to meet this sole representative of their race in the —th Congress, and as he was not one of the old-line colored leaders, but a new star risen on the political horizon, there was a special curiosity to see who he was and what he looked like. Moreover, the Claytons did not often entertain a large company, but when they did, it was on a scale commensurate with their means and position, and to be present on such an occasion was a thing to remember and to talk about. And, most important consideration of all, some remarks dropped by members of the Clayton family had given rise to the rumor that the Congressman was seeking a wife. This invested his visit with a romantic interest, and gave the reception a practical value; for there were other marriageable girls besides Miss Clayton, and if one was left another might be taken.

III

On the evening of April 3d, at fifteen minutes of six o'clock, Mr. Clayton, accompanied by Jack, entered the livery carriage waiting at his gate and ordered the coachman to drive to the Union Depot. He had taken Jack along, partly for company, and partly that Jack might relieve the Congressman of any trouble about his baggage, and make himself useful in case of emergency. Jack was willing enough to go, for he had foreseen in the visitor a rival for Alice's hand,—indeed he had heard more or less of the subject for several days,—and was glad to make a reconnaissance before the enemy arrived upon the field of battle. He had made—at least he had thought so—considerable progress with Alice during the three weeks since her return from Washington, and once or twice Alice had been perilously near the tender stage. This visit had disturbed the situation and threatened to ruin his chances; but he did not mean to give up without a struggle.

Arrived at the main entrance, Mr. Clayton directed the carriage to wait, and entered the station with Jack. The Union Depot at Groveland was an immense oblong structure, covering a dozen parallel tracks and furnishing terminal passenger facilities for half a dozen railroads. The tracks ran east and west, and the depot was entered from the south, at about the middle of the building. On either side of the entrance, the waiting-rooms, refreshment rooms, baggage and express departments, and other administrative offices, extended in a row for the entire length of the building; and beyond them and parallel with them stretched a long open space, separated from the tracks by an iron fence or *grille.* There were two entrance gates in the fence, at which tickets must be shown before access could be had to trains, and two other gates, by which arriving passengers came out.

Mr. Clayton looked at the blackboard on the wall underneath the station clock, and observed that the 7.30 train from Washington was five minutes late. Accompanied by Jack he walked up and down the platform until the train, with the usual accompaniment of panting steam and clanging bell and rumbling trucks, pulled into the station, and drew up on the third or fourth track from the iron railing. Mr. Clayton stationed himself at the gate nearest the rear end of the train, reasoning that the Congressman would ride in a parlor car, and would naturally come out by the gate nearest the point at which he left the train.

"You'd better go and stand by the other gate, Jack," he said to his companion, "and stop him if he goes out that way."

The train was well filled and a stream of passengers poured through. Mr. Clayton scanned the crowd carefully as they approached the gate, and scrutinized each passenger as he came through, without seeing any one that met the description of Congressman Brown, as given by Sadler, or any one that could in his opinion be the gentleman for whom he was looking. When the last one had passed through he was left to the conclusion that his expected guest had gone out by the other gate. Mr. Clayton hastened thither.

"Did n't he come out this way, Jack?" he asked.

"No, sir," replied the young man, "I have n't seen him."

"That's strange," mused Mr. Clayton, somewhat anxiously. "He would hardly fail to come without giving us notice. Surely we must have missed him. We'd better look around a little. You go that way and I'll go this."

Mr. Clayton turned and walked several rods along the platform to the men's waiting-room, and standing near the door glanced around to see if he could find the object of his search. The only colored person in the room was a stout and very black man, wearing a broadcloth suit and a silk hat, and seated a short distance from the door. On the seat by his side stood a couple of valises. On one of them, the one nearest him, on which his arm rested, was written, in white letters, plainly legible,—

H. M. Brown, M. C.
    Washington, D. C.

Mr. Clayton's feelings at this discovery can better be imagined than described. He hastily left the waiting-room, before the black gentleman, who was looking the other way, was even aware of his presence, and, walking rapidly up and down the platform, communed with himself upon what course of action the situation demanded. He had invited to his house, had come down to meet, had made elaborate preparations to entertain on the following evening, a light-colored man,—a white man by his theory, an acceptable guest, a possible husband for his daughter, an avowed suitor for her hand. If the Congressman had turned out to be brown, even dark brown, with fairly good hair, though he might not have desired him as a son-in-law, yet he could have welcomed him as a guest. But even this softening of the blow was denied him, for the man in the waiting-room was palpably, aggressively black, with pronounced African features and woolly hair, without apparently a single drop of redeeming white blood. Could he, in the face of his well-known principles, his lifelong rule of conduct, take this negro into his home and introduce him to his friends? Could he subject his wife and daughter to the rude shock of such a disappointment? It would be bad enough for them to learn of the ghastly mistake, but to have him in the house would be twisting the arrow in the wound.

Mr. Clayton had the instincts of a gentleman, and realized the delicacy of the situation. But to get out of his difficulty without wounding the feelings of the Congressman required not only diplomacy but dispatch. Whatever he did must be done promptly; for if he waited many minutes the Congressman would probably take a carriage and be driven to Mr. Clayton's residence.

A ray of hope came for a moment to illumine the gloom of the situation. Perhaps the black man was merely sitting there, and not the owner of the valise! For there were two valises, one on each side of the supposed Congressman. For obvious reasons he did not care to make the inquiry himself, so he looked around for his companion, who came up a moment later.

"Jack," he exclaimed excitedly, "I'm afraid we're in the worst kind of a hole, unless there's some mistake! Run down to the men's waiting-room and you'll see a man and a valise, and you'll understand what I mean. Ask that darkey if he is the Honorable Mr. Brown, Congressman from South Carolina. If he says yes, come back right away and let me know, without giving him time to ask any questions, and put your wits to work to help me out of the scrape."

"I wonder what's the matter?" said Jack to himself, but did as he was told. In a moment he came running back.

"Yes, sir," he announced; "he says he's the man."

"Jack," said Mr. Clayton desperately, "if you want to show your appreciation of what I've done for you, you must suggest some way out of this. I'd never dare to take that negro to my house, and yet I'm obliged to treat him like a gentleman."

Jack's eyes had worn a somewhat reflective look since he had gone to make the inquiry. Suddenly his face brightened with intelligence, and then, as a newsboy ran into the station calling his wares, hardened into determination.

"*Clarion*, special extry 'dition! All about de epidemic er dipt'eria!" clamored the newsboy with shrill childish treble, as he made his way toward the waiting-room. Jack darted after him, and saw the man to whom he had spoken buy a paper. He ran back to his employer, and dragged him over toward the ticket-seller's window.

"I have it, sir!" he exclaimed, seizing a telegraph blank and writing rapidly, and reading aloud as he wrote. "How's this for a way out?"—

DEAR SIR,—I write you this note here in the depot to inform you of an unfortunate event which has interfered with my plans and those of my family for your entertainment while in Groveland. Yesterday my daughter Alice complained of a sore throat, which by this afternoon had developed into a case of malignant diphtheria. In consequence our house has been quarantined; and while I have felt myself obliged to come down to the depot, I do not feel that I ought to expose you to the possibility of infection, and I therefore send you this by another hand. The bearer will conduct you to a carriage which I have ordered placed at your service, and unless you should prefer some other hotel, you will be driven to the Forest Hill House, where I beg you will consider yourself my guest during your stay in the city, and make the fullest use of every convenience it may offer. From present indications I fear no one of our family will be able to see you, which we shall regret beyond expression, as we have made elaborate arrangements for your entertainment. I still hope, however, that you may enjoy your visit, as there are many places of interest in the city, and many friends will doubtless be glad to make your acquaintance.

With assurances of my profound regret, I am

SINCERELY YOURS,
CICERO CLAYTON.

"Splendid!" cried Mr. Clayton. "You've helped me out of a horrible scrape. Now, go and take him to the hotel and see him comfortably located, and tell them to charge the bill to me."

"I suspect, sir," suggested Jack, "that I'd better not go up to the house, and you'll have to stay in yourself for a day or two, to keep up appearances. I'll sleep on the lounge at the store, and we can talk business over the telephone."

"All right, Jack, we'll arrange the details later. But for Heaven's sake get him started, or he'll be calling a hack to drive up to the house. I'll go home on a street car."

"So far, so good," sighed Mr. Clayton to himself as he escaped from the station. "Jack is a deuced clever fellow, and I'll have to do something more for him. But the tug-of-war is yet to come. I've got to bribe a doctor, shut up the house for a day or two, and have all the ill-humor of two disappointed women to endure until this negro leaves town. Well, I'm sure my wife and Alice will back me up at any cost. No sacrifice is too great to escape having to entertain him; of course I have no prejudice against his color,—he can't help that,—but it is the *principle* of the thing. If we received him it would be a concession fatal to all my views and theories. And I am really doing him a kindness, for I'm sure that all the world could not make Alice and her mother treat him with anything but cold politeness. It'll be a great mortification to Alice, but I don't see how else I could have got out of it."

He boarded the first car that left the depot, and soon reached home. The house was lighted up, and through the lace curtains of the parlor windows he could see his wife and daughter, elegantly dressed, waiting to receive their distinguished visitor. He rang the bell impatiently, and a servant opened the door.

"The gentleman did n't come?" asked the maid.

"No," he said as he hung up his hat. This brought the ladies to the door.

"He did n't come?" they exclaimed. "What's the matter?"

"I'll tell you," he said, "Mary," this to the servant, a white girl, who stood in open-eyed curiosity, "we shan't need you any more to-night."

Then he went into the parlor, and, closing the door, told his story. When he reached the point where he had discovered the color of the honorable Mr. Brown, Miss Clayton caught her breath, and was on the verge of collapse.

"That nigger," said Mrs. Clayton indignantly, "can never set foot in this house. But what did you do with him?"

Mr. Clayton quickly unfolded his plan, and described the disposition he had made of the Congressman.

"It's an awful shame," said Mrs. Clayton. "Just think of the trouble and expense we have gone to! And poor Alice'll never get over it, for everybody knows he came to see her and that he's smitten with her. But you've done just right; we never would have been able to hold up our heads again if we had introduced a black man, even a Congressman, to the people that are invited here tomorrow night, as a sweetheart of Alice. Why, she wouldn't marry him if he was President of the United States and plated with gold an inch thick. The very idea!"

"Well," said Mr. Clayton, "then we've got to act quick. Alice must wrap up her throat—by the way, Alice, how *is* your throat?"

"It's sore," sobbed Alice, who had been in tears almost from her father's return, "and I don't care if I do have diphtheria and die, no, I don't!" and she wept on.

"Wrap up your throat and go to bed, and I'll go over to Doctor Pillsbury's and get a diphtheria card to nail up on the house. In the morning, first thing, we'll have to write notes recalling the invitations for to-morrow evening, and have them delivered by messenger boys. We were fools for not finding out all about this man from some one who knew, before we invited him here. Sadler don't know more than half he thinks he does, anyway. And we'll have to do this thing thoroughly, or our motives will be misconstrued, and people will say we are prejudiced and all that, when it is only a matter of principle with us."

The programme outlined above was carried out to the letter. The invitations were recalled, to the great disappointment of the invited guests. The family physician called several times during the day. Alice remained in bed, and the maid left without notice, in such a hurry that she forgot to take her best clothes.

Mr. Clayton himself remained at home. He had a telephone in the house, and was therefore in easy communication with his office, so that the business did not suffer materially by reason of his absence from the store. About ten o'clock in the morning a note came up from the hotel, expressing Mr. Brown's regrets and sympathy. Toward noon Mr. Clayton picked up the morning paper, which he

had not theretofore had time to read, and was glancing over it casually, when his eye fell upon a column headed "A Colored Congressman." He read the article with astonishment that rapidly turned to
chagrin and dismay. It was an interview describing the Congressman as a tall and shapely man, about thirty-five years old, with an
olive complexion not noticeably darker than many a white man's,
straight hair, and eyes as black as sloes.

"The bearing of this son of South Carolina reveals the polished
manners of the Southern gentleman, and neither from his appearance nor his conversation would one suspect that the white blood
which flows in his veins in such preponderating measure had ever
been crossed by that of a darker race," wrote the reporter, who had
received instructions at the office that for urgent business considerations the lake shipping interest wanted Representative Brown
treated with marked consideration.

There was more of the article, but the introductory portion left
Mr. Clayton in such a state of bewilderment that the paper fell from
his hand. What was the meaning of it? Had he been mistaken? Obviously so, or else the reporter was wrong, which was manifestly
improbable. When he had recovered himself somewhat, he picked
up the newspaper and began reading where he had left off.

"Representative Brown traveled to Groveland in company with
Bishop Jones of the African Methodist Jerusalem Church, who is *en
route* to attend the general conference of his denomination at Detroit next week. The bishop, who came in while the writer was in-
terviewing Mr. Brown, is a splendid type of the pure negro. He is
said to be a man of great power among his people, which may easily
be believed after one has looked upon his expressive countenance
and heard him discuss the questions which affect the welfare of his
church and his race."

Mr. Clayton stared at the paper. " 'The bishop,' " he repeated,
" 'is a splendid type of the pure negro.' I must have mistaken the
bishop for the Congressman! But how in the world did Jack get the
thing balled up? I'll call up the store and demand an explanation
of him.

"Jack," he asked, "what kind of a looking man was the fellow
you gave the note to at the depot?"

"He was a very wicked-looking fellow, sir," came back the answer. "He had a bad eye, looked like a gambler, sir. I am not surprised that you did n't want to entertain him, even if he was a Congressman."

"What color was he—that's what I want to know—and what kind of hair did he have?"

"Why, he was about my complexion, sir, and had straight black hair."

The rules of the telephone company did not permit swearing over the line. Mr. Clayton broke the rules.

"Was there any one else with him?" he asked when he had relieved his mind.

"Yes, sir, Bishop Jones of the African Methodist Jerusalem Church was sitting there with him; they had traveled from Washington together. I drove the bishop to his stopping-place after I had left Mr. Brown at the hotel. I did n't suppose you'd mind."

Mr. Clayton fell into a chair, and indulged in thoughts unutterable.

He folded up the paper and slipped it under the family Bible, where it was least likely to be soon discovered.

"I'll hide the paper, anyway," he groaned. "I'll never hear the last of this till my dying day, so I may as well have a few hours' respite. It's too late to go back, and we've got to play the farce out. Alice is really sick with disappointment, and to let her know this now would only make her worse. Maybe he'll leave town in a day or two, and then she'll be in condition to stand it. Such luck is enough to disgust a man with trying to do right and live up to his principles."

Time hung a little heavy on Mr. Clayton's hands during the day. His wife was busy with the housework. He answered several telephone calls about Alice's health, and called up the store occasionally to ask how the business was getting on. After lunch he lay down on a sofa and took a nap, from which he was aroused by the sound of the door-bell. He went to the door. The evening paper was lying on the porch, and the newsboy, who had not observed the diphtheria sign until after he had rung, was hurrying away as fast as his legs would carry him.

Mr. Clayton opened the paper and looked it through to see if there was any reference to the visiting Congressman. He found what he sought and more. An article on the local page contained a résumé of the information given in the morning paper, with the following additional paragraph:—

"A reporter, who called at the Forest Hill this morning to interview Representative Brown, was informed that the Congressman had been invited to spend the remainder of his time in Groveland as the guest of Mr. William Watkins, the proprietor of the popular livery establishment on Main Street. Mr. Brown will remain in the city several days, and a reception will be tendered him at Mr. Watkin's on Wednesday evening."

"That ends it," sighed Mr. Clayton. "The dove of peace will never again rest on my roof-tree."

But why dwell longer on the sufferings of Mr. Clayton, or attempt to describe the feelings or chronicle the remarks of his wife and daughter when they learned the facts in the case?

As to Representative Brown, he was made welcome in the hospitable home of Mr. William Watkins. There was a large and brilliant assemblage at the party on Wednesday evening, at which were displayed the costumes prepared for the Clayton reception. Mr. Brown took a fancy to Miss Lura Watkins, to whom, before the week was over, he became engaged to be married. Meantime poor Alice, the innocent victim of circumstances and principles, lay sick abed with a suppositious case of malignant diphtheria, and a real case of acute disappointment and chagrin.

"Oh, Jack!" exclaimed Alice, a few weeks later, on the way home from evening church in company with the young man, "what a dreadful thing it all was! And to think of that hateful Lura Watkins marrying the Congressman!"

The street was shaded by trees at the point where they were passing, and there was no one in sight. Jack put his arm around her waist, and, leaning over, kissed her.

"Never mind, dear," he said soothingly, "you still have your 'last chance' left, and I'll prove myself a better man than the Congressman."

———

Occasionally, at social meetings, when the vexed question of the future of the colored race comes up, as it often does, for discussion, Mr. Clayton may still be heard to remark sententiously:—

"What the white people of the United States need most, in dealing with this problem, is a higher conception of the brotherhood of man. For of one blood God made all the nations of the earth."

Cicely's Dream

I

THE OLD WOMAN stood at the back door of the cabin, shading her eyes with her hand, and looking across the vegetable garden that ran up to the very door. Beyond the garden she saw, bathed in the sunlight, a field of corn, just in the ear, stretching for half a mile, its yellow, pollen-laden tassels over-topping the dark green mass of broad glistening blades; and in the distance, through the faint morning haze of evaporating dew, the line of the woods, of a still darker green, meeting the clear blue of the summer sky. Old Dinah saw, going down the path, a tall, brown girl, in a homespun frock, swinging a slat-bonnet in one hand and a splint basket in the other.

"Oh, Cicely!" she called.

The girl turned and answered in a resonant voice, vibrating with youth and life,—

"Yes, granny!"

"Be sho' and pick a good mess er peas, chile, fer yo' gran'daddy's gwine ter be home ter dinner ter-day."

The old woman stood a moment longer and then turned to go into the house. What she had not seen was that the girl was not only young, but lithe and shapely as a sculptor's model; that her bare feet seemed to spurn the earth as they struck it; that though brown, she was not so brown but that her cheek was darkly red with the blood of another race than that which gave her her name and station in life; and the old woman did not see that Cicely's face was as comely as her figure was superb, and that her eyes were dreamy with vague yearnings.

Cicely climbed the low fence between the garden and the cornfield, and started down one of the long rows leading directly away from the house. Old Needham was a good ploughman, and straight as an arrow ran the furrow between the rows of corn, until it vanished in the distant perspective. The peas were planted beside alternate hills of corn, the corn-stalks serving as supports for the climbing pea-vines. The vines nearest the house had been picked more or less clear of the long green pods, and Cicely walked down the row for a quarter of a mile, to where the peas were more plentiful. And as she walked she thought of her dream of the night before.

She had dreamed a beautiful dream. The fact that it was a beautiful dream, a delightful dream, her memory retained very vividly. She was troubled because she could not remember just what her dream had been about. Of one other fact she was certain, that in her dream she had found something, and that her happiness had been bound up with the thing she had found. As she walked down the corn-row she ran over in her mind the various things with which she had always associated happiness. Had she found a gold ring? No, it was not a gold ring—of that she felt sure. Was it a soft, curly plume for her hat? She had seen town people with them, and had indulged in day-dreams on the subject; but it was not a feather. Was it a bright-colored silk dress? No; as much as she had always wanted one, it was not a silk dress. For an instant, in a dream, she had tasted some great and novel happiness, and when she awoke it was dashed from her lips, and she could not even enjoy the memory of it, except in a vague, indefinite, and tantalizing way.

Cicely was troubled, too, because dreams were serious things. Dreams had certain meanings, most of them, and some dreams went by contraries. If her dream had been a prophecy of some good thing, she had by forgetting it lost the pleasure of anticipation. If her dream had been one of those that go by contraries, the warning would be in vain, because she would not know against what evil to provide. So, with a sigh, Cicely said to herself that it was a troubled world, more or less; and having come to a promising point, began to pick the tenderest pea-pods and throw them into her basket.

By the time she had reached the end of the line the basket was nearly full. Glancing toward the pine woods beyond the rail fence, she saw a brier bush loaded with large, luscious blackberries. Cicely was fond of blackberries, so she set her basket down, climbed the fence, and was soon busily engaged in gathering the fruit, delicious even in its wild state.

She had soon eaten all she cared for. But the berries were still numerous, and it occurred to her that her granddaddy would like a blackberry pudding for dinner. Catching up her apron, and using it as a receptacle for the berries, she had gathered scarcely more than a handful when she heard a groan.

Cicely was not timid, and her curiosity being aroused by the sound, she stood erect, and remained in a listening attitude. In a moment the sound was repeated, and, gauging the point from which it came, she plunged resolutely into the thick underbrush of the forest. She had gone but a few yards when she stopped short with an exclamation of surprise and concern.

Upon the ground, under the shadow of the towering pines, a man lay at full length,—a young man, several years under thirty, apparently, so far as his age could be guessed from a face that wore a short soft beard, and was so begrimed with dust and incrusted with blood that little could be seen of the underlying integument. What was visible showed a skin browned by nature or by exposure. His hands were of even a darker brown, almost as dark as Cicely's own. A tangled mass of very curly black hair, matted with burs, dank with dew, and clotted with blood, fell partly over his forehead, on the edge of which, extending back into the hair, an ugly scalp wound was gaping, and, though apparently not just inflicted, was still bleeding slowly, as though reluctant to stop, in spite of the coagulation that had almost closed it.

Cicely with a glance took in all this and more. But, first of all, she saw the man was wounded and bleeding, and the nurse latent in all womankind awoke in her to the requirements of the situation. She knew there was a spring a few rods away, and ran swiftly to it. There was usually a gourd at the spring, but now it was gone. Pouring out the blackberries in a little heap where they could be found again, she took off her apron, dipped one end of it into the spring, and ran back to the wounded man. The apron was clean, and she squeezed a little stream of water from it into the man's mouth. He swallowed it with avidity. Cicely then knelt by his side, and with the wet end of her apron washed the blood from the wound lightly, and the dust from the man's face. Then she looked at her apron a moment, debating whether she should tear it or not.

"I'm feared granny'll be mad," she said to herself. "I reckon I'll jes' use de whole apron."

So she bound the apron around his head as well as she could, and then sat down a moment on a fallen tree trunk, to think what she should do next. The man already seemed more comfortable; he had ceased moaning, and lay quiet, though breathing heavily.

"What shall I do with that man?" she reflected. "I don' know whether he's a w'ite man or a black man. Ef he's a w'ite man, I oughter go an' tell de w'ite folks up at de big house, an' dey'd take keer of 'im. Ef he's a black man, I oughter go tell granny. He don' look lack a black man somehow er nuther, an' yet he don' look lack a w'ite man; he's too dahk, an' his hair's too curly. But I mus' do somethin' wid 'im. He can't be lef' here ter die in de woods all by hisse'f. Reckon I'll go an' tell granny."

She scaled the fence, caught up the basket of peas from where she had left it, and ran, lightly and swiftly as a deer, toward the house. Her short skirt did not impede her progress, and in a few minutes she had covered the half mile and was at the cabin door, a slight heaving of her full and yet youthful breast being the only sign of any unusual exertion.

Her story was told in a moment. The old woman took down a black bottle from a high shelf, and set out with Cicely across the cornfield, toward the wounded man.

As they went through the corn Cicely recalled part of her dream. She had dreamed that under some strange circumstances—what they had been was still obscure—she had met a young man—a young man whiter than she and yet not all white—and that he had loved her and courted her and married her. Her dream had been all the sweeter because in it she had first tasted the sweetness of love, and she had not recalled it before because only in her dream had she known or thought of love as something supremely desirable.

With the memory of her dream, however, her fears revived. Dreams were solemn things. To Cicely the fabric of a vision was by no means baseless. Her trouble arose from her not being able to recall, though she was well versed in dream-lore, just what event was foreshadowed by a dream of finding a wounded man. If the wounded man were of her own race, her dream would thus far have been realized, and having met the young man, the other joys might be expected to follow. If he should turn out to be a white man, then her dream was clearly one of the kind that go by contraries, and she could expect only sorrow and trouble and pain as the proper sequences of this fateful discovery.

II

The two women reached the fence that separated the cornfield from the pine woods.

"How is I gwine ter git ovuh dat fence, chile?" asked the old woman.

"Wait a minute, granny," said Cicely; "I'll take it down."

It was only an eight-rail fence, and it was a matter of but a few minutes for the girl to lift down and lay to either side the ends of the rails that formed one of the angles. This done, the old woman easily stepped across the remaining two or three rails. It was only a moment before they stood by the wounded man. He was laying still, breathing regularly, and seemingly asleep.

"What is he, granny," asked the girl anxiously, "a w'ite man, or not?"

Old Dinah pushed back the matted hair from the wounded man's brow, and looked at the skin beneath. It was fairer there, but yet of a decided brown. She raised his hand, pushed back the tattered sleeve from his wrist, and then she laid his hand down gently.

"Mos' lackly he's a mulatter man f'om up de country somewhar. He don' look lack dese yer niggers roun' yere, ner yet lack a w'ite man. But de po' boy 's in a bad fix, w'ateber he is, an' I 'spec's we bettah do w'at we kin fer 'im, an' w'en he comes to he'll tell us w'at he is—er w'at he calls hisse'f. Hol' 'is head up, chile, an' I'll po' a drop er dis yer liquor down his th'oat; dat'll bring 'im to quicker 'n anything e'se I knows."

Cicely lifted the sick man's head, and Dinah poured a few drops of the whiskey between his teeth. He swallowed it readily enough. In a few minutes he opened his eyes and stared blankly at the two women. Cicely saw that his eyes were large and black, and glistening with fever.

"How you feelin', suh?" asked the old woman.

There was no answer.

"Is you feelin' bettah now?"

The wounded man kept on staring blankly. Suddenly he essayed to put his hand to his head, gave a deep groan, and fell back again unconscious.

"He's gone ag'in," said Dinah. "I reckon we'll hafter tote 'im up ter de house and take keer er 'im dere. W'ite folks would n't want ter fool wid a nigger man, an' we doan know who his folks is. He's outer his head an' will be fer some time yet, an' we can't tell nuthin' 'bout 'im tel he comes ter his senses."

Cicely lifted the wounded man by the arms and shoulders. She was strong, with the strength of youth and a sturdy race. The man was pitifully emaciated; how much, the two women had not suspected until they raised him. They had no difficulty whatever, except for the awkwardness of such a burden, in lifting him over the fence and carrying him through the cornfield to the cabin.

They laid him on Cicely's bed in the little lean-to shed that formed a room separate from the main apartment of the cabin. The old woman sent Cicely to cook the dinner, while she gave her own attention exclusively to the still unconscious man. She brought water and washed him as though he were a child.

"Po' boy," she said, "he doan feel lack he's be'n eatin' nuff to feed a sparrer. He 'pears ter be mos' starved ter def."

She washed his wound more carefully, made some lint,—the art was well known in the sixties,—and dressed his wound with a fair degree of skill.

"Somebody must 'a' be'n tryin' ter put yo' light out, chile," she muttered to herself as she adjusted the bandage around his head. "A little higher er a little lower, an' you would n' 'a' be'n yere ter tell de tale. Dem clo's," she argued, lifting the tattered garments she had removed from her patient, "don' b'long 'roun' yere. Dat kinder weavin' come f'om down to'ds Souf Ca'lina. I wish Needham 'u'd come erlong. He kin tell who dis man is, an' all erbout 'im."

She made a bowl of gruel, and fed it, drop by drop, to the sick man. This roused him somewhat from his stupor, but when Dinah thought he had enough of the gruel, and stopped feeding him, he closed his eyes again and relapsed into a heavy sleep that was so closely akin to unconsciousness as to be scarcely distinguishable from it.

When old Needham came home at noon, his wife, who had been anxiously awaiting his return, told him in a few words the story of Cicely's discovery and of the subsequent events.

Needham inspected the stranger with a professional eye. He had been something of a plantation doctor in his day, and was known far and wide for his knowledge of simple remedies. The negroes all around, as well as many of the poorer white people, came to him for the treatment of common ailments.

"He's got a fevuh," he said, after feeling the patient's pulse and laying his hand on his brow, "an' we'll hafter gib 'im some yarb tea an' nuss 'im tel de fevuh w'ars off. I 'spec'," he added, "dat I knows whar dis boy come f'om. He's mos' lackly one er dem bright mulatters, f'om Robeson County—some of 'em call deyse'ves Croatan Injins—w'at's been conscripted an' sent ter wu'k on de fo'tifications down at Wimbleton er some'er's er nuther, an' done 'scaped, and got mos' killed gittin' erway, an' wuz n' none too well fed befo', an' nigh 'bout starved ter def sence. We'll hafter hide dis man, er e'se we is lackly ter git inter trouble ou'se'ves by harb'rin' 'im. Ef dey ketch 'im yere, dey's liable ter take 'im out an' shoot 'im—an' des ez lackly us too."

Cicely was listening with bated breath.

"Oh, gran'daddy," she cried, with trembling voice, "don' let 'em ketch 'im! Hide 'im somewhar."

"I reckon we'll leave 'im yere fer a day er so. Ef he had come f'om roun' yere I'd be skeered ter keep 'im, fer de w'ite folks 'u'd prob'ly be lookin' fer 'im. But I knows ev'ybody w'at's be'n conscripted fer ten mils 'roun', an' dis yere boy don' b'long in dis neighborhood. W'en 'e gits so 'e kin he'p 'isse'f we'll put 'im up in de lof' an' hide 'im till de Yankees come. Fer dey're comin', sho'. I dremp' las' night dey wuz close ter han', and I hears de w'ite folks talkin' ter deyse'ves 'bout it. An' de time is comin' w'en de good Lawd gwine ter set His people free, an' it ain' gwine ter be long, nuther."

Needham's prophecy proved true. In less than a week the Confederate garrison evacuated the arsenal in the neighboring town of Patesville, blew up the buildings, destroyed the ordnance and stores, and retreated across the Cape Fear River, burning the river bridge behind them,—two acts of war afterwards unjustly attributed to General Sherman's army, which followed close upon the heels of the retreating Confederates.

When there was no longer any fear for the stranger's safety, no more pains were taken to conceal him. His wound had healed rapidly, and in a week he had been able with some help to climb up the ladder into the loft. In all this time, however, though apparently conscious, he had said no word to any one, nor had he seemed to comprehend a word that was spoken to him.

Cicely had been his constant attendant. After the first day, during which her granny had nursed him, she had sat by his bedside, had fanned his fevered brow, had held food and water and medicine to his lips. When it was safe for him to come down from the loft and sit in a chair under a spreading oak, Cicely supported him until he was strong enough to walk about the yard. When his strength had increased sufficiently to permit of greater exertion, she accompanied him on long rambles in the fields and woods.

In spite of his gain in physical strength, the newcomer changed very little in other respects. For a long time he neither spoke nor smiled. To questions put to him he simply gave no reply, but looked at his questioner with the blank unconsciousness of an infant. By and by he began to recognize Cicely, and to smile at her approach. The next step in returning consciousness was but another manifestation of the same sentiment. When Cicely would leave him he would look his regret, and be restless and uneasy until she returned.

The family were at a loss what to call him. To any inquiry as to his name he answered no more than to other questions.

"He come jes' befo' Sherman," said Needham, after a few weeks, "lack John de Baptis' befo' de Lawd. I reckon we bettah call 'im John."

So they called him John. He soon learned the name. As time went on Cicely found that he was quick at learning things. She taught him to speak her own negro English, which he pronounced with absolute fidelity to her intonations; so that barring the quality of his voice, his speech was an echo of Cicely's own.

The summer wore away and the autumn came. John and Cicely wandered in the woods together and gathered walnuts, and chinquapins and wild grapes. When harvest time came, they worked in the fields side by side,—plucked the corn, pulled the fodder, and gathered the dried peas from the yellow pea-vines. Cicely was a phenomenal cotton-picker, and John accompanied her to the fields and stayed by her hours at a time, though occasionally he would complain of his head, and sit under a tree and rest part of the day while Cicely worked, the two keeping one another always in sight.

They did not have a great deal of intercourse with other people. Young men came to the cabin sometimes to see Cicely, but when they found her entirely absorbed in the stranger they ceased their visits. For a time Cicely kept him away, as much as possible, from others, because she did not wish them to see that there was anything wrong about him. This was her motive at first, but after a while she kept him to herself simply because she was happier so. He was hers—hers alone. She had found him, as Pharaoh's daughter had found Moses in the bulrushes; she had taught him to speak, to think, to love. She had not taught him to remember; she would not have wished him to; she would have been jealous of any past to which he might have proved bound by other ties. Her dream so far had come true. She had found him; he loved her. The rest of it would as surely follow, and that before long. For dreams were serious things, and time had proved hers to have been not a presage of misfortune, but one of the beneficent visions that are sent, that we may enjoy by anticipation the good things that are in store for us.

III

But a short interval of time elapsed after the passage of the warlike host that swept through North Carolina, until there appeared upon the scene the vanguard of a second army, which came to bring light and the fruits of liberty to a land which slavery and the havoc of war had brought to ruin. It is fashionable to assume that those who undertook the political rehabilitation of the Southern States merely rounded out the ruin that the war had wrought—merely ploughed up the desolate land and sowed it with salt. Perhaps the gentler judgments of the future may recognize that their task was a difficult one, and that wiser and honester men might have failed as egregiously. It may even, in time, be conceded that some good came out of the carpet-bag governments, as, for instance, the establishment of a system of popular education in the former slave States. Where it had been a crime to teach people to read or write, a school-house dotted every hillside, and the State provided education for rich and poor, for white and black alike. Let us lay at least this token upon the grave of the carpet-baggers. The evil they did lives after them, and the statute of limitations does not seem to run against it. It is but just that we should not forget the good.

Long, however, before the work of political reconstruction had begun, a brigade of Yankee schoolmasters and schoolma'ams had invaded Dixie, and one of the latter had opened a Freedmen's Bureau School in the town of Patesville, about four miles from Needham Green's cabin on the neighboring sandhills.

It had been quite a surprise to Miss Chandler's Boston friends when she had announced her intention of going South to teach the freedmen. Rich, accomplished, beautiful, and a social favorite, she was giving up the comforts and luxuries of Northern life to go among hostile strangers, where her associates would be mostly ignorant negroes. Perhaps she might meet occasionally an officer of some Federal garrison, or a traveler from the North; but to all intents and purposes her friends considered her as going into voluntary exile. But heroism was not rare in those days, and Martha Chandler was only one of the great multitude whose hearts went out toward an oppressed race, and who freely poured out their talents, their money, their lives,—whatever God had given them,—in the sublime and not unfruitful effort to transform three millions of slaves into intelligent freemen. Miss Chandler's friends knew, too, that she had met a great sorrow, and more than suspected that out of it had grown her determination to go South.

When Cicely Green heard that a school for colored people had been opened at Patesville she combed her hair, put on her Sunday frock and such bits of finery as she possessed and set out for town early the next Monday morning.

There were many who came to learn the new gospel of education, which was to be the cure for all the freedmen's ills. The old and gray-haired, the full-grown man and woman, the toddling infant,—they came to acquire the new and wonderful learning that was to make them the equals of the white people. It was the teacher's task, by no means an easy one, to select from this incongruous mass the most promising material, and to distribute among them the second-hand books and clothing that were sent, largely by her Boston friends, to aid her in her work; to find out what they knew, to classify them by their intelligence rather than by their knowledge, for they were all lamentably ignorant. Some among them were the children of parents who had been free before the war, and of these some few could read and one or two could write. One paragon, who could repeat the multiplication table, was immediately promoted to the position of pupil teacher.

Miss Chandler took a liking to the tall girl who had come so far to sit under her instruction. There was a fine, free air in her bearing, a lightness in her step, a sparkle in her eye, that spoke of good blood,—whether fused by nature in its own alembic, out of material despised and spurned of men, or whether some obscure ancestral strain, the teacher could not tell. The girl proved intelligent and learned rapidly, indeed seemed almost feverishly anxious to learn. She was quiet, and was, though utterly untrained, instinctively polite, and profited from the first day by the example of her teacher's quiet elegance. The teacher dressed in simple black. When Cicely came back to school the second day, she had left off her glass beads and her red ribbon, and had arranged her hair as nearly like the teacher's as her skill and its quality would permit.

The teacher was touched by these efforts at imitation, and by the intense devotion Cicely soon manifested toward her. It was not a sycophantic, troublesome devotion, that made itself a burden to its object. It found expression in little things done rather than in any words the girl said. To the degree that the attraction was mutual, Martha recognized in it a sort of freemasonry of temperament that drew them together in spite of the differences between them. Martha felt sometimes, in the vague way that one speculates about the impossible, that if she were brown, and had been brought up in North Carolina, she would be like Cicely; and that if Cicely's ancestors had come over in the *Mayflower,* and Cicely had been reared on Beacon Street, in the shadow of the State House dome, Cicely would have been very much like herself.

Miss Chandler was lonely sometimes. Her duties kept her occupied all day. On Sundays she taught a Bible class in the schoolroom. Correspondence with bureau officials and friends at home furnished her with additional occupation. At times, nevertheless, she felt a longing for the company of women of her own race; but the white ladies of the town did not call, even in the most formal way, upon the Yankee school-teacher. Miss Chandler was therefore fain to do the best she could with such companionship as was available. She took Cicely to her home occasionally, and asked her once to stay all night. Thinking, however, that she detected a reluctance on the girl's part to remain away from home, she did not repeat her invitation.

Cicely, indeed, was filling a double rôle. The learning acquired from Miss Chandler she imparted to John at home. Every evening, by the light of the pine-knots blazing on Needham's ample hearth, she taught John to read the simple words she had learned during the day. Why she did not take him to school she had never asked herself; there were several other pupils as old as he seemed to be. Perhaps she still thought it necessary to protect him from curious remark. He worked with Needham by day, and she could see him at night, and all of Saturdays and Sundays. Perhaps it was the jealous selfishness of love. She had found him; he was hers. In the spring, when school was over, her granny had said that she might marry him. Till then her dream would not yet have come true, and she must keep him to herself. And yet she did not wish him to lose this golden key to the avenues of opportunity. She would not take him to school, but she would teach him each day all that she herself had learned. He was not difficult to teach, but learned, indeed, with what seemed to Cicely marvelous ease,—always, however, by her lead, and never of his own initiative. For while he could do a man's work, he was in most things but a child, without a child's curiosity. His love for Cicely appeared the only thing for which he needed no suggestion; and even that possessed an element of childish dependence that would have seemed, to minds trained to thoughtful observation, infinitely pathetic.

The spring came and cotton-planting time. The children began to drop out of Miss Chandler's school one by one, as their services were required at home. Cicely was among those who intended to remain in school until the term closed with the "exhibition," in which she was assigned a leading part. She had selected her recitation, or "speech," from among half a dozen poems that her teacher had suggested, and to memorizing it she devoted considerable time and study. The exhibition, as the first of its kind, was sure to be a notable event. The parents and friends of the children were invited to attend, and a colored church, recently erected,—the largest available building,—was secured as the place where the exercises should take place.

On the morning of the eventful day, uncle Needham, assisted by John, harnessed the mule to the two-wheeled cart, on which a couple of splint-bottomed chairs were fastened to accommodate Dinah and Cicely. John put on his best clothes,—an ill-fitting suit of blue jeans,—a round wool hat, a pair of coarse broga'ns, a homespun shirt, and a bright blue necktie. Cicely wore her best frock, a red ribbon at her throat, another in her hair, and carried a bunch of flowers in her hand. Uncle Needham and aunt Dinah were also in holiday array. Needham and John took their seats on opposite sides of the cart-frame, with their feet dangling down, and thus the equipage set out leisurely for the town.

Cicely had long looked forward impatiently to this day. She was going to marry John the next week, and then her dream would have come entirely true. But even this anticipated happiness did not overshadow the importance of the present occasion, which would be an epoch in her life, a day of joy and triumph. She knew her speech perfectly, and timidity was not one of her weaknesses. She knew that the red ribbons set off her dark beauty effectively, and that her dress fitted neatly the curves of her shapely figure. She confidently expected to win the first prize, a large morocco-covered Bible, offered by Miss Chandler for the best exercise.

Cicely and her companions soon arrived at Patesville. Their entrance into the church made quite a sensation, for Cicely was not only an acknowledged belle, but a general favorite, and to John there attached a tinge of mystery which inspired a respect not bestowed upon those who had grown up in the neighborhood. Cicely secured a seat in the front part of the church, next to the aisle, in the place reserved for the pupils. As the house was already partly filled by townspeople when the party from the country arrived, Needham and his wife and John were forced to content themselves with places somewhat in the rear of the room, from which they could see and hear what took place on the platform, but where they were not at all conspicuously visible to those at the front of the church.

The schoolmistress had not yet arrived, and order was preserved in the audience by two of the elder pupils, adorned with large rosettes of red, white, and blue, who ushered the most important visitors to the seats reserved for them. A national flag was gracefully draped over the platform, and under it hung a lithograph of the Great Emancipator, for it was thus these people thought of him. He had saved the Union, but the Union had never meant anything good to them. He had proclaimed liberty to the captive, which meant all to them; and to them he was and would ever be the Great Emancipator.

The schoolmistress came in at a rear door and took her seat upon the platform. Martha was dressed in white; for once she had laid aside the sombre garb in which alone she had been seen since her arrival at Patesville. She wore a yellow rose at her throat, a bunch of jasmine in her belt. A sense of responsibility for the success of the exhibition had deepened the habitual seriousness of her face, yet she greeted the audience with a smile.

"Don' Miss Chan'ler look sweet?" whispered the little girls to one another, devouring her beauty with sparkling eyes, their lips parted over a wealth of ivory.

"De Lawd will bress dat chile," said one old woman, in soliloquy. "I t'ank de good Marster I's libbed ter see dis day."

Even envy could not hide its noisome head: a pretty quadroon whispered to her neighbor:—

"I don't b'liebe she's natch'ly ez white ez dat. I 'spec' she's be'n powd'rin'! An' I know all dat hair can't be her'n; she's got on a switch, sho's you bawn."

"You knows dat ain' so, Ma'y 'Liza Smif," rejoined the other, with a look of stern disapproval; "you *knows* dat ain' so. You'd gib yo' everlastin' soul 'f you wuz ez white ez Miss Chan'ler, en yo' ha'r wuz ez long ez her'n."

"By Jove, Maxwell!" exclaimed a young officer, who belonged to the Federal garrison stationed in the town, "but that girl is a beauty." The speaker and a companion were in fatigue uniform, and had merely dropped in for an hour between garrison duty. The ushers had wished to give them seats on the platform, but they had declined, thinking that perhaps their presence there might embarrass the teacher. They sought rather to avoid observation by sitting behind a pillar in the rear of the room, around which they could see without attracting undue attention.

"To think," the lieutenant went on, "of that Junonian figure, those lustrous orbs, that golden coronal, that flower of Northern civilization, being wasted on these barbarians!" The speaker uttered an exaggerated but suppressed groan.

His companion, a young man of clean-shaven face and serious aspect, nodded assent, but whispered reprovingly,—

" 'Sh! some one will hear you. The exercises are going to begin."

When Miss Chandler stepped forward to announce the hymn to be sung by the school as the first exercise, every eye in the room was fixed upon her, except John's, which saw only Cicely. When the teacher had uttered a few words, he looked up to her, and from that moment did not take his eyes off Martha's face.

After the singing, a little girl, dressed in white, crossed by ribbons of red and blue, recited with much spirit a patriotic poem.

When Martha announced the third exercise, John's face took on a more than usually animated expression, and there was a perceptible deepening of the troubled look in his eyes, never entirely absent since Cicely had found him in the woods.

A little yellow boy, with long curls, and a frightened air, next ascended the platform.

"Now, Jimmie, be a man, and speak right out," whispered his teacher, tapping his arm reassuringly with her fan as he passed her.

Jimmie essayed to recite the lines so familiar to a past generation of schoolchildren:—

> "*I knew a widow very poor,*
> *Who four small children had;*
> *The eldest was but six years old,*
> *A gentle, modest lad.*"

He ducked his head hurriedly in a futile attempt at a bow; then, following instructions previously given him, fixed his eyes upon a large cardboard motto hanging on the rear wall of the room, which admonished him in bright red letters to

"Always Speak The Truth,"

and started off with assumed confidence—

"I knew a widow very poor,
  Who"—

At this point, drawn by an irresistible impulse, his eyes sought the level of the audience. Ah, fatal blunder! He stammered, but with an effort raised his eyes and began again:

"I knew a widow very poor,
  Who four"—

Again his treacherous eyes fell, and his little remaining self-possession utterly forsook him. He made one more despairing effort:—

"I knew a widow very poor,
  Who four small"—

And then, bursting into tears, turned and fled amid a murmur of sympathy.

Jimmie's inglorious retreat was covered by the singing in chorus of "The Star-spangled Banner," after which Cicely Green came forward to recite her poem.

"By Jove, Maxwell!" whispered the young officer, who was evidently a connoisseur of female beauty, "that is n't bad for a bronze Venus. I'll tell you"—

" 'Sh!" said the other. "Keep still."

When Cicely finished her recitation, the young officers began to applaud, but stopped suddenly in some confusion as they realized that they were the only ones in the audience so engaged. The colored people had either not learned how to express their approval in orthodox fashion, or else their respect for the sacred character of the edifice forbade any such demonstration. Their enthusiasm found vent, however, in a subdued murmur, emphasized by numerous nods and winks and suppressed exclamations. During the singing that followed Cicely's recitation the two officers quietly withdrew, their duties calling them away at this hour.

At the close of the exercises, a committee on prizes met in the vestibule, and unanimously decided that Cicely Green was entitled to the first prize. Proudly erect, with sparkling eyes and cheeks flushed with victory, Cicely advanced to the platform to receive the coveted reward. As she turned away, her eyes, shining with gratified vanity, sought those of her lover.

John sat bent slightly forward in an attitude of strained attention; and Cicely's triumph lost half its value when she saw that it was not at her, but at Miss Chandler, that his look was directed. Though she watched him thenceforward, not one glance did he vouchsafe to his jealous sweetheart, and never for an instant withdrew his eyes from Martha, or relaxed the unnatural intentness of his gaze. The imprisoned mind, stirred to unwonted effort, was struggling for liberty; and from Martha had come the first ray of outer light that had penetrated its dungeon.

Before the audience was dismissed, the teacher rose to bid her school farewell. Her intention was to take a vacation of three months; but what might happen in that time she did not know, and there were duties at home of such apparent urgency as to render her return to North Carolina at least doubtful; so that in her own heart her *au revoir* sounded very much like a farewell.

She spoke to them of the hopeful progress they had made, and praised them for their eager desire to learn. She told them of the serious duties of life, and of the use they should make of their acquirements. With prophetic finger she pointed them to the upward way which they must climb with patient feet to raise themselves out of the depths.

Then, an unusual thing with her, she spoke of herself. Her heart was full; it was with difficulty that she maintained her composure; for the faces that confronted her were kindly faces, and not critical, and some of them she had learned to love right well.

"I am going away from you, my children," she said; "but before I go I want to tell you how I came to be in North Carolina; so that if I have been able to do anything here among you for which you might feel inclined, in your good nature, to thank me, you may thank not me alone, but another who came before me, and whose work I have but taken up where *he* laid it down. I had a friend,—a dear friend,—why should I be ashamed to say it?—a lover, to whom I was to be married,—as I hope all you girls may some day be happily married. His country needed him, and I gave him up. He came to fight for the Union and for Freedom, for he believed that all men are brothers. He did not come back again—he gave up his life for you. Could I do less than he? I came to the land that he sanctified by his death, and I have tried in my weak way to tend the plant he watered with his blood, and which, in the fullness of time, will blossom forth into the perfect flower of liberty."

She could say no more, and as the whole audience thrilled in sympathy with her emotion, there was a hoarse cry from the men's side of the room, and John forced his way to the aisle and rushed forward to the platform.

"Martha! Martha!"

"Arthur! O Arthur!"

Pent-up love burst the flood-gates of despair and oblivion, and caught these two young hearts in its torrent. Captain Arthur Carey, of the 1st Massachusetts, long since reported missing, and mourned as dead, was restored to reason and to his world.

It seemed to him but yesterday that he had escaped from the Confederate prison at Salisbury; that in an encounter with a guard he had received a wound in the head; that he had wandered on in the woods, keeping himself alive by means of wild berries, with now and then a piece of bread or a potato from a friendly negro. It seemed but the night before that he had laid himself down, tortured with fever, weak from loss of blood, and with no hope that he would ever rise again. From that moment his memory of the past was a blank until he recognized Martha on the platform and took up again the thread of his former existence where it had been broken off.

———

And Cicely? Well, there is often another woman, and Cicely, all unwittingly to Carey or to Martha, had been the other woman. For, after all, her beautiful dream had been one of the kind that go by contraries.

The Passing of Grandison

I

WHEN IT IS SAID that it was done to please a woman, there ought perhaps to be enough said to explain anything; for what a man will not do to please a woman is yet to be discovered. Nevertheless, it might be well to state a few preliminary facts to make it clear why young Dick Owens tried to run one of his father's negro men off to Canada.

In the early fifties, when the growth of anti-slavery sentiment and the constant drain of fugitive slaves into the North had so alarmed the slaveholders of the border States as to lead to the passage of the Fugitive Slave Law, a young white man from Ohio, moved by compassion for the sufferings of a certain bondman who happened to have a "hard master," essayed to help the slave to freedom. The attempt was discovered and frustrated; the abductor was tried and convicted for slave-stealing, and sentenced to a term of imprisonment in the penitentiary. His death, after the expiration of only a small part of the sentence, from cholera contracted while nursing stricken fellow prisoners, lent to the case a melancholy interest that made it famous in anti-slavery annals.

Dick Owens had attended the trial. He was a youth of about twenty-two, intelligent, handsome, and amiable, but extremely indolent, in a graceful and gentlemanly way; or, as old Judge Fenderson put it more than once, he was lazy as the Devil,—a mere figure of speech, of course, and not one that did justice to the Enemy of Mankind. When asked why he never did anything serious, Dick would good-naturedly reply, with a well-modulated drawl, that he did n't have to. His father was rich; there was but one other child,

an unmarried daughter, who because of poor health would probably never marry, and Dick was therefore heir presumptive to a large
estate. Wealth or social position he did not need to seek, for he was
born to both. Charity Lomax had shamed him into studying law,
but notwithstanding an hour or so a day spent at old Judge Fenderson's office, he did not make remarkable headway in his legal
studies.

"What Dick needs," said the judge, who was fond of tropes, as
became a scholar, and of horses, as was befitting a Kentuckian, "is
the whip of necessity, or the spur of ambition. If he had either, he
would soon need the snaffle to hold him back."

But all Dick required, in fact, to prompt him to the most remarkable thing he accomplished before he was twenty-five, was a
mere suggestion from Charity Lomax. The story was never really
known to but two persons until after the war, when it came out because it was a good story and there was no particular reason for its
concealment.

Young Owens had attended the trial of this slave-stealer, or mar-
tyr,—either or both,—and, when it was over, had gone to call on
Charity Lomax, and, while they sat on the veranda after sundown,
had told her all about the trial. He was a good talker, as his career in
later years disclosed, and described the proceedings very graphi-
cally.

"I confess," he admitted, "that while my principles were against
the prisoner, my sympathies were on his side. It appeared that he
was of good family, and that he had an old father and mother, respectable people, dependent upon him for support and comfort in
their declining years. He had been led into the matter by pity for a
negro whose master ought to have been run out of the county long
ago for abusing his slaves. If it had been merely a question of old
Sam Briggs's negro, nobody would have cared anything about it.
But father and the rest of them stood on the principle of the thing,
and told the judge so, and the fellow was sentenced to three years in
the penitentiary."

Miss Lomax had listened with lively interest.

"I've always hated old Sam Briggs," she said emphatically, "ever
since the time he broke a negro's leg with a piece of cordwood.
When I hear of a cruel deed it makes the Quaker blood that came

from my grandmother assert itself. Personally I wish that all Sam Briggs's negroes would run away. As for the young man, I regard him as a hero. He dared something for humanity. I could love a man who would take such chances for the sake of others."

"Could you love me, Charity, if I did something heroic?"

"You never will, Dick. You're too lazy for any use. You'll never do anything harder than playing cards or fox-hunting."

"Oh, come now, sweetheart! I've been courting you for a year, and it's the hardest work imaginable. Are you never going to love me?" he pleaded.

His hand sought hers, but she drew it back beyond his reach.

"I'll never love you, Dick Owens, until you have done something. When that time comes, I'll think about it."

"But it takes so long to do anything worth mentioning, and I don't want to wait. One must read two years to become a lawyer, and work five more to make a reputation. We shall both be gray by then."

"Oh, I don't know," she rejoined. "It does n't require a lifetime for a man to prove that he is a man. This one did something, or at least tried to."

"Well, I'm willing to attempt as much as any other man. What do you want me to do, sweetheart? Give me a test."

"Oh, dear me!" said Charity, "I don't care what you *do,* so you do *something*. Really, come to think of it, why should I care whether you do anything or not?"

"I'm sure I don't know why you should, Charity," rejoined Dick humbly, "for I'm aware that I'm not worthy of it."

"Except that I do hate," she added, relenting slightly, "to see a really clever man so utterly lazy and good for nothing."

"Thank you, my dear; a word of praise from you has sharpened my wits already. I have an idea! Will you love me if *I* run a negro off to Canada?"

"What nonsense!" said Charity scornfully. "You must be losing your wits. Steal another man's slave, indeed, while your father owns a hundred!"

"Oh, there'll be no trouble about that," responded Dick lightly; "I'll run off one of the old man's; we've got too many anyway. It may not be quite as difficult as the other man found it, but it will be just as unlawful, and will demonstrate what I am capable of."

"Seeing's believing," replied Charity. "Of course, what you are talking about now is merely absurd. I'm going away for three weeks, to visit my aunt in Tennessee. If you're able to tell me, when I return, that you've done something to prove your quality, I'll—well, you may come and tell me about it."

II

Young Owens got up about nine o'clock next morning, and while making his toilet put some questions to his personal attendant, a rather bright looking young mulatto of about his own age.

"Tom," said Dick.

"Yas, Mars Dick," responded the servant.

"I'm going on a trip North. Would you like to go with me?"

Now, if there was anything that Tom would have liked to make, it was a trip North. It was something he had long contemplated in the abstract, but had never been able to muster up sufficient courage to attempt in the concrete. He was prudent enough, however, to dissemble his feelings.

"I would n't min' it, Mars Dick, ez long ez you'd take keer er me an' fetch me home all right."

Tom's eyes belied his words, however, and his young master felt well assured that Tom needed only a good opportunity to make him run away. Having a comfortable home, and a dismal prospect in case of failure, Tom was not likely to take any desperate chances; but young Owens was satisfied that in a free State but little persuasion would be required to lead Tom astray. With a very logical and characteristic desire to gain his end with the least necessary expenditure of effort, he decided to take Tom with him, if his father did not object.

Colonel Owens had left the house when Dick went to breakfast, so Dick did not see his father till luncheon.

"Father," he remarked casually to the colonel, over the fried chicken, "I'm feeling a trifle run down. I imagine my health would be improved somewhat by a little travel and change of scene."

"Why don't you take a trip North?" suggested his father. The colonel added to paternal affection a considerable respect for his son as the heir of a large estate. He himself had been "raised" in comparative poverty, and had laid the foundations of his fortune by hard work; and while he despised the ladder by which he had climbed, he could not entirely forget it, and unconsciously manifested, in his intercourse with his son, some of the poor man's deference toward the wealthy and well-born.

"I think I'll adopt your suggestion, sir," replied the son, "and run up to New York; and after I've been there awhile I may go on to Boston for a week or so. I've never been there, you know."

"There are some matters you can talk over with my factor in New York," rejoined the colonel, "and while you are up there among the Yankees, I hope you'll keep your eyes and ears open to find out what the rascally abolitionists are saying and doing. They're becoming altogether too active for our comfort, and entirely too many ungrateful niggers are running away. I hope the conviction of that fellow yesterday may discourage the rest of the breed. I'd just like to catch any one trying to run off one of my darkeys. He'd get short shrift; I don't think any Court would have a chance to try him."

"They are a pestiferous lot," assented Dick, "and dangerous to our institutions. But say, father, if I go North I shall want to take Tom with me."

Now, the colonel, while a very indulgent father, had pronounced views on the subject of negroes, having studied them, as he often said, for a great many years, and, as he asserted oftener still, understanding them perfectly. It is scarcely worth while to say, either, that he valued more highly than if he had inherited them the slaves he had toiled and schemed for.

"I don't think it safe to take Tom up North," he declared, with promptness and decision. "He's a good enough boy, but too smart to trust among those low-down abolitionists. I strongly suspect him of having learned to read, though I can't imagine how. I saw him with a newspaper the other day, and while he pretended to be looking at a woodcut, I'm almost sure he was reading the paper. I think it by no means safe to take him."

Dick did not insist, because he knew it was useless. The colonel would have obliged his son in any other matter, but his negroes were the outward and visible sign of his wealth and station, and therefore sacred to him.

"Whom do you think it safe to take?" asked Dick. "I suppose I'll have to have a body-servant."

"What's the matter with Grandison?" suggested the colonel. "He's handy enough, and I reckon we can trust him. He's too fond of good eating to risk losing his regular meals; besides, he's sweet on your mother's maid, Betty, and I've promised to let 'em get married before long. I'll have Grandison up, and we'll talk to him. Here, you boy Jack," called the colonel to a yellow youth in the next room who was catching flies and pulling their wings off to pass the time, "go down to the barn and tell Grandison to come here."

"Grandison," said the colonel, when the negro stood before him, hat in hand.

"Yas, marster."

"Have n't I always treated you right?"

"Yas, marster."

"Have n't you always got all you wanted to eat?"

"Yas, marster."

"And as much whiskey and tobacco as was good for you, Grandison?"

"Y-a-s, marster."

"I should just like to know, Grandison, whether you don't think yourself a great deal better off than those poor free negroes down by the plank road, with no kind master to look after them and no mistress to give them medicine when they're sick and—and"—

"Well, I sh'd jes' reckon I is better off, suh, dan dem low-down free niggers, suh! Ef anybody ax 'em who dey b'long ter, dey has ter say nobody, er e'se lie erbout it. Anybody ax me who I b'longs ter, I ain' got no 'casion ter be shame' ter tell 'em, no, suh, 'deed I ain', suh!"

The colonel was beaming. This was true gratitude, and his feudal heart thrilled at such appreciative homage. What cold-blooded, heartless monsters they were who would break up this blissful relationship of kindly protection on the one hand, of wise subordination and loyal dependence on the other! The colonel always became indignant at the mere thought of such wickedness.

"Grandison," the colonel continued, "your young master Dick is going North for a few weeks, and I am thinking of letting him take you along. I shall send you on this trip, Grandison, in order that you may take care of your young master. He will need some one to wait on him, and no one can ever do it so well as one of the boys brought up with him on the old plantation. I am going to trust him in your hands, and I'm sure you'll do your duty faithfully, and bring him back home safe and sound—to old Kentucky."

Grandison grinned. "Oh yas, marster, I'll take keer er young Mars Dick."

"I want to warn you, though, Grandison," continued the colonel impressively, "against these cussed abolitionists, who try to entice servants from their comfortable homes and their indulgent masters, from the blue skies, the green fields, and the warm sunlight of their Southern home, and send them away off yonder to Canada, a dreary country, where the woods are full of wildcats and wolves and bears, where the snow lies up to the eaves of the houses for six months of the year, and the cold is so severe that it freezes your breath and curdles your blood; and where, when runaway niggers get sick and can't work, they are turned out to starve and die, unloved and uncared for. I reckon, Grandison, that you have too much sense to permit yourself to be led astray by any such foolish and wicked people."

" 'Deed, suh, I would n' low none er dem cussed, low-down abolitioners ter come nigh me, suh. I'd—I'd—would I be 'lowed ter hit 'em, suh?"

"Certainly, Grandison," replied the colonel, chuckling, "hit 'em as hard as you can. I reckon they'd rather like it. Begad, I believe they would! It would serve 'em right to be hit by a nigger!"

"Er ef I did n't hit 'em, suh," continued Grandison reflectively, "I'd tell Mars Dick, en *he* 'd fix 'em. He 'd smash de face off'n 'em suh, I jes' knows he would."

"Oh yes, Grandison, your young master will protect you. You need fear no harm while he is near."

"Dey won't try ter steal me, will dey, marster?" asked the negro, with sudden alarm.

"I don't know, Grandison," replied the colonel, lighting a fresh cigar. "They're a desperate set of lunatics, and there's no telling what they may resort to. But if you stick close to your young master, and remember always that he is your best friend, and understands your real needs, and has your true interests at heart, and if you will be careful to avoid strangers who try to talk to you, you'll stand a fair chance of getting back to your home and your friends. And if you please your master Dick, he'll buy you a present, and a string of beads for Betty to wear when you and she get married in the fall."

"Thanky, marster, thanky, suh," replied Grandison, oozing gratitude at every pore; "you is a good marster, to be sho', suh; yas, 'deed you is. You kin jes' bet me and Mars Dick gwine git 'long jes' lack I wuz own boy ter Mars Dick. En it won't be my fault ef he don' want me fer his boy all de time, w'en we come back home ag'in."

"All right, Grandison, you may go now. You need n't work any more to-day, and here's a piece of tobacco for you off my own plug."

"Thanky, marster, thanky, marster! You is de bes' marster any nigger ever had in dis worl'." And Grandison bowed and scraped and disappeared round the corner, his jaws closing around a large section of the colonel's best tobacco.

"You may take Grandison," said the colonel to his son. "I allow he's abolitionist-proof."

III

Richard Owens, Esq., and servant, from Kentucky, registered at the fashionable New York hostelry for Southerners in those days, a hotel where an atmosphere congenial to Southern institutions was sedulously maintained. But there were negro waiters in the dining-room, and mulatto bell-boys, and Dick had no doubt that Grandison, with the native gregariousness and garrulousness of his race, would foregather and palaver with them sooner or later, and Dick hoped that they would speedily inoculate him with the virus of freedom. For it was not Dick's intention to say anything to his servant about his plan to free him, for obvious reasons. To mention one of them, if Grandison should go away, and by legal process be recaptured, his young master's part in the matter would doubtless become known, which would be embarrassing to Dick, to say the least. If, on the other hand, he should merely give Grandison sufficient latitude, he had no doubt he would eventually lose him. For while not exactly skeptical about Grandison's perfervid loyalty, Dick had been a somewhat keen observer of human nature, in his own indolent way, and based his expectations upon the force of the example and argument that his servant could scarcely fail to encounter. Grandison should have a fair chance to become free by his own initiative; if it should become necessary to adopt other measures to get rid of him, it would be time enough to act when the necessity arose; and Dick Owens was not the youth to take needless trouble.

The young master renewed some acquaintances and made others, and spent a week or two very pleasantly in the best society of the metropolis, easily accessible to a wealthy, well-bred young Southerner, with proper introductions. Young women smiled on him, and young men of convivial habits pressed their hospitalities; but the memory of Charity's sweet, strong face and clear blue eyes made him proof against the blandishments of the one sex and the persuasions of the other. Meanwhile he kept Grandison supplied with pocket-money, and left him mainly to his own devices. Every night when Dick came in he hoped he might have to wait upon himself, and every morning he looked forward with pleasure to the prospect of making his toilet unaided. His hopes, however, were doomed to disappointment, for every night when he came in Grandison was on hand with a bootjack, and a nightcap mixed for his young master as the colonel had taught him to mix it, and every morning Grandison appeared with his master's boots blacked and his clothes brushed, and laid his linen out for the day.

"Grandison," said Dick one morning, after finishing his toilet, "this is the chance of your life to go around among your own people and see how they live. Have you met any of them?"

"Yas, suh, I's seen some of 'em. But I don' keer nuffin fer 'em, suh. Dey're diffe'nt f'm de niggers down ou' way. Dey 'lows dey 're free, but dey ain' got sense 'nuff ter know dey ain' half as well off as dey would be down Souf, whar dey'd be 'preciated."

When two weeks had passed without any apparent effect of evil example upon Grandison, Dick resolved to go on to Boston, where he thought the atmosphere might prove more favorable to his ends. After he had been at the Revere House for a day or two without losing Grandison, he decided upon slightly different tactics.

Having ascertained from a city directory the addresses of several well-known abolitionists, he wrote them each a letter something like this:—

DEAR FRIEND AND BROTHER:—

A wicked slaveholder from Kentucky, stopping at the Revere House, has dared to insult the liberty-loving people of Boston by bringing his slave into their midst. Shall this be tolerated? Or shall steps be taken in the name of liberty to rescue a fellow-man from bondage? For obvious reasons I can only sign myself,

A FRIEND OF HUMANITY.

That his letter might have an opportunity to prove effective, Dick made it a point to send Grandison away from the hotel on various errands. On one of these occasions Dick watched him for quite a distance down the street. Grandison had scarcely left the hotel when a long-haired, sharp-featured man came out behind him, followed him, soon overtook him, and kept along beside him until they turned the next corner. Dick's hopes were roused by this spectacle, but sank correspondingly when Grandison returned to the hotel. As Grandison said nothing about the encounter, Dick hoped there might be some self-consciousness behind this unexpected reticence the results of which might develop later on.

But Grandison was on hand again when his master came back to the hotel at night, and was in attendance again in the morning, with hot water, to assist at his master's toilet. Dick sent him on further errands from day to day, and upon one occasion came squarely up to him—inadvertently of course—while Grandison was engaged in conversation with a young white man in clerical garb. When Grandison saw Dick approaching, he edged away from the preacher and hastened toward his master, with a very evident expression of relief upon his countenance.

"Mars Dick," he said, "dese yer abolitioners is jes' pesterin' de life out er me tryin' ter git me ter run away. I don' pay no 'tention ter 'em, but dey riles me so sometimes dat I'm feared I'll hit some of 'em some er dese days, an' dat mought git me inter trouble. I ain' said nuffin' ter you 'bout it, Mars Dick, fer I did n' wanter 'sturb yo' min'; but I don' like it, suh; no, suh, I don'! Is we gwine back home 'fo' long, Mars Dick?"

"We'll be going back soon enough," replied Dick somewhat shortly, while he inwardly cursed the stupidity of a slave who could be free and would not, and registered a secret vow that if he were unable to get rid of Grandison without assassinating him, and were therefore compelled to take him back to Kentucky, he would see that Grandison got a taste of an article of slavery that would make him regret his wasted opportunities. Meanwhile he determined to tempt his servant yet more strongly.

"Grandison," he said next morning, "I'm going away for a day or two, but I shall leave you here. I shall lock up a hundred dollars in this drawer and give you the key. If you need any of it, use it and enjoy yourself,—spend it all if you like,—for this is probably the last chance you'll have for some time to be in a free State, and you'd better enjoy your liberty while you may."

When he came back a couple of days later and found the faithful Grandison at his post, and the hundred dollars intact, Dick felt seriously annoyed. His vexation was increased by the fact that he could not express his feelings adequately. He did not even scold Grandison; how could he, indeed, find fault with one who so sensibly recognized his true place in the economy of civilization, and kept it with such touching fidelity?

"I can't say a thing to him," groaned Dick. "He deserves a leather medal, made out of his own hide tanned. I reckon I'll write to father and let him know what a model servant he has given me."

He wrote his father a letter which made the colonel swell with pride and pleasure. "I really think," the colonel observed to one of his friends, "that Dick ought to have the nigger interviewed by the Boston papers, so that they may see how contented and happy our darkeys really are."

Dick also wrote a long letter to Charity Lomax, in which he said, among many other things, that if she knew how hard he was working, and under what difficulties, to accomplish something serious for her sake, she would no longer keep him in suspense, but over-whelm him with love and admiration.

Having thus exhausted without result the more obvious methods of getting rid of Grandison, and diplomacy having also proved a failure, Dick was forced to consider more radical measures. Of course he might run away himself, and abandon Grandison, but this would be merely to leave him in the United States, where he was still a slave, and where, with his notions of loyalty, he would speed-ily be reclaimed. It was necessary, in order to accomplish the pur-pose of his trip to the North, to leave Grandison permanently in Canada, where he would be legally free.

"I might extend my trip to Canada," he reflected, "but that would be too palpable. I have it! I'll visit Niagara Falls on the way home, and lose him on the Canada side. When he once realizes that he is actually free, I'll warrant that he'll stay."

So the next day saw them westward bound, and in due course of time, by the somewhat slow conveyances of the period, they found themselves at Niagara. Dick walked and drove about the Falls for several days, taking Grandison along with him on most occasions. One morning they stood on the Canadian side, watching the wild whirl of the waters below them.

"Grandison," said Dick, raising his voice above the roar of the cataract, "do you know where you are now?"

"I's wid you, Mars Dick; dats all I keers."

"You are now in Canada, Grandison, where your people go when they run away from their masters. If you wished, Grandison, you might walk away from me this very minute, and I could not lay my hand upon you to take you back."

Grandison looked around uneasily.

"Let's go back ober de ribber, Mars Dick. I's feared I'll lose you ovuh heah, an' den I won' hab no marster, an' won't nebber be able to git back home no mo'."

Discouraged, but not yet hopeless, Dick said, a few minutes later,—

"Grandison, I'm going up the road a bit, to the inn over yonder. You stay here until I return. I'll not be gone a great while."

Grandison's eyes opened wide and he looked somewhat fearful.

"Is dey any er dem dadblasted abolitioners roun' heah, Mars Dick?"

"I don't imagine that there are," replied his master, hoping there might be. "But I'm not afraid of *your* running away, Grandison. I only wish I were," he added to himself.

Dick walked leisurely down the road to where the white-washed inn, built of stone, with true British solidity, loomed up through the trees by the roadside. Arrived there he ordered a glass of ale and a sandwich, and took a seat at a table by a window, from which he could see Grandison in the distance. For a while he hoped that the seed he had sown might have fallen on fertile ground, and that Grandison, relieved from the restraining power of a master's eye, and finding himself in a free country, might get up and walk away; but the hope was vain, for Grandison remained faithfully at his post, awaiting his master's return. He had seated himself on a broad flat stone, and, turning his eyes away from the grand and awe-inspiring spectacle that lay close at hand, was looking anxiously toward the inn where his master sat cursing his ill-timed fidelity.

By and by a girl came into the room to serve his order, and Dick very naturally glanced at her; and as she was young and pretty and remained in attendance, it was some minutes before he looked for Grandison. When he did so his faithful servant had disappeared.

To pay his reckoning and go away without the change was a matter quickly accomplished. Retracing his footsteps toward the Falls, he saw, to his great disgust, as he approached the spot where he had left Grandison, the familiar form of his servant stretched out on the ground, his face to the sun, his mouth open, sleeping the time away, oblivious alike to the grandeur of the scenery, the thunderous roar of the cataract, or the insidious voice of sentiment.

"Grandison," soliloquized his master, as he stood gazing down at his ebony encumbrance, "I do not deserve to be an American citizen; I ought not to have the advantages I possess over you; and I certainly am not worthy of Charity Lomax, if I am not smart enough to get rid of you. I have an idea! You shall yet be free, and I will be the instrument of your deliverance. Sleep on, faithful and affectionate servitor, and dream of the blue grass and the bright skies of old Kentucky, for it is only in your dreams that you will ever see them again!"

Dick retraced his footsteps towards the inn. The young woman chanced to look out of the window and saw the handsome young gentleman she had waited on a few minutes before, standing in the road a short distance away, apparently engaged in earnest conversation with a colored man employed as hostler for the inn. She thought she saw something pass from the white man to the other, but at that moment her duties called her away from the window, and when she looked out again the young gentleman had disappeared, and the hostler, with two other young men of the neighborhood, one white and one colored, were walking rapidly towards the Falls.

IV

Dick made the journey homeward alone, and as rapidly as the conveyances of the day would permit. As he drew near home his conduct in going back without Grandison took on a more serious aspect than it had borne at any previous time, and although he had prepared the colonel by a letter sent several days ahead, there was still the prospect of a bad quarter of an hour with him; not, indeed, that his father would upbraid him, but he was likely to make searching inquiries. And notwithstanding the vein of quiet recklessness that had carried Dick through his preposterous scheme, he was a very poor liar, having rarely had occasion or inclination to tell anything but the truth. Any reluctance to meet his father was more than offset, however, by a stronger force drawing him homeward, for Charity Lomax must long since have returned from her visit to her aunt in Tennessee.

Dick got off easier than he had expected. He told a straight story, and a truthful one, so far as it went.

The colonel raged at first, but rage soon subsided into anger, and anger moderated into annoyance, and annoyance into a sort of garrulous sense of injury. The colonel thought he had been hardly used; he had trusted this negro, and he had broken faith. Yet, after all, he did not blame Grandison so much as he did the abolitionists, who were undoubtedly at the bottom of it.

As for Charity Lomax, Dick told her, privately of course, that he had run his father's man, Grandison, off to Canada, and left him there.

"Oh, Dick," she had said with shuddering alarm, "what have you done? If they knew it they'd send you to the penitentiary, like they did that Yankee."

"But they don't know it," he had replied seriously; adding, with an injured tone, "you don't seem to appreciate my heroism like you did that of the Yankee; perhaps it's because I was n't caught and sent to the penitentiary. I thought you wanted me to do it."

"Why, Dick Owens!" she exclaimed. "You know I never dreamed of any such outrageous proceeding.

"But I presume I'll have to marry you," she concluded, after some insistence on Dick's part, "if only to take care of you. You are too reckless for anything; and a man who goes chasing all over the North, being entertained by New York and Boston society and having negroes to throw away, needs some one to look after him."

"It's a most remarkable thing," replied Dick fervently, "that your views correspond exactly with my profoundest convictions. It proves beyond question that we were made for one another."

———

They were married three weeks later. As each of them had just returned from a journey, they spent their honeymoon at home.

A week after the wedding they were seated, one afternoon, on the piazza of the colonel's house, where Dick had taken his bride, when a negro from the yard ran down the lane and threw open the big gate for the colonel's buggy to enter. The colonel was not alone. Beside him, ragged and travel-stained, bowed with weariness and upon his face a haggard look that told of hardship and privation, sat the lost Grandison.

The colonel alighted at the steps.

"Take the lines, Tom," he said to the man who had opened the gate, "and drive round to the barn. Help Grandison down,—poor devil, he's so stiff he can hardly move!—and get a tub of water and wash him and rub him down, and feed him, and give him a big drink of whiskey, and then let him come round and see his young master and his new mistress."

The colonel's face wore an expression compounded of joy and indignation,—joy at the restoration of a valuable piece of property; indignation for reasons he proceeded to state.

"It's astounding, the depths of depravity the human heart is capable of! I was coming along the road three miles away, when I heard some one call me from the roadside. I pulled up the mare, and who should come out of the woods but Grandison. The poor nigger could hardly crawl along, with the help of a broken limb. I was never more astonished in my life. You could have knocked me down with a feather. He seemed pretty far gone,—he could hardly talk above a whisper,—and I had to give him a mouthful of whiskey to brave him up so he could tell his story. It's just as I thought from the beginning, Dick; Grandison had no notion of running away; he knew when he was well off, and where his friends were. All the persuasions of abolition liars and runaway niggers did not move him. But the desperation of those fanatics knew no bounds; their guilty consciences gave them no rest. They got the notion somehow that Grandison belonged to a nigger-catcher, and had been brought North as a spy to help capture ungrateful runaway servants. They actually kidnapped him—just think of it!—and gagged him and bound him and threw him rudely into a wagon, and carried him into the gloomy depths of a Canadian forest, and locked him in a lonely hut, and fed him on bread and water for three weeks. One of the scoundrels wanted to kill him, and persuaded the others that it ought to be done; but they got to quarreling about how they should do it, and before they had their minds made up Grandison escaped, and, keeping his back steadily to the North Star, made his way, after suffering incredible hardships, back to the old plantation, back to his master, his friends, and his home. Why, it's as good as one of Scott's novels! Mr. Simms or some other one of our Southern authors ought to write it up."

"Don't you think, sir," suggested Dick, who had calmly smoked his cigar throughout the colonel's animated recital, "that that kidnapping yarn sounds a little improbable? Is n't there some more likely explanation?"

"Nonsense, Dick; it's the gospel truth! Those infernal abolitionists are capable of anything—everything! Just think of their locking the poor, faithful nigger up, beating him, kicking him, depriving him of his liberty, keeping him on bread and water for three long, lonesome weeks, and he all the time pining for the old plantation!"

There were almost tears in the colonel's eyes at the picture of

Grandison's sufferings that he conjured up. Dick still professed to be slightly skeptical, and met Charity's severely questioning eye with bland unconsciousness.

The colonel killed the fatted calf for Grandison, and for two or three weeks the returned wanderer's life was a slave's dream of pleasure. His fame spread throughout the county, and the colonel gave him a permanent place among the house servants, where he could always have him conveniently at hand to relate his adventures to admiring visitors.

———

About three weeks after Grandison's return the colonel's faith in sable humanity was rudely shaken, and its foundations almost broken up. He came near losing his belief in the fidelity of the negro to his master,—the servile virtue most highly prized and most sedulously cultivated by the colonel and his kind. One Monday morning Grandison was missing. And not only Grandison, but his wife, Betty the maid; his mother, aunt Eunice; his father, uncle Ike; his brothers, Tom and John, and his little sister, Elsie, were likewise absent from the plantation; and a hurried search and inquiry in the neighborhood resulted in no information as to their whereabouts. So much valuable property could not be lost without an effort to recover it, and the wholesale nature of the transaction carried consternation to the hearts of those whose ledgers were chiefly bound in black. Extremely energetic measures were taken by the colonel and his friends. The fugitives were traced, and followed from point to point, on their northward run through Ohio. Several times the hunters were close upon their heels, but the magnitude of the escaping party begot unusual vigilance on the part of those who sympathized with the fugitives, and strangely enough, the underground railroad seemed to have had its tracks cleared and signals set for this particular train. Once, twice, the colonel thought he had them, but they slipped through his fingers.

One last glimpse he caught of his vanishing property, as he stood, accompanied by a United States marshal, on a wharf at a port on the south shore of Lake Erie. On the stern of a small steamboat which was receding rapidly from the wharf, with her nose pointing toward Canada, there stood a group of familiar dark faces, and the look they cast backward was not one of longing for the fleshpots of Egypt. The colonel saw Grandison point him out to one of the crew of the vessel, who waved his hand derisively toward the colonel. The latter shook his fist impotently—and the incident was closed.

Uncle Wellington's Wives

I

UNCLE WELLINGTON BRABOY was so deeply absorbed in thought as he walked slowly homeward from the weekly meeting of the Union League, that he let his pipe go out, a fact of which he remained oblivious until he had reached the little frame house in the suburbs of Patesville, where he lived with aunt Milly, his wife. On this particular occasion the club had been addressed by a visiting brother from the North, Professor Patterson, a tall, well-formed mulatto, who wore a perfectly fitting suit of broad-cloth, a shiny silk hat, and linen of dazzling whiteness,—in short, a gentleman of such distinguished appearance that the doors and windows of the offices and stores on Front Street were filled with curious observers as he passed through that thoroughfare in the early part of the day. This polished stranger was a traveling organizer of Masonic lodges, but he also claimed to be a high officer in the Union League, and had been invited to lecture before the local chapter of that organization at Patesville.

The lecture had been largely attended, and uncle Wellington Braboy had occupied a seat just in front of the platform. The subject of the lecture was "The Mental, Moral, Physical, Political, Social, and Financial Improvement of the Negro Race in America," a theme much dwelt upon, with slight variations, by colored orators. For to this struggling people, then as now, the problem of their uncertain present and their doubtful future was the chief concern of life. The period was the hopeful one. The Federal Government retained some vestige of authority in the South, and the newly emancipated race cherished the delusion that under the Constitution, that enduring rock on which our liberties are founded, and under the equal laws it purported to guarantee, they would enter upon the era of freedom and opportunity which their Northern friends had inaugurated with such solemn sanctions. The speaker pictured in eloquent language the state of ideal equality and happiness enjoyed by colored people at the North: how they sent their children to school with the white children; how they sat by white people in the churches and theatres, ate with them in the public restaurants, and buried their dead in the same cemeteries. The professor waxed eloquent with the development of his theme, and, as a finishing touch to an alluring picture, assured the excited audience that the intermarriage of the races was common, and that he himself had espoused a white woman.

Uncle Wellington Braboy was a deeply interested listener. He had heard something of these facts before, but his information had always come in such vague and questionable shape that he had paid little attention to it. He knew that the Yankees had freed the slaves, and that runaway negroes had always gone to the North to seek liberty; any such equality, however, as the visiting brother had depicted, was more than uncle Wellington had ever conceived as actually existing anywhere in the world. At first he felt inclined to doubt the truth of the speaker's statements; but the cut of his clothes, the eloquence of his language, and the flowing length of his whiskers, were so far superior to anything uncle Wellington had ever met among the colored people of his native State, that he felt irresistibly impelled to the conviction that nothing less than the advantages claimed for the North by the visiting brother could have produced such an exquisite flower of civilization. Any lingering doubts uncle Wellington may have felt were entirely dispelled by the courtly bow and cordial grasp of the hand with which the visiting brother acknowledged the congratulations showered upon him by the audience at the close of his address.

The more uncle Wellington's mind dwelt upon the professor's speech, the more attractive seemed the picture of Northern life presented. Uncle Wellington possessed in large measure the imaginative faculty so freely bestowed by nature upon the race from which

the darker half of his blood was drawn. He had indulged in occasional day-dreams of an ideal state of social equality, but his wildest
flights of fancy had never located it nearer than heaven, and he had
felt some misgivings about its practical working even there. Its desirability he had never doubted, and the speech of the evening before had given a local habitation and a name to the forms his
imagination had bodied forth. Giving full rein to his fancy, he saw
in the North a land flowing with milk and honey,—a land peopled
by noble men and beautiful women, among whom colored men and
women moved with the ease and grace of acknowledged right. Then
he placed himself in the foreground of the picture. What a fine figure he would have made in the world if he had been born at the free
North! He imagined himself dressed like the professor, and passing
the contribution-box in a white church; and most pleasant of his
dreams, and the hardest to realize as possible, was that of the gracious white lady he might have called wife. Uncle Wellington was a
mulatto, and his features were those of his white father, though
tinged with the hue of his mother's race; and as he lifted the
kerosene lamp at evening, and took a long look at his image in the
little mirror over the mantelpiece, he said to himself that he was a
very good-looking man, and could have adorned a much higher
sphere in life than that in which the accident of birth had placed
him. He fell asleep and dreamed that he lived in a two-story brick
house, with a spacious flower garden in front, the whole inclosed
by a high iron fence; that he kept a carriage and servants, and never
did a stroke of work. This was the highest style of living in
Patesville, and he could conceive of nothing finer.

Uncle Wellington slept later than usual the next morning, and the
sunlight was pouring in at the open window of the bedroom, when
his dreams were interrupted by the voice of his wife, in tones meant
to be harsh, but which no ordinary degree of passion could rob of
their native unctuousness.

"Git up f'm dere, you lazy, good-fuh-nuffin' nigger! Is you
gwine ter sleep all de mawnin'? I's ti'ed er dis yer runnin' 'roun' all
night an' den sleepin' all day. You won't git dat tater patch hoed
ovuh ter-day 'less'n you git up f'm dere an' git at it."

Uncle Wellington rolled over, yawned cavernously, stretched

himself, and with a muttered protest got out of bed and put on his clothes. Aunt Milly had prepared a smoking breakfast of hominy and fried bacon, the odor of which was very grateful to his nostrils.

"Is breakfus' done ready?" he inquired, tentatively, as he came into the kitchen and glanced at the table.

"No, it ain't ready, an' 't ain't gwine ter be ready 'tel you tote dat wood an' water in," replied aunt Milly severely, as she poured two teacups of boiling water on two tablespoonfuls of ground coffee.

Uncle Wellington went down to the spring and got a pail of water, after which he brought in some oak logs for the fireplace and some lightwood for kindling. Then he drew a chair towards the table and started to sit down.

"Wonduh what's de matter wid you dis mawnin' anyhow," remarked aunt Milly. "You must 'a' be'n up ter some devilment las' night, fer yo' recommemb'ance is so po' dat you fus' fergit ter git up, an' den fergit ter wash yo' face an' hands fo' you set down ter de table. I don' 'low nobody ter eat at my table dat a-way."

"I don' see no use'n washin' 'em so much," replied Wellington wearily. "Dey gits dirty ag'in right off, an' den you got ter wash 'em ovuh ag'in; it's jes' pilin' up wuk what don' fetch in nuffin'. De dirt don' show nohow, 'n I don' see no advantage in bein' black, ef you got to keep on washin' yo' face 'n' han's jes' lack w'ite folks." He nevertheless performed his ablutions in a perfunctory way, and resumed his seat at the breakfast-table.

"Ole 'oman," he asked, after the edge of his appetite had been taken off, "how would you lack ter live at de Norf?"

"I dunno nuffin' 'bout de Norf," replied aunt Milly. "It's hard 'nuff ter git erlong heah, whar we knows all erbout it."

"De brother what 'dressed de meetin' las' night say dat de wages at de Norf is twicet ez big ez dey is heah."

"You could make a sight mo' wages heah ef you'd 'ten' ter yo' wuk better," replied aunt Milly.

Uncle Wellington ignored this personality, and continued, "An' he say de cullud folks got all de privileges er de w'ite folks,—dat dey chillen goes ter school tergedder, dat dey sets on same seats in chu'ch, an' sarves on jury, 'n' rides on de kyars an' steamboats wid de w'ite folks, an' eats at de fus' table."

"Dat 'u'd suit you," chuckled aunt Milly, "an' you'd stay dere fer de secon' table, too. How dis man know 'bout all dis yer foolis'-ness?" she asked incredulously.

"He come f'm de Norf," said uncle Wellington, "an' he 'spe-unced it all hisse'f."

"Well, he can't make me b'lieve it," she rejoined, with a shake of her head.

"An' you would n' lack ter go up dere an' 'joy all dese privi-leges?" asked uncle Wellington, with some degree of earnestness.

The old woman laughed until her sides shook. "Who gwine ter take me up dere?" she inquired.

"You got de money yo'se'f."

"I ain't got no money fer ter was'e," she replied shortly, becom-ing serious at once; and with that the subject was dropped.

Uncle Wellington pulled a hoe from under the house, and took his way wearily to the potato patch. He did not feel like working, but aunt Milly was the undisputed head of the establishment, and he did not dare to openly neglect his work. In fact, he regarded work at any time as a disagreeable necessity to be avoided as much as possible.

His wife was cast in a different mould. Externally she would have impressed the casual observer as a neat, well-preserved, and good-looking black woman, of middle age, every curve of whose ample figure—and her figure was all curves—was suggestive of re-pose. So far from being indolent, or even deliberate in her move-ments, she was the most active and energetic woman in the town. She went through the physical exercises of a prayer-meeting with astonishing vigor. It was exhilarating to see her wash a shirt, and a study to watch her do it up. A quick jerk shook out the dampened garment; one pass of her ample palm spread it over the ironing-board, and a few well-directed strokes with the iron accomplished what would have occupied the ordinary laundress for half an hour.

To this uncommon, and in uncle Wellington's opinion unneces-sary and unnatural activity, his own habits were a steady protest. If aunt Milly had been willing to support him in idleness, he would have acquiesced without a murmur in her habits of industry. This she would not do, and, moreover, insisted on his working at least half the time. If she had invested the proceeds of her labor in rich food and fine clothing, he might have endured it better; but to her passion for work was added a most detestable thrift. She absolutely refused to pay for Wellington's clothes, and required him to furnish a certain proportion of the family supplies. Her savings were carefully put by, and with them she had bought and paid for the modest cottage which she and her husband occupied. Under her careful hand it was always neat and clean; in summer the little yard was gay with bright-colored flowers, and woe to the heedless pickaninny who should stray into her yard and pluck a rose or a verbena! In a stout oaken chest under her bed she kept a capacious stocking, into which flowed a steady stream of fractional currency. She carried the key to this chest in her pocket, a proceeding regarded by uncle Wellington with no little disfavor. He was of the opinion—an opinion he would not have dared to assert in her presence—that his wife's earnings were his own property; and he looked upon this stocking as a drunkard's wife might regard the saloon which absorbed her husband's wages.

Uncle Wellington hurried over the potato patch on the morning of the conversation above recorded, and as soon as he saw aunt Milly go away with a basket of clothes on her head, returned to the house, put on his coat, and went uptown.

He directed his steps to a small frame building fronting on the main street of the village, at a point where the street was intersected by one of the several creeks meandering through the town, cooling the air, providing numerous swimming-holes for the amphibious small boy, and furnishing water-power for grist-mills and saw-mills. The rear of the building rested on long brick pillars, built up from the bottom of the steep bank of the creek, while the front was level with the street. This was the office of Mr. Matthew Wright, the sole representative of the colored race at the bar of Chinquapin County. Mr. Wright came of an "old issue" free colored family, in which, though the negro blood was present in an attenuated strain, a line of free ancestry could be traced beyond the Revolutionary War. He had enjoyed exceptional opportunities, and enjoyed the distinction of being the first, and for a long time the only colored lawyer in North Carolina. His services were frequently called into requisition by impecunious people of his own race; when they had money they went to white lawyers, who, they shrewdly conjectured, would have more influence with judge or jury than a colored lawyer, however able.

Uncle Wellington found Mr. Wright in his office. Having inquired after the health of the lawyer's family and all his relations in detail, uncle Wellington asked for a professional opinion.

"Mistah Wright, ef a man's wife got money, whose money is dat befo' de law—his'n er her'n?"

The lawyer put on his professional air, and replied:—

"Under the common law, which in default of special legislative enactment is the law of North Carolina, the personal property of the wife belongs to her husband."

"But dat don' jes' tech de p'int, suh. I wuz axin' 'bout money."

"You see, uncle Wellington, your education has not rendered you familiar with legal phraseology. The term 'personal property' or 'estate' embraces, according to Blackstone, all property other than land, and therefore includes money. Any money a man's wife has is his, constructively, and will be recognized as his actually, as soon as he can secure possession of it."

"Dat is ter say, suh—my eddication don' quite 'low me ter understan' dat—dat is ter say"—

"That is to say, it's yours when you get it. It is n't yours so that the law will help you get it; but on the other hand, when you once lay your hands on it, it is yours so that the law won't take it away from you."

Uncle Wellington nodded to express his full comprehension of the law as expounded by Mr. Wright, but scratched his head in a way that expressed some disappointment. The law seemed to wobble. Instead of enabling him to stand up fearlessly and demand his own, it threw him back upon his own efforts; and the prospect of his being able to overpower or outwit aunt Milly by any ordinary means was very poor.

He did not leave the office, but hung around awhile as though there were something further he wished to speak about. Finally, after some discursive remarks about the crops and politics, he asked, in an offhand, disinterested manner, as though the thought had just occured to him:—

"Mistah Wright, w'ile's we' re talkin' 'bout law matters, what do it cos' ter git a defoce?"

"That depends upon circumstances. It is n't altogether a matter of expense. Have you and aunt Milly been having trouble?"

"Oh no, suh; I was jes' a-wond'rin'."

"You see," continued the lawyer, who was fond of talking, and had nothing else to do for the moment, "a divorce is not an easy thing to get in this State under any circumstances. It used to be the law that divorce could be granted only by special act of the legislature; and it is but recently that the subject has been relegated to the jurisdiction of the courts."

Uncle Wellington understood a part of this, but the answer had not been exactly to the point in his mind.

"S'pos'n', den, jes' fer de argument, me an' my ole 'oman sh'd fall out en wanter separate, how could I git a defoce?"

"That would depend on what you quarreled about. It's pretty hard work to answer general questions in a particular way. If you merely wished to separate, it would n't be necessary to get a divorce; but if you should want to marry again, you would have to be divorced, or else you would be guilty of bigamy, and could be sent to the penitentiary. But, by the way, uncle Wellington, when were you married?"

"I got married 'fo' de wah, when I was livin' down on Rockfish Creek."

"When you were in slavery?"

"Yas, suh."

"Did you have your marriage registered after the surrender?"

"No, suh; never knowed nuffin' 'bout dat."

After the war, in North Carolina and other States, the freed people who had sustained to each other the relation of husband and wife as it existed among slaves were required by law to register their consent to continue in the marriage relation. By this simple expedient their former marriages of convenience received the sanction of law, and their children the seal of legitimacy. In many cases, however, where the parties lived in districts remote from the larger towns, the ceremony was neglected, or never heard of by the freedmen.

"Well," said the lawyer, "if that is the case, and you and aunt Milly should disagree, it would n't be necessary for you to get a divorce, even if you should want to marry again. You were never legally married."

"So Milly ain't my lawful wife, den?"

"She may be your wife in one sense of the word, but not in such a sense as to render you liable to punishment for bigamy if you should marry another woman. But I hope you will never want to do anything of the kind, for you have a very good wife now."

Uncle Wellington went away thoughtfully, but with a feeling of unaccustomed lightness and freedom. He had not felt so free since the memorable day when he had first heard of the Emancipation Proclamation. On leaving the lawyer's office, he called at the workshop of one of his friends, Peter Williams, a shoemaker by trade, who had a brother living in Ohio.

"Is you hearn f'm Sam lately?" uncle Wellington inquired, after the conversation had drifted through the usual generalities.

"His mammy got er letter f'm 'im last week; he's livin' in de town er Groveland now."

"How's he gittin' on?"

"He says he gittin' on monst'us well. He 'low ez how he make five dollars a day w'itewashin', an' have all he kin do."

The shoemaker related various details of his brother's prosperity, and uncle Wellington returned home in a very thoughtful mood, revolving in his mind a plan of future action. This plan had been vaguely assuming form ever since the professor's lecture, and the events of the morning had brought out the detail in bold relief.

Two days after the conversation with the shoemaker, aunt Milly went, in the afternoon, to visit a sister of hers who lived several miles out in the country. During her absence, which lasted until nightfall, uncle Wellington went uptown and purchased a cheap oil-cloth valise from a shrewd son of Israel, who had penetrated to this locality with a stock of notions and cheap clothing. Uncle Wellington had his purchase done up in brown paper, and took the parcel under his arm. Arrived at home he unwrapped the valise, and thrust into its capacious jaws his best suit of clothes, some underwear, and a few other small articles for personal use and adornment. Then he carried the valise out into the yard, and, first looking cautiously around to see if there was any one in sight, concealed it in a clump of bushes in a corner of the yard.

It may be inferred from this proceeding that uncle Wellington was preparing for a step of some consequence. In fact, he had fully made up his mind to go to the North; but he still lacked the most important requisite for traveling with comfort, namely, the money to pay his expenses. The idea of tramping the distance which separated him from the promised land of liberty and equality had never occurred to him. When a slave, he had several times been importuned by fellow servants to join them in the attempt to escape from bondage, but he had never wanted his freedom badly enough to walk a thousand miles for it; if he could have gone to Canada by stage-coach, or by rail, or on horseback, with stops for regular meals, he would probably have undertaken the trip. The funds he now needed for his journey were in aunt Milly's chest. He had thought a great deal about his right to this money. It was his wife's savings, and he had never dared to dispute, openly, her right to exercise exclusive control over what she earned; but the lawyer had assured him of his right to the money, of which he was already constructively in possession, and he had therefore determined to possess himself actually of the coveted stocking. It was impracticable for him to get the key of the chest. Aunt Milly kept it in her pocket by day and under her pillow at night. She was a light sleeper, and, if not awakened by the abstraction of the key, would certainly have been disturbed by the unlocking of the chest. But one alternative remained, and that was to break open the chest in her absence.

There was a revival in progress at the colored Methodist church. Aunt Milly was as energetic in her religion as in other respects, and had not missed a single one of the meetings. She returned at nightfall from her visit to the country and prepared a frugal supper. Uncle Wellington did not eat as heartily as usual. Aunt Milly perceived his want of appetite, and spoke of it. He explained it by saying that he did not feel very well.

"Is you gwine ter chu'ch ter-night?" inquired his wife.

"I reckon I'll stay home an' go ter bed," he replied. "I ain't be'n feelin' well dis evenin', an' I 'spec' I better git a good night's res'."

"Well, you kin stay ef you mineter. Good preachin' 'u'd make you feel better, but ef you ain't gwine, don' fergit ter tote in some wood an' lighterd 'fo' you go ter bed. De moon is shinin' bright, an' you can't have no 'scuse 'bout not bein' able ter see."

Uncle Wellington followed her out to the gate, and watched her receding form until it disappeared in the distance. Then he re-entered the house with a quick step, and taking a hatchet from a corner of the room, drew the chest from under the bed. As he applied the hatchet to the fastenings, a thought struck him, and by the flickering light of the pine-knot blazing on the hearth, a look of hesitation might have been seen to take the place of the determined expression his face had worn up to that time. He had argued himself into the belief that his present action was lawful and justifiable. Though this conviction had not prevented him from trembling in every limb, as though he were committing a mere vulgar theft, it had still nerved him to the deed. Now even his moral courage began to weaken. The lawyer had told him that his wife's property was his own; in taking it he was therefore only exercising his lawful right. But at the point of breaking open the chest, it occurred to him that he was taking this money in order to get away from aunt Milly, and that he justified his desertion of her by the lawyer's opinion that she was not his lawful wife. If she was not his wife, then he had no right to take the money; if she was not his wife, he had no right to desert her, and would certainly have no right to marry another woman. His scheme was about to go to shipwreck on this rock, when another idea occurred to him.

"De lawyer say dat in one sense er de word de ole 'oman is my wife, an' in anudder sense er de word she ain't my wife. Ef I goes ter de Norf an' marry a w'ite 'oman, I ain't commit no brigamy, 'caze in dat sense er de word she ain't my wife; but ef I takes dis money, I ain't stealn' it, 'caze in dat sense er de word she is my wife. Dat 'splains all de trouble away."

Having reached this ingenious conclusion, uncle Wellington applied the hatchet vigorously, soon loosened the fastenings of the chest, and with trembling hands extracted from its depths a capacious blue cotton stocking. He emptied the stocking on the table. His first impulse was to take the whole, but again there arose in his mind a doubt—a very obtrusive, unreasonable doubt, but a doubt, nevertheless—of the absolute rectitude of his conduct; and after a moment's hesitation he hurriedly counted the money—it was in bills of small denominations—and found it to be about two hundred and fifty dollars. He then divided it into two piles of one hundred and twenty-five dollars each. He put one pile into his pocket, returned the remainder to the stocking, and replaced it where he had found it. He then closed the chest and shoved it under the bed. After having arranged the fire so that it could safely be left burning, he took a last look around the room, and went out into the moon-light, locking the door behind him, and hanging the key on a nail in the wall, where his wife would be likely to look for it. He then se-cured his valise from behind the bushes, and left the yard. As he passed by the wood-pile, he said to himself:—

"Well, I declar' ef I ain't done fergot ter tote in dat lighterd; I reckon de ole 'oman 'll ha' ter fetch it in herse'f dis time."

He hastened through the quiet streets, avoiding the few people who were abroad at that hour, and soon reached the railroad sta-tion, from which a North-bound train left at nine o'clock. He went around to the dark side of the train, and climbed into a second-class car, where he shrank into the darkest corner and turend his face away from the dim light of the single dirty lamp. There were no passengers in the car except one or two sleepy negroes, who had got on at some other station, and a white man who had gone into the car to smoke, accompanied by a gigantic bloodhound.

Finally the train crept out of the station. From the window uncle Wellington looked out upon the familiar cabins and turpentine stills, the new barrel factory, the brickyard where he had once worked for some time; and as the train rattled through the outskirts of the town, he saw gleaming in the moonlight the white headstones of the colored cemetery where his only daughter had been buried several years before.

Presently the conductor came around. Uncle Wellington had not bought a ticket, and the conductor collected a cash fare. He was not acquainted with uncle Wellington, but had just had a drink at the saloon near the depot, and felt at peace with all mankind.

"Where are you going, uncle?" he inquired carelessly.

Uncle Wellington's face assumed the ashen hue which does duty for pallor in dusty countenances, and his knees began to tremble. Controlling his voice as well as he could, he replied that he was going up to Jonesboro, the terminus of the railroad, to work for a gentleman at that place. He felt immensely relieved when the con-ductor pocketed the fare, picked up his lantern, and moved away. It was very unphilosophical and very absurd that a man who was only doing right should feel like a thief, shrink from the sight of other people, and lie instinctively. Fine distinctions were not in uncle Wellington's line, but he was struck by the unreasonableness of his feelings, and still more by the discomfort they caused him. By and by, however, the motion of the train made him drowsy; his thoughts all ran together in confusion; and he fell asleep with his head on his valise, and one hand in his pocket, clasped tightly around the roll of money.

II

The train from Pittsburg drew into the Union Depot at Groveland, Ohio, one morning in the spring of 187–, with bell ringing and engine puffing; and from a smoking-car emerged the form of uncle Wellington Braboy, a little dusty and travel-stained, and with a sleepy look about his eyes. He mingled in the crowd, and, valise in hand, moved toward the main exit from the depot. There were several tracks to be crossed, and more than once a watchman snatched him out of the way of a baggage-truck, or a train backing into the depot. He at length reached the door, beyond which, and as near as the regulations would permit, stood a number of hackmen, vociferously soliciting patronage. One of them, a colored man, soon secured several passengers. As he closed the door after the last one he turned to uncle Wellington, who stood near him on the sidewalk, looking about irresolutely.

"Is you goin' uptown?" asked the hackman, as he prepared to mount the box.

"Yas, suh."

"I'll take you up fo' a quahtah, ef you want ter git up here an' ride on de box wid me."

Uncle Wellington accepted the offer and mounted the box. The hackman whipped up his horses, the carriage climbed the steep hill leading up to the town, and the passengers inside were soon deposited at their hotels.

"Whereabouts do you want to go?" asked the hackman of uncle Wellington, when the carriage was emptied of its last passengers.

"I want ter go ter Brer Sam Williams's," said Wellington.

"What's his street an' number?"

Uncle Wellington did not know the street and number, and the hackman had to explain to him the mystery of numbered houses, to which he was a total stranger.

"Where is he from?" asked the hackman, "and what is his business?"

"He is f'm Norf Ca'lina," replied uncle Wellington, "an' makes his livin' w'itewashin'."

"I reckon I knows de man," said the hackman. "I 'spec' he's changed his name. De man I knows is name' Johnson. He b'longs ter my chu'ch. I'm gwine out dat way ter git a passenger fer de ten o'clock train, an' I'll take you by dere."

They followed one of the least handsome streets of the city for more than a mile, turned into a cross street, and drew up before a small frame house, from the front of which a sign, painted in white upon a black background, announced to the reading public, in letters inclined to each other at various angles, that whitewashing and kalsomining were "dun" there. A knock at the door brought out a slatternly looking colored woman. She had evidently been disturbed at her toilet, for she held a comb in one hand, and the hair on one side of her head stood out loosely, while on the other side it was braided close to her head. She called her husband, who proved to be the Patesville shoemaker's brother. The hackman introduced the traveler, whose name he had learned on the way out, collected his quarter, and drove away.

Mr. Johnson, the shoemaker's brother, welcomed uncle Wellington to Groveland, and listened with eager delight to the news of the old town, from which he himself had run away many years before, and followed the North Star to Groveland. He had changed his name from "Williams" to "Johnson," on account of the Fugitive Slave Law, which, at the time of his escape from bondage, had rendered it advisable for runaway slaves to court obscurity. After the war he had retained the adopted name. Mrs. Johnson prepared breakfast for her guest, who ate it with an appetite sharpened by his journey. After breakfast he went to bed, and slept until late in the afternoon.

After supper Mr. Johnson took uncle Wellington to visit some of the neighbors who had come from North Carolina before the war. They all expressed much pleasure at meeting "Mr. Braboy," a title which at first sounded a little odd to uncle Wellington. At home he had been "Wellin'ton," "Brer Wellin'ton," or "uncle Wellin'ton"; it was a novel experience to be called "Mister," and he set it down, with secret satisfaction, as one of the first fruits of Northern liberty.

"Would you lack ter look 'roun' de town a little?" asked Mr. Johnson at breakfast next morning. "I ain' got no job dis mawnin' an' I kin show you some er de sights."

Uncle Wellington acquiesced in this arrangement, and they walked up to the corner to the street-car line. In a few moments a car passed. Mr. Johnson jumped on the moving car, and uncle Wellington followed his example, at the risk of life or limb, as it was his first experience of street cars.

There was only one vacant seat in the car and that was between two white women in the forward end. Mr. Johnson motioned to the seat, but Wellington shrank from walking between those two rows of white people, to say nothing of sitting between the two women, so he remained standing in the rear part of the car. A moment later, as the car rounded a short curve, he was pitched sidewise into the lap of a stout woman magnificently attired in a ruffled blue calico gown. The lady colored up, and uncle Wellington, as he struggled to his feet amid the laughter of the passengers, was absolutely helpless with embarrassment, until the conductor came up behind him and pushed him toward the vacant place.

"Sit down, will you," he said; and before uncle Wellington could collect himself, he was seated between the two white women. Everybody in the car seemed to be looking at him. But he came to the conclusion, after he had pulled himself together and reflected a few moments, that he would find this method of locomotion pleasanter when he got used to it, and then he could score one more glorious privilege gained by his change of residence.

They got off at the public square, in the heart of the city, where there were flowers and statues, and fountains playing. Mr. Johnson pointed out the court-house, the post-office, the jail, and other public buildings fronting on the square. They visited the market near by, and from an elevated point, looked down upon the extensive lumber yards and factories that were the chief sources of the city's prosperity. Beyond these they could see the fleet of ships that lined the coal and iron ore docks of the harbor. Mr. Johnson, who was quite a fluent talker, enlarged upon the wealth and prosperity of the city; and Wellington, who had never before been in a town of more than three thousand inhabitants, manifested sufficient interest and wonder to satisfy the most exacting *cicerone*. They called at the office of a colored lawyer and member of the legislature, formerly from North Carolina, who, scenting a new constituent and a possible client, greeted the stranger warmly, and in flowing speech pointed out the superior advantages of life at the North, citing himself as an illustration of the possibilities of life in a country really free. As they wended their way homeward to dinner uncle Wellington, with quickened pulse and rising hopes, felt that this was indeed the promised land, and that it must be flowing with milk and honey.

Uncle Wellington remained at the residence of Mr. Johnson for several weeks before making any effort to find employment. He spent this period in looking about the city. The most commonplace things possessed for him the charm of novelty, and he had come prepared to admire. Shortly after his arrival, he had offered to pay for his board, intimating at the same time that he had plenty of money. Mr. Johnson declined to accept anything from him for board, and expressed himself as being only too proud to have Mr. Braboy remain in the house on the footing of an honored guest, until he had settled himself. He lightened in some degree, however, the burden of obligation under which a prolonged stay on these terms would have placed his guest, by soliciting from the latter occasional small loans, until uncle Wellington's roll of money began to lose its plumpness, and with an empty pocket staring him in the face, he felt the necessity of finding something to do.

During his residence in the city he had met several times his first acquaintance, Mr. Peterson, the hackman, who from time to time inquired how he was getting along. On one of these occasions Wellington mentioned his willingness to accept employment. As good luck would have it, Mr. Peterson knew of a vacant situation. He had formerly been coachman for a wealthy gentleman residing on Oakwood Avenue, but had resigned the situation to go into business for himself. His place had been filled by an Irishman, who had just been discharged for drunkenness, and the gentleman that very day had sent word to Mr. Peterson, asking him if he could recommend a competent and trustworthy coachman.

"Does you know anything erbout hosses?" asked Mr. Peterson.

"Yas, indeed, I does," said Wellington. "I wuz raise' 'mongs' hosses."

"I tol' my ole boss I'd look out fer a man, an' ef you reckon you kin fill de 'quirements er de situation, I'll take yo' roun' dere termorrer mornin'. You wants ter put on yo' bes' clothes an' slick up, fer dey're partic'lar people. Ef you git de place I'll expec' you ter pay me fer de time I lose in 'tendin' ter yo' business, fer time is money in dis country, an' folks don't do much fer nuthin'."

Next morning Wellington blacked his shoes carefully, put on a clean collar, and with the aid of Mrs. Johnson tied his cravat in a jaunty bow which gave him quite a sprightly air and a much younger look than his years warranted. Mr. Peterson called for him at eight o'clock. After traversing several cross streets they turned into Oakwood Avenue and walked along the finest part of it for about half a mile. The handsome houses of this famous avenue, the stately trees, the wide-spreading lawns, dotted with flower beds, fountains and statuary, made up a picture so far surpassing anything in Wellington's experience as to fill him with an almost oppressive sense of its beauty.

"Hit looks lack hebben," he said softly.

"It's a pootty fine street," rejoined his companion, with a judicial air, "but I don't like dem big lawns. It's too much trouble ter keep de grass down. One er dem lawns is big enough to pasture a couple er cows."

They went down a street running at right angles to the avenue, and turned into the rear of the corner lot. A large building of pressed brick, trimmed with stone, loomed up before them.

"Do de gemman lib in dis house?" asked Wellington, gazing with awe at the front of the building.

"No, dat's de barn," said Mr . Peterson with good-natured contempt; and leading the way past a clump of shrubbery to the dwelling-house, he went up the back steps and rang the door-bell.

The ring was answered by a buxom Irishwoman, of a natural freshness of complexion deepened to a fiery red by the heat of a kitchen range. Wellington thought he had seen her before, but his mind had received so many new impressions lately that it was a minute or two before he recognized in her the lady whose lap he had involuntarily occupied for a moment on his first day in Grove-land.

"Faith," she exclaimed as she admitted them, "an' it's mighty glad I am to see ye ag'in, Misther Payterson! An' how hev ye be'n, Misther Payterson, sence I see ye lahst?"

"Middlin' well, Mis' Flannigan, middlin' well, 'ceptin' a tech er de rheumatiz. S'pose you be'n doin' well as usual?"

"Oh yis, as well as a dacent woman could do wid a drunken baste about the place like the lahst coachman. O Misther Payterson, it would make yer heart bleed to see the way the spalpeen cut up a-Saturday! But Misther Todd discharged 'im the same avenin', wid-out a character, bad 'cess to 'im, an' we've had no coachman sence at all, at all. An' it's sorry I am"—

The lady's flow of eloquence was interrupted at this point by the appearance of Mr. Todd himself, who had been informed of the men's arrival. He asked some questions in regard to Wellington's qualifications and former experience, and in view of his recent ar-rival in the city was willing to accept Mr. Peterson's recommenda-tion instead of a reference. He said a few words about the nature of the work, and stated his willingness to pay Wellington the wages formerly allowed Mr. Peterson, thirty dollars a month and board and lodging.

This handsome offer was eagerly accepted, and it was agreed that Wellington's term of service should begin immediately. Mr. Peter-son, being familiar with the work, and financially interested, con-ducted the new coachman through the stables and showed him what he would have to do. The silver-mounted harness, the variety of carriages, the names of which he learned for the first time, the arrangements for feeding and watering the horses,—these appoint-ments of a rich man's stable impressed Wellington very much, and he wondered that so much luxury should be wasted on mere horses. The room assigned to him, in the second story of the barn, was a finer apartment than he had ever slept in; and the salary attached to the situation was greater than the combined monthly earnings of himself and aunt Milly in their Southern home. Surely, he thought, his lines had fallen in pleasant places.

Under the stimulus of new surroundings Wellington applied

himself diligently to work, and, with the occasional advice of Mr.
Peterson, soon mastered the details of his employment. He found
the female servants, with whom he took his meals, very amiable
ladies. The cook, Mrs. Katie Flannigan, was a widow. Her husband,
a sailor, had been lost at sea. She was a woman of many words, and
when she was not lamenting the late Flannigan's loss,—according to
her story he had been a model of all the virtues,—she would turn
the batteries of her tongue against the former coachman. This gentleman, as Wellington gathered from frequent remarks dropped by
Mrs. Flannigan, had paid her attentions clearly susceptible of a serious construction. These attentions had not borne their legitimate
fruit, and she was still a widow unconsoled,—hence Mrs. Flannigan's tears. The housemaid was a plump, good-natured German
girl, with a pronounced German accent. The presence on washdays
of a Bohemian laundress, of recent importation, added another to
the variety of ways in which the English tongue was mutilated in
Mr. Todd's kitchen. Association with the white women drew out all
the native gallantry of the mulatto, and Wellington developed quite
a helpful turn. His politeness, his willingness to lend a hand in
kitchen or laundry, and the fact that he was the only male servant
on the place, combined to make him a prime favorite in the servants' quarters.

It was the general opinion among Wellington's acquaintances
that he was a single man. He had come to the city alone, had never
been heard to speak of a wife, and to personal questions bearing
upon the subject of matrimony had always returned evasive answers. Though he had never questioned the correctness of the
lawyer's opinion in regard to his slave marriage, his conscience had
never been entirely at ease since his departure from the South, and
any positive denial of his married condition would have stuck in his
throat. The inference naturally drawn from his reticence in regard
to the past, coupled with his expressed intention of settling permanently in Groveland, was that he belonged in the ranks of the unmarried, and was therefore legitimate game for any widow or old
maid who could bring him down. As such game is bagged easiest at
short range, he received numerous invitations to tea-parties, where
he feasted on unlimited chicken and pound cake. He used to com-

pare these viands with the plain fare often served by aunt Milly, and the result of the comparison was another item to the credit of the North upon his mental ledger. Several of the colored ladies who smiled upon him were blessed with good looks, and uncle Wellington, naturally of a susceptible temperament, as people of lively imagination are apt to be, would probably have fallen a victim to the charms of some woman of his own race, had it not been for a strong counter-attraction in the person of Mrs. Flannigan. The attentions of the lately discharged coachman had lighted anew the smouldering fires of her widowed heart, and awakened longings which still remained unsatisfied. She was thirty-five years old, and felt the need of some one else to love. She was not a woman of lofty ideals; with her a man was a man—

For a' that an' a' that;

and, aside from the accident of color, uncle Wellington was as personable a man as any of her acquaintance. Some people might have objected to his complexion; but then, Mrs. Flannigan argued, he was at least half white; and, this being the case, there was no good reason why he should be regarded as black.

Uncle Wellington was not slow to perceive Mrs. Flannigan's charms of person, and appreciated to the full the skill that prepared the choice tidbits reserved for his plate at dinner. The prospect of securing a white wife had been one of the principal inducements offered by a life at the North; but the awe of white people in which he had been reared was still too strong to permit his taking any active steps toward the object of his secret desire, had not the lady herself come to his assistance with a little of the native coquetry of her race.

"Ah, Misther Braboy," she said one evening when they sat at the supper table alone,—it was the second girl's afternoon off, and she had not come home to supper,—"it must be an awful lonesome life ye 've been afther l'adin', as a single man, wid no one to cook fer ye, or look afther ye."

"It are a kind er lonesome life, Mis' Flannigan, an' dat's a fac'. But sence I had de privilege er eatin' yo' cookin' an' 'joyin' yo' society, I ain' felt a bit lonesome."

"Yer flatthrin' me, Misther Braboy. An' even if ye mane it"—

"I means eve'y word of it, Mis' Flannigan."

"An' even if ye mane it, Misther Braboy, the time is liable to come when things 'll be different; for service is uncertain, Misther Braboy. An' then you 'll wish you had some nice, clean woman, 'at knowed how to cook an' wash an' iron, ter look afther ye, an' make yer life comfortable."

Uncle Wellington sighed, and looked at her languishingly.

"It 'u'd all be well ernuff, Mis' Flannigan, ef I had n' met you; but I don' know whar I's ter fin' a colored lady w'at 'll begin ter suit me after habbin' libbed in de same house wid you."

"Colored lady, indade! Why, Misther Braboy, ye don't nade ter demane yerself by marryin' a colored lady—not but they're as good as anybody else, so long as they behave themselves. There's many a white woman 'u'd be glad ter git as fine a lookin' man as ye are."

"Now *you 're* flattrin' *me*, Mis' Flannigan," said Wellington. But he felt a sudden and substantial increase in courage when she had spoken, and it was with astonishing ease that he found himself saying:—

"Dey ain' but one lady, Mis' Flannigan, dat could injuce me ter want ter change de lonesomeness er my singleness fer de 'sponsibilities er matermony, an' I'm feared she'd say no ef I 'd ax her."

"Ye 'd better ax her, Misther Braboy, an' not be wastin' time a-wond'rin'. Do I know the lady?"

"You knows 'er better 'n anybody else, Mis' Flannigan. *You* is de only lady I'd be satisfied ter marry after knowin' you. Ef you casts me off I 'll spen' de rest er my days in lonesomeness an' mis'ry."

Mrs. Flannigan affected much surprise and embarrassment at this bold declaration.

"Oh, Misther Braboy," she said, covering him with a coy glance, "an' it's rale 'shamed I am to hev b'en talkin' ter ye ez I hev. It looks as though I 'd b'en doin' the coortin'. I did n't drame that I 'd b'en able ter draw yer affections to mesilf."

"I's loved you ever since I fell in yo' lap on de street car de fus' day I wuz in Groveland," he said, as he moved his chair up closer to hers.

One evening in the following week they went out after supper to the residence of Rev. Cæsar Williams, pastor of the colored Baptist church, and, after the usual preliminaries, were pronounced man and wife.

III

According to all his preconceived notions, this marriage ought to have been the acme of uncle Wellington's felicity. But he soon found that it was not without its drawbacks. On the following morning Mr. Todd was informed of the marriage. He had no special objection to it, or interest in it, except that he was opposed on principle to having husband and wife in his employment at the same time. As a consequence, Mrs. Braboy, whose place could be more easily filled than that of her husband, received notice that her services would not be required after the end of the month. Her husband was retained in his place as coachman.

Upon the loss of her situation, Mrs. Braboy decided to exercise the married woman's prerogative of letting her husband support her. She rented the upper floor of a small house in an Irish neighborhood. The newly wedded pair furnished their rooms on the installment plan and began housekeeping.

There was one little circumstance, however, that interfered slightly with their enjoyment of that perfect freedom from care which ought to characterize a honeymoon. The people who owned the house and occupied the lower floor had rented the upper part to Mrs. Braboy in person, it never occuring to them that her husband could be other than a white man. When it became known that he was colored, the landlord, Mr. Dennis O'Flaherty, felt that he had been imposed upon, and, at the end of the first month, served notice upon his tenants to leave the premises. When Mrs. Braboy, with characteristic impetuosity, inquired the meaning of this proceeding, she was informed by Mr. O'Flaherty that he did not care to live in the same house "wid naygurs." Mrs. Braboy resented the epithet with more warmth than dignity, and for a brief space of time the air was green with choice specimens of brogue, the altercation barely ceasing before it had reached the point of blows.

It was quite clear that the Braboys could not longer live comfortably in Mr. O'Flaherty's house, and they soon vacated the premises, first letting the rent get a couple of weeks in arrears as a punishment to the too fastidious landlord. They moved to a small house on Hackman Street, a favorite locality with colored people.

For a while, affairs ran smoothly in the new home. The colored people seemed, at first, well enough disposed toward Mrs. Braboy, and she made quite a large acquaintance among them. It was difficult, however, for Mrs. Braboy to divest herself of the consciousness that she was white, and therefore superior to her neighbors. Occasional words and acts by which she manifested this feeling were noticed and resented by her keen-eyed and sensitive colored neighbors. The result was a slight coolness between them. That her few white neighbors did not visit her, she naturally and no doubt correctly imputed to disapproval of her matrimonial relations.

Under these circumstances, Mrs. Braboy was left a good deal to her own company. Owing to lack of opportunity in early life, she was not a woman of many resources, either mental or moral. It is therefore not strange that, in order to relieve her loneliness, she should occasionally have recourse to a glass of beer, and, as the habit grew upon her, to still stronger stimulants. Uncle Wellington himself was no teetotaler, and did not interpose any objection so long as she kept her potations within reasonable limits, and was apparently none the worse for them; indeed, he sometimes joined her in a glass. On one of these occasions he drank a little too much, and, while driving the ladies of Mr. Todd's family to the opera, ran against a lamp-post and overturned the carriage, to the serious discomposure of the ladies' nerves, and at the cost of his situation.

A coachman discharged under such circumstances is not in the best position for procuring employment at his calling, and uncle Wellington, under the pressure of need, was obliged to seek some other means of livelihood. At the suggestion of his friend Mr. Johnson, he bought a white-wash brush, a peck of lime, a couple of pails, and a handcart, and began work as a whitewasher. His first efforts were very crude, and for a while he lost a customer in every person he worked for. He nevertheless managed to pick up a living during the spring and summer months, and to support his wife and himself in comparative comfort.

The approach of winter put an end to the whitewashing season, and left uncle Wellington dependent for support upon occasional

jobs of unskilled labor. The income derived from these was very uncertain, and Mrs. Braboy was at length driven, by stress of circumstances, to the washtub, that last refuge of honest, able-bodied
poverty, in all countries where the use of clothing is conventional.

The last state of uncle Wellington was now worse than the first.
Under the soft firmness of aunt Milly's rule, he had not been required to do a great deal of work, prompt and cheerful obedience
being chiefly what was expected of him. But matters were very different here. He had not only to bring in the coal and water, but to
rub the clothes and turn the wringer, and to humiliate himself before the public by emptying the tubs and hanging out the wash in
full view of the neighbors; and he had to deliver the clothes when
laundered.

At times Wellington found himself wondering if his second marriage had been a wise one. Other circumstances combined to change
in some degree his once rose-colored conception of life at the
North. He had believed that all men were equal in this favored locality, but he discovered more degrees of inequality than he had
ever perceived at the South. A colored man might be as good as a
white man in theory, but neither of them was of any special consequence without money, or talent, or position. Uncle Wellington
found a great many privileges open to him at the North, but he had
not been educated to the point where he could appreciate them or
take advantage of them; and the enjoyment of many of them was
expensive, and, for that reason alone, as far beyond his reach as they
had ever been. When he once began to admit even the possibility of
a mistake on his part, these considerations presented themselves to
his mind with increasing force. On occasions when Mrs. Braboy
would require of him some unusual physical exertion, or when too
frequent applications to the bottle had loosened her tongue, uncle
Wellington's mind would revert, with a remorseful twinge of conscience, to the *dolce far niente* of his Southern home; a film would
come over his eyes and brain, and, instead of the red-faced Irishwoman opposite him, he could see the black but comely disk of
aunt Milly's countenance bending over the washtub; the elegant
brogue of Mrs. Braboy would deliquesce into the soft dialect of
North Carolina; and he would only be aroused from this blissful

reverie by a wet shirt or a handful of suds thrown into his face, with which gentle reminder his wife would recall his attention to the duties of the moment.

There came a time, one day in spring, when there was no longer any question about it: uncle Wellington was desperately homesick.

Liberty, equality, privileges—all were but as dust in the balance when weighed against his longing for old scenes and faces. It was the natural reaction in the mind of a middle-aged man who had tried to force the current of a sluggish existence into a new and radically different channel. An active, industrious man, making the change in early life, while there was time to spare for the waste of adaptation, might have found in the new place more favorable conditions than in the old. In Wellington age and temperament combined to prevent the success of the experiment; the spirit of enterprise and ambition into which he had been temporarily galvanized could no longer prevail against the inertia of old habits of life and thought.

One day when he had been sent to deliver clothes he performed his errand quickly, and boarding a passing street car, paid one of his very few five-cent pieces to ride down to the office of the Hon. Mr. Brown, the colored lawyer whom he had visited when he first came to the city, and who was well known to him by sight and reputation.

"Mr. Brown," he said, "I ain' gitt'n 'long very well wid my ole 'oman."

"What's the trouble?" asked the lawyer, with business-like curtness, for he did not scent much of a fee.

"Well, de main trouble is she doan treat me right. An' den she gits drunk, an' wuss'n dat, she lays vi'lent han's on me. I kyars de marks er dat 'oman on my face now."

He showed the lawyer a long scratch on the neck.

"Why don't you defend yourself?"

"You don' know Mis' Braboy, suh; you don' know dat 'oman," he replied, with a shake of the head. "Some er dese yer w'ite women is monst'us strong in de wris'."

"Well, Mr. Braboy, it's what you might have expected when you turned your back on your own people and married a white woman. You were n't content with being a slave to the white folks once, but you must try it again. Some people never know when they've got enough. I don't see that there's any help for you; unless," he added suggestively, "you had a good deal of money."

" 'Pears ter me I heared somebody say sence I be'n up heah, dat it wuz 'gin de law fer w'ite folks an' colored folks ter marry."

"That was once the law, though it has always been a dead letter in Groveland. In fact, it was the law when you got married, and until I introduced a bill in the legislature last fall to repeal it. But even that law did n't hit cases like yours. It was unlawful to make such a marriage, but it was a good marriage when once made."

"I don' jes' git dat th'oo my head," said Wellington, scratching that member as though to make a hole for the idea to enter.

"It's quite plain, Mr. Braboy. It's unlawful to kill a man, but when he 's killed he 's just as dead as though the law permitted it. I 'm afraid you have n't much of a case, but if you 'll go to work and get twenty-five dollars together, I 'll see what I can do for you. We may be able to pull a case through on the ground of extreme cruelty. I might even start the case if you brought in ten dollars."

Wellington went away sorrowfully. The laws of Ohio were very little more satisfactory than those of North Carolina. And as for the ten dollars,—the lawyer might as well have told him to bring in the moon, or a deed for the Public Square. He felt very, very low as he hurried back home to supper, which he would have to go without if he were not on hand at the usual supper-time.

But just when his spirits were lowest, and his outlook for the future most hopeless, a measure of relief was at hand. He noticed, when he reached home, that Mrs. Braboy was a little preoccupied, and did not abuse him as vigorously as he expected after so long an absence. He also perceived the smell of strange tobacco in the house, of a better grade than he could afford to use. He thought perhaps some one had come in to see about the washing; but he was too glad of a respite from Mrs. Braboy's rhetoric to imperil it by indiscreet questions.

Next morning she gave him fifty cents.

"Braboy," she said, "ye've be'n helpin' me nicely wid the washin', an' I 'm going ter give ye a holiday. Ye can take yer hook an' line an' go fishin' on the breakwater. I 'll fix ye a lunch, an' ye needn't come back till night. An' there's half a dollar; ye can buy yerself a pipe er terbacky. But be careful an' don't waste it," she added, for fear she was overdoing the thing.

Uncle Wellington was overjoyed at this change of front on the part of Mrs. Braboy; if she would make it permanent he did not see why they might not live together very comfortably.

The day passed pleasantly down on the breakwater. The weather was agreeable, and the fish bit freely. Towards evening Wellington started home with a bunch of fish that no angler need have been ashamed of. He looked forward to a good warm supper; for even if something should have happened during the day to alter his wife's mood for the worse, any ordinary variation would be more than balanced by the substantial addition of food to their larder. His mouth watered at the thought of the finny beauties sputtering in the frying-pan.

He noted, as he approached the house, that there was no smoke coming from the chimney. This only disturbed him in connection with the matter of supper. When he entered the gate he observed further that the window-shades had been taken down.

" 'Spec' de ole 'oman's been house-cleanin'," he said to himself. "I wonder she did n' make me stay an' he'p 'er."

He went round to the rear of the house and tried the kitchen door. It was locked. This was somewhat of a surprise, and disturbed still further his expectations in regard to supper. When he had found the key and opened the door, the gravity of his next discovery drove away for the time being all thoughts of eating.

The kitchen was empty. Stove, table, chairs, wash-tubs, pots and pans, had vanished as if into thin air.

"Fo' de Lawd's sake!" he murmured in open-mouthed astonishment.

He passed into the other room,—they had only two,—which had served as bedroom and sitting-room. It was as bare as the first, except that in the middle of the floor were piled uncle Wellington's clothes. It was not a large pile, and on the top of it lay a folded piece of yellow wrapping-paper.

Wellington stood for a moment as if petrified. Then he rubbed his eyes and looked around him.

"W'at do dis mean?" he said. "Is I er-dreamin', er does I see w'at

I 'pears ter see?" He glanced down at the bunch of fish which he still held. "Heah 's de fish; heah 's de house; heah I is; but whar 's de ole 'oman, an' whar 's de fu'niture? *I* can't figure out w'at dis yer all means."

He picked up the piece of paper and unfolded it. It was written on one side. Here was the obvious solution of the mystery,—that is, it would have been obvious if he could have read it; but he could not, and so his fancy continued to play upon the subject. Perhaps the house had been robbed, or the furniture taken back by the seller, for it had not been entirely paid for.

Finally he went across the street and called to a boy in a neighbor's yard.

"Does you read writin', Johnnie?"

"Yes, sir, I'm in the seventh grade."

"Read dis yer paper fuh me."

The youngster took the note, and with much labor read the following:—

Mr. Braboy:

In lavin' ye so suddint I have ter say that my first husban' has turned up unixpected, having been saved onbeknownst ter me from a warthry grave an' all the money wasted I spint fer masses fer ter rist his sole an' I wish I had it back I feel it my dooty ter go an' live wid 'im again. I take the furnacher because I bought it yer close is yors I leave them and wishin' yer the best of luck I remane oncet yer wife but now agin

MRS. KATIE FLANNIGAN.

N.B. I'm lavin town terday so it won't be no use lookin' fer me.

On inquiry uncle Wellington learned from the boy that shortly after his departure in the morning a white man had appeared on the scene, followed a little later by a moving-van, into which the furniture had been loaded and carried away. Mrs. Braboy, clad in her best clothes, had locked the door, and gone away with the strange white man.

The news was soon noised about the street. Wellington swapped his fish for supper and a bed at a neighbor's, and during the evening learned from several sources that the strange white man had been at his house the afternoon of the day before. His neighbors intimidated that they thought Mrs. Braboy's departure a good riddance of bad rubbish, and Wellington did not dispute the proposition.

Thus ended the second chapter of Wellington's matrimonial experiences. His wife's departure had been the one thing needful to convince him, beyond a doubt, that he had been a great fool. Remorse and homesickness forced him to the further conclusion that he had been knave as well as fool, and had treated aunt Milly shamefully. He was not altogether a bad old man, though very weak and erring, and his better nature now gained the ascendency. Of course his disappointment had a great deal to do with his remorse; most people do not perceive the hideousness of sin until they begin to reap its consequences. Instead of the beautiful Northern life he had dreamed of, he found himself stranded, penniless, in a strange land, among people whose sympathy he had forfeited, with no one to lean upon, and no refuge from the storms of life. His outlook was very dark, and there sprang up within him a wild longing to get back to North Carolina,—back to the little whitewashed cabin, shaded with china and mulberry trees; back to the wood-pile and the garden; back to the old cronies with whom he had swapped lies and tobacco for so many years. He longed to kiss the rod of aunt Milly's domination. He had purchased his liberty at too great a price.

The next day he disappeared from Groveland. He had announced his departure only to Mr. Johnson, who sent his love to his relations in Patesville.

It would be painful to record in detail the return journey of uncle Wellington—Mr. Braboy no longer—to his native town; how many weary miles he walked; how many times he risked his life on railroad trucks and between freight cars; how he depended for sustenance on the grudging hand of back-door charity. Nor would it be profitable or delicate to mention any slight deviations from the path of rectitude, as judged by conventional standards, to which he may occasionally have been driven by a too insistent hunger; or to refer in the remotest degree to a compulsory sojourn of thirty days in a city where he had no references, and could show no visible means of support. True charity will let these purely personal matters remain locked in the bosom of him who suffered them.

IV

Just fifteen months after the date when uncle Wellington had left North Carolina, a weather-beaten figure entered the town of Patesville after nightfall, following the railroad track from the north. Few would have recognized in the hungry-looking old brown tramp, clad in dusty rags and limping along with bare feet, the trim-looking middle-aged mulatto who so few months before had taken the train from Patesville for the distant North; so, if he had but known it, there was no necessity for him to avoid the main streets and sneak around by unfrequented paths to reach the old place on the other side of the town. He encountered nobody that he knew, and soon the familiar shape of the little cabin rose before him. It stood distinctly outlined against the sky, and the light streaming from the half-opened shutters showed it to be occupied. As he drew nearer, every familiar detail of the place appealed to his memory and to his affections, and his heart went out to the old home and the old wife. As he came nearer still, the odor of fried chicken floated out upon the air and set his mouth to watering, and awakened unspeakable longings in his half-starved stomach.

At this moment, however, a fearful thought struck him; suppose the old woman had taken legal advice and married again during his absence? Turn about would have been only fair play. He opened the gate softly, and with his heart in his mouth approached the window on tiptoe and looked in.

A cheerful fire was blazing on the hearth, in front of which sat the familiar form of aunt Milly—and another, at the sight of whom uncle Wellington's heart sank within him. He knew the other person very well; he had sat there more than once before uncle Wellington went away. It was the minister of the church to which his wife belonged. The preacher's former visits, however, had signified nothing more than pastoral courtesy, or appreciation of good eating. His presence now was of serious portent; for Wellington recalled, with acute alarm, that the elder's wife had died only a few weeks before his own departure for the North. What was the occasion of his presence this evening? Was it merely a pastoral call? or was he courting? or had aunt Milly taken legal advice and married the elder?

Wellington remembered a crack in the wall, at the back of the house, through which he could see and hear, and quietly stationed himself there.

"Dat chicken smells mighty good, Sis' Milly," the elder was saying; "I can't fer de life er me see why dat low-down husban' er yo'n could ever run away f'm a cook like you. It 's one er de beatenis' things I ever heared. How he could lib wid you an' not 'preciate you *I* can't understan', no indeed I can't."

Aunt Milly sighed. "De trouble wid Wellin'ton wuz," she replied, "dat he did n' know when he wuz well off. He wuz alluz wishin' fer change, er studyin' 'bout somethin' new."

"Ez fer me," responded the elder earnestly, "I likes things what has be'n prove' an' tried an' has stood de tes', an' I can't 'magine how anybody could spec' ter fin' a better housekeeper er cook dan you is, Sis' Milly. I'm a gittin' mighty lonesome sence my wife died. De Good Book say it is not good fer man ter lib alone, en it 'pears ter me dat you an' me mought get erlong tergether monst'us well."

Wellington's heart stood still, while he listened with strained attention. Aunt Milly sighed.

"I ain't denyin', elder, but what I 've be'n kinder lonesome myse'f fer quite a w'ile, an' I doan doubt dat w'at de Good Book say 'plies ter women as well as ter men."

"You kin be sho' it do," averred the elder, with professional authoritativeness; "yas'm, you kin be cert'n sho'."

"But, of co'se," aunt Milly went on, "havin' los' my ole man de way I did, it has tuk me some time fer ter git my feelin's straighten' out like dey oughter be."

"I kin 'magine yo' feelin's, Sis' Milly," chimed in the elder sympathetically, "w'en you come home dat night an' foun' yo' chist broke open, an' yo' money gone dat you had wukked an' slaved fuh f'm mawnin' 'tel night, year in an' year out, an' w'en you foun' dat no-'count nigger gone wid his clo's an' you lef' all alone in de worl' ter scuffle 'long by yo'se'f."

"Yas, elder," responded aunt Milly, "I wa'n't used right. An' den w'en I heared 'bout his goin' ter de lawyer ter fin' out 'bout a defoce, an' w'en I heared w'at de lawyer said 'bout my not bein' his wife 'less he wanted me, it made me so mad, I made up my min' dat ef he ever put his foot on my do'-sill ag'in, I'd shet de do' in his face an' tell 'im ter go back whar he come f'm."

To Wellington, on the outside, the cabin had never seemed so comfortable, aunt Milly never so desirable, chicken never so appetizing, as at this moment when they seemed slipping away from his grasp forever.

"Yo' feelin's does you credit, Sis' Milly," said the elder, taking her hand, which for a moment she did not withdraw. "An' de way fer you ter close yo' do' tightes' ag'inst 'im is ter take me in his place. He ain' got no claim on you no mo'. He tuk his ch'ice 'cordin' ter w'at de lawyer tol' 'im, an' 'termine' dat he wa'n't yo' husban'. Ef he wa'n't yo' husban', he had no right ter take yo' money, an' ef he comes back here ag'in you kin hab 'im tuck up an' sent ter de penitenchy fer stealin' it."

Uncle Wellington's knees, already weak from fasting, trembled violently beneath him. The worst that he had feared was now likely to happen. His only hope of safety lay in flight, and yet the scene within so fascinated him that he could not move a step.

"It 'u'd serve him right," exclaimed aunt Milly indignantly, "ef he wuz sent ter de penitenchy fer life! Dey ain't nuthin' too mean ter be done ter 'im. What did I ever do dat he should use me like he did?"

The recital of her wrongs had wrought upon aunt Milly's feelings so that her voice broke, and she wiped her eyes with her apron.

The elder looked serenely confident, and moved his chair nearer hers in order the better to play the rôle of comforter. Wellington, on the outside, felt so mean that the darkness of the night was scarcely sufficient to hide him; it would be no more than right if the earth were to open and swallow him up.

"An' yet aftuh all, elder," said Milly with a sob, "though I knows you is a better man, an' would treat me right, I wuz so use' ter dat ole nigger, an' libbed wid 'im so long, dat ef he'd open dat do' dis minute an' walk in, I'm feared I'd be foolish ernuff an' weak ernuff to forgive 'im an' take 'im back ag'in."

With a bound, uncle Wellington was away from the crack in the wall. As he ran round the house he passed the wood-pile and snatched up an armful of pieces. A moment later he threw open the door.

"Ole 'oman," he exclaimed, "here's dat wood you tol' me ter fetch in! Why, elder," he said to the preacher, who had started from his seat with surprise, "w'at's yo' hurry? Won't you stay an' hab some supper wid us?"

The Bouquet

MARY MYROVER'S FRIENDS were somewhat surprised when she began to teach a colored school. Miss Myrover's friends are mentioned here, because nowhere more than in a Southern town is public opinion a force which cannot be lightly contravened. Public opinion, however, did not oppose Miss Myrover's teaching colored children; in fact, all the colored public schools in town—and there were several—were taught by white teachers, and had been so taught since the State had undertaken to provide free public instruction for all children within its boundaries. Previous to that time, there had been a Freedmen's Bureau school and a Presbyterian missionary school, but these had been withdrawn when the need for them became less pressing. The colored people of the town had been for some time agitating their right to teach their own schools, but as yet the claim had not been conceded.

The reason Miss Myrover's course created some surprise was not, therefore, the fact that a Southern white woman should teach a colored school; it lay in the fact that up to this time no woman of just her quality had taken up such work. Most of the teachers of colored schools were not of those who had constituted the aristocracy of the old régime; they might be said rather to represent the new order of things, in which labor was in time to become honorable, and men were, after a somewhat longer time, to depend, for their place in society, upon themselves rather than upon their ancestors. Mary Myrover belonged to one of the proudest of the old families. Her ancestors had been people of distinction in Virginia before a collateral branch of the main stock had settled in North Carolina. Before the war, they had been able to live up to their pedigree; but the war brought sad changes. Miss Myrover's father—the

Colonel Myrover who led a gallant but desperate charge at Vicks-
burg—had fallen on the battlefield, and his tomb in the white cemetery was a shrine for the family. On the Confederate Memorial Day,
no other grave was so profusely decorated with flowers, and, in the
oration pronounced, the name of Colonel Myrover was always
used to illustrate the highest type of patriotic devotion and self-
sacrifice. Miss Myrover's brother, too, had fallen in the conflict; but
his bones lay in some unknown trench, with those of a thousand
others who had fallen on the same field. Ay, more, her lover, who
had hoped to come home in the full tide of victory and claim his
bride as a reward for gallantry, had shared the fate of her father and
brother. When the war was over, the remnant of the family found
itself involved in the common ruin,—more deeply involved, indeed,
than some others; for Colonel Myrover had believed in the ultimate
triumph of his cause, and had invested most of his wealth in Confederate bonds, which were now only so much waste paper.

There had been a little left. Mrs. Myrover was thrifty, and had
laid by a few hundred dollars, which she kept in the house to meet
unforeseen contingencies. There remained, too, their home, with an
ample garden and a well-stocked orchard, besides a considerable
tract of country land, partly cleared, but productive of very little
revenue.

With their shrunken resources, Miss Myrover and her mother
were able to hold up their heads without embarassment for some
years after the close of the war. But when things were adjusted to
the changed conditions, and the stream of life began to flow more
vigorously in the new channels, they saw themselves in danger of
dropping behind, unless in some way they could add to their meagre income. Miss Myrover looked over the field of employment,
never very wide for women in the South, and found it occupied.
The only available position she could be supposed prepared to fill,
and which she could take without distinct loss of caste, was that of
a teacher, and there was no vacancy except in one of the colored
schools. Even teaching was a doubtful experiment; it was not what
she would have preferred, but it was the best that could be done.

"I don't like it, Mary," said her mother. "It's a long step from
owning such people to teaching them. What do they need with education? It will only make them unfit for work."

"They're free now, mother, and perhaps they'll work better if they're taught something. Besides, it's only a business arrangement, and doesn't involve any closer contact than we have with our servants."

"Well, I should say not!" sniffed the old lady. "Not one of them will ever dare to presume on your position to take any liberties with us. *I'll* see to that."

Miss Myrover began her work as a teacher in the autumn, at the opening of the school year. It was a novel experience at first. Though there had always been negro servants in the house, and though on the streets colored people were more numerous than those of her own race, and though she was so familiar with their dialect that she might almost be said to speak it, barring certain characteristic grammatical inaccuracies, she had never been brought in personal contact with so many of them at once as when she confronted the fifty or sixty faces—of colors ranging from a white almost as clear as her own to the darkest livery of the sun—which were gathered in the schoolroom on the morning when she began her duties. Some of the inherited prejudice of her caste, too, made itself felt, though she tried to repress any outward sign of it; and she could perceive that the children were not altogether responsive; they, likewise, were not entirely free from antagonism. The work was unfamiliar to her. She was not physically very strong, and at the close of the first day went home with a splitting headache. If she could have resigned then and there without causing comment or annoyance to others, she would have felt it a privilege to do so. But a night's rest banished her headache and improved her spirits, and the next morning she went to her work with renewed vigor, fortified by the experience of the first day.

Miss Myrover's second day was more satisfactory. She had some natural talent for organization, though hitherto unaware of it, and in the course of the day she got her classes formed and lessons under way. In a week or two she began to classify her pupils in her own mind, as bright or stupid, mischievous or well behaved, lazy or industrious, as the case might be, and to regulate her discipline accordingly. That she had come of a long line of ancestors who had exercised authority and mastership was perhaps not without its effect upon her character, and enabled her more readily to maintain good order in the school. When she was fairly broken in, she found the work rather to her liking, and derived much pleasure from such success as she achieved as a teacher.

It was natural that she should be more attracted to some of her pupils than to others. Perhaps her favorite—or, rather, the one she liked best, for she was too fair and just for conscious favoritism—was Sophy Tucker. Just the ground for the teacher's liking for Sophy might not at first be apparent. The girl was far from the whitest of Miss Myrover's pupils; in fact, she was one of the darker ones. She was not the brightest in intellect, though she always tried to learn her lessons. She was not the best dressed, for her mother was a poor widow, who went out washing and scrubbing for a living. Perhaps the real tie between them was Sophy's intense devotion to the teacher. It had manifested itself almost from the first day of the school, in the rapt look of admiration Miss Myrover always saw on the little black face turned toward her. In it there was nothing of envy, nothing of regret; nothing but worship for the beautiful white lady—she was not especially handsome, but to Sophy her beauty was almost divine—who had come to teach her. If Miss Myrover dropped a book, Sophy was the first to spring and pick it up; if she wished a chair moved, Sophy seemed to anticipate her wish; and so of all the numberless little services that can be rendered in a schoolroom.

Miss Myrover was fond of flowers, and liked to have them about her. The children soon learned of this taste of hers, and kept the vases on her desk filled with blossoms during their season. Sophy was perhaps the most active in providing them. If she could not get garden flowers, she would make excursions to the woods in the early morning, and bring in great dew-laden bunches of bay, or jasmine, or some other fragrant forest flower which she knew the teacher loved.

"When I die, Sophy," Miss Myrover said to the child one day, "I want to be covered with roses. And when they bury me, I'm sure I shall rest better if my grave is banked with flowers, and roses are planted at my head and at my feet."

Miss Myrover was at first amused at Sophy's devotion; but when she grew more accustomed to it, she found it rather to her liking. It had a sort of flavor of the old régime, and she felt, when she bestowed her kindly notice upon her little black attendant, some of the feudal condescension of the mistress toward the slave. She was kind to Sophy, and permitted her to play the rôle she had assumed, which caused sometimes a little jealousy among the other girls. Once she gave Sophy a yellow ribbon which she took from her own hair. The child carried it home, and cherished it as a priceless treasure, to be worn only on the greatest occasions.

Sophy had a rival in her attachment to the teacher, but the rivalry was altogether friendly. Miss Myrover had a little dog, a white spaniel, answering to the name of Prince. Prince was a dog of high degree, and would have very little to do with the children of the school; he made an exception, however, in the case of Sophy, whose devotion for his mistress he seemed to comprehend. He was a clever dog, and could fetch and carry, sit up on his haunches, extend his paw to shake hands, and possessed several other canine accomplishments. He was very fond of his mistress, and always, unless shut up at home, accompanied her to school, where he spent most of his time lying under the teacher's desk, or, in cold weather, by the stove, except when he would go out now and then and chase an imaginary rabbit round the yard, presumably for exercise.

At school Sophy and Prince vied with each other in their attention to Miss Myrover. But when school was over, Prince went away with her, and Sophy stayed behind; for Miss Myrover was white and Sophy was black, which they both understood perfectly well. Miss Myrover taught the colored children, but she could not be seen with them in public. If they occasionally met her on the street, they did not expect her to speak to them, unless she happened to be alone and no other white person was in sight. If any of the children felt slighted, she was not aware of it, for she intended no slight; she had not been brought up to speak to negroes on the street, and she could not act differently from other people. And though she was a woman of sentiment and capable of deep feeling, her training had been such that she hardly expected to find in those of darker hue than herself the same susceptibility—varying in degree, perhaps, but yet the same in kind—that gave to her own life the alternations of feeling that made it most worth living.

Once Miss Myrover wished to carry home a parcel of books. She had the bundle in her hand when Sophy came up.

"Lemme tote yo' bundle fer yer, Miss Ma'y?" she asked eagerly. "I'm gwine yo' way."

"Thank you, Sophy," was the reply. "I'll be glad if you will."

Sophy followed the teacher at a respectful distance. When they reached Miss Myrover's home, Sophy carried the bundle to the doorstep, where Miss Myrover took it and thanked her.

Mrs. Myrover came out on the piazza as Sophy was moving away. She said, in the child's hearing, and perhaps with the intention that she should hear: "Mary, I wish you wouldn't let those little darkeys follow you to the house. I don't want them in the yard. I should think you'd have enough of them all day."

"Very well, mother," replied her daughter. "I won't bring any more of them. The child was only doing me a favor."

Mrs. Myrover was an invalid, and opposition or irritation of any kind brought on nervous paroxysms that made her miserable, and made life a burden to the rest of the household, so that Mary seldom crossed her whims. She did not bring Sophy to the house again, nor did Sophy again offer her services as porter.

One day in spring Sophy brought her teacher a bouquet of yellow roses.

"Dey come off'n my own bush, Miss Ma'y," she said proudly, "an' I did n' let nobody e'se pull 'em, but saved 'em all fer you, 'cause I know you likes roses so much. I'm gwine bring 'em all ter you as long as dey las'."

"Thank you, Sophy," said the teacher; "you are a very good girl."

For another year Mary Myrover taught the colored school, and did excellent service. The children made rapid progress under her tuition, and learned to love her well; for they saw and appreciated, as well as children could, her fidelity to a trust that she might have slighted, as some others did, without much fear of criticism. Toward the end of her second year she sickened, and after a brief illness died.

Old Mrs. Myrover was inconsolable. She ascribed her daughter's death to her labors as teacher of negro children. Just how the color of the pupils had produced the fatal effects she did not stop to explain. But she was too old, and had suffered too deeply from the war, in body and mind and estate, ever to reconcile herself to the changed order of things following the return of peace; and, with an unsound yet perfectly explainable logic, she visited some of her displeasure upon those who had profited most, though passively, by her losses.

"I always feared something would happen to Mary," she said. "It seemed unnatural for her to be wearing herself out teaching little negroes who ought to have been working for her. But the world has hardly been a fit place to live since the war, and when I follow her, as I must before long, I shall not be sorry to go."

She gave strict orders that no colored people should be admitted to the house. Some of her friends heard of this, and remonstrated. They knew the teacher was loved by the pupils, and felt that sincere respect from the humble would be a worthy tribute to the proudest. But Mrs. Myrover was obdurate.

"They had my daughter when she was alive," she said, "and they've killed her. But she's mine now, and I won't have them come near her. I don't want one of them at the funeral or anywhere around."

For a month before Miss Myrover's death Sophy had been watching her rosebush—the one that bore the yellow roses—for the first buds of spring, and, when these appeared, had awaited impatiently their gradual unfolding. But not until her teacher's death had they become full-blown roses. When Miss Myrover died, Sophy determined to pluck the roses and lay them on her coffin. Perhaps, she thought, they might even put them in her hand or on her breast. For Sophy remembered Miss Myrover's thanks and praise when she had brought her the yellow roses the spring before.

On the morning of the day set for the funeral, Sophy washed her face until it shone, combed and brushed her hair with painful conscientiousness, put on her best frock, plucked her yellow roses, and, tying them with the treasured ribbon her teacher had given her, set out for Miss Myrover's home.

She went round to the side gate—the house stood on a corner—and stole up the path to the kitchen. A colored woman, whom she did not know, came to the door.

"W'at yer want, chile?" she inquired.

"Kin I see Miss Ma'y?" asked Sophy timidly.

"I don't know, honey. Ole Miss Myrover say she don't want no

cullud folks roun' de house endyoin' dis fun'al. I'll look an' see if
she's roun' de front room, whar de co'pse is. You sed down heah an'
keep still, an' ef she's upstairs maybe I kin git yer in dere a minute.
Ef I can't, I kin put yo' bokay 'mongs' de res', whar she won't
know nuthin' erbout it."

A moment after she had gone, there was a step in the hall, and
old Mrs. Myrover came into the kitchen.

"Dinah!" she said in a peevish tone; "Dinah!"

Receiving no answer, Mrs. Myrover peered around the kitchen,
and caught sight of Sophy.

"What are you doing here?" she demanded.

"I—I'm-m waitin' ter see de cook, ma'am," stammered Sophy.

"The cook isn't here now. I don't know where she is. Besides,
my daughter is to be buried to-day, and I won't have any one visiting the servants until the funeral is over. Come back some other
day, or see the cook at her own home in the evening."

She stood waiting for the child to go, and under the keen glance
of her eyes Sophy, feeling as though she had been caught in some
disgraceful act, hurried down the walk and out of the gate, with her
bouquet in her hand.

"Dinah," said Mrs. Myrover, when the cook came back, "I don't
want any strange people admitted here to-day. The house will be
full of our friends, and we have no room for others."

"Yas'm," said the cook. She understood perfectly what her mistress meant; and what the cook thought about her mistress was a
matter of no consequence.

The funeral service were held at St. Paul's Episcopal Church,
where the Myrovers had always worshiped. Quite a number of
Miss Myrover's pupils went to the church to attend the services.
The building was not a large one. There was a small gallery at the
rear, to which colored people were admitted, if they chose to come,
at ordinary services; and those who wished to be present at the funeral supposed that the usual custom would prevail. They were
therefore surprised, when they went to the side entrance, by which
colored people gained access to the gallery stairs, to be met by an
usher who barred their passage.

"I'm sorry," he said, "but I have had orders to admit no one until the friends of the family have all been seated. If you wish to wait

until the white people have all gone in, and there's any room left, you may be able to get into the back part of the gallery. Of course I can't tell yet whether there'll be any room or not."

Now the statement of the usher was a very reasonable one; but, strange to say, none of the colored people chose to remain except Sophy. She still hoped to use her floral offering for its destined end, in some way, though she did not know just how. She waited in the yard until the church was filled with white people, and a number who could not gain admittance were standing about the doors. Then she went round to the side of the church, and, depositing her bouquet carefully on an old mossy gravestone, climbed up on the projecting sill of a window near the chancel. The window was of stained glass, of somewhat ancient make. The church was old, had indeed been built in colonial times, and the stained glass had been brought from England. The design of the window showed Jesus blessing little children. Time had dealt gently with the window, but just at the feet of the figure of Jesus a small triangular piece of glass had been broken out. To this aperture Sophy applied her eyes, and through it saw and heard what she could of the services within.

Before the chancel, on trestles draped in black, stood the sombre casket in which lay all that was mortal of her dear teacher. The top of the casket was covered with flowers; and lying stretched out underneath it she saw Miss Myrover's little white dog, Prince. He had followed the body to the church, and, slipping in unnoticed among the mourners, had taken his place, from which no one had the heart to remove him.

The white-robed rector read the solemn service for the dead, and then delivered a brief address, in which he dwelt upon the uncertainty of life, and, to the believer, the certain blessedness of eternity. He spoke of Miss Myrover's kindly spirit, and, as an illustration of her love and self-sacrifice for others, referred to her labors as a teacher of the poor ignorant negroes who had been placed in their midst by an all-wise Providence, and whom it was their duty to guide and direct in the station in which God had put them. Then the organ pealed, a prayer was said, and the long cortège moved from the church to the cemetery, about half a mile away, where the body was to be interred.

When the services were over, Sophy sprang down from her

perch, and, taking her flowers, followed the procession. She did not walk with the rest, but at a proper and respectful distance from the last mourner. No one noticed the little black girl with the bunch of yellow flowers, or thought of her as interested in the funeral.

The cortège reached the cemetery and filed slowly through the gate; but Sophy stood outside, looking at a small sign in white letters on a black background:—

"*Notice.* This cemetery is for white people only. Others please keep out."

Sophy, thanks to Miss Myrover's painstaking instruction, could read this sign very distinctly. In fact, she had often read it before. For Sophy was a child who loved beauty, in a blind, groping sort of way, and had sometimes stood by the fence of the cemetery and looked through at the green mounds and shaded walks and blooming flowers within, and wished that she might walk among them. She knew, too, that the little sign on the gate, though so courteously worded, was no mere formality; for she had heard how a colored man, who had wandered into the cemetery on a hot night and fallen asleep on the flat top of a tomb, had been arrested as a vagrant and fined five dollars, which he had worked out on the streets, with a ball-and-chain attachment, at twenty-five cents a day. Since that time the cemetery gate had been locked at night.

So Sophy stayed outside, and looked through the fence. Her poor bouquet had begun to droop by this time, and the yellow ribbon had lost some of its freshness. Sophy could see the rector standing by the grave, the mourners gathered round; she could faintly distinguish the solemn words with which ashes were committed to ashes, and dust to dust. She heard the hollow thud of the earth falling on the coffin; and she leaned against the iron fence, sobbing softly, until the grave was filled and rounded off, and the wreaths and other floral pieces were disposed upon it. When the mourners began to move toward the gate, Sophy walked slowly down the street, in a direction opposite to that taken by most of the people who came out.

When they had all gone away, and the sexton had come out and locked the gate behind him, Sophy crept back. Her roses were faded now, and from some of them the petals had fallen. She stood there irresolute, loath to leave with her heart's desire unsatisfied, when, as her eyes sought again the teacher's last resting-place, she saw lying beside the new-made grave what looked like a small bundle of white wool. Sophy's eyes lighted up with a sudden glow.

"Prince! Here, Prince!" she called.

The little dog rose, and trotted down to the gate. Sophy pushed the poor bouquet between the iron bars. "Take that ter Miss Ma'y, Prince," she said, "that's a good doggie."

The dog wagged his tail intelligently, took the bouquet carefully in his mouth, carried it to his mistress's grave, and laid it among the other flowers. The bunch of roses was so small that from where she stood Sophy could see only a dash of yellow against the white background of the mass of flowers.

When Prince had performed his mission he turned his eyes toward Sophy inquiringly, and when she gave him a nod of approval lay down and resumed his watch by the graveside. Sophy looked at him a moment with a feeling very much like envy, and then turned and moved slowly away.

The Web of Circumstance

I

WITHIN A LOW CLAPBOARDED HUT, with an open front, a forge was glowing. In front a blacksmith was shoeing a horse, a sleek, well-kept animal with the signs of good blood and breeding. A young mulatto stood by and handed the blacksmith such tools as he needed from time to time. A group of negroes were sitting around, some in the shadow of the shop, one in the full glare of the sunlight. A gentleman was seated in a buggy a few yards away, in the shade of a spreading elm. The horse had loosened a shoe, and Colonel Thornton, who was a lover of fine horseflesh, and careful of it, had stopped at Ben Davis's blacksmith shop, as soon as he discovered the loose shoe, to have it fastened on.

"All right, Kunnel," the blacksmith called out. "Tom," he said, addressing the young man, "he'p me hitch up."

Colonel Thornton alighted from the buggy, looked at the shoe, signified his approval of the job, and stood looking on while the blacksmith and his assistant harnessed the horse to the buggy.

"Dat's a mighty fine whip yer got dere, Kunnel," said Ben, while the young man was tightening the straps of the harness on the opposite side of the horse. "I wush I had one like it. Where kin yer git dem whips?"

"My brother brought me this from New York," said the Colonel. "You can't buy them down here."

The whip in question was a handsome one. The handle was wrapped with interlacing threads of variegated colors, forming an elaborate pattern, the lash being dark green. An octagonal ornament of glass was set in the end of the handle. "It cert'n'y is fine," said

Ben; "I wish I had one like it." He looked at the whip longingly as Colonel Thornton drove away.

" 'Pears ter me Ben gittin' mighty blooded," said one of the by-standers, "drivin' a hoss an' buggy, an' wantin' a whip like Colonel Thornton's."

"What's de reason I can't hab a hoss an' buggy an' a whip like Kunnel Tho'nton's, ef I pay fer 'em?" asked Ben. "We colored folks never had no chance ter git nothin' befo' de wah, but ef eve'y nigger in dis town had a tuck keer er his money sence de wah, like I has, an' bought as much lan' as I has, de niggers might 'a' got half de lan' by dis time," he went on, giving a finishing blow to a horseshoe, and throwing it on the ground to cool.

Carried away by his own eloquence, he did not notice the approach of two white men who came up the street from behind him.

"An' ef you niggers," he continued, raking the coals together over a fresh bar of iron, "would stop wastin' yo' money on 'scursions to put money in w'ite folks' pockets, an' stop buildin' fine chu'ches, an' buil' houses fer yo'se'ves, you'd git along much faster."

"You're talkin' sense, Ben," said one of the white men. "Yo'r people will never be respected till they've got property."

The conversation took another turn. The white men transacted their business and went away. The whistle of a neighboring steam sawmill blew a raucous blast for the hour of noon, and the loafers shuffled away in different directions.

"You kin go ter dinner, Tom," said the blacksmith. "An' stop at de gate w'en yer go by my house, and tell Nancy I'll be dere in 'bout twenty minutes. I got ter finish dis yer plough p'int fus'."

The young man walked away. One would have supposed, from the rapidity with which he walked, that he was very hungry. A quarter of an hour later the blacksmith dropped his hammer, pulled off his leather apron, shut the front door of the shop, and went home to dinner. He came into the house out of the fervent heat, and, throwing off his straw hat, wiped his brow vigorously with a red cotton handkerchief.

"Dem collards smells good," he said, sniffing the odor that came in through the kitchen door, as his good-looking yellow wife opened it to enter the room where he was. "I've got a monst'us good appetite ter-day. I feels good, too. I paid Majah Ransom de intrus' on de mortgage dis mawnin' an' a hund'ed dollahs besides, an' I spec's ter hab de balance ready by de fust of nex' Jiniwary; an' den we won't owe nobody a cent. I tell yer dere ain' nothin' like propputy ter make a pusson feel like a man. But w'at's de matter wid yer, Nancy? Is sump'n' skeered yer?"

The woman did seem excited and ill at ease. There was a heaving of the full bust, a quickened breathing, that betokened suppressed excitement.

"I—I—jes' seen a rattlesnake out in de gyahden," she stammered.

The blacksmith ran to the door. "Which way? Whar wuz he?" he cried.

He heard a rustling in the bushes at one side of the garden, and the sound of a breaking twig, and, seizing a hoe which stood by the door, he sprang toward the point from which the sound came.

"No, no," said the woman hurriedly, "it wuz over here," and she directed her husband's attention to the other side of the garden.

The blacksmith, with the uplifted hoe, its sharp blade gleaming in the sunlight, peered cautiously among the collards and tomato plants, listening all the while for the ominous rattle, but found nothing.

"I reckon he's got away," he said, as he set the hoe up again by the door. "Whar's de chillen?" he asked with some anxiety. "Is dey playin' in de woods?"

"No," answered his wife, "dey've gone ter de spring."

The spring was on the opposite side of the garden from that on which the snake was said to have been seen, so the blacksmith sat down and fanned himself with a palm-leaf fan until the dinner was served.

"Yer ain't quite on time ter-day, Nancy," he said, glancing up at the clock on the mantel, after the edge of his appetite had been taken off. "Got ter make time ef yer wanter make money. Didn't Tom tell yer I'd be heah in twenty minutes?"

"No," she said; "I seen him goin' pas'; he didn' say nothin'."

"I dunno w'at's de matter wid dat boy," mused the blacksmith over his apple dumpling. "He's gittin mighty keerless heah lately; mus' hab sump'n' on 'is min',—some gal, I reckon."

The children had come in while he was speaking,—a slender, shapely boy, yellow like his mother, a girl several years younger, dark like her father: both bright-looking children and neatly dressed.

"I seen cousin Tom down by de spring," said the little girl, as she lifted off the pail of water that had been balanced on her head. "He come out er de woods jest ez we wuz fillin' our buckets."

"Yas," insisted the blacksmith, "he's got some gal on his min'."

II

The case of the State of North Carolina *vs.* Ben Davis was called. The accused was led into court, and took his seat in the prisoner's dock.

"Prisoner at the bar, stand up."

The prisoner, pale and anxious, stood up. The clerk read the indictment, in which it was charged that the defendant by force and arms had entered the barn of one G. W. Thornton, and feloniously taken therefrom one whip, of the value of fifteen dollars.

"Are you guilty or not guilty?" asked the judge.

"Not guilty, yo' Honah; not guilty, Jedge. I never tuck de whip."

The State's attorney opened the case. He was young and zealous. Recently elected to the office, this was his first batch of cases, and he was anxious to make as good a record as possible. He had no doubt of the prisoner's guilt. There had been a great deal of petty thieving in the county, and several gentlemen had suggested to him the necessity for greater severity in punishing it. The jury were all white men. The prosecuting attorney stated the case.

"We expect to show, gentlemen of the jury, the facts set out in the indictment,—not altogether by direct proof, but by a chain of circumstantial evidence which is stronger even than the testimony of eyewitnesses. Men might lie, but circumstances cannot. We expect to show that the defendant is a man of dangerous character, a surly, impudent fellow; a man whose views of property are prejudicial to the welfare of society, and who has been heard to assert that half the property which is owned in this county has been stolen, and that, if justice were done, the white people ought to divide up the land with the negroes; in other words, a negro nihilist, a communist, a secret devotee of Tom Paine and Voltaire, a pupil of the anarchist propaganda, which, if not checked by the stern hand of the law, will fasten its insidious fangs on our social system, and drag it down to ruin."

"We object, may it please your Honor," said the defendant's attorney. "The prosecutor should defer his argument until the testimony is in."

"Confine yourself to the facts, Major," said the court mildly.

The prisoner sat with half-open mouth, overwhelmed by this flood of eloquence. He had never heard of Tom Paine or Voltaire. He had no conception of what a nihilist or an anarchist might be, and could not have told the difference between a propaganda and a potato.

"We expect to show, may it please the court, that the prisoner had been employed by Colonel Thornton to shoe a horse; that the horse was taken to the prisoner's blacksmith shop by a servant of Colonel Thornton's; that, this servant expressing a desire to go somewhere on an errand before the horse had been shod, the prisoner volunteered to return the horse to Colonel Thornton's stable; that he did so, and the following morning the whip in question was missing; that, from circumstances, suspicion naturally fell upon the prisoner, and a search was made of his shop, where the whip was found secreted; that the prisoner denied that the whip was there, but when confronted with the evidence of his crime, showed by his confusion that he was guilty beyond a peradventure."

The prisoner looked more anxious; so much eloquence could not but be effective with the jury.

The attorney for the defendant answered briefly, denying the defendant's guilt, dwelling upon his previous good character for honesty, and begging the jury not to prejudge the case, but to remember that the law is merciful, and that the benefit of the doubt should be given to the prisoner.

The prisoner glanced nervously at the jury. There was nothing in their faces to indicate the effect upon them of the opening statements. It seemed to the disinterested listeners as if the defendant's attorney had little confidence in his client's cause.

Colonel Thornton took the stand and testified to his ownership of the whip, the place where it was kept, its value, and the fact that it had disappeared. The whip was produced in court and identified by the witness. He also testified to the conversation at the blacksmith shop in the course of which the prisoner had expressed a desire to possess a similar whip. The cross-examination was brief, and no attempt was made to shake the Colonel's testimony.

The next witness was the constable who had gone with a warrant to search Ben's shop. He testified to the circumstances under which the whip was found.

"He wuz brazen as a mule at fust, an' wanted ter git mad about it. But when we begun ter turn over that pile er truck in the cawner, he kinder begun ter trimble; when the whiphandle stuck out, his eyes commenced ter grow big, an' when we hauled the whip out he turned pale ez ashes, an' begun to swear he did n' take the whip an' did n' know how it got thar."

"You may cross-examine," said the prosecuting attorney triumphantly.

The prisoner felt the weight of the testimony, and glanced furtively at the jury, and then appealingly at his lawyer.

"You say that Ben denied that he had stolen the whip," said the prisoner's attorney, on cross-examination. "Did it not occur to you that what you took for brazen impudence might have been but the evidence of conscious innocence?"

The witness grinned incredulously, revealing thereby a few blackened fragments of teeth.

"I've tuck up more'n a hundred niggers fer stealin', Kurnel, an' I never seed one yit that did n' 'ny it ter the las'."

"Answer my question. Might not the witness's indignation have been a manifestation of conscious innocence? Yes or no?"

"Yes, it mought, an' the moon mought fall—but it don't."

Further cross-examination did not weaken the witness's testimony, which was very damaging, and every one in the court room felt instinctively that a strong defense would be required to break down the State's case.

"The State rests," said the prosecuting attorney, with a ring in his voice which spoke of certain victory.

There was a temporary lull in the proceedings, during which a bailiff passed a pitcher of water and a glass along the line of jury-men. The defense was then begun.

The law in its wisdom did not permit the defendant to testify in his own behalf. There were no witnesses to the facts, but several were called to testify to Ben's good character. The colored witnesses made him out possessed of all the virtues. One or two white men testified that they had never known anything against his reputation for honesty.

The defendant rested his case, and the State called its witnesses in rebuttal. They were entirely on the point of character. One testified that he had heard the prisoner say that, if the negroes had their rights, they would own at least half the property. Another testified that he had heard the defendant say that the negroes spent too much money on churches, and that they cared a good deal more for God than God had ever seemed to care for them.

Ben Davis listened to this testimony with half-open mouth and staring eyes. Now and then he would lean forward and speak perhaps a word, when his attorney would shake a warning finger at him, and he would fall back helplessly, as if abandoning himself to fate; but for a moment only, when he would resume his puzzled look.

The arguments followed. The prosecuting attorney briefly summed up the evidence, and characterized it as almost a mathematical proof of the prisoner's guilt. He reserved his eloquence for the closing argument.

The defendant's attorney had a headache, and secretly believed his client guilty. His address sounded more like an appeal for mercy than a demand for justice. Then the State's attorney delivered the maiden argument of his office, the speech that made his reputation as an orator, and opened up to him a successful political career.

The judge's charge to the jury was a plain, simple statement of the law as applied to circumstantial evidence, and the mere statement of the law foreshadowed the verdict.

The eyes of the prisoner were glued to the jury-box, and he looked more and more like a hunted animal. In the rear of the crowd of blacks who filled the back part of the room, partly concealed by the projecting angle of the fireplace, stood Tom, the blacksmith's assistant. If the face is the mirror of the soul, then this man's soul, taken off its guard in this moment of excitement, was full of lust and envy and all evil passions.

The jury filed out of their box, and into the jury room behind the judge's stand. There was a moment of relaxation in the courtroom. The lawyers fell into conversation across the table. The judge beckoned to Colonel Thornton, who stepped forward, and they conversed together a few moments. The prisoner was all eyes and ears in this moment of waiting, and from an involuntary gesture on the part of the judge he divined that they were speaking of him. It is a pity he could not hear what was said.

"How do you feel about the case, Colonel?" asked the judge.

"Let him off easy," replied Colonel Thornton. "He's the best blacksmith in the county."

The business of the court seemed to have halted by tacit consent, in anticipation of a quick verdict. The suspense did not last long. Scarcely ten minutes had elapsed when there was a rap on the door, the officer opened it, and the jury came out.

The prisoner, his soul in his eyes, sought their faces, but met no reassuring glance; they were all looking away from him.

"Gentlemen of the jury, have you agreed upon a verdict?"

"We have," responded the foreman. The clerk of the court stepped forward and took the fateful slip from the foreman's hand.

The clerk read the verdict: "We, the jury impaneled and sworn to try the issues in this cause, do find the prisoner guilty as charged in the indictment."

There was a moment of breathless silence. Then a wild burst of grief from the prisoner's wife, to which his two children, not understanding it all, but vaguely conscious of some calamity, added their voices in two long, discordant wails, which would have been ludicrous had they not been heart-rending.

The face of the young man in the back of the room expressed relief and badly concealed satisfaction. The prisoner fell back upon the seat from which he had half risen in his anxiety, and his dark face assumed an ashen hue. What he thought could only be surmised. Perhaps, knowing his innocence, he had not believed conviction possible; perhaps, conscious of guilt, he dreaded the punishment, the extent of which was optional with the judge, within very wide limits. Only one other person present knew whether or not he was guilty, and that other had slunk furtively from the court room.

Some of the spectators wondered why there should be so much ado about convicting a negro of stealing a buggy-whip. They had forgotten their own interest of the moment before. They did not realize out of what trifles grow the tragedies of life.

It was four o'clock in the afternoon, the hour for adjournment, when the verdict was returned. The judge nodded to the bailiff.

"Oyez, oyez! this court is now adjourned until ten o'clock to-morrow morning," cried the bailiff in a singsong voice. The judge left the bench, the jury filed out of the box, and a buzz of conversation filled the court room.

"Brace up, Ben, brace up, my boy," said the defendant's lawyer, half apologetically. "I did what I could for you, but you can never tell what a jury will do. You won't be sentenced till to-morrow morning. In the meantime I'll speak to the judge and try to get him to be easy with you. He may let you off with a light fine."

The negro pulled himself together, and by an effort listened.

"Thanky, Majah," was all he said. He seemed to be thinking of something far away.

He barely spoke to his wife when she frantically threw herself on him, and clung to his neck, as he passed through the side room on his way to jail. He kissed his children mechanically, and did not reply to the soothing remarks made by the jailer.

III

There was a good deal of excitement in town the next morning. Two white men stood by the post office talking.

"Did yer hear the news?"

"No, what wuz it?"

"Ben Davis tried ter break jail las' night."

"You don't say so! What a fool! He ain't be'n sentenced yit."

"Well, now," said the other, "I've knowed Ben a long time, an' he wuz a right good nigger. I kinder found it hard ter b'lieve he did steal that whip. But what's a man's feelin's ag'in the proof?"

They spoke on awhile, using the past tense as if they were speaking of a dead man.

"Ef I know Jedge Hart, Ben'll wish he had slep' las' night, 'stidder tryin' ter break out'n jail."

At ten o'clock the prisoner was brought into court. He walked with shambling gait, bent at the shoulders, hopelessly, with downcast eyes, and took his seat with several other prisoners who had been brought in for sentence. His wife, accompanied by the children, waited behind him, and a number of his friends were gathered in the court room.

The first prisoner sentenced was a young white man, convicted several days before of manslaughter. The deed was done in the heat of passion, under circumstances of great provocation, during a quarrel about a woman. The prisoner was admonished of the sanctity of human life, and sentenced to one year in the penitentiary.

The next case was that of a young clerk, eighteen or nineteen years of age, who had committed a forgery in order to procure the means to buy lottery tickets. He was well connected, and the case would not have been prosecuted if the judge had not refused to allow it to be nolled, and, once brought to trial, a conviction could not have been avoided.

"You are a young man," said the judge gravely, yet not unkindly, "and your life is yet before you. I regret that you should have been led into evil courses by the lust for speculation, so dangerous in its tendencies, so fruitful of crime and misery. I am led to believe that you are sincerely penitent, and that, after such punishment as the law cannot remit without bringing itself into contempt, you will see the error of your ways and follow the strict path of rectitude. Your fault has entailed distress not only upon yourself, but upon your relatives, people of good name and good family, who suffer as keenly from your disgrace as you yourself. Partly out of consideration for their feelings, and partly because I feel that, under the circumstances, the law will be satisfied by the penalty I shall inflict, I sentence you to imprisonment in the county jail for six months, and a fine of one hundred dollars and the costs of this action."

"The jedge talks well, don't he?" whispered one spectator to another.

"Yes, and kinder likes ter hear hisse'f talk," answered the other.

"Ben Davis, stand up," ordered the judge.

He might have said "Ben Davis, wake up," for the jailer had to touch the prisoner on the shoulder to rouse him from his stupor. He stood up, and something of the hunted look came again into his eyes, which shifted under the stern glance of the judge.

"Ben Davis, you have been convicted of larceny, after a fair trial before twelve good men of this county. Under the testimony, there can be no doubt of your guilt. The case is an aggravated one. You are not an ignorant, shiftless fellow, but a man of more than ordinary intelligence among your people, and one who ought to know better. You have not even the poor excuse of having stolen to satisfy hunger or a physical appetite. Your conduct is wholly without excuse, and I can only regard your crime as the result of a tendency to offenses of this nature, a tendency which is only too common among your people; a tendency which is a menace to civilization, a menace to society itself, for society rests upon the sacred right of property. Your opinions, too, have been given a wrong turn; you have been heard to utter sentiments which, if disseminated among an ignorant people, would breed discontent, and give rise to strained relations between them and their best friends, their old masters, who understand their real nature and their real needs, and to whose justice and enlightened guidance they can safely trust. Have you anything to say why sentence should not be passed upon you?"

"Nothin', suh, cep'n dat I did n' take de whip."

"The law, largely, I think, in view of the peculiar circumstances of your unfortunate race, has vested a large discretion in courts as to the extent of the punishment for offenses of this kind. Taking your case as a whole, I am convinced that it is one which, for the sake of the example, deserves a severe punishment. Nevertheless, I do not feel disposed to give you the full extent of the law, which would be twenty years in the penitentiary,* but, considering the fact that you have a family, and have heretofore borne a good reputation in the community, I will impose upon you the light sentence of imprisonment for five years in the penitentiary at hard labor. And I hope that this will be a warning to you and others who may

---

* There are no degrees of larceny in North Carolina, and the penalty for any offense lies in the discretion of the judge, to the limit of twenty years.

be similarly disposed, and that after your sentence has expired you may lead the life of a law-abiding citizen."

"O Ben! O my husband! O God!" moaned the poor wife, and tried to press forward to her husband's side.

"Keep back, Nancy, keep back," said the jailer. "You can see him in jail."

Several people were looking at Ben's face. There was one flash of despair, and then nothing but a stony blank, behind which he masked his real feelings, whatever they were.

Human character is a compound of tendencies inherited and habits acquired. In the anxiety, the fear of disgrace, spoke the nineteenth-century civilization with which Ben Davis had been more or less closely in touch during twenty years of slavery and fifteen years of freedom. In the stolidity with which he received this sentence for a crime which he had not committed, spoke who knows what trait of inherited savagery? For stoicism is a savage virture.

IV

One morning in June, five years later, a black man limped slowly along the old Lumberton plank road; a tall man, whose bowed shoulders made him seem shorter than he was, and a face from which it was difficult to guess his years, for in it the wrinkles and flabbiness of age were found side by side with firm white teeth, and eyes not sunken,—eyes bloodshot, and burning with something, either fever or passion. Though he limped painfully with one foot, the other hit the ground impatiently, like the good horse in a poorly matched team. As he walked along, he was talking to himself:—

"I wonder what dey 'll do w'en I git back? I wonder how Nancy 's s'ported the fambly all dese years? Tuck in washin', I s'ppose,— she was a monst'us good washer an' ironer. I wonder ef de chillun 'll be too proud ter reco'nize deir daddy come back f'um de penetenchy? I 'spec' Billy must be a big boy by dis time. He won' b'lieve his daddy ever stole anything. I'm gwine ter slip roun' an' s'prise 'em."

Five minutes later a face peered cautiously into the window of what had once been Ben Davis's cabin,—at first an eager face, its coarseness lit up with the fire of hope; a moment later a puzzled face; than an anxious, fearful face as the man stepped away from the window and rapped at the door.

"Is Mis' Davis home?" he asked of the woman who opened the door.

"Mis' Davis don' live here. You er mistook in de house."

"Whose house is dis?"

"It b'longs ter my husban', Mr. Smith,—Primus Smith."

" 'Scuse me, but I knowed de house some years ago w'en I wuz here oncet on a visit, an' it b'longed ter a man name' Ben Davis."

"Ben Davis—Ben Davis?—oh yes, I 'member now. Dat wuz de gen'man w'at wuz sent ter de penitenchy fer sump'n er nuther,— sheep-stealin', I b'lieve. Primus," she called, "w'at wuz Ben Davis, w'at useter own dis yer house, sent ter de penitenchy fer?"

"Hoss-stealin'," came back the reply in sleepy accents, from the man seated by the fireplace.

The traveler went on to the next house. A neat-looking yellow woman came to the door when he rattled the gate, and stood looking suspiciously at him.

"W'at you want?" she asked.

"Please, ma'am, will you tell me whether a man name' Ben Davis useter live in dis neighborhood?"

"Useter live in de nex' house; wuz sent ter de penitenchy fer killin' a man."

"Kin yer tell me w'at went wid Mis' Davis?"

"Umph! I 's a 'spectable 'oman, I is, en don' mix wid dem kind er people. She wuz 'n' no better'n her husban'. She tuk up wid a man dat useter wuk fer Ben, an' dey 're livin' down by de ole wagon-ya'd, where no 'spectable 'oman ever puts her foot."

"An' de chillen?"

"De gal's dead. Wuz 'n' no better 'n she oughter be'n. She fell in de crick an' got drown'; some folks say she wuz 'n' sober w'en it happen'. De boy tuck atter his pappy. He wuz 'rested las' week fer shootin' a w'ite man, an' wuz lynch' de same night. Dey wa'n't none of 'em no 'count after deir pappy went ter de penitenchy."

"What went wid de proputty?"

"Hit wuz sol' fer de mortgage, er de taxes, er de lawyer, er sump'n,—I don' know w'at. A w'ite man got it."

The man with the bundle went on until he came to a creek that crossed the road. He descended the sloping bank, and, sitting on a stone in the shade of a water-oak, took off his coarse brogans, unwound the rags that served him in lieu of stockings, and laved in the cool water the feet that were chafed with many a weary mile of travel.

After five years of unrequited toil, and unspeakable hardship in convict camps,—five years of slaving by the side of human brutes, and of nightly herding with them in vermin-haunted huts—Ben Davis had become like them. For a while he had received occasional letters from home, but in the shifting life of the convict camp they had long since ceased to reach him, if indeed they had been written. For a year or two, the consciousness of his innocence had helped to make him resist the debasing influences that surrounded him. The hope of shortening his sentence by good behavior, too, had worked a similar end. But the transfer from one contractor to another, each interested in keeping as long as possible a good worker, had speedily dissipated any such hope. When hope took flight, its place was not long vacant. Despair followed, and black hatred of all mankind, hatred especially of the man to whom he attributed all his misfortunes. One who is suffering unjustly is not apt to indulge in fine abstractions, nor to balance probabilities. By long brooding over his wrongs, his mind became, if not unsettled, at least warped, and he imagined that Colonel Thornton had deliberately set a trap into which he had fallen. The Colonel, he convinced himself, had disapproved of his prosperity, and had schemed to destroy it. He reasoned himself into the belief that he represented in his person the accumulated wrongs of a whole race, and Colonel Thornton the race who had oppressed them. A burning desire for revenge sprang up in him, and he nursed it until his sentence expired and he was set at liberty. What he had learned since reaching home had changed his desire into a deadly purpose.

When he had again bandaged his feet and slipped them into his shoes, he looked around him, and selected a stout sapling from among the undergrowth that covered the bank of the stream. Taking from his pocket a huge clasp-knife, he cut off the length of an ordinary walking stick and trimmed it. The result was an ugly-looking bludgeon, a dangerous weapon when in the grasp of a strong man.

With the stick in his hand, he went on down the road until he approached a large white house standing some distance back from the street. The grounds were filled with a profusion of shrubbery. The negro entered the gate and secreted himself in the bushes, at a point where he could hear any one that might approach.

It was near midday, and he had not eaten. He had walked all night, and had not slept. The hope of meeting his loved ones had been meat and drink and rest for him. But as he sat waiting, outraged nature asserted itself, and he fell asleep, with his head on the rising root of a tree, and his face upturned.

And as he slept, he dreamed of his childhood; of an old black mammy taking care of him in the daytime, and of a younger face, with soft eyes, which bent over him sometimes at night, and a pair of arms which clasped him closely. He dreamed of his past,—of his young wife, of his bright children. Somehow his dreams all ran to pleasant themes for a while.

Then they changed again. He dreamed that he was in the convict camp, and, by an easy transition, that he was in hell, consumed with hunger, burning with thirst. Suddenly the grinning devil who stood over him with a barbed whip faded away, and a little white angel came and handed him a drink of water. As he raised it to his lips the glass slipped, and he struggled back to consciousness.

"Poo' man! Poo' man sick, an' sleepy. Dolly b'ing f'owers to cover poo' man up. Poo' man mus' be hungry. W'en dolly get him covered up, she go b'ing poo' man some cake."

A sweet little child, as beautiful as a cherub escaped from Paradise, was standing over him. At first he scarcely comprehended the words the baby babbled out. But as they became clear to him, a novel feeling crept slowly over his heart. It had been so long since he had heard anything but curses and stern words of command, or the ribald songs of obscene merriment, that the clear tones of this voice from heaven cooled his calloused heart as the water of the brook had soothed his blistered feet. It was so strange, so unwonted a thing, that he lay there with half-closed eyes while the child brought leaves and flowers and laid them on his face and on his breast, and arranged them with little caressing taps.

She moved away, and plucked a flower. And then she spied another farther on, and then another, and, as she gathered them, kept increasing the distance between herself and the man lying there, until she was several rods away.

Ben Davis watched her through eyes over which had come an unfamiliar softness. Under the lingering spell of his dream, her golden hair, which fell in rippling curls, seemed like a halo of purity and innocence and peace, irradiating the atmosphere around her. It is true the thought occurred to Ben, vaguely, that through harm to her he might inflict the greatest punishment upon her father; but the idea came like a dark shape that faded away and vanished into nothingness as soon as it came within the nimbus that surrounded the child's person.

The child was moving on to pluck still another flower, when there came a sound of hoof-beats, and Ben was aware that a horseman, visible through the shrubbery, was coming along the curved path that led from the gate to the house. It must be the man he was waiting for, and now was the time to wreak his vengeance. He sprang to his feet, grasped his club, and stood for a moment irresolute. But either the instinct of the convict, beaten, driven, and debased, or the influence of the child, which was still strong upon him, impelled him, after the first momentary pause, to flee as though seeking safety.

His flight led him toward the little girl, whom he must pass in order to make his escape, and as Colonel Thornton turned the corner of the path he saw a desperate-looking negro, clad in filthy rags, and carrying in his hand a murderous bludgeon, running toward the child, who, startled by the sound of footsteps, had turned and was looking toward the approaching man with wondering eyes. A sickening fear came over the father's heart, and drawing the ever-ready revolver, which according to the Southern custom he carried always upon his person, he fired with unerring aim. Ben Davis ran a few yards farther, faltered, threw out his hands, and fell dead at the child's feet.

Some time, we are told, when the cycle of years has rolled around, there is to be another golden age, when all men will dwell together in love and harmony, and when peace and righteousness shall prevail for a thousand years. God speed the day, and let not the shining thread of hope become so enmeshed in the web of circumstance that we lose sight of it; but give us here and there, and now and then, some little foretaste of this golden age, that we may the more patiently and hopefully await its coming!

Baxter's Procrustes

BAXTER'S PROCRUSTES is one of the publications of the Bodleian Club. The Bodleian Club is composed of gentlemen of culture, who are interested in books and book collecting. It was named, very obviously, after the famous library of the same name, and not only became in our city a sort of shrine for local worshipers of fine bindings and rare editions, but was visited occasionally by pilgrims from afar. The Bodleian has entertained Mark Twain, Joseph Jefferson, and other literary and histrionic celebrities. It possesses quite a collection of personal mementos of distinguished authors, among them a paperweight which once belonged to Goethe, a lead pencil used by Emerson, an autograph letter of Matthew Arnold, and a chip from a tree felled by Mr. Gladstone. Its library contains a number of rare books, including a fine collection on chess, of which game several of the members are enthusiastic devotees.

The activities of the club are not, however, confined entirely to books. We have a very handsome clubhouse, and much taste and discrimination have been exercised in its adornment. There are many good paintings, including the portraits of the various presidents of the club, which adorn the entrance hall. After books, perhaps the most distinctive feature of the club is our collection of pipes. In a large rack in the smoking-room—really a superfluity, since smoking is permitted all over the house—is as complete an assortment of pipes as perhaps exists in the civilized world. Indeed, it is an unwritten rule of the club that no one is eligible for membership who cannot produce a new variety of pipe, which is filed with his application for membership, and, if he passes, deposited with the club collection, he, however, retaining the title in himself. Once a year, upon the anniversary of the death of Sir Walter Raleigh, who, it will be remembered, first introduced tobacco into England, the full membership of the club, as a rule, turns out. A large supply of the very best smoking mixture is laid in. At nine o'clock sharp each member takes his pipe from the rack, fills it with tobacco, and then the whole club, with the president at the head, all smoking furiously, march in solemn procession from room to room, upstairs and downstairs, making the tour of the clubhouse and returning to the smoking-room. The president then delivers an address, and each member is called upon to say something, either by way of a quotation or an original sentiment, in praise of the virtues of nicotine. This ceremony—facetiously known as "hitting the pipe"—being thus concluded, the membership pipes are carefully cleaned out and replaced in the club rack.

As I have said, however, the *raison d'être* of the club, and the feature upon which its fame chiefly rests, is its collection of rare books, and of these by far the most interesting are its own publications. Even its catalogues are works of art, published in numbered editions, and sought by libraries and book collectors. Early in its history it began the occasional publication of books which emphasis should be laid upon the qualities that make a book valuable in the eyes of collectors. Of these, age could not, of course, be imparted, but in the matter of fine and curious bindings, of hand-made linen papers, of uncut or deckle edges, of wide margins and limited editions, the club could control its own publications. The matter of contents was, it must be confessed, a less important consideration. At first it was felt by the publishing committee that nothing but the finest products of the human mind should be selected for enshrinement in the beautiful volumes which the club should issue. The length of the work was an important consideration—long things were not compatible with wide margins and graceful slenderness. For instance, we brought out Coleridge's *Ancient Mariner*, an essay by Emerson, and another by Thoreau. Our *Rubáyát of Omar Khayyám* was Heron-Allen's translation of the original manuscript in the Bodleian Library at Oxford, which though less poetical than Fitz-Gerald's was not so common. Several years ago we began to publish the works of our own members. Bascom's *Essay on Pipes* was a very creditable performance. It was published in a limited edition of one hundred copies, and since it had not previously appeared elsewhere and was copyrighted by the club, it was sufficiently rare to be valuable for that reason. The second publication of local origin was Baxter's *Procrustes*.

I have omitted to say that once or twice a year, at a meeting of which notice has been given, an auction is held at the Bodleian. The members of the club send in their duplicate copies, or books they for any reason wish to dispose of, which are auctioned off to the highest bidder. At these sales, which are well attended, the club's publications have of recent years formed the leading feature. Three years ago, number three of Bascom's *Essay on Pipes* sold for fifteen dollars—the original cost of publication was one dollar and seventy-five cents. Later in the evening an uncut copy of the same brought thirty dollars. At the next auction the price of the cut copy was run up to twenty-five dollars, while uncut copy was knocked down at seventy-five dollars. The club had always appreciated the value of uncut copies, but this financial endorsement enhanced their desirability immensely. This rise in the *Essay on Pipes* was not without a sympathetic effect upon all the club publications. The Emerson essay rose from three dollars to seventeen, and the Thoreau, being by an author less widely read, and by his own confession commercially unsuccessful, brought a somewhat higher figure. The prices, thus inflated, were not permitted to come down appreciably. Since every member of the club possessed one or more of these valuable editions, they were all manifestly interested in keeping up the price. The publication, however, which brought the highest prices, and, but for the sober second thought, might have wrecked the whole system, was Baxter's *Procrustes*.

Baxter was, perhaps, the most scholarly member of the club. A graduate of Harvard, he had traveled extensively, had read widely, and while not so enthusiastic a collector as some of us, possessed as fine a private library as any man of his age in the city. He was about thirty-five when he joined the club, and apparently some bitter experience—some disappointment in love or ambition—had left its mark upon his character. With light, curly hair, fair complexion and gray eyes, one would have expected Baxter to be genial of temper, with a tendency toward wordiness of speech. But though he had occasional flashes of humor, his ordinary demeanor was characterized by a mild cynicism, which, with his gloomy, pessimistic philosophy, so foreign to the temperament that should accompany his physical type, could only be accounted for upon the hypothesis of some secret sorrow such as I have suggested. What it might be no one knew. He had means and social position, and was an uncommonly handsome man. The fact that he remained unmarried at thirty-five furnished some support for the theory of a disappointment in love, though this the several intimates of Baxter who belonged to the club were not able to verify.

It had occured to me, in a vague way, that perhaps Baxter might be an unsuccessful author. That he was a poet we knew very well, and typewritten copies of his verses had occasionally circulated among us. But Baxter had always expressed such a profound contempt for modern literature, had always spoken in terms of such unmeasured pity for the slaves of the pen, who were dependent upon the whim of an undiscriminating public for recognition and a livelihood, that no one of us had ever suspected him of aspirations toward publication, until, as I have said, it occurred to me one day that Baxter's attitude with regard to publication might be viewed in the light of effect as well as of cause—that his scorn of publicity might as easily arise from failure to achieve it, as his never having published might be due to his preconceived disdain of the vulgar popularity which one must share with the pugilist or balloonist of the hour.

The notion of publishing Baxter's *Procrustes* did not emanate from Baxter—I must do him the justice to say this. But he had spoken to several of the fellows about the theme of his poem, until the notion that Baxter was at work upon something fine had become pretty well disseminated throughout our membership. He would occasionally read brief passages to a small coterie of friends in the sitting room or library—never more than ten lines at once, or to more than five people at a time—and these excerpts gave at least a few of us a pretty fair idea of the motive and scope of the poem. As I, for one, gathered it, it was quite along the line of Baxter's philosophy. Society was the Procrustes which, like the Greek bandit of old, caught every man born into the world, and endeavored to fit him to some preconceived standard, generally to the one for which he was least adapted. The world was full of men and women who were merely square pegs in round holes, and vice versa. Most marriages were unhappy because the contracting parties were not properly mated. Religion was mostly superstition, science for the most part sciolism, popular education merely a means of forcing the stupid and repressing the bright, so that all the youth of the rising generation might conform to the same dull, dead level of democratic mediocrity. Life would soon become so monotonously uniform and so uniformly monotonous as to be scarce worth the living.

It was Smith, I think, who first proposed that the club publish Baxter's *Procrustes*. The poet himself did not seem enthusiastic when the subject was broached; he demurred for some little time, protesting that the poem was not worthy of publication. But when it was proposed that the edition be limited to fifty copies, he agreed to consider the proposition. When I suggested, having in mind my secret theory of Baxter's failure in authorship, that the edition would at least be in the hands of friends, that it would be difficult for a hostile critic to secure a copy, and that if it should not achieve success from a literary point of view, the extent of the failure would be limited to the size of the edition, Baxter was visibly impressed. When the literary committee at length decided to request formally of Baxter the privilege of publishing his *Procrustes*, he consented, with evident reluctance, upon condition that he should supervise the printing, binding, and delivery of the books, merely submitting to the committee, in advance, the manuscript, and taking their views in regard to the bookmaking.

The manuscript was duly presented to the literary committee. Baxter having expressed the desire that the poem not be read aloud at a meeting of the club, as was the custom, since he wished it to be given to the world clad in suitable garb, the committee went even farther. Having entire confidence in Baxter's taste and scholarship, they, with great delicacy, refrained from even reading the manuscript, contenting themselves with Baxter's statement of the general theme and the topics grouped under it. The details of the bookmaking, however, were gone into thoroughly. The paper was to be of handmade linen, from the Kelmscott Mills; the type black-letter, with rubricated initials. The cover, which was Baxter's own selection, was to be of dark green morocco, with a cap-and-bells border in red inlays, and doublures of maroon morocco with a blind-tooled design. Baxter was authorized to contract with the printer and superintend the publication. The whole edition of fifty numbered copies was to be disposed of at auction, in advance, to the highest bidder, only one copy to each, the proceeds to be devoted to paying for the printing and binding, the remainder, if any, to go into the club treasury, and Baxter himself to receive one copy by way of remuneration. Baxter was inclined to protest at this, on the ground that his copy would probably be worth more than the royalties on the edition, at the usual ten percent, would amount to, but was finally prevailed upon to accept an author's copy.

While the *Procrustes* was under consideration, someone read, at one of our meetings, a note from some magazine which stated that a sealed copy of a new translation of Campanella's *Sonnets*, published by the Grolier Club, had been sold for three hundred dollars. This impressed the members greatly. It was a novel idea. A new work might thus be enshrined in a sort of holy of holies, which, if the collector so desired, could be forever sacred from the profanation of any vulgar or unappreciative eye. The possessor of such a treasure could enjoy it by the eye of imagination, having at the same time the exaltation of grasping what was for others the unattainable. The literary committee were so impressed with this idea that they presented it to Baxter in regard to the *Procrustes*. Baxter making no objection, the subscribers who might wish their copies delivered sealed were directed to notify the author. I sent in my name. A fine book, after all, was an investment, and if there was any way of enhancing its rarity, and therefore its value, I was quite willing to enjoy such an advantage.

When the *Procrustes* was ready for distribution, each subscriber received his copy by mail, in a neat pasteboard box. Each number was wrapped in a thin and transparent but very strong paper, through which the cover design and toolings were clearly visible. The number of the copy was endorsed upon the wrapper, the folds of which were securely fastened at each end with sealing-wax, upon which was impressed, as a guarantee of its inviolateness, the monogram of the club.

At the next meeting of the Bodleian a great deal was said about the *Procrustes*, and it was unanimously agreed that no finer specimen of bookmaking had ever been published by the club. By a curious coincidence, no one had brought his copy with him, and the two club copies had not yet been received from the binder, who, Baxter had reported, was retaining them for some extra fine work. Upon resolution, offered by a member who had not subscribed for the volume, a committee of three was appointed to review the *Procrustes* at the next literary meeting of the club. Of this committee it was my doubtful fortune to constitute one.

In pursuance of my duty in the premises, it of course became necessary for me to read the *Procrustes*. In all probability I should have cut my own copy for this purpose, had not one of the club auctions intervened between my appointment and the date set for the discussion of the *Procrustes*. At this meeting a copy of the book, still sealed, was offered for sale and bought by a non-subscriber for the unprecedented price of one hundred and fifty dollars. After this a proper regard for my own interests would not permit me to spoil my copy by opening it, and I was therefore compelled to procure my information concerning the poem from some other source. As I had no desire to appear mercenary, I said nothing about my own copy, and made no attempt to borrow. I did, however, casually remark to Baxter that I should like to look at his copy of the proof sheets, since I wished to make some extended quotations for my review, and would rather not trust my copy to a typist for that purpose. Baxter assured me, with every evidence of regret, that he had considered them of so little importance that he had thrown them into the fire. This indifference of Baxter to literary values struck me as just a little overdone. The proof sheets of "Hamlet," corrected in Shakespeare's own hand, would be well-nigh priceless.

At the next meeting of the club I observed that Thompson and Davis, who were with me on the reviewing committee, very soon brought up the question of the *Procrustes* in conversation in the smoking-room, and seemed anxious to get from the members their views concerning Baxter's production, I supposed upon the theory that the appreciation of any book review would depend more or less upon the degree to which it reflected the opinion of those to whom the review should be presented. I presumed, of course, that Thompson and Davis had each read the book—they were among the subscribers—and I was desirous of getting their point of view.

"What do you think," I inquired, "of the passage on Social Systems?" I have forgotten to say that the poem was in blank verse, and divided into parts, each with an appropriate title.

"Well," replied Davis, it seemed to me a little cautiously, "it is not exactly Spencerian, although it squints at the Spencerian view, with a slight deflection toward Hegelianism. I should consider it an harmonious fusion of the best views of all the modern philosophers, with a strong Baxterian flavor."

"Yes," said Thompson, "the charm of the chapter lies in this very quality. The style is an emanation from Baxter's own intellect—he has written himself into the poem. By knowing Baxter we are able to appreciate the book, and after having read the book we feel that we are so much the more intimately acquainted with Baxter—the real Baxter."

Baxter had come in during this colloquy and was standing by the fireplace smoking a pipe. I was not exactly sure whether the faint smile which marked his face was a token of pleasure or cynicism; it was Baxterian, however, and I had already learned that Baxter's opinions upon any subject were not to be gathered always from his facial expression. For instance, when the club porter's crippled child died, Baxter remarked, it seemed to me unfeelingly, that the poor little devil was doubtless better off, and that the porter himself had certainly been relieved of a burden; and only a week later the porter told me in confidence that Baxter had paid for an expensive operation, undertaken in the hope of prolonging the child's life. I therefore drew no conclusions from Baxter's somewhat enigmatical smile. He left the room at this point in the conversation, somewhat to my relief.

"By the way, Jones," said Davis, addressing me, "are you impressed by Baxter's views on Degeneration?"

Having often heard Baxter express himself upon the general downward tendency of modern civilization, I felt safe in discussing his views in a broad and general manner.

"I think," I replied, "that they are in harmony with those of Schopenhauer, without his bitterness; with those of Nordau, without his flippancy. His materialism is Haeckel's, presented with something of the charm of Omar Khayyám."

"Yes," chimed in Davis, "it answers the strenuous demand of our day—dissatisfaction with an unjustified optimism—and voices for us the courage of human philosophy facing the unknown."

I had a vague recollection of having read something like this somewhere, but so much has been written that one can scarcely discuss any subject of importance without unconsciously borrowing, now and then, the thoughts or the language of others. Quotation, like imitation, is a superior grade of flattery.

"The *Procrustes*," said Thompson, to whom the metrical review had been apportioned, "is couched in sonorous lines, of haunting melody and charm; and yet so closely interrelated as to be scarcely quotable with justice to the author. To be appreciated the poem should be read as a whole—I shall say as much in my review. What shall you say of the letter-press?" he concluded, addressing me. I was supposed to discuss the technical excellence of the volume from the connoisseur's viewpoint.

"The setting," I replied judicially, "is worthy of the gem. The dark green cover, elaborately tooled, the old English lettering, the heavy linen paper, mark this as one of our very choicest publications. The letter-press is of course De Vinne's best—there is nothing better on this side of the Atlantic. The text is a beautiful, slender stream, meandering gracefully through a wide meadow of margin."

For some reason I left the room for a minute. As I stepped into the hall, I almost ran into Baxter, who was standing near the door, facing a hunting print, of a somewhat humorous character, hung upon the wall, and smiling with an immensely pleased expression.

"What a ridiculous scene!" he remarked. "Look at that fat old squire on that tall hunter! I'll wager dollars to doughnuts that he won't get over the first fence!"

It was a very good bluff, but did not deceive me. Under his mask of unconcern, Baxter was anxious to learn what we thought of his poem and had stationed himself in the hall that he might overhear our discussion without embarrassing us by his presence. He had covered up his delight at our appreciation by this simulated interest in the hunting print.

When the night came for the review of the *Procrustes* there was a large attendance of members, and several visitors, among them a young English cousin of one of the members, on his first visit to the United States; some of us had met him at other clubs, and in society, and had found him a very jolly boy, with a youthful exuberance of spirits and a naïve ignorance of things American that made his views refreshing and, at times, amusing.

The critical essays were well considered, if a trifle vague. Baxter received credit for poetic skill of a high order.

"Our brother Baxter," said Thompson, "should no longer bury his talent in a napkin. This gem, of course, belongs to the club, but the same brain from which issued this exquisite emanation can produce others to inspire and charm an appreciative world."

"The author's view of life," said Davis, "as expressed in these beautiful lines, will help us to fit our shoulders for the heavy burden of life, by bringing to our realization those profound truths of philosophy which find hope in despair and pleasure in pain. When he shall see fit to give to the wider world, in fuller form, the thoughts of which we have been vouchsafed this foretaste, let us hope that some little ray of his fame may rest upon the Bodleian, from which can never be taken away the proud privilege of saying that he was one of its members."

I then pointed out the beauties of the volume as a piece of bookmaking. I knew, from conversation with the publication committee, the style of type and rubrication, and could see the cover through the wrapper of my sealed copy. The dark green morocco, I said, in summing up, typified the author's serious view of life, as a thing to be endured as patiently as might be. The cap-and-bells border was significant of the shams by which the optimist sought to delude himself into the view that life was a desirable thing. The intricate blind-tooling of the doublure shadowed forth the blind fate which left us in ignorance of our future and our past, or of even what the day itself might bring forth. The black-letter type, with rubricated initials, signified a philosophic pessimism enlightened by the conviction that in duty one might find, after all, an excuse for life and a hope for humanity. Applying this test to the club, this work, which might be said to represent all that the Bodleian stood for, was in itself sufficient to justify the club's existence. If the Bodleian had done nothing else, if it should do nothing more, it had produced a masterpiece.

There was a sealed copy of the *Procrustes*, belonging, I believe, to one of the committee, lying on the table by which I stood, and I had picked it up and held it in my hand for a moment, to emphasize one of my periods, but had laid it down immediately. I noted, as I sat down, that young Hankin, our English visitor, who sat on the other side of the table, had picked up the volume and was examining it with interest. When the last review was read, and the generous applause had subsided, there were cries for Baxter.

"Baxter! Baxter! Author! Author!"

Baxter had been sitting over in a corner during the reading of the reviews, and had succeeded remarkably well, it seemed to me, in concealing, under his mask of cynical indifference, the exultation which I was sure he must feel. But this outburst of enthusiasm was too much even for Baxter, and it was clear that he was struggling with strong emotion when he rose to speak.

"Gentlemen, and fellow members of the Bodleian, it gives me unaffected pleasure—sincere pleasure—someday you may know how much pleasure—I cannot trust myself to say it now—to see the evident care with which your committee have read my poor verses, and the responsive sympathy with which my friends have entered into my views of life and conduct. I thank you again, and again, and when I say that I am too full for utterance—I'm sure you will excuse me from saying any more."

Baxter took his seat, and the applause had begun again when it was broken by a sudden exclamation.

"By Jove!" exclaimed our English visitor, who still sat behind the table, "what an extraordinary book!"

Everyone gathered around him.

"You see," he exclaimed, holding up the volume, "you fellows said so much about the bally book that I wanted to see what it was like; so I untied the ribbon and cut the leaves with the paper knife lying here and found—and found that there wasn't a single line in it, don't you know!"

Blank consternation followed this announcement, which proved only too true. Everyone knew instinctively, without further investigation, that the club had been badly sold. In the resulting confusion Baxter escaped, but later was waited upon by a committee, to whom he made the rather lame excuse that he had always regarded uncut and sealed books as tommy-rot, and that he had merely been curious to see how far the thing could go; and that the result had justified his belief that a book with nothing in it was just as useful to a book-collector as one embodying a work of genius. He offered to pay all the bills for the sham *Procrustes*, or to replace the blank copies with the real thing, as we might choose. Of course, after such an insult, the club did not care for the poem. He was permitted to pay the expense, however, and it was more than hinted to him that his resignation from the club would be favorably acted upon. He never sent it in, and, as he went to Europe shortly afterwards, the affair had time to blow over.

In our first disgust at Baxter's duplicity, most of us cut our copies of the *Procrustes*, some of us mailed them to Baxter with cutting notes, and others threw them into the fire. A few wiser spirits held on to theirs, and this fact leaking out, it began to dawn upon the minds of the real collectors among us that the volume was something unique in the way of a publication.

"Baxter," said our president one evening to a select few of us who sat around the fireplace, "was wiser than we knew, or than he perhaps appreciated. His *Procrustes*, from the collector's point of view, is entirely logical, and might be considered as the acme of bookmaking. To the true collector, a book is a work of art, of which the contents are no more important than the words of an opera. Fine binding is a desideratum, and, for its cost, that of the *Procrustes* could not be improved upon. The paper is above criticism. The true collector loves wide margins, and the *Procrustes*, being all margin, merely touches the vanishing point of the perspective. The smaller the edition, the greater the collector's eagerness to acquire a copy. There are but six uncut copies left, I am told, of the *Procrustes*, and three sealed copies, of one of which I am the fortunate possessor."

After this deliverance, it is not surprising that, at our next auction, a sealed copy of Baxter's *Procrustes* was knocked down, after spirited bidding, for two hundred and fifty dollars, the highest price ever brought by a single volume published by the club.